Joanna Adam was born in Edinburgh and grew up on the west coast of Scotland. She has travelled, living in Switzerland, New York, and Scotland before settling with her husband outside London.

KEPT

Joanna Adam

Copyright © 2023 Joanna Adam
All rights reserved.

ISBN 978-1-7395131-1-5

This novel is entirely a work of fiction. The names, characters, and incidents portrayed in it are the work of the author's imagination. Any resemblance to actual persons, living or dead, or events or localities is entirely coincidental.

*For Mike
and my creative team
Charlotte, James, Lizzie & Prim*

Part 1

'Hello, darling. Lovely to see you. How is the little one?'

'Hi. May-May. It's me, Laura, remember? No children.'

Behind her, the door closed slowly on dry hinges as she entered her grandmother's room. For a moment, Laura hovered uneasily in the stifling air wondering where to put her coat. She glanced around at the familiar furniture in this unfamiliar setting. Laura crossed the room, as she bent down to kiss her grandmother, Laura caught a faint, sharp reek.

'Of course, darling, silly me. Sit down and tell me all about what you're up to.' Her grandmother smiled and raised her hand to touch Laura's cheek. Despite the heat of the room, May-May's hand felt cool.

'How's school?'

'Not school, May-May. I'm working now at an ad agency.'

'Yes, oh yes.'

Laura put her coat on an empty seat, swept a stray lock of hair behind her ear, and settled herself in the nursing chair near her grandmother. Laura studied May-May's pale face. Her white hair was curled and set. She had powder and lipstick applied and was wearing her pearls. May-May was sitting upright in the old wingback armchair, which was positioned so she could look out through the tall French windows to the garden beyond. With the light behind her, her grandmother looked regal.

'How are you, May-May?'

'Can't complain, my darling. I was admiring the crocuses.' May-May turned to look out at the swathe of purple that rippled across the lawn under the ancient cypress. 'They do look splendid, don't they?' A smile deepened across May-May's face.

'Very pretty,' said Laura. She began to pull a large, fat, burgundy book, stamped on the front in gold with "Nether Place", from a carrier, shaking the book from the slippery hold of the plastic bag. 'Mum gave me a family photograph album for us to look through together.'

'How is your mother?' May-May turned back into the room. 'She hasn't been to see me in such a long time.'

'Same as ever. Mum said she came earlier in the week.'

'Really? It seems such an age since I've seen her, years even.' May-May laughed lightly, but Laura thought she looked sad.

'Shall we look at the old photographs?'

'Lovely idea, darling ... actually, I'm a bit thirsty, could you fill my glass? There should be a jug of juice, behind you, on the chest of drawers.'

Laura took May-May's glass from the table beside her and filled it from the jug. When Laura turned back, May-May's head was leaning against the wing of the chair; her eyes were closed. Laura quietly placed the glass of juice on the coaster on the side table and sat down. Her mother had warned her that her pills made May-May sleepy.

'Stop being a wuss,' Mum had said, 'it's your grandmother you're going to see, not some hobgoblin.'

'Do I have to?' Laura had moaned, 'I've got so much to do at the flat; I want to paint my bedroom this weekend.'

'You can go between coats, while the paint dries. This is your chance to explore the foreign land of old age. Take the old photo album to get her talking. Your grandmother may be a bit forgetful, but she's sharp as a tack on the past... oh and take a book in case she drops off.'

May-May looked peaceful, her face relaxed as she dozed. Laura looked around the room. She tried to remember how it used to be when it was May-May's home. Dividing walls now broke up the elegant old drawing room into three-bedroom suites. There had been parquet, which Laura's Mary-Janes had tapped on so satisfyingly. Now the floor was covered in a pale green carpet. Ceiling tiles had been installed too. They hid the intricate mouldings she remembered radiating from the ornate, central rose where a chandelier had hung. Mum had sold the enormous light on eBay when the house was being prepared for sale. The French windows were the only detail that reminded Laura of what the room had once been. Beyond the window, she could see the grey stone of the terrace. Shallow steps led down to lawns that ran between the trees, through the swathes of crocuses to the lake.

May-May slept. Laura was not quite sure how long she should stay. She fished out her book from her bag and settled down to read, but she had hardly finished a page before May-May woke.

'Hello, darling. Lovely to see you. How is the little one?'

'Hello, May-May. It's me, Laura.' She slipped her book back into her handbag and picked up the photograph album. 'Would you like to look at this now? You can tell me about the people in the pictures?'

'Lovely idea, darling ...' Her grandmother picked up her juice. The glass trembled in her hand as she sipped, threatening to spill.

Laura resisted reaching out and grabbing the glass. Instead, she opened the album.

'My goodness, where did you find this?' asked May-May.

Laura pulled her chair closer to her grandmother and turned the book towards her.

'Mum dug it out, she has all the family albums.'

'Now, what do we have here?' May-May asked.

The album had opened to a photograph of a round-faced baby in a long white gown.

Laura studied the photograph. 'It must be my christening. Me, Laura.'

'So, this is you?' May-May lingered over the picture of the baby. 'Lovely whitework, the dress had been in Dennis' family for generations.'

Laura pointed to the following photograph on the adjacent page. Her father, Max, tall and handsome, stood centre frame, looking like a movie star in his smart church suit. He was flanked by the sisters. The older, Beth, whose happy open face drew one into the picture, was holding the baby. On Max's other side, standing slightly apart, was Tina, petite and delicate.

'Here's Mum, carrying me, with Dad and Aunt Tina coming out of the church,' Laura laughed. 'They look so young!'

'Yes, Max, between my lovely girls.'

'How old is everyone here?' Laura asked.

May-May's gnarled fingers hesitated, hovering over the page.

'Well, let me think… Beth would have been over thirty, perhaps thirty-two, your father, older, mid-forties? Beth was so thrilled when you came along; you can see it on her face. She'd waited so long to have a baby.'

'Is that you and Grandpa behind, in the archway?' In the background Laura could make out her grandparents, Dennis, and Esme, leaving the church.

'Oh yes, Dennis, and me in my fur. I remember it was a cold day.' May-May glanced down at her hands, where her wedding band and sapphire engagement ring sat loose on her fine fingers. 'Dennis was a lovely man,' she said.

Laura watched the juice sloshing in the glass as May-May took another sip of her drink. When she finished, Laura rescued the tumbler and placed it back on the table.

'Oh look, here's a picture of my three together, Beth with Duncan and Tina. So glad I had a boy.' May-May glanced up at Laura and said, 'Not that there's anything wrong with girls, but after Beth, Dennis was so pleased,' May-May turned back to the photograph. 'Beth always so serious, Duncan always wanting what was not, and my beautiful surprise, Tina.' Her fingers trailed tenderly over the three fresh faces. Then she looked up at Laura confused. 'Do you know where they are? My babies? It's been such a long time….'

Laura felt a wave of panic.

'Don't worry, May-May. Mum will be here on Wednesday,' Then Laura then pointed at the photographs again. 'Tina looks so young here, doesn't she? Just a girl.'

May-May turned to the photograph. Looking at the pictures seemed to bring her back into the moment. 'Yes, well, she must have been ... how old? Almost twenty.'

'So glamorous. I love Tina's hat. Cool!'

'She always managed to look chic, Tina. Though I think she borrowed that hat from me. Wanted to be grown up. Like her older siblings,' May-May smiled. 'Tina moved to Milan; you know. To do something in art. She came back after a while, settled in London.' May-May paused, touched Tina's face in the photograph, and then lifted her hand to stifle a yawn. 'You know, darling, would you mind? I feel rather tired.'

'Of course,' Laura took back the album. She saw her grandmother's eyes were misty, and May-May's face looked as grey as the interleaving tissue paper that separated the pages of photographs in the album. Laura smoothed the crinkled surfaces carefully before closing the book.

'I'll leave the album here with you, if that's okay, then next time I come, we can look through some more photographs. That is if you'd like to.'

'Thank you, my darling. That would be lovely.'

After Laura left, May-May sat back in the old wingback chair and closed her eyes. The late sun, sneaking low through the French windows, warmed her bones. She remembered the christening well. It had been a happy occasion, though she couldn't think now why it shouldn't have been. It had been a lovely English late autumn day with high blue skies, beautiful with an ethereal light. There had been enough of a chill in the air so that she could wear her fur but not so much wind that she needed more than a few pins to hold her hat. Everyone had behaved well, cool and calm, like the weather. The church had looked splendid. Beth had organised the event, so of course, everything went smoothly. The flowers were heavenly. When May-May closed her eyes, she could feel the coolness of the church interior and smell the sweet spiciness of the flowers mixed with the mustiness of old hymn books.

Max and Beth were so happy with their new baby, Laura Marie. Tina was Godmother. She wasn't on good form that day, rivalries with her older sister re-surfacing. Tina was beautiful but spoilt, always wanting to be the centre of attention. That must be my fault, she thought. Mothers always spoil their youngest, don't they?

She recalled now; Tina, for some reason, thought the baby should be called Lara. She had got herself in quite a state when she realised Beth and Max had chosen to name the baby Laura. Duncan had been unhappy too, itching to be elsewhere, already wanting to escape his father's authority.

When the christening tea was over, Beth and Max took Laura home, and Duncan and Meredith left with little Gareth. Alone with her parents, Tina had had a tantrum. Dennis could never abide a scene. Now, did Tina want to go back to Milan or had Dennis sent her? She remembered Tina flouncing out of the room, slamming the door behind her. It's funny what you remember, she thought, the noises, the smells, the emotion in the room.

'Well, that's it!' Dennis had said. 'She can't very well stay here. Tina needs to be off somewhere else, doing her own thing, not moping about. Pity she didn't do better in her exams.'

'Perhaps Tina and I could take a trip. Go on a cruise or something?' she remembered suggesting.

'No, no! We can't fix this for her. She must decide for herself,' said Dennis.

Soon after the christening he arranged for Tina to go and do an art course in Florence. A one-way ticket and a small allowance. In the end, Tina was away for nearly five years. She hadn't come home often enough. Duncan and Meredith had gone to the States with Gareth a few years after. She had felt her children were deserting her, but Beth and Max had stayed close with their new baby. Max had been such a support then and over the years. She couldn't now remember how Beth met Max, perhaps in a pub like all the young. He had been such a find.

1982 – 1987

White Wine

The three secretaries from the third floor went to the same pub every Friday after work. It was Beth's first job after qualifying from Queen's College, where she'd won a prize for her speeds. Beth had found shorthand easy. For her, Pitman was like a secret language, a code for a game of subterfuge. Beth loved the loops and curls that wriggled across the page as she took dictation. Her typing skills had been excellent too.

The girls found a free table in a corner of the pub. Beth caught glints of light from the bar through the smoke and the wall of suits.

'What would everybody like?' she asked. 'The usual?'

The pub would only get busier as the evening progressed, and she hated the scrum to the bar; better to get it over and done with. The room was already filling up with testosterone. Beth pushed through the noisy forest of self-absorbed men brandishing beers and cigarettes towards the barmen, who commanded the room, handing out drinks like favours.

'Excuse me.' Beth arrived at the counter. It had been designed for someone at least five inches taller than her. She had her tenner ready in her hand to attract the attention of a bartender, but time after time, she was passed over. Men on either side of her leant in to shout their orders. Beth felt as though she was shrinking, squeezed between tweed and worsted shoulders, as the barmen's focus floated over her.

'What'll you have?' said a barman to a man standing next to her.

'You're next, aren't you?' The man waved a cigarette in her direction.

'Oh,' said Beth to the herringbone shoulder, 'yes, yes I am, thank you.'

'Yes?' said the barman, turning towards her.

Beth took a breath. She had wrapped herself in indignation while she had been ignored and had to unravel herself from her outrage before she could respond. The barman tapped the counter and gave her a withering look.

'Three white wines, please,' she said, in a rush, though she really felt like tea.

'We only have house.'

'Fine.' It was easy. She was back at the table with almost all the wine, having spilt only a drop or two on the way.

'God, pubs are gross,' said Angie, taking her glass of wine from Beth. 'It's enough to make you take up smoking,'

'At least we'd smell like the decor,' said Penny looking around. 'All this horse memorabilia on the walls. What do you think the effect they are going for is? Hackney cab meets brewer's dray?'

The vanilla-coloured wallpaper was bronzed with nicotine, accentuating the relief embossed on the walls. Beth raised her knees one after the other, allowing her shoes to be released by the sticky carpet. 'How much spilt beer does it take?'

'And the noise, why does everyone have to shout?' said Penny, raising her voice above the growing hubbub.

'And is this actually wine or vinegar?' Angie said, lifting her glass so the ceiling light caught the sallow liquid within. 'But,' she said, looking first at Penny and then at Beth. 'We are independent young women; we can go out to the pub if we like.'

Beth and Penny raised their glasses and they all joined in a toast.

'To independence!' they laughed.

'You forgot your change.' A deep voice interrupted the toast, holding out a fiver and some coins to Beth. She looked up at him with incomprehension and then she recognised his jacket tweed.

'You left it on the bar,' he said. 'I grabbed it before the barman thought it was for him. Much too generous for a tip.'

'Thanks,' said Beth, rising awkwardly and turning to take the money from his hand. 'That was kind.' His self-assurance was disarming. She silently cursed her blotchy skin, knowing she would be scarlet. This man with his ease and control of the situation was disconcerting. However independent she thought she was and however confident she ought to be, Beth always felt the need to gird herself when entering the masculine domain of a pub. Now, she felt unable to think of any suitable small talk and so, nodding a further thanks, she turned back to her friends. She could sense him behind her for a moment, a lovely woodsy smell, before he turned back to the bar.

'What a hunk, straight out of a Jackie Collins. Doesn't look like your typical City boy,' said Penny, leaning over and nudging Beth. 'Perhaps you should get the second round too. Go and introduce yourself while you're up.'

'But I don't know him,' said Beth horrified.

After much goading from Angie and Penny, Beth did get the next round. The voice was still by the bar, drinking with his friends. He stubbed out his cigarette in an ashtray on the counter, then came towards her and introduced himself. He was called Max. They stood shouting at each other over the din and Beth felt herself standing taller next to him reaching to hear his words. He was a paediatric surgeon at St Thomas'. He had come out for a drink with friends after their regular game of tennis. When the barman arrived, Max took over the order and paid for the round. It was extraordinary the difference Beth felt being next to someone. Talking to him, she felt shy but having him beside her gave her assurance. Beth and Max carried the drinks over and, pulling up chairs, the group of tennis blokes joined Beth and her friends. The three girls were no longer isolated; they had become part of the crowd.

At the end of the evening, Max took Beth's number.

Over the weekend, he called her.

'I thought we should go out to dinner,' he said.

At first, Beth was intimidated by the sheer scale of Max. It wasn't that he was especially tall or broad, though he was next to her, but she wasn't used to having someone so vivid in her life. He was good-looking, with such striking blue eyes that in the beginning she had found him hard to look at. But something raffish in the angle of his eyebrows, an eruption of tufty unruliness, made her pause. It suggested something wild in him that made her feel cautious, but also, by breaking the symmetry of his face, revealed the possibility of discourse. Before, Beth had never had a problem speaking up, her father had called her forthright more than once, but she wasn't quite sure how to be with Max. She determined not to be flighty or needy like some of the nurses at the hospital that Max mentioned in disparaging tones, but Beth found she missed him if the days passed, and they didn't meet.

'So?' Penny asked as they made coffee in the office kitchen a few weeks after they had all met in the pub.

'No, not yet,' said Beth.

'Why not?' Penny asked some days later as they waited for the photocopier as it churned away.

'I just want to get to know him a bit first,' said Beth. 'Want him to know me too.' She was terrified she would become too invested in this new relationship, and then, when she felt they had something real together, Max would discover how boring she was and move on.

One weekend at his flat, while rummaging through his classical LP collection, Beth discovered Max had an Abba album, Waterloo. It seemed unlikely, an old girlfriend must have given it to him, but Max declared he was a staunch fan when she jokingly asked him about it.

'They're great,' he said. 'Almost as good as Johann Strauss.'

They had laughed together and that seemed to settle their relationship on something solid and tangible. Some months later, Max took Beth to Austria for her birthday to listen to the Vienna Philharmonic perform.

'So you can compare the two greatest dance bands ever.'

Beth had never been to Vienna, so Max insisted they take a horse-drawn tour of the city. Beth had no intention of doing anything so embarrassingly touristy, but once she was seated in the carriage next to Max, their knees wrapped together in a woolly blanket, she forgot that people might stop and stare or that the coachman could overhear their conversation and she enjoyed herself. Afterwards, they had hot chocolate in Café Schwarzenberg.

When they returned to London, Beth took the plunge and brought Max home to Nether Place. Beth usually took the train, but they drove down together in Max's sports car, it was exhilarating. Beth seldom felt glamorous, but sitting beside Max in his swanky car, she felt sophisticated. Beth smiled across at Max, she felt if she reached up, she would be able to touch the silver linings of the clouds as they roared past with the roof down and the heating on high. She wasn't anxious, Beth knew her parents would like Max, but she wanted to keep the knowing of him to herself. Max was hers, her privilege, warming her heart, until she shared him. Of course, when they met him, her parents were delighted.

'Darling, he's like Clarke Cable with more hair and without the moustache,' said Ma as Beth helped her mother fetch coffee from the kitchen after lunch. Ma boiled the kettle, and Beth smiled at each delicate cup and matching, colourful saucer as she collected them from the cupboard and arranged them on the tray.

When they returned to the drawing room, Max was listening attentively to Pa talking about the history of Nether Place and the Parteger family. That afternoon, they all went for a walk and on the way back, Max helped Pa bring in more wood for the fire.

'Quite a catch, Beth,' said Pa later. 'Nice chap, and a doctor too,'

With her father's approval, Beth felt she had finally done something right.

Then Pa said, 'Don't muck it up.'

Beth felt her happiness diminish as the tone of her father's praise twisted into incredulity. The feeling reminded her of years ago when she was about fifteen and the hunt had met at Nether Place. The first and last time, the excitement of hosting overcoming concerns for the lawn. Beth had been commandeered to hand round the stirrup cup. As she manoeuvred carefully amongst the horses offering port, she had heard Mrs Johnson's braying laugh and overheard her father congratulating her on her mount.

'Handsome filly,' she heard her father say as he patted the horse on its shoulder. 'Good breeding stock.' At that moment, he had caught Beth's eye. He seemed to pause as if sizing her up before tipping his hat to Mrs Johnson and moving off. Beth later wondered if her father had been talking about the horse, herself or perhaps Mrs Johnson, two of whose four children were riding with the hunt. Not long after, as the hunt made to move off, a horse had taken fright and bolted across the lawn, digging divots out of the turf as it went.

When Beth was alone with Max, she felt sure of her feelings. She felt happy and safe with him; when they were together, he was funny and attentive. But when they were under the scrutiny of her parents, Max was on his best behaviour and became more formal, and Beth, in response, seemed to grow untidy emotions that threatened to leak out and spoil everything. It made her wonder what Max really felt. Sometimes he was so impressively self-contained and calm.

'I can see what I see in you,' Beth said to Max one chilly evening later that spring. They were sitting on the terrace at Nether

Place, bundled in sweaters and rugs, sipping white wine. Beth turned away from Max's inquiring eyes and looked out over the lawn. Low crisp light added clarity to the bright new green of the trees reflected in the mirror-smooth lake. A fish rose with a splash and was gone as quickly, leaving concentric rippling circles that radiated across the water's surface. Her heart glowed. She wasn't sure she wanted Max to see how much he mattered to her. But she needed him to share her feelings because she wasn't sure she could go on holding them all to herself. 'But … I don't know –'

'You make me feel real.' Max took her wine and placed it next to his on the terrace. Then he took her hand, cold and damp from the icy glass and kissed her fingertips. 'You make me feel ready to settle, ready to start the rest of my life.'

Tina

The first time I met you was in the spring before a long golden summer. Do you remember, Max? You had already been down to Nether Place and met my parents while I'd been away at school.

'He's a bit of a dish,' Ma had said to me in the Easter break. 'And at ten years older than Beth, he'll be a steadying influence.'

Beth was solid as a rock as it was, but I didn't say anything. How could she marry someone so old? To me, Beth at twenty-six was ancient, so you I thought must be antique.

Later the next term, home for an exeat from school, I couldn't believe how happy Beth looked. She literally glowed. Beth had been out shopping with Ma for a wedding dress all afternoon. That evening, we were at the front door waiting for you to arrive. I was ready to be seriously unimpressed. Then, you swept down the drive in your green sports car, raking the gravel as you pulled up at the door. You leapt out of the car, bounded up the steps, and hugged Beth. Over her shoulder, you winked at me.

'And you must be little Tina,' you said, breaking away from Beth and shaking my hand.

I scowled at being called 'little'. You glanced at Beth and you both laughed.

'Age is not so important,' I said.

'I have to talk to Mrs Simms about food for the wedding with Ma,' Beth said after lunch on Sunday. 'I know it might be a bit boring for you, darling,' she said to you in a stage whisper I could hear across the room, 'But perhaps you could help Tina with her tennis, play a game?' She glanced across the room at me and said more loudly, 'You said you wanted to make the school team this summer, didn't you, Tina? Perhaps Max can give you some tips. He plays tennis every week.'

While everybody disappeared about the house: Beth and Ma to the kitchen, Pa to his study, I followed you to the back porch where we scrabbled around for tennis shoes and rackets. Then we ambled out to the court that Pa had put in beyond the walled garden. We started with a knock-up. I can still remember how awkward I was, how uncoordinated I seemed to become under your gaze. I missed so many shots. After we had collected all the stray balls for the umpteenth time, you came to see how I held my racket and took hold of my wrist. You altered the angle of the racket in my hand.

'Like this, see, don't let the racket move in your hand, hold it firmly, but not too tight, don't grip it. Do that, and it'll make it much easier to hit the ball consistently well.'

I looked at the taped handle of the racket in my hand. You held the racket head in one hand and my wrist in the other. I nodded. I played better after that.

'What really lets my play down are my serves,' I admitted when we attempted a game. Again, you came to my side of the net and held my racket hand. Together we traced the arc of my swing, up and over, again and again.

'Muscle memory. This is what it should feel like. You need to stretch to reach the ball; it will give power to your serve.'

'The trouble is I can never throw the ball in the right place,' I grumbled.

'Like this.' You threw the ball up, 'it needs to land here. See.' You pointed to the court, 'you need to practice just throwing.' You demonstrated letting the ball rise, fall and bounce, catching it and tossing it up again, letting it bounce in the same place at your feet. 'Over and over. Practice. A lot. Okay, let's try together.'

You stood behind me and took my left hand holding the ball in your left hand, and my right hand with the racket in your right.

'Together,' you said in my ear. You smelt of cigarette smoke and faintly of some woody aftershave. We threw and swung and hit; the ball went in. We went through the motions a couple more times.

'Now, have a go on your own.'

You moved back and stood behind me to watch. I threw the ball up and struck. The ball went in. I served again, hitting the ball harder. 'Bravo!' you said, 'you learn quickly, Tina. If you hit the ball like that, you'll definitely make the school team.'

By the end of the afternoon, I was smitten. I remember feeling quite miffed when I had to leave for school. You and Beth were sitting out on the lawn under the cedar having tea with Ma, late spring shadows stretching across the lawn. Pa helped me get my bag into the car for the boring drive. I wished it was you who was taking me back to school in your snazzy green sports car. I imagined the stir our arrival would cause amongst my friends.

I did make the school tennis team that summer and every summer after. Do you remember? You came to watch me play.

Moving

The first years after Beth married were idyllic. Looking back there seemed to be an endless stream of balmy summer days and perfect weekends ideal for picnics and barbeques. Beth and Max moved out of London, finding a crooked cottage on the outskirts of Cobham on the fast line to Waterloo and not far from her parents in Faygate. Together they decorated, Max reaching the high bits, though the ceilings were so low he hardly needed a ladder. Beth subscribed to Country Living magazine and was inspired to try sponging and rag rolling in different rooms with varied success. She had borrowed Ma's old singer and sewed flouncy curtains with swags and tails, making a home stitch by stitch, ruffle by ruffle. She couldn't have been happier, rushing back to the cottage from work at the end of the day to get on with the next project. Max held onto his flat near the hospital. Sometimes he needed to stay the night in London if he was on call or had early surgery.

The cottage was not far from Penny's place, Beth's friend from work. Penny had married John, and they lived in a mid-terrace, two-up two-down near the station. Beth was relieved that Max liked John, and the two couples often met on weekends. It was good to have local friends. Sometimes Beth would bump into Penny at the station, and they would travel in to work together. Penny chatting loudly about her plans while Beth mumbled, and the carriage listened all the way to London.

Over lunch at work, Beth and Penny sometimes discussed; when would be the right moment to start a family. They agreed that it was definitely before they hit thirty, but they could never quite decide exactly when. They envisaged having children simultaneously and bringing them up together as friends. So, Beth was surprised when one Sunday lunch at the pub, Penny announced that she was pregnant. Champagne was ordered.

'Already?' Beth said. 'How marvellous!' Beth looked at Penny's sunny face and beamed back, raising the glass John had handed her. Beth had been trying too. She smiled to herself. It wouldn't be long; she would be next.

Penny could talk of nothing else. Beth couldn't blame her. If it were her, she would be the same. Penny had great plans, many concerning her pregnancy, what she should eat or not eat, and what she should drink. Beth listened. She knew it all already. She had read the books too. Together they poured over the catalogues discussing the benefits of different cribs and pushchairs. They spent their lunch hour in Mothercare. Penny confided that when the baby arrived, she intended to start her own business, an interior design company, so she could stay at home with the baby. She had begun developing her ideas already. It was something she had always wanted to do.

'I've never felt brave enough,' Penny said. 'But now John has made partner at his firm …'

Then, Penny and John moved to a larger Georgian house on the other side of the village, with plenty of scope for a budding interior designer.

Beth felt she had some catching up to do, but she wasn't sure why. It wasn't a race. Soon after, Max and Beth traded up to a detached house in a nearby town. It had lovely bay windows and ceilings high enough for Max, a good enough garden for Beth, who was beginning to understand her mother's obsession with plants and plenty of bedrooms for a family. It was the perfect nest. Beth wasn't pregnant yet, but it wasn't for lack of trying, and surely, she would join the club soon.

'Weren't they ghastly?' said Beth driving through the dark country lanes. Max and Beth were returning from a dinner at Penny and John's. There had been another couple there. Beth had found them unbearable.

'Oh, I don't know,' said Max.

Although they no longer saw so much of each other, Beth and Penny still kept in touch. Beth was godmother to Penny's little girl, Mia; she had taken her a gift, a stuffed bunny.

'The woman was so smug,' said Beth, swerving slightly to avoid a pothole. 'And it was a bit awkward when she started breastfeeding. I noticed you and John sidled off.'

'Hmm,' said Max.

'And that little boy! What a horror! He never sat still.'

'I believe that is the nature of boys. The house looked very grand. I love the minimalist look Penny has gone for.'

'The renovations have taken forever, but it all looks fabulous now. Penny does have an eye,' said Beth, wondering if Max thought their home cluttered and if he was tired of the warm peachy hues she loved. 'And the husband was so …. gross.'

'That's a bit harsh …. the baby was cute,' said Max.

'Yes.' Beth had tried not to obsess over the adorable little hand that had appeared above the satin hem of the blue, waffle knit blanket and flexed in ecstasy over the proffered breast. Beth had looked at the perfect bubble of motherhood at the other end of the sofa. They were so close Beth could lift her hand, reach out and touch, but of course, she didn't. She didn't know the woman. 'Yes, he was,' Beth said. 'Very cute.'

'Darling, honestly, you shouldn't worry. Our time will come!'

Beth huffed.

There had been an exquisite moment that evening. Before dinner was served, Mia had been instructed to say goodnight to her godmother and thank her for her gift, and Beth had received a slobbery bedtime kiss. Then John picked Mia up, dangling her upside-down as he carried her giggling, clutching her bunny, up to bed. Beth had held onto the feeling of the wriggly little body she had embraced for the shortest of moments. The smell and flutter of childhood had filled her senses.

'It was a lovely evening and good to see Penny and John,' said Max.

Beth slowed the car down as they neared the speed limit sign and entered their street.

'It was a lovely evening, and she is amazing.' Beth said. '…. But I can't believe Penny invited people over so close to her due date.' Beth was aware of Max turning to look at her, but she kept her eyes firmly on the road. Max said nothing.

Marmalade

Beth and Max drove down to Nether Place. Her brother, Duncan and his wife, Meredith, would be there with their toddler, Gareth. After lunch on Saturday, Duncan suggested a dog walk. Meredith decided to go as well; Gareth would be having a rest. Max went with them; Ma forbade smoking in the house. Beth volunteered to stay behind and keep an eye on Gareth. The walkers set out, and Beth lifted her nephew up so he could wave to his parents. They strode down the back drive with Max to the fields and hills beyond. The dogs circled around their ankles, and cigarette smoke wafted around their heads as Max raised his hand to return Beth's wave.

Beth would generally have enjoyed getting some fresh air, but it was a chance to have her nephew to herself. After the walkers left, she sat with Gareth in front of the fire and played with his toys, but he was tired and began to grizzle. So, Beth gave in and took him upstairs for a nap. She held the sleepy boy in her arms as she carried him slowly to his cot. His fair, straight hair fell over his wide forehead as he leaned against her shoulder. She relished the weight of him in her arms. He was hot with exhaustion, and his eyelashes fluttered in dreams over his flushed cheeks. He was such a miracle; birth was an extraordinary thing. Beth couldn't believe how her friends could treat pregnancy so casually. She breathed in the musky scent of childhood, reluctant to put him down, but he was fast asleep; she had no more excuses. She gently lowered him into his cot and returned downstairs to join her mother in the kitchen.

Ma planned to make marmalade that afternoon, and at Nether Place, making marmalade was a team activity. The kitchen was warm, and the big old aluminium pot was ready by the Aga. Beth joined her mother at the island and together, they started preparing the oranges and weighing the sugar.

'Do all babies smell of heaven?' asked Beth, her head bent close to Ma's as they chopped the fruit at the kitchen island.

'All my babies smelled delicious. Even Duncan, made from slugs and snails and puppy-dog's tails.' Ma poured the cut orange slices into the pot. Her back turned, she asked. 'Any news?'

'No, Ma, no,' said Beth. It was lovely that her mother cared, but her enquiries had become a nagging reminder to Beth of her continued failure. 'You know I would tell you. I'd tell you first ... after Max.'

'Darling, you shouldn't worry; babies come when you least expect them,' said Ma filling the scales with sugar. 'Look at Tina; she took her time to arrive.'

'Well –'

The door to the kitchen swung open and Tina bounced into the room.

'Speak of the devil,' said Beth. Why was Tina so gorgeous? Tina, still a teenager, made life look effortless. She was already taller than Beth and had Ma's slender frame and eye for colours and clothes, all basic female skills that Beth seemed to lack.

When it had only been Beth and Duncan, Ma had seemed bemused by her children, as though she hadn't expected such a self-reliant, sturdy daughter as Beth or such an imaginative, artistic son as Duncan. They had been brought up by Nanny. Her parents were absent and glamorous, like ancient Gods. In Beth's memory, her parents posed at the top of a golden staircase against sunlit skies in evening dress and gave forth didactic orders.

'Your coat must be longer than the hem of your skirt, Beth.'

'Don't brush your hair in the kitchen.'

'Never borrow other people's shoes.'

'Walk on the outside of the pavement, Duncan, let your sister be on the inside. A gentleman looks after a lady.'

To Beth, these commands seemed unrelated to her actual life and the hurly burly of the village school playground. No one ever explained why they needed to follow these rules. It seemed it was more important that she and Duncan be trained to take orders without question than that they should think for themselves.

When years later, Tina came along, it had surprised them all. This new baby seemed to fill Ma's expectations of what a child of hers should be. Now she was older, Beth could see that perhaps by that stage in her life, it was simply that Ma had more time to spend with the new baby, but to Beth, who was nearly twelve, it had felt like a betrayal. At the same time, Beth was sent away to boarding school, and this new, tiny person captivated her mother and absorbed all her attention.

Once when Beth had been invited into Pa's study to have her school report read, Tina had toddled into the room in tears with a broken toy, and Beth lost any attention that had been hers. Another time, Beth had been chatting with Ma about clothes for a party when Tina had come in and tried on all Beth's clothes that were lying out, pulling them about. It had become a game between Ma and Tina, and Beth felt excluded. Beth remembered those tiny cuts; it happened over and over. If she took time over her homework, Ma would tell her to get a move on, or if her room was messy, she couldn't go outside until it was tidy. And if she was late for anything, her father could be explosive. But Tina could throw her juice about and leave a trail of toys and clothes around the house. There were different rules for different daughters. Beth could see that Tina was just a baby, and she did love her, but it was impossible not to be jealous. The baby always came first. Tina sucked the joy out of Beth's world.

'What do you think, Ma?' Tina asked now as she twirled around the kitchen table. She was wearing a white frilly blouse and a purple miniskirt that made Beth gasp.

'I wasn't asking you.' Tina pouted at Beth as she danced around them. 'You have no idea about anything,' she muttered as she swung away.

'There just seems so much of you,' Beth faltered. 'On show.'

Beth would never have been allowed to wear anything so revealing when she was a teenager, not that she would have wanted to. Beth tossed the orange rind she had sliced into the pot.

'Do you like the skirt, Ma? It came out all right, didn't it?' Tina asked. Turning to Beth, she said, 'No need to get your knickers in a twist! Ma helped me sew the skirt, so it has parental approval. And anyway, I'll be wearing tights … probably.'

'Tina's going to a party tonight, a sixteenth,' said Ma.

'Can I borrow your boots, Ma? The ones that come over the knee.'

'Of course, you can, darling.'

'Your suede ones, Ma? She'll ruin them. She's only just fifteen.' Beth took the sugar from the scales and furiously stirred it into the pan of fruit and lifted the pan onto the hotplate.

Tina stuck her tongue out at Beth as she pirouetted past.

'Oh, but Ma,' said Tina, 'I won't be able to stay over anymore. It's a full house.'

'You'll have to ask your father if he'll collect you, but he won't want to be too late,' said Ma.

'I can pick up Tina,' said Max. The walkers were back, letting cold air slip into the room with the dogs, who padded mud over the kitchen floor before Duncan called them back into the boot room to be left amongst the abandoned wellies by the backdoor.

'I'd like to take the car out for a run. Where are you going anyway?' asked Max.

Tina rocked back on her heels and looked up at him through wisps of blond hair. Beth wondered if Tina knew how ridiculous she looked, showing off, it was preposterous.

'A party,' she said. 'It'll be late.'

Beth dropped the lemons she had been chopping into the pan, noisily clattering the knife on the cutting board.

'Looking very fancy, Tina,' said Duncan coming back into the room. 'You'll look the part in Max's flashy MG.'

'For God's sake, don't encourage her,' said Beth to her brother.

'How was Gareth?' asked Meredith standing by Beth and looking into the pan of simmering fruit.

'Out like a light,' said Beth. She looked up at the kitchen clock. 'He's been down for nearly an hour now.'

'I'll go and see how he is,' said Meredith.

'See ya!' said Tina as she did a final twirl and left the kitchen too.

'Anyone want tea?' asked Ma, filling the kettle up at the kitchen sink.

Tina

You picked us up from the party, do you remember? Mary and I staggered to your car, giggling. I remember Mary sat beside you, and I squeezed sideways across the back, behind the front seats. We had to carry Mary into her house, one of us on either side, trying not to wake her parents. We were conspirators helping the prisoner break back into the yard. After we dropped Mary off, I sat in the front with you, and we drove back to Nether Place.

You rested your hand on my knee. I can still feel the heat of that touch where you burned me, branded me.

'You look gorgeous, Tina, turning into quite the lady,' you said. I floated on your words. We turned into the drive, your hand slid up my leg, and your fingers gripped my thigh as the car took the turn. It didn't seem so odd; I was dizzy and needed to be anchored.

When we got home, you helped me out of the car. You supported me as we went in and helped me climb the stairs to my room. Then you put me to bed, undressing me slowly. You took great care, your hands caressing my skin as you removed every piece of clothing. First, you took off my shirt, as you undid the buttons the backs of your knuckles grazing my skin, then my skirt. It was almost as my mother used to undress me at the end of the day when I was a child, but there was something in your touch that my mother never showed; a desire to linger.

You sat me down and lifted my legs onto the bed. Then took off Ma's high suede boots, one by one. Your hands grasping the zipper heads at my inner thigh and sliding them down the length of my legs. You held the foot of the boots and, tipping the soles up, let my feet drop back onto the bed. There was only my underwear left. You took off my bra first, sliding the straps over my shoulders. You were very close as you leaned over to reach behind and unhook the clasp. I could feel the warmth of your breath on me and smell your aftershave and your cigarettes. Your arm brushed a nipple as you dropped my bra on the floor. I felt myself arch towards you, but, at that moment, you sat back and moved down the bed. You slipped off my knickers and just sat, looking at me. Then as I began to prickle with the cold of the night, you leant over me and tucked a stray strand of hair behind my ear. Your hand trailed down over my body, your touch like a feather.

'Beautiful Tina,' you said. 'Almost all grown up.'

My body cool, your hand hot. When your hand rested on my thigh, heavy, my whole body felt light, waiting I wasn't sure what for. After a moment, you pulled my duvet over me, got up and left. In the doorway, you looked back.

'Sleep well,' you said before closing the door.

A Liability

Beth had known it was the beginning of the end but not when the end would come. It had taken over a week of awkwardness and uncertainty. Although she knew what would happen, until the moment it did, she couldn't help but hope that, perhaps, it might not. Now she felt empty.

It had all started to go wrong when she had been down at Nether

Place. Ma was weeding the long border, and Beth had sat nearby on the lawn. They had talked about the family. How Tina was enjoying sixth form. How happy her father was that Duncan had settled in so well at the company firm, Farthingale & Parteger, establishing himself and getting noticed by the partners already. That the arrival of Gareth had brought Duncan and Meredith stability.

'And what are you now? Ten, twelve weeks? How lovely it will be when you will have a little one too.' Ma looked around at the flower bed. 'I think I've finished here. Shall we go in and get tea?'

Beth stood up to walk with Ma back to the house. Her mother picked up her trug. Beth paused, feeling uneasy. She felt a spasm, a single cramp. Beth wouldn't have noticed, would have thought nothing of it if she hadn't felt this way before. She placed a hand on her stomach and looked at Ma, who stopped pulling her gardening gloves off and stared back over the delphiniums.

'Oh, darling, not again.'

After her third, her doctor had joked that she was a liability; Beth had tried to smile. He had referred her to a specialist. When the tests came back, they showed that there wasn't anything wrong.

The morning it all started; Beth woke with intense cramps. She curled onto her side and sobbed into the pillow. 'Stay, stay, stay.'

Beth begged with each ragged breath she gasped until well after she knew there was no going back. When her breathing calmed, she felt the stickiness, Beth lifted herself up, tear-stained and smeary, and perched on the edge of the bed. She checked that her legs would hold her before staggering to the bathroom, dripping. Beth slumped on the loo, elbows on her knees, head in her hands, looking at the trail of spots and splashes across the floor that marked her path. 'Don't go,' she whined, but no one was listening. Weariness washed over her.

Beth sat in the bathroom, staring into nothingness. She wasn't sure how long she'd been there, but she finally got herself up and into the shower. She needed to phone Max. He had had an early start that morning and had left without waking her. She would clean up first, though, she always felt better when everything was tidy and in its place. When she was dressed, Beth looked at the bed. It couldn't be described as a sea of blood exactly, but it was a mess, a heart-wrenching mess. In tears, she bundled the bed linen and mattress cover together to take downstairs. Beth tried to stick to the practicalities. If she could do that, the day might hold together. Beth filled the utility sink, adding a splash of bleach to the detergent. As she pushed the stained linen into the hot water with a wooden spoon to soak, acrid steam swirled up and caught in the back of her throat and tears gathered at her chin. Then she returned upstairs and cleaned the bathroom, but it was not the distraction she'd hoped it would be. She struggled to think of the words she could use; a way to tell Max that wouldn't end in tears. He had been so pleased. They had wanted this so much. This time she had felt good. This time she had been so sure.

'Hi Max,' she said into the phone as she sat in the kitchen with an undrunk cup of coffee in front of her, the washing machine gurning in the background. 'Oh, Miss Pritchard.' Beth tried to sound more upbeat, 'sorry to disturb you. I thought this was Max's number. Is he around?' She must have called the office line in her distress, but no, Miss Pritchard said Max was in the operating theatre this morning and had asked her to answer his calls. She'd get him to call Beth back when he was free.

'Everything all right?' Miss Pritchard asked. Beth put down the handset. She didn't want to talk to Max's smart secretary.

Beth blew her nose. It was as if she held a pot with all their hopes and fears swirling around inside. All Beth could do was try not to spill a drop, but she did time and time again. Max would know why she had called and would try and hide his disappointment. He acted as though they were trying for Beth, but she knew he wanted this as much as she did. She knew he wanted a child of his own, a shot at eternity. All his protestations and care would only make her feel worse. She was the leaky vessel letting him down.

While she waited for Max to call, Beth phoned her GP and then her mother.

'Oh, darling, I'm so, so sorry,' said Ma with a sigh. What else could she have said?

Beth had never thought about having a family; it was a given. She had started her marriage to Max with the idea that their life together would be unique while never quite admitting that although their love for each other was exceptional, she hoped their path would be conventional. Beth thought it would be easy to be happy and to do what everyone else did. She barely noticed when she had begun to be left behind. But suddenly, she was surrounded by friends with beautiful, perfect babies. The trouble was that when the natural became impossible, it became vital.

The phone rang; Beth reached for it with a lurch, pulling herself into the present.

'Darling,' Max said. 'Are you alright?'

Beth sighed. How can you mourn the loss of something you've never had. Her breath broke, she gasped. 'No.'

Raspberries

The sun was hot on their backs as Beth and Meredith wandered between the raspberry canes picking fruit. Ma had sent them out after tea with old, empty plastic ice cream tubs selected from the cracked and chipped Tupperware that Mrs Simms kept under the sink in the pantry. With Gareth toddling behind, Beth and Meredith had meandered, through the jumble of soft flowers and tangled greens of the herbaceous borders that Ma loved, to the walled garden. Here, Burr, who had been the gardener at Nether Place for as long as Beth could remember, kept the kitchen garden regimented and organised with straight rows of vegetables, fruit, and showy flowers for cutting. There were three rows of raspberries. Beth and Meredith had been asked to gather as much fruit as possible; friends were coming to dinner. They started picking from the end nearest the greenhouses where the stoned fruit grew. Beth and Meredith took different sides of the middle row, where red dots of the bright fruit beckoned from among the coarse green leaves. The two women chatted as they slowly moved down the row.

'You're a lovely colour, Beth,' said Meredith as both women's arms reached out over the canes, 'but you haven't been away yet this year, have you?'

Beth caught the sun easily and seldom burned.

'No, just gardening. We haven't managed to get away yet. Max has a break at the end of the month, so we'll try and go abroad then.'

'You're so lucky. I go red at the slightest,' said Meredith. Beth looked across at her sister-in-law, whose auburn hair was tucked beneath her straw hat, her white face dappled with bright triangles of sunshine from gaps in the woven brim. The movement of her gold cross caught Beth's eye; the only jewellery Meredith wore. It swung back and forth as she leant to pick the berries.

Beth and Duncan had not been brought up to be particularly religious. The family went to Easter and Christmas services. Her parents went more often; her father was a warden now, and her mother was on the flower rota. Duncan had always been open and friendly, up for trying new things and making friends. Looking for somewhere to fit in. Flying from one thing to another, trying one type of life before flitting to the next. Duncan had been working in London at an advertising agency when he had met Meredith at a charity event organised by the business. His wings had caught in Meredith's web. There was something about Meredith, a certainty, that Beth could see would appeal to Duncan. Meredith was quiet, but she had an assurance that was attractive, particularly if you were looking for somewhere to belong. Their parents had been surprised. Duncan was relatively young, just out of university, and they were unprepared for him to leave home and set up house with someone new. But their marriage was a success. Duncan and Meredith were happy, and now they had Gareth.

'We haven't planned anything yet either. Without children to slow you down, you can go anywhere. For us it's like a military operation! To do anything with Gareth, we have to be so organised,' said Meredith. 'I suppose we might get to Cornwall.' They continued down the line of fruit. 'Take advantage and get away as much as you can before you get hampered with babies. They're such a tie.'

Beth plucked furiously at the raspberry bushes.

'You're still trying, aren't you?' Meredith gave Beth a rather sly look, but perhaps it was just the angle of her hat.

'When will you be having another?' asked Beth more aggressively than she'd intended; it wasn't a competition, after all.

'Oh, one is enough for me, for sure. Gareth is always so busy; I can't keep up.'

'He's lovely, such a happy little boy.'

'It's great that we can come down here, where there's space, and he can run around. He needs constant entertaining; he never sleeps. I'm completely worn out.'

Despite her claim to be exhausted, Meredith seemed to be pulling ahead of Beth down the line of raspberries.

'I'm sure if you had two, they would entertain each other,' said Beth as she hurried forward to catch up.

'Oh no, Gareth is a handful. Kids are such hard work, Beth; you've no idea. I have to keep my eyes on him all the time.' Meredith looked up from the bushes. 'Where is he?'

'He was here a moment ago,' said Beth. She had seen him toddling on unsteady legs between the canes. 'Gareth,' she called, looking out over the green for his tow-coloured head, her heart pounding.

'Boo!' Gareth squealed from behind her. 'I'm here!'

'Meredith, he's here,' Beth called out.

'Great,' said Meredith continuing to pick fruit, 'as long as he's in the walled garden.'

Beth turned back to Gareth; his round face peered up at her. He must have run the length of the bed and come back around the next row behind her. He showed her what he had in his pot, a few green berries and a leaf before he helped himself to the fruit in her tub with a greedy hand. Beth lifted her pot higher.

'Hello there,' she said.

Gareth, chuckled at his bravado, then squashed the fruit into his mouth. He turned and capered back up the row, his little legs swinging wildly as he ran.

Beth watched him go, then turned back to the raspberry canes. She needed to pick up speed if she was to catch up with Meredith. As they neared the bottom of the row, Gareth reappeared in front of his mother and laugh uproariously before speeding away back up towards the greenhouses.

'Shall we call it a day?' Meredith said. 'My pots quite full.'

'Good idea,' said Beth. Together, they walked up between the raspberry canes, following the small, ribbed footprints in the soft earth made by Gareth's retreating plimsols. Meredith's tub of raspberries was indeed fuller than Beth's. They entered the warmth of the long south-facing greenhouse that leant against the garden wall. Gareth was at the far end, splashing his pot in the water of the old sink; a green raspberry leaf floated on the swell. Burr was working at the raised bed.

'I wonder if we should take a few of these peaches up to the house too, they look delicious,' said Meredith pulling Gareth's wet arms out of the water and rolling up the sleeves of his sweater.

'What a good idea; Ma loves her peaches.' Beth reached up to pick a perfect golden peach nestled against the warm wall.

'I wouldnae touch that,' said Burr stalling Beth's outstretched arm. 'She'll no be wanting the fruit this weekend.'

'No?' Beth turned to Burr.

'Mrs Parteger knows the peaches are no for eating. I've got my show on Sunday.'

'The show?'

'I'll be taking the fruits for the village show,' he said. 'I always win the stone fruit category. And don't go picking the dahlias either; they're spoken for. I've already taken cut flowers up to the house.'

Onions

Beth was in the old pantry at Nether Place. They were down for the weekend. That morning, Pa had taken Max to the Johnsons. Colonel Johnson was master of the local hunt. He was going to take them to see the hounds in their kennels. Beth suspected Max could think of better ways to spend a Saturday morning, but he was a good guest and would be enthusiastic. Besides, they would spend time back at the Johnson's, and Beth knew that Mrs Johnson made a mean cup of coffee with a decent slug of alcohol added; that would cheer up Max.

Ma getting lunch together, she had sent Beth to find something to go with the lamb they were having. Beth breathed in the cool air of the pantry. The healthy mushroom smell of the earthy vegetables made her feel like she was underground. The long slate slab that ran the length of the room was no longer used just to keep food fresh. Tins and packets had begun to trespass, but at the far end, under the mesh-covered window, Beth saw a creamy brie that was starting to ooze. It would be perfect for the evening. Beth looked under the slab where basket drawers on metal runners held the dry vegetables and rootled around.

Having found what she needed Beth returned to the kitchen. She sniffed, wiping her right eye with the back of her hand as she chopped the onions.

'I've decided to look into IVF,' Beth said. 'Max isn't keen. He doesn't think it's appropriate, but I'm thinking of going ahead -'

'Oh ....' Ma rolled out some pastry that had been resting in the fridge, turning, and rolling until the circle of dough grew to fit the pie dish. 'Is that wise?'

'It's been nearly five years, Ma.'

'It seems .... imprudent to contemplate something so significant for both of you if .... Max isn't supportive.' Ma placed the pastry in the oven, weighted with pottery beads, to bake blind.

'I know, but .... I just want to see what it would involve.' Beth added the garlic she had chopped to the frying onions and turned back to slice the courgettes and tomatoes. 'Max is heartbroken too. He'd love to have children.'

'There's always adoption?' Her mother's voice floated out from the fridge where she was gathering bits and pieces for their lunch. 'You and Max are in a position to offer some poor child a proper home.' Ma said as she brought the olives and tomatoes to the kitchen island.

'We've talked a bit about that, but we want our own children. Max says he doesn't think he'd have the patience to bring up someone else child.'

When Beth had her goddaughter, Mia, sitting on her knee as she read her a story, or held any of her friends' children, she felt a surge of protectiveness that she knew would easily turn to unconditional love. If she was given a child, she would be able to make a family, but Max didn't feel that way. For him there needed to be a reason, there needed to be a motivation beyond love for love's sake. 'I've decided I want to look at the options; the science is moving forward all the time.'

'From what little I know about IVF,' said Ma, 'it would take its toll on you, all those hormones you'd have to take.'

'But to have a baby, that's our own. A baby I could give Max. That would be the best.'

'I read an article in Harpers recently. You should read it. It was about a girl on her third round of IVF. It described all the ups and downs of the treatment. Only to end unhappily. And so expensive. Sorry to be a pessimist, darling, but IVF may not be the panacea you think it may be.'

'Why is everyone so dead set against me trying,' said Beth sucking her finger where she'd nicked herself with the knife.

Tina

Do you remember the carol service? Was that the beginning, or had it begun earlier? You and Beth came with Ma and Pa to the end-of-term service at my school. The chapel was beautiful, filled with candles precariously perched on sloping window ledges and pew ends. Some were placed at the sides of the aisle where rising flames teased sweeping gowns. It was my last year, and the whole sixth form sang the Leavers' Carol, even though we had another six months to go. I remember Beth cried through the solos and was seriously blotchy by the time the service was over and we went through for the sixth form tea.

'It always does me in,' Beth sniffled into the white handkerchief you handed her. 'Children singing is way too emotional, and coupled with carols, I don't stand a chance.'

The handkerchief looked quite ragged by the time we reached the common room, and Beth scuttled off to the ladies to repair herself. You and Dennis fetched tea and brought it to the table that Ma and I had found.

'Pass the tea, Dennis,' I said.

'Don't call me Dennis,' said Dennis passing around plates and cups. 'I'm your father.'

My roommate Bella called her father by his Christian name. Bella was seriously cool. She lived in London.

You sat beside me, and leaning back, you rested your arm along the back of my chair. You flicked my ponytail from time to time like you used to do when I was younger. Beth appeared and joined us at the table, still looking pink but having dealt with her mascara. You sat up a bit straighter.

After tea, students could go home. Ma, "Don't call me Dennis", and Beth went to get the car. You followed me up the steep staircase to my room to help with my bags. We reached the landing as Bella was just leaving with her parents. We all said hello and inching around each other on the narrow landing, said goodbye. Then Bella and her parents clattered down the stairs. In the packed-up room, my bags sat on my stripped bed. The only sign of a busy term were the torn remains of my timetable and a few desultory strands of tinsel blue-tacked to the wall around Bella's abandoned George Michael posters.

I slung my hold all over my shoulder before grabbing my big bag. You bend down your warm hand closed tight over mine.

'Let me help you with that,' you said, smiling, our faces level. You were very close to me in that attic room. I held my breath, but after a moment, you turned and went down the stairs with my case. I followed, and we joined the others as if nothing had happened at all.

I didn't see you for a while, until the drinks party that my parents gave every year for the neighbours on Christmas Eve. You came early with Beth. She went on and on about the holly she'd brought that had berries as though it was special, as though the garden and woods weren't full of holly. She started to decorate the hall and drawing room, balancing branches on the mantlepiece and around candles. You went off to help Pa get the drinks together. Ma was in the kitchen with Mrs Simms, preparing the nibbles.

'Can you help me, Tina?' Beth asked. 'I could do with a hand if I'm to finish in time. If you hold the ladder for me, I could maybe get some holly on the chandelier.'

I was late getting ready, so I left her to it. She was so capable.

Beth never really wanted any help. She was always happier getting things done on her own, in her own way. Later, when I came downstairs, Ma was telling Beth what a good job she'd done.

'I could have done with some help with the ladder. I couldn't reach anywhere high.' Beth said.

'It all looks perfect, darling,' said Ma. 'No one will be examining the ceiling. Oh, there you are, Tina. What have you been up to?' I showed her my mauve nails. I was wearing a fabulous purple, halter-neck mini dress from Biba that Bella had leant me.

'Your hair looks very pretty up like that,' said Ma. 'Very sixties. And I love your nails.'

'You'll freeze,' said Beth.

'You look lovely, Tina,' you said, coming into the hall carrying a tray of glasses. 'Sorry if I'm a bit late to help. Dennis was showing me his wine collection. We were looking for a wine for tomorrow's lunch. He has some excellent reds stored away.'

'Tasting rather than looking, I think,' said Beth.

'Darling, you look lovely too. Would you like a drink?' you asked Beth. Then you turned to me and winked.

'Glass of red for me, please,' said Beth. 'You'll have a sherry, won't you, Ma? Tina?'

'Nothing for me,' I said. 'I'm not drinking tonight.' The truth was, I hated the taste of the stuff back then.

'Only drink when you're out with your under-age friends at pubs?'

'Honestly, Max, leave her alone,' said Beth. 'Pop that tray down and come and help me move the coffee table before someone trips over it.'

At the party, in the crowded room of guests, you ran a finger down my bare spine as we stood talking to some older neighbours. Your hand continued down my dress before you moved off to talk to someone else. I could feel my heart beating hard while I answered dull questions about school.

Later in bed, reading, I heard the third step on the attic staircase creak and knew you were coming to see me. You grinned from the door, swaying slightly. I leant up on my elbow, holding the sheets high.

'I've brought the remains of a bottle of Champagne from the party. Thought you and I could celebrate a little longer. Everyone else seems to have gone to sleep.'

'I've already brushed my teeth,' I said.

'God, you can do better than that. You sound just like Beth.' You handed me the bottle. I smiled back at you and vowed not to be like prissy Beth. I took a swig from the thick, heavy glass bottle, trying not to gag as you watched.

'That's more like it,' you said.

You prowled around my room, humming carols to yourself, glancing at me every now and then.

'Have some more,' you said, 'enjoy yourself.' I took another heavy drink. You looked at my books and picked up ornaments as you wandered, even fingered the fabric of my dress that hung on the wardrobe door. At the window, you saw the ice in the corner of the pane. With your nail, I saw you draw a heart in the frost on the glass. Then you kicked off your shoes and slipped off your jacket.

'It's cold in here.' You shivered. 'Budge up.' You took off your trousers and got into bed beside me. 'You can warm me up,' you said. You took the champagne bottle from me and put it on the floor beside the bed. Then you turned and brushed a stray lock of hair from my face. 'Beautiful Tina, Happy Christmas!'

I wanted so much to be grown-up, Max to be part of the world outside school and childhood. How could I have known there was no shortcut to living life?

Tinker's Wood

Beth took a cup of coffee to the drawing room and sat in the armchair by the French window in the fitful sunlight, reading the papers. All the supplements were spread out on the floor around her. She looked up from time to time, her eye caught by dancing leaves, and she would gaze out at the scudding clouds. It looked like it might rain later. She watched for a mistle thrush that kept returning to crush the shells of snails on the stone steps outside. Max was on call at the hospital that weekend staying at the flat, but Duncan was at Nether Place, so Beth had come down too. This afternoon, the house was quiet. Ma was out to tea with a friend. Meredith had taken Gareth to a soft play centre, and Duncan was ensconced with Pa in his study. Beth was halfway through the garden supplement when she heard the study door slam and steps marching across the hall parquet. She jumped up and tracked Duncan to the boot room, where he was pulling on his Barbour.

'Going for a walk,' he said. 'I'll take the dogs.'

'Can I come?' Beth didn't get Duncan to herself very often. She raced to get ready, pulling on some old wellies and grabbing her anorak as Duncan collected leads, called the dogs, and they started out the door.

The clouds were darkening as Beth followed Duncan down the drive and along the fork to Home Farm. She struggled to match his stride. They walked through the farmyard in silence. She followed him on the single-track road out the other side. Duncan had always been like this. He would be oblivious to those around him, needing to obstinately grind through whatever was troubling him. Beth had learnt to hold fast; wait till he was ready. At the end of the road, they joined the footpath that ran between a stand of oaks and a bare winter field. It began to spit, the sharp wind driving the drops across the field and through to the woods behind. Duncan looked up to call the dogs to heel. Marching ahead, he took the path through an old beech copse and over the stile and onto the open heath. He let the dogs run free.

As they broke cover and began to climb up the steep hill to the pines of Tinker's Wood, the rain intensified, throwing down heavy drops from which there was no escape. Duncan didn't pause but pushed on. He seemed oblivious to the weather. Beth pulled her hood up and followed. They crossed the scrub. The path narrowed to no more than a sheep track between the gorse. Beth, head down, watched the rain drip off the hem of Duncan's coat as she trudged up the steep hill behind him. By the time they reached the cover of the trees, raindrops were caught in her eyelashes and dripped off the end of her nose.

They stood close to the dark, rippling bark of the pines for shelter and watched as the wind blew the rain away, a grey curtain being pushed across the valley. Afternoon sunshine broke through the remnants of tattered clouds in sharp shards of brightness. High above them, the rooks rose from the topmost branches of the trees of Tinker's Wood to surf the gusts of wind, cackling to each other.

'I'm thinking of handing in my notice at Farthingale and Parteger,' Duncan said.

'Oh?'

Beth studied her wellies; flexing her toes, she spotted a crack in the right boot near the instep.

'Have been for a while…'

Her brother had recently begun muttering about the difficulties of working with their father, but Beth had presumed Duncan was committed to the company and his role in continuing the family connexion. She had thought Duncan relished the role as much as he enjoyed complaining.

They looked out over the valley. The landscape below was now clear and sharp. To the left, Beth could see the chimney pots of Nether Place nestled in the trees. Far off, rods of sunlight on a field of stubble caught a flock of pigeons that lifted and banked into the sun, flashing white against the dark, receding clouds.

'I love this view, even in the rain,' he said. 'It's always here, constantly changing, but always the same.'

'Like people's faces,' Beth, persuaded the rain was over, pushed her hood back and shook the water from her hair.

'No, not like faces,' said Duncan smiling, mock dodging the pellets of rain that spun from Beth. 'You're worse than the dogs.'

'I guess you mean the permanence of this view, but someone could build a motorway right through the middle of it one day. Faces are fascinating because people are so unpredictable. You know, say one thing but mean another.'

She wasn't upset about Duncan's personal decision to stand back from working with their father in the business. That was his choice, but she was concerned about the consequences for the rest of the family.

'When I'm up here, I feel as though I could lift off and soar with the rooks.' Duncan raised his arms and leant forward into the wind. 'Rise above everything and float away.'

'Whereas I prefer to keep my feet solidly on the ground,' said Beth, stamping her feet that were growing cold.

As they watched, the sun faded, and the valley returned to a misty blend of tired winter greys and browns. Beth shivered.

'Time for tea,' she said, calling the dogs, but they were busy under the yellowing gorse bushes and ignored her. She turned and started walking back to the house. Duncan took a last look at the view, whistled, and the wet dogs slunk out from their rabbiting and followed him down the hill.

'Have you told Pa?'

'Not yet. You know I've tried to be who Pa wants, I really have, but it's not for me.'

'What will Pa say, do you think?' she asked as she climbed the stile. Jumping down, Beth landed in a puddle and felt dampness creep in the crack in her wellie. They both knew that their father's ambition was for there to be a Parteger at Farthingale & Parteger for generations to come. Pa had tried to mould Duncan from the start, taking an interest in his choice of school subjects and pushing him towards those studies that would fit with the family business.

'There's not much he can say,' Duncan said. 'I've made up my mind.' He swung round to look at her, his expression unflinching as if defying her to contradict him. 'I've given it almost five years.' He turned and resumed walking. 'It was fun at the beginning, learning all the different aspects of the business. But as soon as I was moved into management, I realised it was not for me.' He shrugged. 'The whole environment, ethos, everything.'

'Are you really sure?' she asked.

'Every time I want to try something new, I get swept aside. Of course, the management doesn't want change, and God knows, a little wouldn't hurt.'

They walked through the beech wood towards the field.

'I mean, I've known for years, forever really, that I was a square peg, wouldn't be cut out for the job,' he said. 'You've probably known too. You'd be much better at carrying on the family tradition. You are loyal and interested in a way that I am not.'

'What does Meredith think?' Beth thought about families and responsibility and the expectations that entailed. Max would talk over any big decision; he wouldn't keep anything from her. Meredith had married someone with an established career path. She and Duncan had a house; they had a child.

'She's okay about me trying to find something different,' he sighed, 'she knows I'm not happy where I am. Anyway, I'll look around first. I will only leave F & P if I have something to go to.'

'Have you any idea what you want to do?'

'I'd prefer something more creative,' he said, 'perhaps back into advertising.'

Beth remembered Duncan being happy at the advertising firm in London where he had worked for a couple of years. He had been carefree, wild even, before he joined F & P and settled down, before he met Meredith.

They reached the field and splashed through puddles and mud.

Beth's sock in her broken boot was sodden. Duncan called the dogs to heel again. As they left the wood, he knocked against branches that scattered hanging, jewel-like raindrops heavily onto them both.

'What I really want to do, what I'd like, would be to try something different, somewhere different,' he said. 'Somewhere where it isn't so god-damned wet all the time.'

Beth caught her breath, 'Somewhere different?'

'Yes, the States, possibly.' Duncan held the gate for her as they crossed onto the track that led back to the farm.

'And Meredith is keen?'

'We haven't talked about moving country.'

'She's very close to her family.' Beth said. Max wouldn't surprise her with something important, like moving country, they'd talk it over.

'We can always visit. We would visit.' After a moment Duncan asked. 'And you, Beth, do you and Max have any plans?'

'Nothing special,' she said. 'Just more of the same.' Checking dates, looking at the calendar, but she didn't go into that with her brother.

As they crossed the yard at Home Farm and headed down the drive towards the house, Duncan said, 'Not a word, Beth.'

'Right,' she said, feeling honoured that he had confided in her, but uncomfortable that she knew more than Meredith.

'I'm not ready. Just wanted to run it past you, warn you what I am thinking about.'

'I shall miss you,' she said as though he had already left.

Ice Cream

Beth took Mia's hand, picked up the car seat, and walked back to her car. She helped the little girl into the back seat, making sure she was comfortable and the seatbelt secure.

'Thanks so much,' called Penny from her front door, 'We'll have a cup of tea when you drop Mia back. We can catch up then.'

Beth waved to Penny before getting in the car. It was Mia's sixth birthday treat.

'What made you choose the zoo this year?' said Beth once their journey was underway.

'I just love animals, Godmother Beth.'

'I do too,' said Beth. She pulled onto the dual carriageway and pushed the car to join the faster traffic. Beth looked at Mia in the rear-view mirror. Mia was holding her stuffed bunny, rubbing it gently along her chin while she looked out the car window, 'You know you don't have to call me godmother every time, Mia. You can just call me Beth or Auntie Beth if you prefer. Godmother Beth is a bit of a mouthful.'

'But you're my godmother, not my aunt. Mummy says it's very special to have a special godmother like you, Godmother Beth.'

Beth managed to park close to the gates. They picked up a map at the zoo entrance and sat on a bench in the sun, deciding what they would like to see and what route they should take.

'I want to see the giraffes.'

'Good idea,' said Beth. 'They are such an outrageous combination of grace and awkwardness.'

'And the monkeys, and the goats, and the snakes.'

'Okay,' said Beth. 'Let's go.'

As they walked together in the warm spring sunshine visiting Mia's favourite animals, the smell of the creatures, their food and their waste were rich and bestial and, to Beth, suddenly crushing. There were calves and kids everywhere. A reminder that life went on all around her, even as she seemed to stand still. It was a relief when they arrived in the reptile house. After they had spent far too long searching for snakes in the terrariums, they went to the cafe. Mia poked at her sandwich for a bit before Beth ordered the prerequisite ice cream.

'Mummy is going to have another baby,' said Mia.

'Another one?' Penny hadn't said anything. She probably couldn't bear the thought of Beth's strained congratulations, accompanied by the grimace Beth caught herself using when she knew she should be looking happy. Now, she tried to ignore the sharp pain that twisted inside.

'I'm so cross,' said Mia. 'Jack is so annoying. I really don't want another brother.'

'I suppose you might get a baby sister; that would be fun.'

'No, it's going to be another boy, baby, Mummy said.' Mia dug her spoon deeper into her ice cream, then lifted and turned it to lick the narrow, pointed head. Beth watched the melted ice cream snake its way back down the long handle dripping on the table as it went.

'Why don't you have children, Godmother Beth?' Mia asked, waving the spoon about as she licked her fingers.

'I guess I haven't had the right opportunity.'

'But you're old like Mummy, and you're married.'

'That's true, but not everyone gets what they want in life.'

'Mummy says you shouldn't say want, you should say, please may I have. Perhaps you didn't ask nicely enough.'

'Perhaps.'

'Well, I think you're so lucky. You might have got some beastly boys.'

'Or I might have had a gorgeous girl like you.'

'That's true,' Mia looked thoughtful.

'Actually, I think I'm very lucky to have you as my goddaughter. I really enjoy our days out, and, I'm having great fun visiting the zoo with you today.'

'So really, you are doubly lucky.'

Beth wiped Mia's sticky fingers with some wet wipes fished out of her bag.

'Shall we go and see if we can find a friend for your rabbit in the gift shop?' Beth said.

Tina

It was the Easter holidays; I was home from school. When I told you, you had smiled like a cat with cream. We were sitting side by side on my bed in my room up under the eaves. You touched my stomach, laying your warm hand flat against me. I was happy you were pleased. I had thought you might be cross.

'I have a baby?' you said, as though you couldn't believe it could be true. 'Show me.'

I stood up and took my clothes off while you watched. I was thrilled that you looked at me steadily, with eyes that knew me so completely. You made me feel special, grown-up. I never thought of Beth then; why would I? To me, she was boring and moaned constantly about absolutely everything. You must have thought her dull too, or you wouldn't have come to me. I'd never imagined you touching her like you touched me. Now, I thought, things would change.

'Turn,' you said, 'so I can see.'

I showed you the small beginnings, my swollen belly a silhouette against the light from the window.

'Beautiful, so slender, and then this beginning ... this is a first for me,' you said, watching me for a moment. 'I've always wanted ...' You gulped, but real men don't cry, do they, Max? You reached out and pulled me towards you, between your legs. You kissed my stomach tenderly and ran your hand between my thighs.

'My lovely Tina,' you said, looking up at me. You licked your fingers and then lowered me to my knees. You kissed my lips while you undid your flies. You pushed me down, holding my head, cupped in your hands, gentle but firm.

'Say nothing to anyone,' you said after you had come. 'About this. Don't even tell your mother — ever.'

'I ... I want to tell Ma,' I said.

'There's no need to tell anyone anything yet, is there? We could keep this precious secret to ourselves for a while longer, don't you think?' You held me by my shoulders. 'You are my greatest secret, Tina.' You stood and eased past me, fastening your trousers. Then you pulled me up to you and kissed me slowly. 'And I'm your greatest secret. Aren't I?'

'But —'

'You know how much you mean to me,' you said.

You folded my nakedness into your smoky embrace, and I could feel the warmth of you as you held me tight, the taste of you still in my mouth and your belt buckle cold against my new stomach.

'Your parents don't need to know about us; we'd never be able to see each other again if they did. You wouldn't want that, would you?'

The words grazed my skin as your lips moved over my neck. My hair moved under your breath, I felt submerged in the musky smell of you. I felt comfort in your certainty.

'This, between us, has always been special. Hasn't it?' you said.

I nodded.

'You don't want anyone in your family to get hurt, do you? You understand? I don't need to ask you to promise me you won't talk, do I? As adults, we can agree this is the best thing to do.'

It was as if you looked into the very part of me where hopes grew and gently blew the first frosty breath on any filaments of growth. You released me and walked across the room.

'When you have to,' you said, 'say it was some boy at the school dance or something, and … no more skipping meals. My baby needs a healthy start.' you paused at the door smiling again and added. 'But not a word — or all this, that we have together, will be over. Be sensible, and nothing need change,' you said.

You opened the door and left.

Elephants

'She's pregnant!' said Beth. There was a slight pause in the rhythmic tinkle of cutlery and china from the surrounding tables.

'Shh, darling,' said her mother, leaning in and covering Beth's hand with her own.

'I don't believe it!'

'I didn't mean to upset you,' said Ma. 'I just thought you would want to know.'

'Are you sure?'

Beth sat back, pulling her hand out from under her mother's and pushing her plate away. She looked around at the happy faces chattering away at the surrounding tables as though nothing had changed. Her mother must have chosen the crowded, noisy cafe at Peter Jones so Beth would not be able to overreact. Ma needn't have put so much thought into it. Beth wouldn't cause a scene; she felt utterly deflated.

They often met up for lunch when Ma was up in town shopping or meeting friends. This evening her mother was due to go to the theatre with Pa.

'I've a wedding present to choose this afternoon at the General Trading Company,' Ma said, 'And I might pick up some ornaments for the orangery too. They have those amazing china elephants, I'm sure you've seen them, with the howdahs, in blue and green.'

Beth couldn't believe her mother was being so sanguine. Perhaps she had railed and wept and beaten her chest till no emotion was left, but sometimes Ma took English stoicism too literally. Ma was giving her time to collect herself, Beth understood, and she had seen the elephants. Beth had thought they were fabulous, partly because they were so large. They would look impressive in the orangery at Nether Place.

'How pregnant is she?' Beth asked.

'Six months, give or take. The school called, and we had to pick her up. They were *not* impressed.'

'Why didn't anyone notice? Someone must have seen —'

'Well, we weren't looking; it wasn't a consideration.'

'How? When?' Beth asked. She needed to know the details. 'And who with?'

'She's not telling, being very vague,' Ma said, 'You are not the only one who is upset. This is less than ideal for everyone. Your father is apoplectic! As a matter of fact, the only person who seems to be taking things calmly is Tina.'

Beth gazed into her coffee as if the dark liquid might hold the answer to the dull ache that seemed to be growing inside her. This should be her baby. She was older and had been trying for so long. She found it hard to suppress the jealousy she felt towards her sister. The moment Tina arrived; Beth felt she had been replaced. After all these years, she was disappointed that she couldn't let go of the childhood bitterness. Even now, her thoughts gurned with misery and petulance.

'It's not fair,' Beth muttered.

'Nothing's fair, you know that...' said Ma, pouring herself some more tea. 'I wonder if the GTC will deliver all the way to Nether Place.'

'What has been decided? Has anything been discussed?' asked Beth.

'It's too far along to get rid of, not that she wants to. Tina seems to think she can carry on, finish her exams, not that the school will let her, and bring up the baby herself. Another coffee, darling?'

'No, no thanks. What will Tina do about her university place? Will she be able to defer? She was doing so well.' Beth had missed out on going to university, a combination of a lack of application and a desire to get into the workplace and be independent. She had been so proud of Tina. Now Beth resented Tina throwing away the opportunity. 'And where will she live? Nether Place?'

'So many questions! If you could come down this weekend, your father and I thought we could have a proper family discussion.

Meredith can't make it, but Duncan will be there. Would you both be able to come?'

'Of course.' Beth glanced at her watch. 'I'd better get back to work.'

'You'll let Max know, won't you, darling?' said Ma as Beth stood, and they kissed their goodbyes. 'It would be good to have him there too. He sees things so clearly.'

That evening at home, Beth tried to speak to Max but felt her throat tighten each time she searched for words.

'What is it, darling?' asked Max as they sat down to supper, 'you've been unusually ... quiet this evening.'

'She's pregnant,' Beth eventually managed to mumble.

'She? Who's, what?'

'Tina is pregnant.'

'Oh!'

'I can't believe it,' Beth said.

They ate in silence. The clash and scrape of cutlery the only sound.

'I'm not surprised,' said Max as they finished their meal.

'You're not?'

'Well,' Max looked thoughtful, 'to be honest, I've always thought Tina was a bit of a slut.'

'A slut! Really?' Yesterday Beth would have been outraged if anyone had called her sister a slut, but tonight it didn't seem so incongruous.

'Well, slut may be a bit strong, but that evening I collected her from the party. I never liked to say, but her behaviour didn't seem appropriate. I didn't want to upset you at the time, but she was in a right state and carrying on.'

'Carrying on? What do you mean?'

'You know, all those girls, her friends too, wearing hardly any clothes, showing yards of flesh, and plastered ... what right-minded teenage boy would not make a move.'

'That was ages ago, and all the girls like to show off.' Beth collected and stacked their plates. 'You know, Tina's so young, and she has her whole life ahead of her.'

'And now she's pregnant.'

Later that evening, passing the open door of his study on her way upstairs, Beth saw Max sitting at his desk, smoking a cigar from the pretty Cuban box on his desk. He'd been given the cigars by grateful parents after he had led the consultation team that had performed a successful operation on their sick daughter. Beth hesitated at the door but didn't call out to him as she usually would. Max looked deep in thought, his head surrounded by drifting cigar smoke like wraiths caught in the light from the desk lamp.

By the time he came upstairs, Beth was drowsy, almost asleep. She saw him briefly, dark against the landing light before he closed the door and entered the dusky bedroom. She felt his weight press down on the mattress as he sat beside her on the bed. He slid his arm gently around her and bent to kiss her temple. The smoky smell from his cigar enveloped her.

'You know,' he said, in his throaty growl, 'I've been thinking.'

She rolled over so she could make out his face in the gloom. 'What about?'

He kissed her again on the lips, and his hand slid down over the slope of her hip.

'Max, I'm asleep.' She curled away, back into the cosy duvet.

He got up from the bed, unbuttoning his shirt and said, 'I've been thinking about us going down to see your parents this weekend to talk about Tina.' Beth heard a rustle and a thunk of the belt buckle as Max tossed his trousers on the back of the bedroom chair. She watched him through her eyelashes as he paced the room discarding his clothes as he went. It made a difference, all that tennis and joining the new gym. Some of her friend's husbands, younger than Max, seemed to have given up, but not Max. Beth stretched under the covers like a sleepy cat.

'You know I have never been keen on adoption,' said Max to the still-life above the chest of drawers before turning back toward Beth, 'but I think it might be the right solution for Tina. She can't really keep the baby, not if she wants to continue her studies.'

Beth curled up into a foetal ball again, thinking about the many times she'd tried to persuade Max that adoption might be a good idea. It was the only thing they'd ever argued about.

'You've never –'

'I've always thought,' Max said. 'Well, I'd just prefer to know what the challenge was. If there's no direct genetic link, how'd you know what you've got.'

'Tina should go to university,' Beth said, rocking her head into her pillow to wipe a tear. 'I agree; adoption would definitely be best for her.'

Max hopped slightly, then regained his balance as he pulled off his socks.

'We wouldn't be able to see the baby, watch it grow, or vet the other family, of course, but it would be the best outcome.' He pulled on his pyjamas and slid into bed beside her, switching off his bedside light. Beth was thinking about her babies, who, one after the other, had slipped away before she'd got to know them.

'Yes,' said Beth, with a sigh. 'I think that is probably what will happen. I can't see my parents putting up with a new-born at Nether Place.'

'Extraordinary to think of Tina having a baby. A new, tiny life,' Max spooned in behind her and nuzzled her ear. 'It will be your nephew or niece.' He bit her earlobe tenderly.

Beth still saw Tina as a child at school, and here she was, effortlessly managing the one thing Beth had been unable to achieve. She felt the heartache twist in her chest. It should be me, thought Beth; this should be my baby.

After a while, Beth said, 'I wonder …'

'Mmm?'

'Wonder whether we.… whether this might be the time.'

'Time for what?' He kissed her shoulder.

'But you've never liked the idea.' She nestled into him.

'What, adoption?' Max held her close but very still.

'But we… we could, couldn't we? She rolled round to face him. 'Adopt.'

'Adopt?' He pulled back from her slightly. 'Adopt … us adopt Tina's baby? They lay still. In the dim bedroom light, Beth searched his face to see if he agreed.

'Well, there's an idea,' he said at last.

'You've never wanted to take on someone else's child,' she said.

'Yes, but I suppose … I mean, this would be your sister's baby. It would be as close as you could get to having your own child.' Max propped himself up on his elbow and let his other hand stroke up and down her arm. 'I love your genes.'

'We don't know who the father is. Would that worry you?' she said.

'He is probably some arrogant public-school boy with an impeccable pedigree.'

'We could make sure there were opportunities, all sorts of life chances that perhaps another family couldn't provide.'

'It is an opportunity for us too …' Max looked deep in thought.

'I think it would be a wonderful idea.'

'After all you've been through, darling, trying to have your own baby,' said Max, 'are you sure you want to bring up someone else's child?'

'Yes,' she said, her breath catching, 'yes, I think I do.'

He kissed her and said, 'Well, if it's what you really want, darling, of course I'll support you.'

'There will be sacrifices. For a start, you'll have to give up smoking, Max, if there's a baby in the house.'

'Anything for you, my darling.' He kissed the back of her neck.

In the car on the way down to Nether Place, Max said, 'I can talk to your parents if you like. You know, it might seem a bit unorthodox. The idea might take some getting used to, but I can persuade them. You won't have to say a word. Do you trust me?'

'Of course I trust you! In this and everything.' She leant across and squeezed Max's hand where it rested on the round head of the gear stick. Beth knew that she would trust Max through thick and thin. What was left in a relationship if there was no trust?

'Good,' said Max, turning to give her a quick smile. 'You give me carte blanche!'

She heard something in his voice that perhaps sounded like pride or satisfaction, but she didn't dwell on where it might come from. She, too, felt pride in their marriage and satisfaction with the warmth of her feelings for Max. She nestled back into her seat, the more Beth thought about adopting Tina's baby, the more she knew it really was the perfect solution.

Tina

I was staying in a private clinic tucked away in a quiet suburb of a provincial town, far from home, but I didn't feel isolated. I was glad. I did not want any visitors. Not even you, Max. I wanted this precious time for myself to get to know this new little person who had entered my life.

The breeze had lifted the curtains all day, bringing light and laughter into the room from the street outside. Now the light was changing. The sky was losing its brightness, and cool air flowed in and pooled on the floor. I slipped out of bed, my bare feet cold on the linoleum, and crossed the room to close the window. I didn't want my baby to catch a chill. I didn't want anything bad to happen to my little girl. As I turned, there was a fidgeting from the bassinet. I leaned in, wrapped my baby in her blanket, and carried her back to my bed. I sat cross-legged and cradled her, allowing her small fingers to curl around one of my own. What an extraordinary tiny being she was. Her little face turned towards me, rubbing against me, searching. I undid my top and settled back into the pillows to feed her. I felt the draw of milk and gazed down at the contented baby in my arms. We nestled together, and it felt as though we were still one, that we were not quite separate yet. I wondered how anyone could give their child away.

At Easter, when I was home for the school holidays, I had realised my body was changing. I had denied what I already knew. I had become a shapeshifter, morphing slowly from one being to the next so gradually that no one around me noticed. That was when I told you, Max, that I was going to have your child. It was only when I got back to school, later, during the exams, on a sweltering, stuffy day, that my disguise was uncovered; I fainted. The school was not pleased. My parents collected me from sickbay and took me home. I was not allowed to say goodbye to my friends.

Not long after, on a clear summer's day, I left home. I thought I might be sick on the ferry, but I wasn't. Maybe the salty air and a new sense of purpose contributed to my feeling of being grounded even as the boat rocked around me.

Pa had organised everything. It was as if suddenly he couldn't stand the sight of me. I had sat sullen and uncommunicative, slouched on an itchy tapestry chair in his study while he rang a friend in Italy and arranged for me to be sent away. I was to have a job at a Pensione, to help with general cleaning and looking after summer visitors until my baby arrived.

On the day my school friends would have been opening the envelopes containing the results that would unlock their lives, I was in the hot kitchen of the Pensione, heating up brioche for holiday guests. A month or so later, my waters broke. Madame Castellini took me to the clinic as my father had instructed. The doctor said I had nothing to worry about. He was right; the pain of labour was nothing compared to the pain of the loss I was already feeling for this little person who was now arriving, this little person I hadn't yet met.

I finished feeding my baby, winded her as I had been taught, and carefully put her back in the cot by my bed. I stroked Lara's cheek, and she smiled back at me. The nurse told me it was wind, but I knew it was a smile, a shared secret between us.

There was a quiet knock on the bedroom door. You entered with a nurse.

'I'm here to take the baby home,' you said.

The nurse lifted my sleepy girl out of her crib.

'Lara,' I said, 'she's called Lara.'

'What?' you said without looking at me, absorbed by the baby. Taking my child, you left the room.

As the heavy door closed behind you, all the tiny snuffling, mewling babble that had become my life was gone. It was over. I sat on the bed. I couldn't move. The quiet in the room closed in on me, pressing into me. The blunt silence shredded me. I held myself tight with misery. There was nothing I could do.

It had been finalised months ago. There had been a gathering at Nether Place; we were in the drawing room. Beth sat with Duncan and Ma on the sofa opposite me, Pa in his wingback chair by the fire. You paced around the room behind me, a dark presence waiting to pounce.

Pa spoke at length. He was decisive and authoritative, talking in his work voice of damage limitation as though I was a financial problem.

'Darling,' Ma said every time Pa's rhetoric spun off at a tangent or became particularly choleric. She leaned over and placed her hand on his arm, and he would pause, look at her and start again, back on track. 'The worry you've put your mother through …'

He insisted I give up the baby.

I sat on my own. I listened as everyone discussed what should happen to me. No one asked me how I felt or what I wanted.

Then Duncan spoke up, interrupted Pa, tried to suggest a compromise. With a flicker of sympathy, he suggested if I stayed at Nether Place, I could perhaps resit my exams later in the year. Pa dismissed the idea that I could continue to live with my baby at Nether Place.

'We're not living in the '50s anymore,' Duncan said, but of course, Pa still did.

I looked across at Beth. All this time, she had sat looking at the rug. She had said nothing, nothing to support me. She wouldn't even look at me. I was so cross with them all. I burst into tears of frustration; a torrent of self-pity poured out of me. I couldn't bear the thought of relinquishing the life growing inside me to strangers, however convenient that might be for my parents.

When I'd calmed down, you stepped in with the perfect solution. A collective sigh seemed to wrap everyone in the room. As I listened to you, I felt myself shrink into the corner of the sofa. I had long ago given up hope that you might have supported me, but I didn't think you would take from me. When you finished speaking, there was silence in the room as your words were digested. I could see nods of reason, heavy heads bouncing with hope, and I heard faint sighs of relief like shingle running back to the sea. I knew I had lost; I started to cry again. Then Ma came and sat beside me and took my hand.

'As difficult as it might be to give up your baby, think how much better both of your lives will be. Your heart might break, but your child will have more support, more care, more advantages in a proper family,' said Ma. She touched her pearls. 'Some decisions in life are harder than one might think possible to bear, but you are only a child yourself. This way, you will be able to have a life of your own too.'

You, Max, suggested your name be put on the birth certificate to negate the need for going through the adoption system.

Later, after you had gone, taking Lara with you, as the light in the room slowly faded, turning grey with dusk, I uncurled from my pain. I noticed the cigarette packet and the slim silver lighter I had given you the previous Christmas on the chest of drawers. You must have left them behind. Slowly, I got off the bed, crossed the room, picked them up and moved to the window; lighting up, coughing, I took my first ash-filled breath.

Part 2

May-May had dozed off. She lay in bed, pale against the white pillows.

'Not one of her good days, I'm afraid,' said the nurse who welcomed Laura.

While Laura waited for May-May to wake, she studied her grandmother's room. May-May's wardrobe with the etched border to the oval glass, the matching dressing table, and the chair Laura sat in all came from May-May's old bedroom. The other incidental furniture had come from different rooms at Nether Place. Laura had always loved the inlaid console table with its intricate floral design, but it had been placed in front of the radiator. From where she sat, Laura could see that the delicate swirls of leaves and petals had begun to lift; the inlay had buckled and looked like a scattering of potpourri across the surface. In front of the window, beside the wingback chair, which had been her grandfather's, was a round side table. Aunt Tina had given May-May the porcelain shepherdess with her sheep that danced across the polished surface of the table between family photographs.

May-May was still asleep. Laura pushed herself up from the low chair and wandered over to the side table. When she was younger, she had never been allowed to touch the delicate figurine. The words "Don't touch" seemed to follow her through her childhood. Now, she reached down and picked it up. Other than May-May's shallow breath, the room was quiet. Laura's fingers curved over the cool, smooth china. Laura sighed; everyone missed her Aunt Tina. Laura looked down at the figurine in her hands and noticed a small chip in one of the frills of the shepherdess' dress. She gently replaced the ornament and went to look for the photograph album. Laura flicked through the pages and found the picture she was looking for. It was of her mother, May-May, Tina, and herself. They were sitting on rugs spread out on the grass in the shade of the vast cedar that still stretched its limbs over the lawn. Laura must have been four, nearly five. She remembered it had been an exciting day. It was the day that her Aunt Tina had come home.

Her father had been teaching Gareth how to play croquet, playing as a team against her Uncle Duncan and his wife, Meredith. The coloured balls bashed and thunked across the lawn. The game ended when Gareth hit a ball hard and it rolled away slowly at first, then gaining momentum till it trickled down the slope and into the lake with a splash. Laura remembered the ball was red. Duncan went to find the gardener, Burr, and a net.

Burr, under Duncan's instruction, their silhouettes dark against the silvery lake sparkling in the afternoon sunshine, was fishing the ball out of the murky lake when Tina arrived. Laura remembered hearing a call and, turning back towards the grey stone house, saw Tina waving, tall and golden. She gracefully strolled across the lawn towards them. Tina kicked off her shoes and settled on the rug beside Laura in a rustle of fabric and a veil of scent. Her father went to get folding chairs from the pavilion. Even her grandfather joined them, lured from his study, to celebrate Tina's return. He brought an ice bucket and champagne. Mrs Simms followed him across the grass bearing glasses on a tray.

Tina had brought gifts for the children.

Laura didn't only remember that day because Tina brought presents, but it helped. She remembered her mother being a little cross that there were presents at all when it wasn't someone's birthday. Gareth had torn into the wrapping-up paper on his gift and been over the moon with the remote-controlled car he'd been given. He had whooped with excitement, and Mrs Simms had been sent to find batteries. Laura remembered the pop as the thick plastic casing had released the car from its hold, and her uncle had untwisted all the black ties that fixed the car to the cardboard mounting while Gareth became more and more impatient.

Laura, after carefully removing the wrapping-paper, had been entranced by her present, a doll, a little girl with silky hair, wearing a red dirndl dress.

Her mother had reminded her to thank Tina.

'Thank you, Aunt Tina,' both the children had chanted in unison.

'What are you going to call your new friend?' her father had asked Laura.

'I'm going to call her Alix, like May-May's doll.' Laura said.

'Alix, the doll left behind on the train. When did you tell Laura that story, Ma?' asked her mother.

'It's not much of a story,' May-May had said.

'Shall I help you take her out of the box?' her father asked. Laura shook her head. She wanted to keep the beautiful doll in its box until she got home. How she had loved that doll. Laura had recently come across Alix when packing up to move into the flat in Earls Court. After a nostalgic reunion, she had rewrapped the doll reverently back in its tissue paper and put it in the pile of things to take with her.

Laura was drawn back into the room by tinkering sounds, chinks, and clunks. She lifted her eyes from the album on her lap. May-May was awake, her ringed hand nudging on her bedside table among the bits and pieces, a glass, her watch, a photograph of Dennis, and some books, all crowded together.

'Hello,' said Laura.

'Hello?' said May-May blinking across the room, her hand hovering. 'Who's that?'

'It's me, Laura. How are you?' She closed the album leaving it on the floor beside her chair and got up and came towards the bed. 'You've been dozing. What are you looking for? Would you like a drink?' Laura helped her grandmother sit up, pulling the pillows around her for support.

'Ah, Laura.' May-May looked up at her. 'Yes, please, my darling. There should be a jug of squash somewhere.'

Laura found the juice and poured some into the glass on the

bedside table, making sure May-May could reach it.

'I was just looking through the album and came across the photo of the day Tina returned from Italy. Do you remember?' Laura asked.

'A glorious day, I do remember,' said May-May, nodding.

'Tina gave me that lovely doll.' Laura put the jug down and swept a stray strand of her hair behind her ear. 'Tell me the story again about your Alix and the concert tour.'

'Gosh, that was so long ago, my darling. I left Russia when I was very young. How old are you now?'

'I'm twenty-five, May-May.'

'I must have been almost the same age. I played the piano.' May-May smiled, lifting her gnarled hands. 'Hard to imagine now, with my arthritis, but I did.' She looked at her fingers, twisting them in the light, then dropped them back onto the bedspread. 'I was a member of a regional orchestra. I don't know how we got permission to tour abroad, but it was a great opportunity. Uncle Nesti organised the trip. He was a bit of a hustler.' May-May looked at Laura, 'is that a word that's still used?'

'Oh yes,' said Laura settling in the chair near her grandmother's bed, 'if you mean a sharp operator.'

'My mother travelled with me to Moscow on the train.'

'And you had Alix with you too?'

'Yes, in those days, Alix came with me everywhere. Although I was no longer a child, I brought Alix to remind me of the childhood I was leaving behind.'

'That's understandable. You were setting off on a great adventure into the unknown.'

'Then, I didn't know I wouldn't be going back. Then, I thought I would be home in a few months.'

'But you knew there might be an opportunity to stay?'

'In those days, we all hoped.'

'Tell me about the train,' said Laura. She loved to hear details of her grandmother's past.

'My mother had brought pickled herring and hard-boiled eggs to eat.' May-May leant back against her pillows, and her eyes became unfocused as if searching her thoughts for the right story, her mind ticking back into the past. 'My mother had a napkin, red and white that she'd embroidered herself, beautiful needlework. She spread the napkin out on her knees and peeled the eggs. The little pieces of shell fell on the patterned cloth.' May-May's hand swept across the bedspread, and she trickled her fingers through the air to illustrate her story. 'It reminded me of the pale rose petals that, at the end of the day, would drop onto the Turkish carpet in the parlour of our dacha.' May-May's voice cracked, and she took a sip of her squash before continuing. 'To season the eggs, my mother brought a tiny salt cellar and a matching pepper pot, one white, one black, each with a little painted flower. You would have loved them.' May-May smiled at Laura and reached out to pat her hand. 'When we had finished our lunch, my mother slid open the train window and shook the napkin through the gap scattering the shell in the wind and letting the cold air into the compartment.' May-May was quiet for a while. 'I'm afraid to say I was ashamed of my provincial mother with her picnic, and I was aloof, not engaging with her as I should have done. I stared very hard out the window. Though the truth was I was afraid of the journey ahead.'

'And excited,' prompted Laura.

'And excited.' May-May nodded and sipped her juice again, 'My mother was so thrilled that I had this opportunity, but also so sad.' May-May looked at Laura, 'When I look back, I can see how upset she was. She cloaked her sadness with the joy of her jolly little picnic.'

May-May finished her drink, and Laura helped put the glass back on the bedside table.

'We were late into Moscow, and I had to rush to catch the next train. My mother gave me her prayer book. There, you see, I still have it.' May-May pointed towards the bedside table where the small, rather battered leather book nestled among her other belongings. 'My mother said to me, "Put this in your purse, remember your valise and run. I'll bring Alix and find a porter for your heavy bag. Bless you, my darling!" She smiled at me as I set off.'

'How did you know where to go, what to do?'

'I found Uncle Nesti on the international platform organising everyone in our group. He was wearing his big coat with the fur collar, waving his silver-tipped cane in one hand, and had a fistful of passports in the other. He was shouting over the noise of the trains and travellers. Uncle Nesti hustled me onto the train with the other stragglers and jumped up behind us. I felt the train lurch. I pushed my way to the window. My mother was standing on the platform with a porter and my bag. I waved and waved. Travelling away from everything I knew, travelling towards my future and your grandfather, Dennis.'

'So, you left home and travelled into the unknown with only an overnight case?'

'I had to leave my past behind. My lilac leather gloves and matching scarf, my dark dresses, and accessories for the concerts, all in my big travelling bag, and little Alix too, everything I had brought for the journey, all left on the platform with my mother. I didn't get to say goodbye properly, just a hasty wave from the window as the train picked up speed and left the station.' May-May looked at Laura with watery eyes. 'I couldn't look back, you understand. It was a different time.'

May-May reached a hand toward the photograph of her husband on the table next to her. 'I had this opportunity, and I took it. I met your grandfather, and together we started our own new family.'

'But you still played the piano?' said Laura.

'Oh yes. Your grandfather bought me the most beautiful grand as a wedding present.'

May-May closed her eyes and settled back on her pillows, her fingers plucked at her blankets as though she were sitting at a keyboard.

Laura stared out the window at the garden beyond. The world had moved on. Today, the window was closed against the cold wind. May-May had once been accomplished and capable, but now the years had tumbled past, leaving her vulnerable. Laura turned back to May-May and soothed her grandmother's agitated hand, stroking the thin, veined skin. The clever fingers were now marred by arthritis. Her grandmother had fallen asleep, the breath fluttering in her chest as if it couldn't decide to settle.

Laura sighed and looked around the stifling room. Nether Place had changed too. The former elegant proportions of the old drawing room had been obliterated, with inserted walls and lowered ceiling. When Laura was young, the piano was on the left as you came into the room from the hall, its nose nudging into the bay window. If it were still here, it would be taking up a good part of Major Whittaker's room next door. She wondered if Major Whittaker was musical. She thought not, but maybe all those whiskers hid a sensitive disposition. May-May's room was the mid-section of the old drawing room; she had the lovely French window but a smaller bathroom due to the boxed-in fireplace. Lady Wetherstone had the third section, the grandest part, with the two large windows beside which the drinks cabinet and the record player had once stood. May-May did love being in the room next to a Lady; it almost made up for her change in circumstances.

1989 – 1996

Silver Spoon

Laura was wobbling around the coffee table on springy knees playing with a silver teaspoon. Beth was still tremulous with the miracle that had brought Laura into her life. Or was it exhaustion? Even though Laura was a good sleeper, Beth seemed to spend every night with one ear open.

'Gorgeous. A darling of a little girl,' said Ma. 'What a joy she is.'

'She is perfect,' said Beth. 'Don't bang that spoon, Laura.'

'She won't do any harm.'

Beth had brought Laura over to see her mother at Nether Place. They were in the drawing room. Beth eyed uneasily ornaments that had casually been left at toddler level. The tea things were in the middle of the table; Beth had ensured they were out of Laura's reach. Ma sipped from the teacup she held high as Laura bobbed past, tracking around the table, humming to herself.

'What would you like to be called by Laura, Ma? Grandma Esme?'

'Goodness, that sounds far too much of a mouthful for such a little girl. She'll decide on something herself. I expect she'll use May-May, like Gareth, nothing wrong with that. I rather like having a pet name.'

'She is adorable, and we have such a good time together.' Beth smiled at Laura, who gurgled back. 'But, looking after a toddler …

it's not quite as much ... unadulterated fun as I imagined.'

'Nothing worthwhile is easy. You know that ...,' said Ma. 'You must enjoy the moment. This is a fabulous time for you, darling, don't spoil it by worrying about what you are missing out on. Laura will have left home before you know it.'

'It's not the caring and cuddling; we love a hug, don't we, Laura?' Beth slid her hand over the impossible silkiness of Laura's fair hair as she bounced past on her journey around the coffee table. 'It's the monotony, the everyday .... you know, I feel quite guilty saying this, but I hadn't realised how bored I would be.' Beth watched Laura wobble, trying to put the spoon in her mouth while not falling over. 'I never thought I would miss work quite so much.'

'All that easy socialising. I suppose being on your own with a baby can be isolating. Of course, I had Nanny to help me with you and Duncan.' Ma sipped her tea, 'But there are all sorts of mother and baby groups nowadays, aren't there?'

'Yes, we do go to one locally,' said Beth. Initially, she had found these gatherings stressful. She had wondered if someone would spot that she didn't really belong, that she wasn't a proper mother. But no one had challenged her, and now she was used to the hurley burley of the playgroup and realised that, despite all the mother and baby books they read that they could all quote from, most of the mothers were working out parenting as they went along.

'How about your friend, Penny? You must see quite a bit of her.'

'Of course. Mia is at school now, Jack is four, and Toby is just a little older than Laura. Those boys are quite a challenge.'

The last time they had met up, while Jack emptied the cupboards in Beth's kitchen, she had tried to talk about her frustrations. Penny had said Beth should try having more than one; then, she wouldn't have time to be bored. Then Penny changed the subject quickly. She must have remembered that it wasn't quite so easy for Beth to have babies. Beth knew Penny wasn't insensitive, she just had so much going on in her own life. After Beth had waved them off, she put Laura in her highchair and gave her a rusk to gnaw on. Then Beth crawled around the kitchen floor, putting everything back in the cupboards so the kitchen would be tidy before Max got home.

'Once they've been over, I have a job getting the house back in order.' Beth said. She didn't mention how demoralising it was to talk to Penny, who managed to run her interior design business and looked after three children – though she did have an au pair and a cleaner. As Beth wasn't working, she did not feel she deserved any help. Surely, she should be able to keep her house, feed her family and look after one baby, shouldn't she?

'Boys will be boys,' said Ma.

'Well, I'm not sure … Duncan was never destructive, was he?'

'Of course not! Nanny would never have allowed it.'

Years ago, Beth remembered sitting almost exactly where she was now. In the drawing room after Sunday lunch, she and Duncan were expected to behave for all the empty, endless childhood afternoon. In winter, a fire smouldered in the vast fireplace, and they would lean in towards the roaring heat that seemed to dissipate quickly in the unwavering chill of the large room. In summer, their mother hid the grate with a gilt-framed screen that an aged aunt had covered in floral tapestry years before.

Whatever the season, their father would sit in his wingback chair to the right of the hearth. Beth would watch Pa's head playing peek-a-boo behind the newspapers as he wrestled the sheets. Beth would try not to giggle because she knew reading the newspapers was a serious business. Pa would rustle the pages and grumble about the news, the price of heating oil, the trouble in Vietnam, and the endless student protests in America and France. Ma would sit at the grand and play slow, soothing melodies over the commotion. Beth would listen with her heart open. Mesmerised, she would sit up straight beside Duncan and, side by side on the sofa, toes skimming the Persian carpet, they would sway along to their mother's playing like two Indian snakes.

'Your mother was a concert pianist when I met her, an outstanding concert pianist,' their father would say, 'but instead of pursuing a career, she came all the way from Russia to make her life here with us.'

Beth remembered watching her mother sitting at the piano, her grey eyes concentrating on the sheet music. To Beth, Ma was a magician who could command the notes to do extraordinary things. It was as though the little, black dots might come alive, rise off the paper, and fly through the air to settle wherever her mother chose. Beth used to imagine the notes taking wing and landing on the mantlepiece amongst the family photographs or drifting over the rug behind the sofa table, and if the window was open, perhaps they would fly out and sing with the birds.

'Do you still practice every day,' Beth asked her mother, pointing towards the black, shiny monster of a piano that still dominated the corner of the room.

'Oh, yes,' said her mother. 'You never know. I may get a call from the Wigmore Hall yet.'

There was a bump, and a crash as Laura landed heavily on her nappy-padded bottom. The teaspoons she had been holding hit the table with a loud bang. She looked up with surprise.

'Whoops-a-daisy, up you get.' Laura smiled up at her grandmother.

'Oh no!' Beth swooped, tutting. Laura gave a whimper as she turned to her mother for a hug.

Honey

The following year, Duncan had gone for a job interview in Austin. Later, his new job secured, he and Meredith returned to the States to look for a house. Gareth went with them to visit schools. Then they used the long summer school holiday to pack up and send their belongings on the slow boat across the Atlantic. Duncan's new employers were expecting him to start after Labor Day, at the beginning of September. For the last two weeks of August, while the container wended its way, Duncan and Meredith joined the rest of the family for a holiday at a villa their father had rented in France.

'It's been great to have this time together,' Duncan said on their last night as he pushed his chair back away from the table and the remains of the meal. 'This has been a fabulous holiday. It has been a very special send-off. It does seem a very final farewell, almost as if you wanted to see the back of us. But we're not going forever. We'll be back every summer to see you all, particularly if it's to a villa as lovely as this!'

'We aim to please,' said Pa through the burbled agreement that it had been an excellent couple of weeks. Beth looked at her father, sitting behind his wine glass; he always seemed solid and in control. Pa had taken Duncan's departure from Farthingale & Parteger well enough. Beth suspected there must have been fireworks behind the scenes, but to family and friends, he had shown a calm resignation that betrayed no bitterness. The family line was that although this was an exciting opportunity for Duncan, he would doubtless be back in time. Beth wondered about that; she couldn't think of a more comprehensive way for Duncan to cut himself off from family obligations than by moving to a different country. With space, he would be able to create himself in his own image and there would be no need for him ever to come home.

Pa refilled Ma's glass, his own, and then reached across the table, his extended arm bearing the chilled bottle; he offered everyone more rosé. Max took the dripping bottle from him and made sure everyone's glass was filled.

'To a favourable journey and successful future.' Pa raised his glass to Duncan and Meredith. They all joined in the toast. Beth looked round the table. Duncan looked happier than he had for a while, ready for his new adventure, and Gareth seemed enthusiastic about his new school. Meredith was smiling too. She was supportive of Duncan, but she had not spoken about her own feelings, and Beth knew Meredith was very close to her own family in Wales and probably didn't relish moving quite so far away from home.

'You will write to me, won't you, Beth,' Meredith had said. 'Keep in touch. Let me know what's going on. Duncan is so hopeless at keeping me in the loop.'

Beth had promised she would write. She thought it strange that the Duncan she knew, who was so garrulous in social situations and a skilled salesman, should be taciturn with Meredith. Perhaps Duncan thought Meredith could work out what was going on by osmosis or telepathy. Beth thought how lucky she was; she seldom disagreed with Max. She smiled across the table at him now. He was talking to Ma about the extraordinary blue of the agapanthus growing in huge pots along the terrace. Then, without skipping a beat, he looked up and winked at Beth; she felt a deep pleasure.

As the conversation rippled around her, Beth sat back and basked. The sky was turning dark purple, and the air was cooling, and yet it was still warm enough to linger at the table. Chatter from the children floated out from the open bedroom window above. Below the terrace, the automatic cleaner chuntered around the lit swimming pool, the underwater lights sending a blue glow into the surrounding garden. Little citronella candles burned on the table. Beth caught a trace of the sharp oil as it diffused into the warm Mediterranean night. The air felt gentle on her skin. Everyone she loved was here, together; even Tina, who was surveying them all from the end of the table. Beth caught Tina's eye and raised her glass. As she always did, Beth wondered how Tina felt about seeing Laura with her and Max. Not-knowing made Beth feel apprehensive about family get-togethers, but Laura was happy, and Tina was free; so really, there couldn't be a better arrangement. Now, Tina responded in kind, lifting her glass, and taking a sip of her wine. In her other hand, Tina held a cigarette; she flicked her ash away down the terrace. Tina had flown in from Italy for their final weekend. She hadn't had enough holiday time to come for the whole trip, but she was here now.

Earlier in the day, Pa had taken the grandchildren with him when he went shopping for the final barbeque. Ma went too, to make sure he bought some vegetables and salad not just a vast amount of meat. At the last moment, Beth had leapt into the car.

'It will be the last time I have a chance to go to the market,' she said as she pulled the car door shut. She squished next to Gareth, cajoling him to move over next to Laura in her car seat. No one would be taken in, her parents would suspect she didn't trust them with the children, but Beth knew the market would be busy, and her parents easily distracted. She didn't want Laura, who was only three, wandering off when no one was looking.

The market was packed. They were too late for the locals, but the stalls were crowded with tourists. Beth heard English and German voices among the French as they wove their way through the packed lanes that led to the central square and the main food halls.

'Mummy, you're squeezing my hand too tightly,' said Laura, 'and you're walking too fast.'

'Sorry, sweetheart.' Beth stopped pushing forward through the throng and looked down at Laura. Beth tried to relax her grip on Laura's small slippery hand. 'Shall we get some honey?' she asked. 'French honey is very special. It's made from lavender.'

'Don't be silly, Mummy, honey is made from bees. May-May told me that.'

Beth looked up. Pa was surging ahead. Beth could see his blue bucket hat moving away from her above the crowd. Gareth would be bouncing at his heels, holding onto Ma's hand. Despite the crowd, Beth would have no trouble finding them later. She turned back to Laura.

'By bees, that's right. There's a honey stall over there. Shall we have a look?'

The stall holder's English filled the gaps in Beth's schoolgirl French and when Laura had selected a pot from the pyramid of jars, Beth handed over some francs, pulling the large notes out of her purse, before tucking the change away again and zipping her bag closed, thinking about the warning signs about pickpockets.

Beth and Laura caught up with the others by the butcher's stand.

'Mercy boocoo,' said Pa to the stall holder before handing Beth the damp bag of meat he'd bought for the barbeque. She tipped the soggy package into a spare carrier. Then Pa took Gareth and Laura on a tour of the open-air market with its myriad stalls of colourful vegetables looking fresh and vibrant, flowers standing tall in high tubs, and livestock waiting to be slaughtered. Laura found some kittens, mewling balls of fluff, in a cardboard box left by a pillar and Gareth saw a little, black-spotted pig. Beth watched as he leaned over the fence and reached out to scritch the piglet's scratchy back, Gareth's feet lifting him onto his toes his body balancing on the top rail. Beth fought an urge to grab his t-shirt to make sure he didn't topple into the pen. She thought that pigs, even small ones, wouldn't turn up their noses at little boys for breakfast.

'Come on,' said Pa. 'They won't let you take a pig on the plane back to America.'

On the way home, Beth bought some peaches. The stallholder flicked open the brown paper bag with a crack and dropped the fruit inside.

As they had left for the market, the rest of the family had been enjoying a leisurely breakfast. While they were out, Duncan was taking Meredith to visit a nearby museum with an exhibition of local fabrics. Max was going for a jog through the lavender fields beyond the villa and up into the hills. Tina was going to chill; this was her first break of the summer, and she wanted to relax and spend the day by the pool.

When they returned from the market, Beth peeled herself off the hot car seat while the children ran into the villa. Beth helped her parents carry the shopping in. Then, she had promised to take the children swimming.

'Do you want to come too?' she asked Max, when she got back to their room, as she changed into her costume, but he said he'd already been for a swim when he got back from his run. He'd had a shower, dressed, and was putting on his watch. He said he would help unpack the shopping and get the meat marinating for the barbeque. Beth left the room with her towel and went to look for the children.

In the pool, Beth held onto Laura even though she was wearing armbands. Gareth, three years older, was leaping into the water, showering them with waves and droplets making Laura shriek with glee.

'Gareth, stop that!' said Meredith as she and Duncan came to join them by the pool.

'No need to get your aunt wetter than she already is,' said Duncan.

Later, after Meredith and Beth had fed and bathed the children and got them into their pyjamas, Max came to read them a story. Beth listened to the children's chatter as she headed off to shower. She heard Laura telling Max that she really did want him to be read one of Gareth's stories about dinosaurs fighting spacemen. She was lucky that Max was so hands-on with Laura; Duncan was mixing cocktails.

On her way to the kitchen, changed and ready to help get supper ready, Beth walked past Tina's bedroom: her door was open. Tina was lounging on the bed, leaning against the headboard, book in one hand, cigarette in the other, looking guilty. She was wrapped in a towel, her blood-red painted toenails peeking out from amongst the rumpled sheets. Beth surveyed the muddle; Tina's clothes scattered around the room looked alluring, seductive even. Beth knew that her own rumpled clothes left lying about would look like dirty washing.

'I'll close the door,' said Beth. 'Ma will have a fit if she finds out you've been smoking in the house.' She pulled the door to and wondered how her sister could live in such a mess. Beth had made her and Max's bed as soon as they'd had breakfast. It was clear Tina was still a child. She could never have looked after Laura. She couldn't even keep her room tidy, and passive smoking was so bad for children. Beth felt a moment of self-satisfaction but standing for a moment in the corridor looking at the closed door, she felt deflated. Another chance to connect missed.

Max and Duncan commandeered the barbecue that evening. Cooking the steaks, chicken and sausages that Dennis had bought at the butcher.

'Are you sure everything is cooked properly,' said Ma every time someone took a helping of chicken from the heavy terracotta dish, but everyone tucked in. Tina was the only one who picked at her food. Now, Tina sat back, slightly away from the table, holding her cigarette high, so the smoke didn't get in anyone's way, smudges of grey floated off into the night sky.

Tomorrow they would go their separate ways. Beth and Max would fly back to the U.K with Laura. Duncan and his family were flying straight to the States. Ma and Pa were driving home, meeting up with friends and sightseeing on the way. Tina was returning to Italy. Beth helped herself to a peach from the large bowl in the centre of the table. When they were gone, any uneaten fruit would be left to moulder in the bowl.

Christmas Cards

Max brought Beth a glass of wine.

'Thought you could do with a drink,' he said, 'how are you getting on?'

'Ploughing through.'

Beth sat in the warm glow of the fire feeling festive. She smiled a thank you at Max and sipped the mellow red wine. Beth had the gate-legged table opened in front of her; it was covered in all the paraphernalia of the season. Beth knew that she ought to find writing Christmas cards a chore, but she secretly enjoyed everything about Advent. She liked the excess and the gaudiness and loved witnessing Laura's excitement now that she was old enough to know what was happening. Laura sat at her feet, amusing herself with a music box she'd been given at nursery; it played tinny carols.

'Very festive!' said Max to Laura, who beamed up at him as he settled in the chair near the fire.

'Why are you writing so much?' Max asked, 'I thought a "Happy Christmas and much love" was all that was required.'

'Oh, this one is for Duncan and Meredith. Meredith enclosed a letter with hers. You remember I showed you the photograph of the house. I thought I should reply in kind.'

'Show me again.'

'Here it is, see, quite chatty, deserves a proper response.' She picked up the A4 sheet and passed it across to Max.

'Are you sure they are expecting a long reply? This looks like a round-robin. They've probably sent one to everyone.' He sniffed the thin shiny paper. 'It smells like they used a Gestetner; didn't know anybody still used those.'

'Oh, I think a proper letter is in order.' Beth knew Meredith would want to hear all their news, and Beth had promised to keep in touch. Though perhaps that was just how Beth would feel if she was on the other side of the world and not coming home for Christmas.

'House looks amazing, doesn't it? Low-built and spread out, ultra-modern. I like the covered veranda, but it's odd there's no planting around the house and no hedge or fence or anything, just straight onto the road.'

'It looks very dry too, but that could be the exposure,' said Beth,

'Turn over, it's both sides. Meredith writes quite a bit about what they're up to.'

'She does, doesn't she. Duncan's completed his trial period and has been offered a permanent position in the PR department; that's good, but we already knew that. He's also taken up golf and tennis. I don't think I've ever known Duncan to do more than take the dogs for a walk. What has got into him?'

'I guess it's a good way to meet people.'

'Gareth seems to have won several school prizes.' Max looked across at Beth. 'That seems unlikely; he's only been there a term.'

'He's very young; perhaps at that age in America, they get prizes for taking part.'

'Hmm, that would make sense. He gets a star for Math and a rosette for Legos construction. Meredith has adopted the American spelling, I see.'

'I guess it's a bit of a joke.'

'Well, to my mind, Americans run fast and loose with their 's's, or lack of them.'

Beth wrote in her letter to Meredith about Laura's first Christmas ballet show and then added more about Max's upcoming department drinks.

'Meredith doesn't write anything about herself, does she, apart from the fact that she's unpacked,' said Max.

'I noticed that too,' said Beth, 'I'm sure it takes time to unpack everything and make a home. I do hope she's happy. It will make all the difference to Duncan. There's a photo of them all together at the bottom of the page.'

'So there is. They look happy enough. Don't know what you're worried about.'

In the photograph, Duncan's family appeared stranded, glowing in white t-shirts against the orange backdrop of the picture. They looked as if they had landed somewhere alien and were hanging on to each other, hoping they would survive if they stuck together.

'Now, Laura,' said Max, 'When shall we get a tree; this

weekend?'

'You know we don't really need a tree if we are going to Nether Place,' said Beth.

'Of course we need a tree.' said Max and Laura in unison.

'It will be a very different Christmas without Duncan and his family. We must be on good form to keep Ma and Pa cheerful.'

'Well, that won't be hard. We are always on good form.' Max said.

'Aunt Tina will be there,' said Laura.

'Yes, she'll with us this year at Nether Place,' Beth said. 'That will be fun, won't it?'

It would be the first Christmas together since Laura had come into their lives. Beth wondered how Tina would feel about celebrating with them, Beth, Max, and Laura, as a family. Tina had never been good at sharing, aloof, so maybe she wouldn't feel left out. After all, she was busy, moving from Italy to Nether Place, looking for a job; she wouldn't want Laura back. Tina was never sentimental; she wouldn't get emotional now. It had been so long ago now that Laura had come into their lives; Beth had nothing to fear.

Max looked at the clock. 'Bath time, Laura.'

He stood, and as Laura grumbled about getting ready for bed, he crossed the rug and drew Beth to her feet. 'Hug?'

'Always,' she said, allowing herself to be pulled towards him.

'Are you OK?' he growled into her ear. 'Happy?'

'Very,' Beth always felt more herself when Max held her close; she could feel his warmth and breathe him in, and somehow that made her feel more real. 'I'm so lucky.'

'We're so lucky.'

'Me too!' said Laura, pushing between their legs. Max bent down and picked her up.

'Family hug!' he said. He smiled at Beth, as she smiled back, Laura gave them each a damp kiss. Together the three of them were strong, a tripod, sturdy against the storm.

Max bent to give her a kiss then swung Laura up and away for her bath. Beth returned to her Christmas cards.

Tina

'I will not have you disrupting our lives,' you said.

We had barely sat down at the table.

Before I could reply, the waiter arrived, gliding across the pale patterned carpet of the large, almost empty, oak-panelled room. He bowed slightly as he gave us the menus with white-gloved hands. You ordered drinks for us both, gins to sip while we thought about what we might like to eat, as though we were civilised people.

'You can't just turn up and expect to see Laura.'

'Beth is my sister. I can see her whenever I want. If she is concerned, she would have said something to me, herself,' I said. 'Besides, I'd never –'

'It doesn't matter what you want or what you think Beth wants. I will not have you nosing in where I do not want you. We are a family now. While you have been away in Italy, gadding around, we have been building our relationship with Laura. I don't want you swanning in and upsetting the boat.'

'I wasn't gadding.' I didn't mean to sound so petulant, but, although I had agreed to it, your possession of Laura rankled.

The waiter appeared silently and asked if we were ready to order.

'Five more minutes,' you said with a dismissive wave of your hand.

'I've been building my career.'

'Working as a receptionist in an art gallery is hardly a career. When you came back, Tina, I was hopeful we could re-establish our friendship. But I didn't think you would set out to upset us.' You studied the menu. 'You can't just come over whenever you want and take Laura out.'

'I'm a gallery assistant!'

'That's what I said.' You finished your gin, folding your lips over the last drops. Then you replaced your empty glass on the white tablecloth giving me a look that challenged me to disagree.

'You can't stop me seeing my own sister and child, you know. All I'm asking for is to visit every now and then ...'

In truth, when I had visited Beth, and we had sat over tea while Laura played at our feet, I had felt oddly indifferent. I couldn't understand why. The child she was now was so far from the tiny baby I had held so many years ago when for just one moment, she was truly mine. Although I had seen Laura intermittently over the years, I could not reconcile this child with my memory of my baby. What I felt was not maternal love for Laura but jealousy towards Beth, who could so effortlessly create a home and a family for Laura, something beyond my grasp.

'Yes, two mozzarella salads, followed by the steak, rare,' you said to the waiter who had reappeared, notebook in hand.

'Actually, I would like the monkfish,' I said.

You stared at me for a moment before acceding and told the waiter that we would have one steak, one monkfish and a bottle of Beaujolais.

'No claret or burgundy then,' you said. 'If you're having fish.'

'I'm no longer a child, Max. You can't bully me,' I said. 'I can choose for myself what I want and what I do.'

The waiter brought our salads to the table, placing the plates down carefully, twisting them to ensure the pattern of the border was aligned with the table setting. Another brought the wine, making a show of removing the cork from the bottle. I sat quietly as you went through the pantomime of tasting before the wine was poured.

'And how are you going to do that? You can hardly be independent while living with your parents. What are you now, twenty-two, twenty-three?'

'I'm going to get a job in London.'

'At an art gallery,' you scoffed. 'That will hardly pay for the lifestyle you aspire to. Art gallery girls have private incomes. And where will you live? You won't be able to commute from Nether Place, it's too far. And if you think you can stay in my flat you've another thing coming. In the short term, possibly, but being there full time is quite another.'

'Don't want me disturbing your little escapades?' I dared to say. You didn't flinch, didn't even look up from your food. When I first went to Italy, I thought I was special, the only one. I thought it was all a mistake, and you would turn around and come back for me. As the months and years passed, I came to realise how naive I had been. I couldn't have been the only one, not the first. Maybe the first to have a baby, but not the first. I spent a good deal of time thinking about you at your work, surrounded by keen, young nurses. That had hurt.

'I can share with Bella. And, once I have a job, I plan to persuade Pa to help me find a flat.'

'Good luck with that. I can't imagine your father has much ready cash. Asset rich, cash poor,' you said as you chased a tomato around your plate. 'Where would you look?'

'I'm not ... it's none of your business. Anyway, it won't be for a bit till I'm more settled.'

'I can't quite see how you will afford London. Possibly I could help, increase what we already agreed on ... perhaps,' you said, taking a sip of wine and looking across the table at me over the top of your glass. You arched your wayward eyebrow. Those blue eyes, when did you learn to use them as a weapon, Max? 'Perhaps, when the time comes, I could help you move in?'

'The fish for Mademoiselle and the steak for Monsieur,' said the waiter as our salad plates were removed and replaced with the next course.

'It's blackmail.' I felt outraged. Though I couldn't work out if I was angry at you for deceiving Beth or myself for being complicit.

Knowing that whatever you said or did, however much I tried to dissent, some part of me would always be open to you.

'What it is, is practical,' you said, waving your fork at me.

'You ought to tell her,' I said. 'Surely she deserves to know.'

'That's no concern of yours. Besides, it would only upset her, and Beth is very happy with Laura. And let's face it, you are happy with your life too. A little extra, my contribution, would mean you could treat yourself.' You stabbed the last morsel of steak and finished it off. 'You don't want to be encumbered with a child. You can hardly look after yourself,' you said, finishing your wine. 'I can help you, Tina.'

The waiter refilled your glass; I put my hand over mine.

Perhaps I was too selfish. When I watched Beth with Laura, I felt I could never be a proper mother.

'I don't want your help,' I said, sounding childish.

The waiter bought the dessert menu.

'Nothing,' you said.

'I thought I might –'

'No, we are fine.' you repeated to the waiter.

'You have a lovely slim figure, Tina. Best to keep it that way.'

You ordered coffee; I declined.

'Hasn't Beth guessed? Surely, she suspects?'

'No, why would she? She trusts me.'

'And she doesn't trust me, her sister?'

'What? The flirty little tramp who got pregnant at a Christmas school disco. I don't think so. Anyway, she doesn't need to trust you to be your sister.'

A waiter cleared the table, and another brought your coffee. I had come to this lunch thinking I could stand up to you, but it was like looking at the sun. And it dawned on me; however much I understood it wasn't good for me, I loved to bask in the warmth of the sun.

'Whereas, as a couple, a family. It is to our mutual advantage to trust each other and build on that trust,' you said.

'You mean look the other way.'

'Not at all. To be in a strong relationship, one doesn't need to know everything about the other person. Though perhaps,' you conceded, 'it helps to concentrate on the good bits.'

'Deceiving Beth, denying what you know to be the truth,' I said.

'Truth, trust; trust, truth, what's the difference if everyone is happy. Beth doesn't need to know the truth. She trusts me, I trust her, and we are happy as things are,' you said to the tablecloth, tracing the raised stitching of the jacquard with your finger. Then without looking up, you raised your hand to ask for the bill. When you did raise your head, you held my gaze.

'You are irresistible, you know, Tina. You can't blame me; being as delectable as you are.'

I felt a little pulse in my heart, betraying me. You reached across the table and patted my hand. 'Now you are back, find yourself a job and a little flat, if you like. I'd like to come and see you from time to time. I can help, make a contribution, a healthy contribution; London can be expensive. I'll help you get back on your feet,' you said, 'you will be so busy you won't have time to worry about Laura. You'll see her at family events, not every weekend; give your excuses. Once or twice a year should be enough. No need to upset Beth.'

'Really, Max, you are not listening to me.'

'So, you don't want my help?' You leaned in and stroked my cheek and, with your thumb, gently wiped away the tear of frustration and defeat that was silently sliding on my skin. 'Really? You are so lovely, Tina, such a beauty, but you need to be looked after; you deserve a proper lifestyle. I can help make that happen,' you said, 'London can be lonely.'

And with that one touch, I was yours again.

Kite

It was a bright, blustery summer day, and the children wore coloured duffle coats like little bears from Peru. They were sitting in the sunshine on the edge of the terrace, making a kite. That morning, Gareth had found two broken kites in an old toy box in one of the outhouses and had brought them into the house for inspection. Beth recognised the tattered remnants. She remembered what fun it had been, running all over the lawn chasing Duncan, shrieking in the wind dragging her red kite along the ground behind her. Her kite had seemed heavier than the wind. Duncan's kite had been blue and soared easily. They had been given them at the start of a long summer holiday, as an encouragement to spend time outside. She remembered the kites had been a huge success but had been discarded years ago. Now they were to be resurrected.

Max loved a project. He and Gareth had a long conversation at lunch and agreed the smartest idea would be to take the best parts of both the broken kites and make them into one. As Ma didn't like mess in the house and felt strongly that children should get plenty of fresh air, they had set up their workshop outside on the terrace. Gareth had brought Sellotape from Mrs Simms's special drawer in the kitchen. Laura had brought one of the hair ribbons from her collection for the tail, and Pa had provided a large ball of string from the deep drawer of his study desk.

'It's going to be a supersonic kite. Isn't it Uncle Max?' They heard Gareth shout. He leapt up and ran in circles on the lawn, arms extended like a jet engine.

'Well –,' said Max.

'Just like in my book, Daddy, where the children have a kite with a really, really, long tail,' said Laura, waving her ribbon ineffectively in the air.

'Is that a supersonic kite?' asked Max, smiling down at Laura as he manhandled the frame of the kite.

'It doesn't have to be actually supersonic,' said Gareth.

'That's good,' said Max. 'Pass the Sellotape, Gareth.'

Gareth leapt forward and passed the tape over before plonking himself down next to Max. The three of them sat side by side, their heads bent happily over their project.

Beth and her mother were standing at the French windows of the drawing room, watching the children's antics, and listening to the chat.

'He is an angel. You are so lucky, Beth,' Ma said, closing the window against the sharp wind. 'A great find. I said so when you got engaged, and he hasn't let you down.'

'He's so good with Laura,' Beth said. 'Not all my friends have such helpful husbands. Max has a plan most weekends. They set off together on an adventure and have great fun. It gives me some time to myself.'

'Lovely to have the families together too. Generally, cousins have good relationships: a certain obligation without being too familiar. And beneficial for them both to spend time together, being only children. Meredith mentioned something about Gareth finding it hard to make friends at his new school. I remember him being very keen when they first went, but Americans are surprisingly different.'

'Children can be foul,' said Beth, 'particularly if someone is new, a bit different or speaks with another accent.'

'Such a shame Tina couldn't join us for the weekend,' said Ma. 'It would have been good to have got everyone together.'

Beth had hardly seen Tina. Christmas had gone surprisingly well. Tina had been aloof and disinterested, which had suited Beth. They had amicable chats with the rest of the family at mealtimes but no heart to hearts. Tina had practically ignored Laura. Since then, Tina had been impossible to get hold of. She was always so busy going back and forth to London, staying with Bella, going to job interviews looking for somewhere to live.

'I gave Max Bella's number and asked him if he could see what

Tina was up to when he was last in London. I thought he might be able to persuade her to come down. He said she is frightfully difficult to get hold of. Max tries to keep an eye on her for me, but he tells me he rarely manages to see her. She is apparently catching up with old school friends this weekend.'

'She's supposed to be looking for a job. That's why she's in London, not to go to a party. I never was sure Bella was a good influence,' said Ma.

'Max implied Tina has been out on a date.'

'Goodness, well, I suppose it would be lovely for her to meet someone. I do think she feels left out sometimes.'

Duncan appeared with Meredith, who carried in a tray of coffee things which she put down on the sofa table. Beth and her mother joined them. Ma poured the coffee out into the colourful demi-tasse.

'Were you watching the saintly Max entertaining the children,' said Duncan, drawn to the window by the children's voices. From within the warm silence of the room their high chirps sounded like the busy starlings in the woods. With cup and saucer in hand, Duncan rocked on his toes. 'How does he do it? Five minutes with Gareth, and I'm ready to tear my hair out.'

'He's just energetic,' said Ma. 'It's normal for a boy to be boisterous.'

'His school told us he's got ADHD or something. They insist he takes drugs to calm him down, or they won't let him attend.'

'Really! What sort of drugs?' asked Beth.

'Ritalin, apparently quite a few of the kids in his class are on it.'

'It's a nonsense,' said Meredith from the sofa where she had settled, 'they just don't have the space for the kids to run around. If they had more outdoor playtime, Gareth would be able to run off all his excess energy and settle down in class just fine.'

'What does it mean: ADHD?' asked Ma, sitting opposite Meredith.

'Basically, as far as I can tell, short attention span and bad social skills,' said Meredith.

'That doesn't seem very specific,' said Ma.

'I guess if you have a room full of kids to teach, you quickly notice any who are specifically demanding,' said Duncan.

'This is not something I remember hearing about when you were young,' said Ma. 'It must have been around; perhaps people just didn't talk about it then.'

'I always get confused between ADHD and autism.' said Beth. She crossed the room and sat beside Meredith on the sofa. 'And I'm not sure we talk about either much now,'

Duncan also turned into the room and moved towards the chairs by the fire with Ma.

'Well, watch this space; everything that starts in the States makes its way here sooner or later. All the kids here will be on Ritalin too before you know it,' said Duncan.

'Talking of exuberance, you're looking very colourful, Duncan,' said Beth. 'Is that also something we should look forward to, brightly dressed men?'

'It's a Hawaiian shirt, a summer shirt.' Duncan held his arms wide, revealing the full glory of the pattern.

'I was thinking you were looking very dapper,' said Ma.

'Duncan is becoming quite the exhibitionist,' Meredith added, flicking through a magazine.

'By the way, where is Tina?' asked Duncan.

'We were just wondering ourselves,' said Beth.

'What's her relationship like with Laura?'

For a moment, Beth was taken aback. She wondered if Duncan could hear the cogs in her brain as they fell into place. In those early years, when Tina was away, Beth had made Laura entirely her own. Since Tina's return Beth and Max had not talked over what they felt the relationship between Tina and Laura should be. With hardly any consideration, Beth had managed to forget that Tina had any claim.

'She never comes to see her.' Beth said, thinking that she should make more of an effort to get Tina over.

'Well, she possibly doesn't want to rock the boat,' said Duncan.

'Tina's probably waiting for an invitation to a villa in the South of France,' said Dennis coming into the room. He chuckled, but no one else joined in. 'I thought I could smell coffee.'

Was Pa going to make the same joke every year, rolling out the banter?

Duncan told Beth it was good to come home to Nether Place. From here, they could easily travel on to Meredith's parents in Wales, and if Tina was in London, they could meet up with her too.

But Beth knew Duncan would prefer to meet up with the family on neutral ground, somewhere without memories or expectations waiting to ambush him.

Whisky

The following summer, when the family was together once more, Pa asked Beth and Duncan to join him for coffee in his study. Ma slipped away with the dirty lunch dishes to the kitchen and the company of Mrs Simms. Meredith was already in Wales with Gareth to see her parents.

Beth had often seen Duncan disappear into the study when he had worked with their father, but she rarely had reason to step inside the room herself. On the threshold, forgotten childhood anxieties caused her to pause, this was the room of retribution. The room smelt faintly of cigar or pipe smoke, though as far as she knew no one had lit up in the room since her grandfather had died. Above the fireplace, her bewigged great-grandfather's spectral face shone out of a sea of black paint. To her left, the lower section of the tall window was obscured by piles of scientific and engineering magazines balanced on a dark, carved chest. The other walls of the room were lined with heavy floor-to-ceiling bookcases. On Pa's solid desk, which dominated the room, a metal Anglepoise lamp leaned over the large ink-flecked blotter, his fountain pen in a brass stand at its head. On the right was a silver tray with a half-full whisky decanter and glasses. On the left of the blotter, a heavy-duty stapler weighed down a pile of manila folders. The upright chairs that faced her father's desk were covered in tapestry. Beth remembered the wool itchy on the back of her bare, swinging legs as she waited to hear what punishment was to be meted out for some misdemeanour.

How had Duncan managed to grow up so much that he could stand in the middle of the room on the paisley-patterned rug holding his coffee while talking to their father about the number of pheasant poults to buy in for the autumn shoots. The last time they had been in this room together was to hear their school reports read.

'Duncan is a bright and social child; in class he could do better,' their father would intone. You must be disappointed with your grades, Duncan. You haven't applied yourself like your sister.'

Then it would be Beth's turn. 'No one likes a know-it-all, young lady. There's nothing attractive about a girl with her nose in a book.'

Neither of them was musical like their mother.

'Come in, Beth, for goodness sake, don't stand there in the door, come in, come in,' said Pa now as he poured Duncan and himself a whisky. Beth and Duncan settled themselves side by side on the two tapestry chairs. Feeling guilty for no earthly reason, Beth sat straight-backed, perched near the edge of her seat her ankles crossed.

'I want to talk to you both about money,' said Pa. Beth glanced at Duncan and saw he, too, was relieved; family money was a safe subject.

'You know that together you are the named executors of my estate. And I'm sure you know that Tina now has a flat in London. I wanted to reassure you how that was financed.' He coughed and sipped his whisky. 'As you both know, the bulk of the estate and the family stake in Farthingale & Parteger will go to Duncan. I just wanted to reassure you, Duncan, that none of the money used to buy the flat came out of your inheritance.'

'Pa, I'm not really into all that primogenitor stuff. Both girls should –'

'Nonsense.' Beth saw her father still hoped that Duncan would change his mind, come back, and take over at F & P., he wasn't going to discuss an alternative. Dennis placed both his hands firmly on his desk in a solid, decisive movement. Then Pa's fingertips slid forward to pull some papers he had laid out on the blotter towards him.

'Now, there is a parcel of investments set aside for Beth and Tina. It is out of this pot that the money came to buy the flat. Don't worry, provision has been made. The pot was broken to redeem Tina's share, but the remainder has been re-invested. Any costs involved in the transactions have been shouldered by Tina, as it was at her behest that the original trust was broken. When the time comes, any assets paid out will be adjusted, weighted in your favour Beth, to take into account that Tina already has, well, pretty much all of her share.'

'Pa, really, I'd rather not talk about inheritance. All this stuff is years off worrying about,' said Beth.

'Beth, I appreciate you probably don't like talking about money, but it's important you should try to understand. I wanted you both to know that there has been no favouritism here. Tina asked for her due early, and after consideration, I released funds. Given the nature of the request, I have set up a further trust which actually owns the flat.'

'So, it doesn't belong to Tina?' asked Beth.

'She's what, only twenty-three, twenty-four. Tina has the benefit of the flat but given the nature of the investment and her previous impulsive behaviour, I felt it responsible to place the flat in a trust. Tina asked that Laura be the eventual sole beneficiary. So, the flat will remain within the family should anything happen to Tina. It is a closed trust; no one can be added to the bequest.'

'What if Tina marries and has more children. Wouldn't she want the option to add additional beneficiaries?' asked Beth.

'Apparently not,' said Pa. 'Duncan, I have put you as a named signatory of the trust. I'll need you to sign some papers I have here.'

Beth watched as her brother signed the necessary forms.

'It's very kind of Tina to name Laura as beneficiary. I wonder if she'll regret taking her share now and having it all tied up later,' said Beth, as they left the room and crossed the hall.

'What price independence. I should think Pa made those the conditions for freeing up the cash. Pa is just as intransigent as ever,' said Duncan. 'He really ought to be thinking about the bigger picture. Move with the times. Don't you think? Apart from anything else, it should be you he's talking to. You, he's getting involved. You are much savvier, and more business minded than I am. I remember you were always top in Maths at school. By the way, how's it going at F & P? How long have you been there now?'

'Oh, I'm loving it, just getting started really, but it's great to be back working now Laura's at school.'

Beth had been at Farthingale and Parteger for almost six months and had enjoyed every minute. Being considered useful again after the years of being at home was liberating. Observing something her father might have discussed with her over Sunday lunch percolate down through the company made her proud to have even minimal input. Farthingale and Pateger was somewhere Beth felt she belonged. When she passed her accountancy exams, Beth hoped she would be rewarded with more opportunities within the firm. This feeling of possibilities made her magnanimous towards her father.

'Pa is irascible, but he's spent his whole life working for the family, not himself. I don't think he can quite let that go,' she said.

'You mean, let me go,' said Duncan. 'Well, he should. I'm not coming back. You know that don't you.'

'I do, but we miss you so much,' she said. Beth linked her arm in his as they stood in the hall by the round table with one of Ma's beautiful flower arrangements in its centre. They had grown up arm in arm and then Beth could not have imagined a time when one of them would not have instinctively know what the other was thinking. But now Duncan's ambitions seemed so very far from her own. He had lost faith in F & P a long time ago, for her the journey was just beginning. With her free hand, Beth picked a fallen bud from the polished table and crushed the damp petals.

'And how is Austin working out?'

'It's fantastic. There's something about America, the can-do attitude. And it's a relief to be back in advertising.'

'I'm not surprised. For you at school, it was design and acting that you loved. But how is Meredith really getting on?' Beth wasn't sure that Meredith was of a mindset to embrace a can-do approach to life. So far, Beth had not managed to get Meredith alone to find out how she was really liking Texas.

'She's okay. She struggled to begin with. I'm the one with the green card, so, she isn't allowed to work, which doesn't help. But she's started volunteering at a local church, helping with the admin at a charity, beginning to make friends.'

'That's good.'

Beth marvelled at how the whole family could say so much without getting to the heart of an issue, but then he said. 'I thought moving abroad would bring us closer together, but it doesn't seem to be working out that way. Our interests, if anything, seem to be diverging.'

'Sometimes,' said Beth. 'It works better when a couple has something different to bring to the table.'

'Sometimes … you know …'

She thought Duncan might be about to confide in her, but he moved away. He gave her an apologetic smile before disentangling his arm and heading out the front door into the garden, taking any chance of a heartfelt exchange with him. Instead, he whistled to the dogs, lounging in the sun on the warm front steps, to join him for a walk. Beth watched him lope away into the brightness, the dogs swooping at his feet. Beth threw the crumpled flower that she still held crushed in her hand into the urn by the door, relieved that she hadn't had to deal with a problematic heart to heart after all. Other people's relationships were beyond understanding. How lucky she was, she thought; she and Max had no secrets. He was a better communicator than she was. He always told her what he was thinking, what was on his mind.

Christmas Show

Max brought the post with him as he came in from work and popped it down on the kitchen counter along with his briefcase. Beth was getting supper ready, and Laura sat at the kitchen table doing her homework.

'You're early… that's good,' said Beth, leaving off what she was doing to give him a kiss, wooden spoon held aloft. 'We can eat together.'

'The department meeting was cancelled; too many people couldn't make it.' He went to the sink and washed his hands. 'Hello, Laura, what are you up to?' Max came and stood beside her as he dried his hands.

'Homework.' Laura's head was bent over her books. A stray strand of golden hair had escaped her ponytail and trickled down the side of her face.

'What sort of homework?'

'I have five words and have to look them up in a dictionary and write a proper sentence for each one, said Laura, 'it's very hard.'

'Maybe you could write one sentence that used all the words together; that would be much quicker.'

'But probably not easier,' said Beth. They made a pretty picture,

Max bending down to read over Laura's shoulder, his dark head against her blond hair, so much like Tina's.

'Or proper,' said Laura giving her father a nudge.

'How long till supper?' asked Max.

'Fifteen minutes,' said Beth turning back to the stove to furiously stir a cheese sauce for the cauliflower.

'Need any help?'

'No, I'm fine.' Beth preferred to work on her own in the kitchen, she had organised everything perfectly to suit her cooking methods and found it hard to give ground to anyone else.

'White okay?' Max had opened the fridge and waved a half-full bottle in Beth's direction.

'Lovely, thanks.'

He fetched some glasses and poured them each a glass of wine.

'When was this opened?' Max sniffed his glass.

'Sunday evening, remember. That's why we didn't finish it. You had an early start … an operation Monday.'

'We should be having red this close to Christmas. Only a month to go! Have you got your list ready for Santa, Laura?'

'I really want my ears pierced, but Mummy says no.'

'Yes, I say no,' said Beth. 'Six is far too young!'

'Clare has her ears pierced.' Laura pulled a face at Beth.

'Not sure Santa does piercings, but maybe he'll give you a fabulous pair of diamond earrings you can keep till you're older.' Max pulled the post towards him and started going through it, separating the letters, buff envelopes with a typed address were usually for him and hand-written envelopes were generally addressed to Beth.

'Or a cat. I'd really like a kitten with whiskers,' said Laura.

'And a tail?' said Max. He gave Beth a wink. Beth had found a breeder of British Blues, and she was due to pick up a kitten for Laura on Christmas Eve. Max slipped his mail into his jacket pocket and picked up a thick envelope addressed to the family. Beth thought it absurd, this habit of Max's to squirrel away his post.

She was not interested in his mail, but Max could be cagy about his private letters.

'Is this the first card of the year?' As he held up a glittery Christmas scene; a folded sheet of paper slipped out onto the counter.

'Oh, that looks like it's from Duncan and Meredith,' said Beth, picking up the fallen letter from the kitchen top. 'Duncan is so lousy at being in touch. I've no idea what they're up to.'

Max went through the rest of the post, putting the Christmas catalogues on one side.

'Shall I throw these?' he asked.

'I'll have a look later; you never know….' Beth looked up from the round robin from Texas. There was always something in the catalogues, and she still had presents to buy.

'What does Meredith say?' said Max.

'Hmmm, Duncan's really enjoying his job and has taken up jogging! There's a group at his work that go out together.'

'Along with golf and tennis? Sounds unlikely.'

'I guess with guaranteed good weather, exercise is more appealing; look, here's a photo.' She showed him the letter. 'He's actually jogging in the picture. It must be for a competition; he has a number on his shirt. And there's another picture of Gareth with some school project he's won a prize for.'

'Science Fair, he's got a first. Well done, Gareth.' Max gave the letter back.

'Oh, and he has his green belt in taekwondo, whatever that is. And has joined the school chess club and taken up the clarinet.'

'Sounds busy. How about it, Laura? Fancy joining any after-school clubs.'

'I already do ballet, you know that, Daddy. Are you coming to my Christmas Show this year?'

Max looked at the family calendar on the fridge. 'Hmm, the 15th; unfortunately, I think I'm working late that night.'

'You never come! Mummy always enjoys it. You should come

too.'

'Don't fret, Laura, May-May's coming. She loves watching you dance.'

'Would you like to take up an instrument, like Gareth, the flute perhaps?' said Max.

'Then you could not come to my concerts, as well,' said Laura.

'As long as it's not the double bass,' said Beth imagining herself struggling with a huge case across the school car park late at night for some recital.

'What else?' asked Max, turning back to Beth, who still held the round-robin in her hand, 'How's Meredith?'

'Well, they are all doing a terrific amount, terrifically well, but as usual, she's not written much about herself. Just a postscript, really, saying she's enjoying being involved in a local church charity. And there's a lovely photo of them all together in front of their tree,' Beth studied the picture. They looked stiff, posed for the photograph, each standing slightly apart from the other, like separate planets orbiting around a celestial tree. 'They're going to have a barbecue on Christmas day.'

'I can never get used to the idea of a hot Christmas; they'll be wearing t-shirts.'

'I love their white tree,' said Laura who was standing on her chair to look over her mother's shoulder.

'Down you get! Have you finished your homework? It's suppertime,' said Beth fetching a cloth to wipe the table.

Tina

You were probably more interested in Just William and Alistair Maclean or those commando books that Duncan enjoyed. For me, it was fairy tales. When I was young, I had a collection of stories written in dialect from around the British Isles. I loved that book and would pester Ma all the time to read them to me. There weren't so many tales about princesses; the book was about common folk making good or getting their comeuppance. The midwife who helped a fairy family or the boy who tried to trick a leprechaun out of his pot of gold.

There was one story that used to scare me. It didn't really make sense when I was young. It was about a woman sitting at her spinning wheel, and all she does is sit and spin and wish for company. When I was young, I couldn't fathom why she didn't get up and do something. But I didn't know then what I know now. All day, I spin webs of guilt to torture myself with, wondering why I gave up my child. At night, my thoughts coil into cravings for you that keep me awake.

In the tale, a monster of a man comes into the room bit by bit while the woman sits and spins. And all the while, as the creature assembles itself, she keeps spinning, still hoping for company. He takes that as an invitation and inveigles his way into her home, feet first. I think of your dress shoes tossed across the room when you came to me after a medical dinner. Then shins and knees, and I see you kneeling above me, your hair falling over your eyes as you bend to kiss me. Next, the hips and I laugh at the explanation I had to give to the handyman who replaced the broken shelf in my hall that fell when you arrived late one night, and we were too impatient to make it to the bedroom. The broad shoulders and firm hands follow, and I long to be pinned to the bed while you grazed over me. All the way up to the huge head. And all I can think of is you. Not Beth, who I'm jealous of while owing the most incredible debt, nor Laura, my own child, but you. Your eyes and lips and my desire for you. It is I who am the monster.

Whenever I find your socks in my laundry basket, I think of that fool woman. Whenever I see one of your shirts hanging ghostlike in my wardrobe, emitting essence of Max, the most seductive scent of all, I want to put it on, wrap myself in you and forget the world outside. I used to console myself that I had no responsibility for myself because you had taken advantage of me, but now I'm not so sure. Despite the evidence that all is not well, the woman in the tale keeps spinning and wishing for company. Even as a child, I thought, run, woman, run; run while you can, but she can't. And that is where we are the same, of course, I want you. I want your company. I invited you in.

When the monster is fully assembled, feet, body, and head, they can begin to talk. At last, she asks, 'What did you come for?' And the monster says, 'For you!'

Now, I weep as I sit here yearning for the luxury of afternoon sex or the feel of a silky dress sliding over my skin as I walk towards you. The woman in the story had to sit alone and wait too. Wait for some bloody monster who slunk into her affections and took over, bit by bit. That's what I did, Max, I gave you control. You didn't have much work to do on me. Who am I, a woman who would rather have a lover than look after her own child? A woman who loves her sister while wishing to rip her heart out. Yes, I am the monster in my own story.

I think I hate you, and then you touch me. Brush my hand, cup my breast, send a hand to linger over my arse, and I'm glad I'm in my Aubade lingerie, something to make me a sexy parcel for you to unwrap, lighting me up as you go. When you're not here, I ache for you. My body wants to be touched. It is as though my sole purpose is to be fucked by you. And I want it. My love for you swings back and forth, but my body is constant in its desire. When I reason, I can see your influence, but I know you just let the real me out of the box.

At first, I was in awe; I was amazed you condescended to pay me attention. Then, I believed I was in love with you and you with me. Now, I want to be wanted and need to be needed. I must be in love with you. I ache for you.

Disney World

Beth was in the vast sunshine outside the turnstiles with Laura. They were covered in lotion and had their hats with them. Beth checked her bag again. She had sun cream, a bottle of water, tissues, and sunglasses. Chattering adults with excited children were beginning to trickle past them from the car park towards the turnstiles. Max had gone to get their passes for the day. She saw him now, striding back towards her across the warming pink tarmac holding two coffees.

'Thank you. We did say 8.30, didn't we?' Beth asked, taking one of the drinks from his outstretched hand.

'Yes,' said Max. '8.30.'

'And it's now, what?' She grimaced as she sipped the coffee. Why did the coffee taste as though it had been boiled for hours?

'8.35.'

'They're late,' said Beth. She had been awake for hours with Laura, who had woken early and snuggled up with Beth in her half of the giant bed. Beth had quietly read under her breath to Laura, so they didn't disturb Max. He hadn't slept on the plane and had fallen asleep as soon as they reached the hotel room.

'Only just,' said Max.

'Do you think they'll be very late, Daddy?' asked Laura.

'I shouldn't think so,' said Max.

They arrived at last, Gareth charging across the car park towards them, hallooing and waving his cap.

'Well, this is exciting,' said Duncan shaking Max's hand and giving Beth a peck and a hug. 'It's so good to see you over here for a change. So great to have this time together.'

'Good to see you too,' said Beth. She glanced at her watch; it was nearly nine.

'We're not late, are we?' said Duncan smiling broadly. 'Meredith wanted to finish breakfast.'

'No worries,' Beth said, smiling back at Duncan. Without a doubt, they were going to have a fabulous holiday together.

'Sorry,' said Meredith to Beth as they set off towards the park, joining the stream of eager families. 'Gareth is supposed to eat in a calm, relaxed environment. His psychologist says if he starts in the morning in an unpressurised way, it will enable him to have better outcomes throughout the day.'

'Gosh,' said Beth. 'I didn't realise Gareth was seeing someone. He's only a child.'

'The school suggested it. He's supposed to learn coping strategies.'

'Oh,' said Beth wondering what issues might be problematic for Gareth.

'I just thought, as he's been so excited about this holiday, I should try and slow him down before he gets overwrought,' said Meredith.

They merged with the crowds pushing into the park and regrouped under the statue of Walt Disney and Mickey Mouse. Duncan and Max had the map open and were discussing what they should do and see and in what order.

'We should do the Magic Kingdom first?' Beth said. 'I think Laura will enjoy that bit best, and when she's used to the rides, we can try something more adventurous.' Beth had already studied the map of Disney World and had a definite plan of what they should be doing.

'I'm not a baby, Mummy,' said Laura tucking a stray strand of hair behind her ear. 'I'm seven. I want to go on all the rides.'

'Gareth won't mind what we do, will you, Gareth?' said Meredith. 'We haven't been before, so everything is an adventure.'

'Best have your say, Gareth. Enjoy yourself while you're young. It'll be downhill from now on.' said Duncan.

'For goodness sake, Duncan, don't be such a killjoy,' said Meredith.

'See what I mean,' said Duncan.

'I want to see the pirates first!' said Gareth.

'The Pirates of the Caribbean it is,' said Beth. It wasn't first on her list, but the guide indicated it was a gentle enough ride. They set off past the tropical-themed stands and play area to join the queue for the boat ride.

As the day progressed, they perfected a system of the adults queueing for alternate rides to speed up the wait time for the children. Then as lunchtime approached, Beth hurried them to their reservation.

'I hope you don't mind, Gareth,' said Beth. 'There are other character meals at different restaurants, but this was the one I thought Laura would like best.'

'Why would Gareth mind a dozen or so princesses attending to his every need while he has lunch?' asked Duncan.

'No need to put ideas in his head,' said Meredith. 'Of course, he won't mind. Will you, Gareth?' Gareth wasn't listening. He was running around wielding a plastic cutlass Duncan had bought him.

There was an edge in Meredith's voice, a hint of a threat. Beth wasn't sure who Meredith was trying to get at, but it didn't bother Beth one way or the other. Laura was always doing what her older cousin wanted, hanging on Gareth's every word and this time, this holiday, Beth wanted to make sure Laura got to do some of the things she wanted to do too.

'How about the rest of us,' added Max. 'Do we get a say in whether we want to be fawned over by simpering teenage girls in crinolines?'

Beth glared at Max, but he had been very good about the holiday. She had thought he might find the Disney experience over the top. Max was fifty, not their target audience. Beth was surprised by how much fun he seemed to be having, but Max had embraced all things Disney. If anything, it was she who was struggling. Beth didn't know why she was being such a spoilsport, but too much fun seemed obnoxious, and the rank commercialisation was outrageous. At the end of every ride, the shop was a gauntlet to run with all the gaudy, shiny toys, waiting to catch children's hearts and parents' pockets.

After lunch, Gareth wanted to go on Splash Mountain. It was not on Beth's list. She didn't want to spin around uncontrollably on a boat and had no intention of getting wet, even if the sun was hot enough to dry them quickly.

'You go,' she said to the others. 'I'll just have a pit stop with Laura.' And she started to haul Laura off in the opposite direction.

'Mum,' said Laura, straining, digging in her heels and pouting. 'I want to go on the ride.'

'Really? Are you sure?' asked Beth. 'You'll get wet.'

'I'll take Laura,' said Max. 'We'll meet you at the end.'

Beth was left alone in the crowd of mingling, happy families as the others hurried onto the ride. She glowered angrily at the passing faces and went to buy herself a coffee. Beth sat near the end of the ride, where she could see people leaving in various states of dampness. Her coffee was hardly finished when Gareth appeared, dripping, with Laura chasing behind him, soaked and laughing.

'You don't mind, do you, Mummy,' said Laura. 'It was Daddy's fault. He's so heavy.' What a wet blanket I am, thought Beth. Did Laura really think she'd be cross?

'Honestly, Duncan and Max were like schoolboys,' said Meredith. 'Rocking the boat, getting everyone much wetter than was necessary.'

'I thought part of the fun was getting wet,' said Duncan.

'Sometimes, Duncan, you just don't know when everyone has had enough of your antics,' said Meredith.

'Anyone want an ice cream?' Beth asked.

Beth was in the queue outside Space Mountain, waiting for the others to finish their ride and join her near the front of the line. They had made it to Tomorrowland on the promise that it would be the last stop of the day.

'I'm going to sit this one out,' said Beth.

'Really,' said Duncan. 'Again, it's meant to be fantastic. A rollercoaster in the dark, what could be more exciting.'

'I think I've reached my limit.'

'Come on, darling,' said Max and added, whispering, 'Don't be such a misery, Laura really wants to go on this ride, and she'll be upset if you chicken out.'

'Chicken, chicken,' sang Gareth.

'That's enough, Gareth,' said Meredith.

They had now reached the front of the queue.

'On you go,' said Beth backing away from the entrance to the ride. She had felt increasing apprehension as they neared the entrance gate. 'Honestly, I've really had enough for the day.'

'Nothing to do with this being the first proper rollercoaster?' asked Max. 'Come on, give it a go, don't be a scaredy cat.'

'Scaredy cat, scaredy cat,' sang Gareth.

'Enough, Gareth,' said Duncan. 'Or you can wait outside with your aunt.'

'I've just had such a lovely day and don't want to spoil everything by getting queasy now,' said Beth. She did feel feeble, but she knew she would be horribly scared and dreadfully sick if she went on the ride. Just looking at it made her feel faint.

Meeting at Disney World had been her idea. A way to see Duncan and Meredith away from Nether Place and for the children to have fun together. Beth hadn't thought the other adults would want to go on all the rides. She thought they would have a civilised time, perhaps sit and chat over coffee while the children enjoyed themselves. But even Max wanted to experience everything. That evening, she asked him what the appeal was.

'Why wouldn't I want to have fun?' Max said. 'I've never been to Disney World before. It's a whole new adventure for me. I'm having a great time and loving watching Laura enjoying herself too. You need to loosen up, Beth. You should open yourself up to trying new things. Then you might not be so terrified of everything and wouldn't make yourself sick.'

Christmas Drinks

'So lovely Tina could be here,' said Mrs Johnson to Beth. It was the annual Christmas drinks party at Nether Place and the room was full of local friends mingling. 'I haven't seen her for such a long time. Since she was a child, really.' Mrs Johnson sipped the glass of champagne Tina had brought her.

Beth watched Tina crossing the room, gliding between people, slinking like a cat, handing out drinks. Mr Johnson leered as Tina handed him a glass of champagne. Tina must realise the impact she had, that red dress was so provocative, but Beth saw Tina was oblivious of Mr Johnson.

'Bob doesn't usually drink bubbly, more a whisky man,' said Mrs Johnson clasping the knot of her pearls that swung on her bosom. She turned to Beth and continued. 'I'm surprised she hasn't married. Such a pretty girl. She has a lovely figure, like her mother.'

Dismay crossed Mrs Johnson's face. 'Not that you don't look pleasant too, dear.' Mrs Johnson's eyes hunted the wallpaper behind Beth's head as if searching for an appealing reason for Beth to take after her father. Having found a thought amongst the damask, she said, 'But having children does take its toll, doesn't it.' And she patted her own stomach. 'My four have definitely left their mark.'

Beth smiled, hoping she looked sympathetic. Mrs Johnson was older than her mother and had always looked magnificent with a fine embonpoint. But her Edwardian deportment could no longer disguise that now, she was becoming quite stout. Perhaps Mrs Johnson had never been told of Beth's difficulties or had forgotten. Still, there was no denying that Beth was a Parteger. It was not such a bad deal; the family was chock-full of handsome women. Beth knew she could hold her own just not with the sensitive frailness and wistful beauty of her mother - and Tina.

Beth glanced at Tina, who brushed the front of her silk dress as if sweeping away crumbs, then tucked a golden strand of hair behind an ear before picking up a fresh bottle and crossing the room towards Pa and Max. Tina walked with grace. Beth required effort to move, whereas Tina seemed to waft between the chairs like the wind through the reeds by the lake. Tina poured Pa some champagne before turning to Max. She must have said something amusing to Max as she refilled his glass; he bent towards her, laughing. Beth couldn't hear above the din in the room. She must ask Max later what Tina had said that was so entertaining.

Mrs Johnson was rattling through what each of her children was up to. Beth remembered the quartet of Johnson children. There had been childhood teas when the families had got together. If they met at Nether Place, Beth and Duncan would be charged with entertaining the visiting children, and if they had gone to the Johnsons, they would be whisked off to play in an alien and fascinating world. As teenagers, the families had sent their children to different boarding schools, and when the holidays rolled around, they seemed to forget their shared childhood and begrudged being bundled together as a group where awkward school rivalries were exposed, and boredom was de rigueur. Younger than the youngest Johnson, Tina had missed out on these enforced get-togethers.

'I bumped into Edith the other day in Peter Jones. She was buying school uniform,' said Beth. They had been going opposite ways on adjacent escalators but had recognised each other and caught a coffee before Edith Johnson, who was now married with her own brood, had dashed away. Edith had looked harried but had been amazingly normal. Beth rather wondered why they hadn't managed to continue to be friends. The stigma of one's parents being friends cast a long shadow.

Tina drifted towards them with the champagne and filled Mrs Johnson's glass.

'You look charming tonight, Tina, my how you've grown.'

'Thank you, Mrs Johnson.'

'You must call me Olive.'

Tina gave Beth that sideways smile, and Beth couldn't help smiling back. Neither of them would ever be able to call Mrs Johnson, Olive.

Catch Up

Beth pulled Meredith's Christmas letter towards her and wondered how to reply. It had been so hectic before they left for Nether Place that Beth only had time to send a card. Laura had been in the usual festive ballet show, and this year Beth had volunteered to help with the costumes. Only to find herself making thirty baby blue tutus for a class of five-year-olds, nothing to do with Laura's performance. Beth had survived, they had made it to her parents for the annual drinks, and she had enjoyed Christmas. Though Tina's penchant for giving everyone extravagantly expensive presents always grated. She didn't know how Tina could afford it. Beth felt undermined but refused to play a war of escalation. After lunch, Beth and Max had driven to see Max's parents before returning home for a round of parties to celebrate festivities. Beth had invited far too many friends over for dinner on New Year's Eve. So even now, though well into January, Beth felt she was still catching up.

Tonight, Laura was sleeping over at a friend, and Max was staying in London. He had a late meeting and a dinner, then an early operation in the morning. So, Beth had no excuse; she must settle down and write replies to her Christmas cards. Churchill was there to help, he would normally be upstairs with Laura, but as she was away, he had to settle for Beth. He had looked grumpily at her, pacing around the room before deciding that her lap would have to do. As she stroked him, soft grey fur loosened and floated up to tickle her nose. She couldn't move with him on her lap, wouldn't move now till the letters were done. On top of the pile was Duncan and Meredith's card. Beth had spoken to Duncan on the family call on Christmas day along with the rest of the family, but Beth must reply to Meredith. She wanted to keep in touch.

Meredith's letter started off with Gareth. There were several photographs of him. The first showed his fist around the neck of a twisting snake at some sandy outdoor reptile zoo. Another showed him in a gym, looking very pleased with himself, wearing a white kimono and holding a neatly folded red belt. The third was with the school basketball team. Gareth was so much shorter than the other boys that Beth wondered if perhaps he was the mascot. Gareth was twelve. He would surely have a growth spurt soon. There then followed a short passage about how busy Duncan was. He had the promotion he was after, and his new job involved a great deal of travel. There was a photo of Duncan surrounded by strangers. He'd completed a marathon and stood foil-caped and smiling, holding his finisher's medal. There was a final photograph of Meredith with her choir in front of the church Christmas tree. Something about the letter reminded Beth of an afternoon on one her own family holidays. Beth had been left on the beach while Max had taken Laura kite surfing. It was something that Beth had no interest in doing, yet, even so, she felt left out, even with a good book to keep her company.

'Well, I'm glad she's happy with her Church. They do look a rather jolly bunch,' Max had said when Beth showed him the photograph.

'Yes, she says her local Christian community has been a great support,' said Beth. 'But what do you suppose she means by "Unfortunately, Duncan's actions are incompatible with their practices" that I don't quite understand.'

'Well, Duncan has never been a holy roller. Perhaps they object to his customary whisky on a Sunday night.'

'It's a shame there isn't a photograph of them all together this year.' Beth said.

Though she knew how hectic it could be at family events. When everyone was enjoying themselves there wasn't always time to ask someone to capture the moment. But better to live life fully than record every instant, for who in posterity would appreciate that minute with as much pleasure as those who were there themselves.

Tina

I no longer pretended to look at the menu. I took a slow sip of water and contemplated whether to go ahead and order lunch, eat on my own, or give up and go back to the flat. It would be a shame not to see you, I had dressed with care as always for you, Max. Then, with a scurry of air, the door of the wine bar shot open and in you wandered.

'Sorry, the meeting overran,' you said, dropping your jacket over the back of the vacant chair opposite me.

'Ah, Max.' I looked up at you, relieved not to have been abandoned. 'How do you cope with all these meetings, all these committees, all this importance?'

'I'm here now, Tina.' You sat down and smiled. 'I'm all yours.' You picked up the menu and glanced at your watch. 'Have to get a move on, though. I'm picking Beth up later; we're driving down to Nether Place this afternoon.'

'With Laura?' I asked, always hoping for news.

'Laura's staying with a friend this weekend.' Without looking up, intently tracing the wood grain of the table with a finger, you said. 'You could come too, you know.'

'I'm working tomorrow.'

'The gallery's dead, even at the weekend, *especially* at the weekend. And they pay you a pittance! Come on, skip a day. Come to the country. The weather is meant to be good.'

'It's my job, Max. It matters to me.'

'Then come down Saturday evening. Your mother has asked the

Johnsons and that neighbour with the lawyer husband. I will be going out of my mind.'

'You have my sympathy,' I said. 'But you'll have Beth to protect you.'

'Beth isn't you,' you said, looking at me at last. 'I like that shirt, or rather the décolleté. You are looking very lovely, Tina.' You reached across the table and lifted my hand in yours. You turned my hand, exposing the vulnerable palm and toyed with my fingers. 'I want you to be there.'

'Honestly, you ask too much.'

'You must come,' you said. 'How will I manage without you?'

Despite myself, I felt my heart lift a little.

On Saturday, I caught the train after work.

'How lovely to see you, darling,' Ma said with a peck. 'We have a full house. The Johnsons are staying over after supper. So, I've put you in your old room in the attic. I thought you'd prefer that anyway.'

I took my overnight bag and headed up the stairs.

'And darling,' Ma called after me, 'no smoking in the house, remember.'

I nodded and kept going up along the upper hall and took the narrow wooden stairs to my old room, avoiding the creaky step. This part of the house always felt neglected. As though the cold had seeped into the stones and now lay waiting to bleed into my bones and drag me back into the past. I dumped my bag on the bed and trailed around the room, re-engaging with my adolescent self. The room felt unloved and deserted, despite the host of memories lurking in every corner.

I picked up my old journal from the bedside table. Inside the cover, in my loopy, teenage script, the front page declared this diary belongs to Tina Parteger, Nether Place, Faygate, The World, The Universe. Turquoise and pink ink scrawled over the pages between pasted cut-outs from magazines. Loaded with content but no emotion, nothing to embarrass you here, Max. Though I don't think my mother would have looked. Beth might be less scrupulous, but I couldn't imagine her making the journey up the extra flight of stairs.

How I used to idolise Beth. When I was a teenager, I would glance at her sideways, terrified she'd catch me looking. Beth was self-assured, she had a job and a husband, all while I was still at school.

I lifted my bag and found my cigarettes and lit up. Smoking always made me feel grown up, though at twenty-five you would have thought I didn't need confirmation anymore. I sauntered to the window wondering when we would have sex. I pushed up the sash, breathing smoky breath out into the late afternoon sky. Voices rose from the garden below. Wrapped in the damp smell of putty from the dormer, I looked down at the lawn streaked by the low evening sun and beyond to the shimmering lake turning dark as the light faded. I saw you trudging up the path from the walled garden, deep in talk with the boring lawyer. His wife and Beth walked a little behind, chatting, Beth carrying greenery in an open trug. You stopped and turned, drawing the two women into your talk. Then, as you strolled on, you pulled Beth close to you, your arm around her shoulders. You looked up at the house, smiling. I drew back into the shadows.

At dinner, you stood so close; you always stand too close. I was at the sideboard helping myself from the dishes on the hot plate when you came over and stood next to me, helping yourself to potatoes as though you couldn't decide how much was enough. You didn't look at me. You didn't say anything, but I could feel you, a heat at my side through the cool of my summer frock. I waited as you dithered. When I edged away, you moved closer. I didn't look at you, but I breathed you in, and I breathed you out. The serving spoon I was holding fell too loudly back into its dish. Why do you do this? Exert your aura; make me stumble. I turned to look at you, to say something. But your back was to me. You had turned to the table to ask Beth if you could bring her something.

'Why does Beth get everything,' I muttered under my breath. I couldn't imagine Beth making you feel like I could. I was beginning to despise her. All I could think was how stupid she was. How could she not be aware? I felt so alert, so engaged by your presence. How could no one else see?

'What?' You turned.

'Nothing.' I met your gaze before taking my plate to my seat.

Conversation rippled as we ate, rising and dipping, louder each time the wine was passed around. I pushed a potato through congealed gravy and watched you with silent eyes.

I was part of the family, but my time away in Italy somehow changed everything. The last time Duncan was over from Texas, we had met for lunch in London.

'What happened, Tina? Duncan had asked. 'You never used to avoid family get-togethers. You're so quiet now. You used to have views and opinions, too many as I remember; you were never lost for words. Life and soul. What happened?'

I hadn't thought I had changed that much. If I had, I hadn't thought anyone had noticed. I didn't know how to respond.

'Oh, I don't know. I guess I talk all day at the gallery,' I said, knowing that if I started to speak if I was to say what I really felt, I wasn't sure I'd be able to stop. 'Perhaps, now I'm older, I don't feel I have an automatic right to speak out anymore.'

'Hmmm, older and wiser?'

'Perhaps, I just gave all the words away.' I replied at last. It was impossible for me to reconcile what I didn't have with what I wanted. Max thought he had devised the perfect way to have both Beth and Laura, and me. I couldn't begin to explain that to Duncan without tearing the family apart, but I wasn't happy.

'Come to the States sometime … come and stay,' Duncan said after a moment, but I had gathered he had problems of his own.

Beth helped Ma clear the plates. Pa was asking me about the

flat. You were talking to Mrs Johnson, who sat next to you. She was large and blousy, a friend of Ma's, far too hearty. You, Max, were being charming. You looked very distinguished, leaning in, captivating Mrs Johnson, who giggled at something you said. You always looked good in a suit, and your hair was still dark, just the right amount of salt and pepper at your temples. Fifty, is that how old you are? More or less. You didn't look it. I wondered; did you use Grecian 2000?

I watched you from beneath lowered lids. When you knew you had my attention, you quietly played with your cutlery and placed your fork at an angle, just so, just for a moment. I knew what that meant. I looked across the room at Beth, who was returning with cream for the pudding. How had I reached a place where I could treat her so badly? When I was younger, it had been easy to discount Beth. As a teenager, I had been a ball of spite and selfishness. It never occurred to me then that Beth might have feelings. To me, my relationship with you had been all that mattered. It was the only true love in Nether Place, Faygate, The World, The Universe.

Much later, I heard the creaky step.

You came in the dark, I let you, and I hated myself. I knew you would come, and I would accept you like I always did because I needed you so much. It would be like it had always been because, for a moment, I felt part of something bigger. Afterwards, I felt very small and said to myself, never, never again.

Part 3

As Laura pushed open the familiar oak door, childhood memories flooded back. When Nether Place was her grandmother's home, a heavy round table had stood firmly in the centre of the panelled hall. On the table, there had always been a huge vase of flowers picked from the garden with an abundance of loose greenery, ready to be painted by some Dutch master. The soft drifting floral scents mixed with the smell of beeswax. Persian carpets had wrinkled across the polished floors leading down corridors that led into the depths of the house.

Now, the hall was an antiseptic reception area painted cream. A tall, thin display of highly scented lilies wavered in a cheap vase on the modern desk as if they knew they shouldn't be there, like a nervous guest at an upmarket party wearing too loud a perfume. Usually, someone would be sitting behind the desk to encourage visitors to sign the log-in book, but sometimes the nurses were busy elsewhere. Today no one sat at the desk. Laura would have to go in search of tea or use the coffee station by the library door. A bruised petal fell from a fading lily onto the check-in book as Laura signed herself in.

'Hello, my darling,' said May-May. 'How good of you to come. I have been sitting here in the sunshine, thinking it would be so lovely to share the afternoon with someone. And here you are!'

May-May looked well today. She sat poised in her chair. Her clothes were neat, her hair had been set, she was wearing her pearls, and there was more colour in her cheeks than when Laura had last seen her.

'Hi, May-May. Sorry, I'm late, there was a problem with the train.'

'What a bore for you but not an issue for me, darling. I wasn't going anywhere. I was just thinking, I hadn't seen anyone for ages.'

'Wasn't Mum here in the week?' said Laura as she shrugged off her coat and hung it over the back of a chair.

'I don't think so.' May-May looked out the window. Her hands lay in her lap, loosely holding her ancient Russian prayer book. Then, after a moment, she said, 'Maybe she was.'

'I managed to find that friendly nurse, Sharon. I asked her if she could bring us some tea; if she had a moment.'

'Good idea, darling.' May-May's gaze returned to the room; she placed the book on the table beside her, pushing the shepherdess over to make room. 'Why don't you sit down?'

'I'm looking for the album. We could look at some more photos if you like?' When her mother had first suggested she should visit her grandmother, Laura hadn't wanted to; thought she would find it too depressing. But she had enjoyed listening to May-May's stories and the photographs had proved a good way to prompt an anecdote or two.

'I think it might have been tidied away. Is it under those glossies?'

Laura found the album beneath the stack of shiny fashion magazines. She pulled it out, sat down with it, and began leafing through the pages. She found a large formal photograph of all the family.

'When was this taken, May-May?' asked Laura.

'Let's see. That was ... well, it was here at Nether Place. I recognise the fireplace.' She paused for a moment. 'No, I can't remember when.' May-May gazed out of the window again as if chasing some forgotten thought. She sighed. The sunshine had swept over her armchair and stopped to pick out the gold lettering embossed on the prayer book. A moment later, May-May said. 'Was it to mark Beth's birthday, her fortieth?'

'I think it might be a bit later,' said Laura. 'Perhaps Grandpa's birthday?'

'Oh, yes! It was taken at Dennis' seventy-fifth.' May-May turned to look at the photograph, her hand passed over the family group. 'This was the moment we were a perfect family. All my children are here, happy with their partners, and I had two adorable grandchildren. Look at you! Look at us all.'

'You still have two adorable grandchildren,' said Laura.

'I do, I do,' said May-May with a smile. Her grandmother cupped Laura's cheek in her tissue paper hand. After a moment, May-May turned back to the photograph.

'Mrs Simms must have taken this because we are all here, even Tina.' May-May's finger jabbed the photo. 'And that is Freddie. They were late. Their flight was delayed. They'd flown in from somewhere exotic that morning.'

'Was that... was that the first time you'd met Freddie?'

'No, Tina had already brought him down to Nether Place several times. We were all so happy she'd met someone who seemed suitable. Someone who really cared for her. What a disaster!'

'And here are Duncan, Meredith, and Gareth. They came back to visit pretty often, didn't they? I remember being in awe of Gareth.'

'Every summer. Meredith liked to see her family.' May-May shifted slightly in her chair and Laura repositioned the heavy album. 'Duncan was always itching to get back to work. Always had something else he needed to be doing. He said he only got a short amount of holiday. It upset your grandfather that he didn't stay longer.'

'I think that's right, though. The States are notoriously stingy with paid leave.'

'Somehow, I remember feeling he was always running away, wanting to be somewhere else.'

'I'm sure he didn't mean to give that impression.'

May-May searched in her sleeve for a handkerchief and dabbed her nose.

'Did Grandpa have balloons and cake for his birthday?' asked Laura.

'You must remember, you were, what? About eight or nine?'

'Twelve! I do remember, particularly the cake. It was huge and covered in hundreds and thousands.'

'Mrs Simms loved to bake ... any excuse.'

The door opened, brushing the carpet, and Sharon brought in the tea. Even the noises of the house had changed, Laura thought, once everything had echoed: latches clicking, voices ringing, footsteps resounding on the parquet. Now every sound was hushed, smothered, as though a "do not disturb" sign had been placed over the building. When tea was set, the nurse left, and the soft-close mechanism of the door whooshed shut.

'Tell me about the birthday? Did Grandpa enjoy himself? Did he have a good time?'

'Oh yes, it was a lovely day,' said May-May. 'It was wonderful to have everyone together. We had champagne before lunch in the drawing room. Gareth, rather enthusiastically, helped Duncan fill the glasses. Everyone was on good form. It made your grandfather so very happy to have the family together, chatting and laughing. Mrs Simms had cooked Beef Wellington, Dennis' favourite. It was delicious.' May-May looked thoughtful for a moment, sliding her jaw. 'We don't get much beef here ...' she smiled, her hand resting on her chin. 'Though I doubt I could manage it now.'

'Would you like some tea, May-May, before it gets too strong?'

'Thank you, darling.' May-May held out her cup. Laura steadied the trembling saucer as she poured.

'I remember Beth insisted on getting the meat from her butcher in London for Dennis' lunch. It rather put Mrs Simms out. Beth wasn't supposed to be involved, but you know how she does love to organise everything.' May-May sipped her tea.

'Then, after lunch, it was time for presents and the glorious cake,' prompted Laura.

'You and Gareth were very excited, but you had to wait. Your grandfather wanted to make a speech.'

'A celebration of his life?'

'More an announcement. Dennis had been thinking about stepping down from Farthingale and Parteger. We'd talked it over; it troubled your grandfather. He'd come to realise that Duncan really wasn't interested in the family business and wasn't going to return from America, but it hurt. When they first went out, Meredith wasn't happy in Austin, and we didn't think they'd stay long.' May-May paused and gazed out the window again. Laura looked at the garden too. The crocuses had gone over and been mowed; the lawn looked pristine. But the sky was no longer blue; the odd cloud had begun to gather. 'To be honest, we thought Meredith would have fitted right in with all those mid-westerners, with her prudish beliefs and socks and sandals.'

'You can't say that May-May!'

'Why not? It was what we thought at the time. Anyway, we didn't realise it, but the facts were, Meredith was miserable, but Duncan wanted to stay. If Duncan had been involved in F & P, Dennis would have stepped back, but when Duncan applied for his green card, we knew he had gone for good. Your grandfather couldn't bear not having some link to the company. It had been his whole life.'

'Wasn't Mum supposed to take over? Didn't she work at F & P for years?'

'Oh no. I don't think that was ever on the cards.'

'I thought she enjoyed working for Grandpa?'

'Yes, she did, but sadly, she'd had to leave F & P just before Dennis' birthday.'

'Why was that? I never realised she *had* to leave. I thought she decided to spend more time at home.'

'It was so long ago now.' May-May looked into her empty cup, which tinkled against the saucer in her unsteady hand. Laura rescued them and put them back on the tray.

'Thank you, darling. I remember, at first, Beth was thrilled to be working at the family firm.' May-May leaned back in her chair and closed her eyes.

'Was Grandpa thinking Mum could organise everything for him?'

May-May turned, opening her pale, watery grey eyes to look at

Laura.

'I think your grandfather thought it would be good for Beth. She'd been finding it hard to find a flexible job that she could fit around your school runs. He was helping her out.'

'So, how did that go? What went wrong?' Laura leaned forward.

'To begin with, it all went very well. Beth worked in the finance department as a trainee. She'd been studying at home, some correspondence course in accounting. She needed practical experience to qualify, which she did. Then, being keen, Beth spotted some minor irregularities. Regrettably, it transpired Mr Bennett was skimming the accounts; had been for years. Such a shame, a charming man, he'd been here for lunch.'

'You can't get anything past Mum,' said Laura.

'Quite. So, she told your grandfather, and he dealt with it.'

'How?'

'Luckily, Mr Bennett was not far off retirement, and he was given a watch, and everyone was told he was leaving for personal reasons.'

'Even though he'd been cheating the firm?' Laura asked.

'That's how things were done. Everyone was happy.'

'Except Mum, I imagine.'

'Well, Beth was then asked to move to some other department, where she looked after staff.'

'Personnel?'

'That's right. And that went well for a while until one of the secretaries came to her and told her that old Mr Farthingale couldn't keep his hands to himself, and she wondered if she should talk to the press.'

'What?'

'I know! The press, I ask you,' said May-May. 'It wasn't really such a surprise, but Beth wouldn't let it go. She complained to your grandfather over Sunday lunch when she was back at Nether Place one weekend; she said it wasn't on. I remember thinking it wasn't on to talk about such things at the dining table. Dennis said it was a private matter and had nothing to do with good practice. Beth thought that was quite funny. She said she was sure Mr Farthingale had had plenty of practice. But the truth was, the firm couldn't afford a lawsuit.'

'So, what happened?'

'I think the girl ended up with a very nice flat in Sloane Square, two red-headed children, like their father, and eventually a slice of Mr Farthingale's will. She did very well out of it.' May-May turned to look out the window again. Laura saw it had clouded over completely, the cedar a dark giant, the lake a flat, ominous grey.

'And Mum?'

'Your grandfather thought it best if she stood down. Dennis suggested she get more involved in her charity work.' May-May closed her eyes again.

Her mother must have been devastated. At the time, Laura had just noticed the house looking much tidier.

'What are you thinking, May-May? Have I tired you out? You were going to tell me what Grandpa said in his speech?'

'Oh, yes, well, Dennis thanked everyone for their kind birthday wishes and announced that although he had formally retired, he intended to stay on at F & P as a non-executive director. And he very sweetly said what a terrific asset Beth had been.'

'Wow, how did Mum take that?'

'I'm not sure now. I seem to remember Gareth had a meltdown about the cake or something, and Meredith had to take him away.'

Heavy raindrops began to spot the pale flagstones of the terrace. May-May put her hand out and touched Laura's arm, 'Darling, would you mind? I feel quite tired all of a sudden.'

On the train back to London, Laura remembered the first time she had met Freddie. He had licked his lips with his tongue and looked at her as if little girls were lunch. She was glad to be holding her father's hand. Freddie shone, and his braying laugh seemed to splinter the sunlit air.

It was half term; Laura and her mother were in London. They had spent the morning at the British Museum because Laura was studying the ancient Egyptians at school. Then, her father joined them for lunch, and afterwards, they walked through Fitzrovia to The Wigmore Hall. Laura had recently taken up the cello. She didn't feel very musical, but her mother hoped she would be.

'Talent often skips a generation. You could be musical like your grandmother,' Mum had said and bought tickets for a concert with a cello soloist.

Her Aunt Tina had asked if she could join them. She wanted them all to meet her new man.

Laura and her father were left waiting with Freddie in the entrance of the concert hall while her mother and aunt went to the cloakroom.

'Come up to the big smoke for a bit of culture, have you? A day out with the missus and this little lady?' Freddie asked her father and grinned at Laura with too many teeth. 'So glad we could join you.'

Laura felt her father become still, his hand holding hers tightened.

Before her father could reply, her mother and aunt joined them. In a moment, Freddie was at her Aunt Tina's side, his voice soft, his actions considerate.

After the concert, they all went to have tea in a nearby, smart hotel where the chink of teacups on saucers echoed through the entrance hall. They sat on pale blue chairs in a pale blue room with the panelling picked out in white. Laura thought they could have been sitting in one of the blue Wedgwood bowls her grandmother had in the drawing room at Nether Place. A waiter brought the tea and placed it between them on an inconveniently low table. Laura sat beside her mother on a sofa and watched the grown-ups. Her father was on her other side. His chair didn't look very comfortable; he sat very upright. Aunt Tina perched on the brink of her chair, her legs crossed at the ankle; she looked as fine as the bone china teacup and saucer she was holding. Freddie's armchair completed the circle. He sat with his legs spread wide, so his paunch had room to drop. His pink-striped shirt was straining; the buttons looked ready to fly. Freddie held forth about his work in the City. He gesticulated expansively. Laura's mother looked mesmerised, lips slightly parted, frowning as if trying to make sense of Freddie's words. Her father turned and gave Laura a wink. Laura had juice and biscuits while the grown-ups drank tea. Nobody but Freddie had cake; crumbs littered the blue carpet.

On the way home in the car, her parents were unusually quiet. Eventually, her mother said,

'Well, what did you....'

'He's one of those people who stands too close ... did you manage to work out what he actually does?' asked her father. 'Something in the City?'

'Didn't understand a word,' said her mother.

Her father guffawed. And they laughed and laughed, sniggering, like children in a playground.

1997 – 2000

Skydiving

'It's just a local charity dinner,' Beth said as she turned her back to Max and lifted up her hair. 'Can you …? It's not like I'm asking you –'

'You know I hate this sort of thing.' Max pulled up the zipper on the back of her dress.

'We spoke about this, ages ago.' Beth knelt, struggling in her tight dress, and pulled out the shoe box with her courts from the bottom of the wardrobe. 'It's been in the diary for months.'

Beth and Penny had signed up to help at a local charity years before. They'd rattled tins together outside the supermarket and the library. Penny had stepped back when babies and her design company took over her life, but Beth was still involved. As time had gone on, she'd got to know the members of the committee and had recently found herself being put forward to take the role of treasurer.

'I won't even be able to drink,' Max said. 'How is my tie? Straight?'

'Enough. I'm sorry, but you didn't have surgery booked for the next day when I organised the table. And you promised.' Max was inclined to sign up for all sorts of commitments at work that appeared in the diary without warning.

'I can't say no if there is an emergency.'

'I know, darling, I'm sorry. If I wasn't on the committee, I wouldn't be so insistent.'

They turned up at the church hall half an hour later. Beth ran up the stone steps to the front door.

'There's nobody here,' said Max shuffling behind her in his dress shoes with his hands in his pockets like a recalcitrant schoolboy.

'You know I need to be early.' She held open the door for him.

'It's still daylight outside...'

'For goodness' sake, darling, just get over it and enjoy the evening. John and Penny will be here soon. You can talk to them.' They crossed the hollow entrance, Beth's heels clipping on the tiled floor. She smiled as she passed the large, splendid floral arrangement on the side table. She had brought it in earlier that afternoon. In the hall, the polished wood floor was covered with numerous tables laid out for bingo, pads of paper and pencils ready at every place.

'There's Helen. I must have a word.' Beth gestured to the end of the room, where a woman was setting out the paraphernalia for the evening's games, a massive cage of numbered balls taking pride of place on a table in the centre of the stage.

'You said you wouldn't leave me alone,' said Max.

'You know I have the odd thing to attend to,' she said. Honestly, she didn't know why Max was being so very difficult. He usually quite enjoyed these events, particularly if Beth had managed to arrange for them to be with friends. 'Have a look around. The silent auction is along the far wall; go and have a look. I thought we could put in a bid for the cottage in the Lake District.'

In the end, the evening was a success and the funds raised exceeded expectations. Even Max had cheered up and got into the spirit of things. It was only when she saw him laughing at one of John's anecdotes that she realised Max had been morose of late, quite grumpy, really. Beth wondered if something had happened at work. Perhaps Beth should suggest Max take up golf.

'Skydiving? Really?' Beth asked as they drove home. 'You put a bid in on the skydiving? What was wrong with the cottage?'

'Didn't like the pictures; it looked damp. This will be fun; you'll love it,' Max said. 'Think of it as an early birthday present. You're going to be forty. It's quite a milestone; it needs to be celebrated properly.'

'You can do it. You bid on it. You know I hate heights.' Really this was exasperating.

'No, no, I got it for you for your birthday.' Max grinned at her. 'You need to challenge yourself sometimes. Try something new before it's too late. Besides, I've got patients that day.'

'I can't … I won't do it,' she said, feeling pale at the thought. 'And stop smirking. You do things like this to annoy me on purpose.'

'Come on, darling. If you jump, I'll make you a birthday cake. Anyway, you can't really get out of it. John and Penny have already said they'll sponsor you.'

Beth indicated and turned the car into their road. It was true; she could use the event to raise awareness for the charity. As a committee member, she was supposed to actively fundraise. She must talk to Penny about spreading the word. But then, as she parked the car, Beth remembered that she would actually have to leap out of a plane and felt pale all over again.

'It's old Mr Rashford's plane. It's tiny. It barely looks safe.'

'He takes people up all the time. Besides, the more you hate the idea, the more money you'll raise. I bet there'll be a crowd to see you do it.'

Max was right. On the day of Beth's skydive, quite a few people turned up to see her jump. Beth was chatting to her friends, hiding in the crowd, when Mr Rashford called out that they were ready, and Penny pushed her forward. Beth tried to be jaunty as she waved to her friends, but as she turned to walk across the tarmac, tears filled her eyes, and her mouth was dry. She tried to swallow.

The plane was tiny, and the sky large. Mr Rashford greeted her. Two others were making the jump that day, young men down from London. They had jumped before. Mr Rashford introduced his nephew, Alan, who would fly the plane. Beth glanced at Alan; he looked about fourteen. Beth tried to breathe. Then she was introduced to Ben, who would be her buddy. At least he looked reliable, she thought, sturdy.

'Okay, let's go,' said Mr Rashford.

The passengers accompanied Alan towards the plane. Beth's supporters cheered. Penny waved from the side lines; she had driven Beth to the aerodrome.

'I'm so jealous,' Penny had said, 'it's such an amazing experience. You'll be blown away.'

'I hope not,' said Beth. She suspected Max had asked Penny to take her to the airfield to make sure she got on the plane.

Her hand touched the door frame as she climbed the short steps up to the aircraft, and Beth was overwhelmed with an urge to run away. She felt as the cat must do when she forced him into his carrier to go to the vet. Churchill would brace his legs at the edge of the opening and push away with all his strength. It was an instinctive action, a desire for self-preservation. But Beth was bundled on board the plane by Ben before she could come up with a plan of resistance.

The plane was noisy, so noisy she couldn't really hear what anyone was saying. Ben was talking; she hoped whatever was being said wasn't important. Beth thought the two young men were way too cheerful, bouncing about needlessly. She felt nauseous and gripped her seat, staring straight ahead.

When the plane reached the proper height, Ben undid his seatbelt, leapt up, and flung open the door. Beth shrank back into the wall of the aircraft in horror. The two young men readied themselves and, laughing together, vanished from sight as they jumped out of the plane.

Ben motioned to Beth to join him for their tandem jump. She

undid her seatbelt, prised herself away from the safety of her chair and crawled towards him.

Afterwards, Penny drove her home.
'So, how was it?' Penny asked in the car.
Beth couldn't speak; she was still finding it hard to breathe. The moment she had taken the insane step into nothingness still filled her with horror. In her hands, Beth held a photograph taken after the jump, showing herself and Ben with his arm over her shoulders, smiling in front of the landed plane. She couldn't remember the photograph being taken.
'You must have loved it, really. The space, the feeling of freedom ... amazing, something you'll remember for the rest of your life,' said Penny.
Beth thought about how quiet the sky was after the noise of the plane, how scarily tranquil, just the air pushing past. To Beth, it sounded like death. Then the jolt as the parachute opened.
'Yes,' she managed to squeeze the words out through her clenched lips. 'It was exhilarating.'

The following month, it was Beth's actual birthday. She was sitting on the sofa in front of the fire in the living room, trying to relax. Laura had made her a cup of coffee, and Max had brought her some glossy magazines. She was supposed to be enjoying her special day. She was to sit back and do nothing; Beth seemed to itch all over. She sipped the pallid coffee and flicked through the magazines. There was very little editorial content and page after page of terribly thin, androgynous models wearing expensive clothes, nothing for anyone with a little girth and ample years. Beth preferred interiors magazines with house adverts at the back. There was less pretence, and the sun-filled photographs invited you in. Although everything was expensive, it was conceivable that she could book a chic boutique hotel somewhere exotic and get a taste of the luxury lifestyle or buy some new cushion covers and change the entire look of her living room. In contrast, the fashion plates seemed to taunt her, you should be thinner, you should be smarter, you should be taller, but she couldn't be, ever. They were selling dreams, but none that she could aspire to. Beth took another sip of her now tepid coffee, grimaced and slipped across the room to pour the remainder out the window. She would take the magazines to her mother the next time she visited; Ma would appreciate them.

Tina was coming over for tea later. Thinking about Tina set Beth on edge. Since Tina had met her new man, she had seemed to pull away from Beth. The few moments when they connected seemed fewer, as though, now she belonged with someone else, Tina was no longer interested in finding common ground. Tina always could be wilful and churlish; now, it was a given. It was natural and a good thing as far as Beth was concerned; Tina was growing up. Though Beth did struggle when Tina was unappreciative. But the less interested Tina was in Beth, the less interested she might be in Laura. Beth paused in her thoughts, distracted by a faint stain on the sleeve of her dress. She scratched it with her nail; it would come out in the next wash. Although they would always share Laura, *she* was Laura's mother; *she* was bringing her up. To Beth, Tina had hatched Laura, not spent months with a life growing inside her. Beth had to think of it that way. The birth and transfer had to be impersonal so Beth could claim maternity. Beth was to blame; she had started it. She had undone the links to childhood that they had shared as sisters so that she could write a future for herself with Laura. Now their life experiences and expectations seemed so disparate, and their individual interpretation of events could be so contrasting it was laughable. There were only ten years between them in age, and yet they seemed to have grown up in different families.

Before the birthday tea, Laura was supposed to be finishing her school project at the kitchen table, and Max was cooking. He was baking Beth the promised cake for her momentous birthday. It seemed incredible to Beth that she was this old. Forty was middle-aged; life was hurtling past. Beth didn't feel she had achieved anything significant, but when she thought of her happy marriage, Laura and now her work, Beth could feel that she was accomplishing something more than just endlessly producing meals.

After lunch, she had been banished, told to keep out of the way. Max had donned the pink frilly apron and chef's hat that Laura had been given for her last birthday by her grandmother. He would be playing the fool, entertaining Laura, trying to distract her from her homework. Beth ground her teeth and listened to the ruckus. She had left the doors open to keep an ear on what was going on.

'I've never seen you cook anything other than steak, Dad.' Beth heard Laura say. 'Mum says you can't even load the dishwasher properly.'

'Anyone who can read can cook,' said Max, 'and I only put the dirty dishes in the wrong place to tease your mother.'

Beth sighed. She heard the blender turn on, whining at top speed. She imagined yellow balls of hard butter being tossed out of the mixing bowl, like rocks of lava thrown from a volcano.

'It's often the small things that make life worthwhile, the little crumbs.' Beth heard Max shout above the noise of the machine. 'Right, add the eggs. Besides, your mother *likes* to rearrange the dishwasher. It makes her feel in control.'

Finally, Beth heard Max turn the mixer off.

'Does it look all right to you?' Max asked.

'I think that looks about right.'

'Really?' said Max. 'It looks a bit like scrambled eggs. Oops, it says here to heat the oven and grease the cake tins before you start. They should put these instructions in bold.'

A short while later, Max popped his head around the sitting room door.

'All good,' he said, 'cakes are in the oven. Done the washing up. Going to catch up on some work till the buzzer goes. Laura's finishing her homework and will help me with the icing later. No peeking!' He crossed the hall to his study.

Beth wondered when she would be allowed into the kitchen to clear up. Shortly after, Laura wandered through and switched on the telly.

'You don't mind, do you, Mum?' she asked.

'Not at all, if you've finished your project. How did the cooking go?'

'Oh, okay,' said Laura sounding very unconcerned. She curled up on the sofa beside Beth burrowing under her arm. Beth stroked Laura's hair away from her face where a lock had fallen into her eyes. Beth felt so lucky to have this amazingly beautiful child in her life, let alone on her sofa. Shortly before the end of Laura's programme, there came a buzz from the kitchen.

'Right, come on, Miss, time to see to these cakes.' Max called, and Laura scampered to the kitchen.

'I thought they'd be puffier somehow,' Beth heard Max say.

'When Mum's cakes don't rise, she pads them out with icing,' said Laura.

'Ah, tricks of the trade,' said Max.

Beth heard the beater on high again, and her heart sank. There would be icing sugar everywhere.

Max said, 'Where are the hundreds and thousands?'

'Can I lick the beaters?' said Laura.

There was a crunch of gravel and the noise of a car outside. Shortly after that, the doorbell rang, followed by the clatter of Laura's shoes on the tiles as she raced to open the door.

'Hi, Aunt Tina! How are you?'

'Smells wonderful in here,' said Tina coming into the room with a large tote.

'Hello, Tina,' said Beth, she pushed up the sleeves of her dress to hide the stain in the folds of fabric and rose to give her sister a kiss.

'Happy Birthday!' Tina looked immaculate, surrounded by a

cloud of scent. She leant towards Beth, to one side of her face and then the other, then Tina settled on the sofa as though avoiding touching anything. Max brought in a tray with tea which he placed on the low table in front of Beth. Then he moved to the window and pushed aside the heavy fabric to reach the cord to close the curtains against the darkening sky. He remained standing, aloof, Beth thought as she sat back down and poured the tea.

'I heard you did a skydive,' said Tina. 'I can't believe it. I never saw you as a risk-taker. Everyone knows you hate heights. Tell me all about it.'

'It was exhilarating,' said Beth.

'That's it?'

'To be honest, that's all I remember. All I want to remember.'

'You enjoyed it, really.' Max smiled at her. 'You were pleased as punch when you got home.'

'I was so relieved it was over.' Beth looked over at her husband. Why had Max insisted on her making the jump? A test to prove herself worthy of his love, or was it just one of his games?

'Best present ever,' Laura said, 'Penny said Mum was amazing.'

Beth smiled at Laura's upturned face.

'So, now that you're being adventurous, I got these for you.' Tina produced a present from her bag. 'Happy Birthday.'

'Thank you,' said Beth. She untied the ribbon and folded back the crisp, glossy wrapping paper to expose a plain brown box. Beth turned the box over and read the white, italic script that ran across the top. 'Louboutin,' she lifted the lid to reveal the iconic black shoes with red-lacquered soles. 'Wow! Gosh, they're beautiful ... look at the heels! They are like something out of a magazine."

'I know you don't normally wear anything higher than an inch or so, but I thought, at forty, surely, it's the perfect age to have some fun; be a bit rebellious.'

'Thank you,' repeated Beth. She took the impeccable shoes with the impossible heels and placed them on the table in front of her. She straightened them. They were a perfectly glossy black, the tapering heels like parallel ice picks. The red soles reflected in the glass of the tabletop.

'Cool, try them on, Mum,' said Laura, then she asked Tina, 'How did you know what size to get?'

'Well, I do hope they fit,' said Tina. 'Beth is half a size smaller than me, has been since I was fourteen. What did you give your mother?'

'I gave her some special soap that Daddy told me she likes. And Daddy gave her a new watch. Show her Mummy.' Beth extended her arm.

'Very nice,' said Tina.

'It must be time for "C-A-K-E",' said Max, and Laura leapt up and followed him out to the kitchen, 'Do you know where Mummy keeps the candles?' Beth heard Max ask Laura as he pulled the door to behind them.

'You don't like them, do you?' said Tina as soon as the door was closed. 'I'm only trying to bring a little excitement into your life.'

'No, no, I'm sure I'll have fun wearing ....'

'No need to pretend if they're not your thing.'

'I'm not pretending, Tina. I'm just not sure when I'll wear them,' said Beth. Why was it always so difficult to talk to her sister?

'How about in the bedroom?' said Tina. 'If you don't like them, Max might. But you haven't even tried them on.'

'That's none of you busi ... I don't know why you are being so aggressive, Tina.'

Tina gave a loud sigh and re-crossed her legs allowing the silence to stretch.

'Here we are having such a lovely birthday tea, and you seem to want to accentuate the differences. I feel you are judging me. You ooze indignation,' said Beth. 'Are you cross with me?'

'Am I cross?'

'I thought, after all this time, you'd be happy and happy for us. Perhaps even show some gratitude.'

'Gratitude?' Tina's voice sharpened, and then she laughed. The sound was like a thousand brittle tears of glass splintering from some enormous mirror. Beth looked at the coffee table surface. It still reflected the unbroken image of the shoes a red and black smear in the glass. Now, she felt she would never wear them, if ever she did, she would hear Tina's heart-breaking laugh.

'After all, Laura has a loving, stable home. I thought you'd be glad,' said Beth trying to find more solid ground and get back to what she knew to be true. She nudged one of the shoes to adjust them into a perfect, opposing pair. 'I thought you'd at least be happy for her.'

'I just –'

'I mean, it was years ago, it no longer matters, but we did pick up the pieces … anyway, it is such a long time ago now –'

The door shot open, and the master baker and his assistant entered the room. They carried the cake, with forty blazing candles melting into the icing.

'HAPPY BIRTHDAY TO YOU!' they sang. Beth blew out the candles on the caramel-coloured pancake sitting proud in a lake of icing covered in a layer of hundreds and thousands.

'Who'd like a slice of this amazing cake?' Beth asked as she raised the cake knife with a flourish.

'Me, me,' said Laura.

Beth watched Tina as she considered her hands, twisting her fingers in her lap. Then Tina looked up at Beth and smiled.

'Unfortunately, I have to go now,' Tina said.

Tina

When I looked at Laura, I could see traces of myself. In the tiny things, the way Laura pushed her hair behind her ear or sucked at her bottom lip when she was concentrating. The years had passed, and she was a child. Had I really given birth to this whole, complete person? Beth's presence constantly reminded me of how enraged I was when I was denied the right to raise my own child. Letting go had been hard, but I had to admit Beth was a good mother, and Laura was happy. I could see that; it made it easier to stand back. But I wondered that no one else had ever picked up on any similarity to you, Max. On the surface, Laura has the look of a Parteger. She has my fair colouring and slender frame, just as I am like Ma. But Laura doesn't have our grey eyes.

Every now and then, Laura would turn and look at me or would move suddenly, and I saw you in her so very clearly. When she smiled, it came slowly, teasing from the left side of her mouth as though her lips were persuading her to smile. I wondered how old you were, Max, when you realised the potential of that shy smile. Of course, I couldn't mention or draw attention to any resemblance, but my mother brought it up once.

'I am amazed how similar, on occasion, Laura is to Max. She has picked up many of his gestures,' Ma had said.

'They spend so much time together,' said Beth, as though that was explanation enough. 'Always making and doing stuff. They adore each other.'

I had to bite my tongue. At night, when even London was quiet, I would pace my flat and hanker after Laura. I would dream of claiming her back, telling Beth everything, but I knew it would destroy her. So, for now, I let them live their fantasy.

Duncan might have been the one to spot it if he had been around. He wasn't particularly keen on children, but he was curious about people and interested in detail. But Duncan, like everyone else, respected you, the surgeon, every day saving children's lives. I'm sure he appreciated that you made Beth happy, but I shouldn't think he thought about you for long enough to know if he liked you, Max, or to consider your mannerisms. Anyway, Duncan was far away and had his own challenges. And, after all, everyone enjoys the status quo. Even Duncan was invested in not asking too many awkward questions. And I, the only person who might have had something to say, didn't have a voice.

When I came back from Italy, I thought I might be able to start again with Laura, that some primaeval instinct would pull us together. It came to nothing, not just because you forbade it. It seems I had been in love with the idea of love. Love doesn't need to be reciprocated. But it turns out that for me a mismatched relationship is no relationship at all.

Nostalgia

Beth was hiding in the morning room. She had a new Country Living, an Interiors magazine, and a cup of coffee; she was very happy. As the rest of the family had set out on the customary postprandial walk in the drizzle, she had given everyone the slip and snuck away on her own. It was always great to see Duncan, but this holiday had been fraught. Not only was Duncan at loggerheads with Pa, but he and Meredith didn't seem to be getting on either.

It seemed that Duncan wanted to carve a modern path in an innovative world. He reviled everything to do with duty and veneration. Beth couldn't agree, for her objects were like photographs, memories in solid form. She rubbed the shiny wooden arms of the chair she was sitting in. How many Parteger hands had done the same. Beth couldn't throw everything away as Duncan was doing, with each announcement alienating all the family held dear. For Beth, the past lingered in every corner of

Nether Place, a comfort, and a reassurance. Each generation had left its mark, a scratch here or a stain there. Beth was sure her grandmother's memories were enfolded in the coming-out gown kept in the faded eau de nil Debenham & Freebody box, still tied with the original ribbon, and stored in the attic. Knowing that her great aunt had been the last to undo the clasp on the broken opal bracelet at the back of her mother's jewellery drawer gave her satisfaction. Beth even felt sympathy for the creaky step on the back stair to the attic. Over the years, countless maids would have skipped over it on their way up and down to the kitchen. Memories seemed to float in the very air, breathed in and out by the house as it warmed and cooled with every season. What had happened previously, however mundane, could not be discounted just because the world had moved on. Beth sipped her coffee; the world wouldn't be the same without such treasures.

Over lunch, Duncan had expounded on the merits of America, the 'can do' attitude and the opportunities for all. Beth had watched her father's complexion as he huffed and puffed in response.

'Blair getting in is a new start. He's a Conservative dressed in a Labour suit. Can't wait to see what he achieves,' said Duncan.

'Politicians inevitably make promises they can never push through parliament,' said Pa, who was rankled. 'I'm not sure you have the right to expound on U.K. politics, now you have been away so long.'

'Thank God Thatcher got the unions under control,' Duncan said, carrying on blithely. He seemed to be enjoying the spat. 'Gives Blair an opportunity without having to rely on their support.'

'We can agree on that,' said Pa.

'All those strikes in the 70s were dreadful,' said Beth. 'Do you remember toasting marshmallows over the fire while we did our homework by candlelight?'

'Thank goodness the aga ran on oil, or we would have had nothing to eat,' said Ma.

'How did you cope in Wales?' Beth asked Meredith.

'My Nan knitted us all sweaters,' she said, and turned back to her shepherd's pie.

'And selling off council houses was brilliant, creating easy capital for the masses. It's all about the individual now and what each person can achieve. It's invigorating,' said Duncan.

Beth thought about her Parish Council, the Primary School Board, and the village church. She was involved with all these venerable institutions. The interconnectivity of small-town life was essential to her. It was her support system. Mrs Terry at the village grocers would always let her know if Laura had spent all her pocket money on sweets or stuck within the agreed limit.

'I like the idea of a church, a post office, and a village school,' said Beth.

'I agree. Isn't community a good thing?' Meredith said. 'Takes a village to raise a child and all that.'

'But after it has grown up, that child should be able to lead the life they want, should have aspirations,' said Duncan. 'Not be stuck in some parochial hellhole, constantly judged by narrow-minded neighbours with outmoded moral convictions.'

'But if everyone has left the village to seek their fortune, who will bring up the next generation of children?' said Beth.

'There will always be someone with antiquated ideas. They can hold the provincial fort,' said Duncan.

'It's the responsibility you can't bear. You want to be free, but you don't really want everyone else to be,' said Pa, 'you want some underclass to do all the dirty work while a liberal elite goes off and enjoys itself. That won't work. There will be a revolution if the connection between the haves and have-nots is lost.'

'Sometimes, I feel as though I might drown under the weight of previous generations and their expectations,' said Duncan. 'In America, you can be who you want to be. Your past is irrelevant; it's what you make of yourself in the here and now.'

Now, Beth heard the walkers return and went to see how they had got on. She leaned her shoulder against the boot room door and watched the fracas. They were all crowded by the back door. Everyone was struggling to get out of their wet coats, reaching for pegs. The dogs were weaving between the family, wagging their tails, and licking the faces that came in range as the walkers bent down to take off their wellies. Duncan called the dogs away. Meredith hung up Dennis' dripping Barbour that she had borrowed. Gareth was stripping off his wet things and dropping them on the floor; Beth went to help. As she straightened, clutching Gareth's coat, she looked across the boot room and saw Max helping a chattering Laura. He bent over and gave her a cuddle as he pinched her little boots between his own, and she pulled her feet out of her wellies. Max glanced up at Beth and winked. She smiled back.

Once they had hung up their coats, the walkers, ruddy-faced and fresh, left the muddy dogs in the boot room, closing the door against their frantic need to be included. Beth put the kettle on. As soon as the tea was made, the grown-ups were sent to the drawing room with the tray of tea things so Mrs Simms could give the children their supper.

'I'm not really a child anymore.' Beth heard Gareth complain to Mrs Simms as she placed a plate of food in front of him. 'Where's the ketchup?'

Gareth, at thirteen, would still be much happier with fish fingers than with the pheasant they were having for dinner, thought Beth as she carried the silver teapot through to the drawing room.

Ma presided over tea, set out on the gate-legged table. When the formality of filling everyone's cup was completed, Beth and Meredith took their tea to the chairs by the window, leaving Max and Duncan with Ma and Pa and the cake and biscuits.

'Tell me about this new job you're going for. Will it be a promotion?' Max asked Duncan. 'If you get it, will you still be based in Austin?'

'It's a great opportunity,' said Duncan, 'I'd be heading up my own division. The company is expanding. If the situation continues to accelerate, I may have to move to the head office in San Francisco. As it is, I already have to do a great deal of travel.'

'He's not normally so pushy, you know,' said Meredith to Beth, leaning in so she would not be overheard. 'It's only here that he sounds so pretentious. I think it's the wood panelling that brings it out in him. By the way, Max was brilliant with Gareth on the walk earlier; I can never calm him down once he's in a sulk.'

'Duncan has become surprisingly outspoken,' said Beth. 'He seems to have nurtured views that will specifically rile Pa. I would have thought he would know better. He's become so American. It must be exhausting trying to remember who he is.'

'Not the half of it,' whispered Meredith. 'Old insecurities about the family business and general self-doubt about not living up to parental expectations. Talking of which, how are you enjoying working at F & P?'

'Oh, well, I've moved department,' said Beth.

'Really, why? I thought you were enjoying working in the accounts department.'

'I was, but there was a bit of a personality clash, and a sidestep seemed a good idea. I'm now working in personnel, getting to know everyone who works in the business. It's interesting to see how a variety of departments work. Particularly if I want to move into management.' Beth looked in her empty cup and rather wondered when she'd finished her tea. 'I felt, as a Parteger, that if I saw something that I didn't feel was right or good for the company ... well, I was in a unique position, and if necessary, I ought to say something.'

'Hmm, not an easy position to be in.'

'Personnel suits me better anyway. It is more time flexible, which is ideal, what with all the school runs, ballet, etc. The company has been very accommodating with my working hours, though I always get in early to compensate.'

'I guess being a doctor doesn't leave Max much time to help

out during the week.'

'Yes, poor Max, he still works long, hard hours. All that saving the lives of little children.'

'Ah, yes, Max, the saint,' said Meredith.

'He loves the work as well as the accolades,' Beth added, not wanting to sound disloyal. She had not meant to sound ironic. 'He works long hours and often doesn't make it home at night. Luckily, we held onto the flat.'

'That must be handy if he were to have an assignation,' Meredith gave her a sly smile. 'Or a late meeting.'

'Well, I don't think Max has enough time for assignations! But there are late meetings and sometime a collegiate dinner.' Whatever did Meredith think was going on, perhaps Duncan was playing the field, and she was compensating. Though when Beth thought about it, she'd never seen Duncan flirting, it seemed inconceivable.

'We make sure we have good family times at the weekend. I'm sure it's the same with you. Are you happy Duncan is applying for this promotion?'

'Oh, I am used to his socialising and his sports club - all that boy's own stuff. Duncan's a great schmoozer. Like Max, he's out all the time, but he always comes home. Do you ever go up to London to stay at the flat? Tina was there for a while, wasn't she? Where is she living now?'

'Oh, no, when she was up in town, she used to stay with her friend Bella, she only stayed at our flat if Bella was away and then Max would be there too, to let her in. She's never had a key.' Beth felt outraged at the idea of Tina having a key to the flat, even though Beth seldom went there. 'Her new flat is near Earls Court. I haven't seen it, but Max has. He tells me it's in a slightly grotty area, but Tina's convinced it's "up and coming".'

'Hmm. Where is she, by the way?'

'It's a shame, but the gallery wanted her to work this weekend, and she's often busy in the evenings. She has some new boyfriend.'

'Perhaps Duncan will meet her for lunch, or something, on his way back when I'm staying with my parents in Wales.'

'I'm sure she'd love that,' said Beth.

Tina

All the years, I waited for you, Max, all the years. I had always wanted someone of my own. I wanted someone who cared for me alone. When my heart first stirred, you had been there. You had planted a seed of a perfect love, but like a canker, the idea of love had grown within me as I grew. You were entangled in my being; I couldn't get free. I had trampled over my sister and lied to my family ... for years. I wanted to feel ashamed, but I couldn't. In fact, I felt a perverse glee that although Beth might have Laura, you still wanted me. I could lure you away from your happy home. Although I was sure Beth was ignorant, or refused to see what was going on under her nose, it felt like we were in a dance together, and we danced around you. I resented that Beth had Laura, and I could not deny you because you were fundamental to my life. I could not be distracted. I could not find someone as compelling as you. Then one day, Freddie walked into the art gallery.

When I told Bella I had met someone, had met someone really nice, she had been sceptical.

'All this hanging around, being a mistress to some selfish pig, has left you vulnerable, Tina,' Bella said. 'Don't make the same mistake. City men work and play hard and fast, be careful you don't get flattened in the rush.'

I knew Freddie was serious right away. I could see he was planning ahead. It was thrilling to be the centre of someone's attention, to be the only one. I had never liked sharing. When I was young, Ma had doted on me, particularly when Beth and Duncan went away to school. I wanted to be pampered, adored, and Freddie wanted to spoil me.

It was a thrill to be out in public, something I'd never been able to do with you, Max. The joy of holding hands in a crowd or hugging outside a tube station. Just walking in the street with Freddie was an experience you and I, Max, had never shared.

Freddie was so much fun to be with. He had this fabulous City salary, and he wanted to spend it. We went to the races, we went to the tennis, we went out to Le Gavroche and stayed at Le Manoir aux Quat'Saisons. Freddie liked acquiring things; he was the consummate consumer. He expected me to look the part and loved shopping with me. He wanted me to look chic and desirable. He wanted me to ooze sex. Freddie liked sex too. He might not have been as assiduous as you, but Freddie liked fun. He liked experimenting. Freddie wanted to experience everything – except children. He told me early on. We were out to dinner at Nobu, and he took my hand and told me.

'I hope you're not disappointed,' he said.

Well, why would he say something like that unless he wanted to spend years and years with me?

'Perhaps I might get a little dog if I feel the need. Would that fit in with your life plan?' I asked.

'My darling, anything but a baby. My childhood was unhappy. My parents were abroad. I was brought up by my boarding school and passed around to various aunts in the holidays. I'm not sure I would know how to be a parent. Also, I wouldn't like to burden the world with a little Freddie or Frederica. Can you imagine!' Freddie chortled. 'But I want to meet all your family, your parents, your siblings. I want to know everything about you.'

And I told him everything, well almost everything.

And you, Max, you were not pleased; you were so indignant. So it would be clear to you that things had changed, I finessed a meeting as soon as I could, with Beth and Laura there too so you couldn't make a scene, but within the week you arranged to meet me at the flat.

'You're delusional,' you said. 'He's fake, a caricature. He's too loud and too large, and he'll squash you.'

'Come off it, Max, you're behaving badly. Just because I've found someone who makes me happy.'

'I make you happy,' you said.

'You are too busy carving yourself up, giving a small part to everybody.'

'That's not true. I can take care of Beth and look after you. You've never said you weren't happy.'

'The sex was good; great! But I wasn't happy. I'm no longer prepared to share.'

'Nobody gets all of me, not the children I operate on, or Beth, or you, but I give everyone as much of me as they need.'

'Well, I need more. Now, I look forward to seeing Freddie, and he doesn't disappoint me. With you, I was constantly waiting.'

'If you choose to continue with Freddie, he will let you down. It's what he does, I can tell.'

You hadn't made me laugh often, Max. It was a freedom. Freddie had broken the spell you had cast over me. You threw the keys to the Earls Court flat across the table at me and strode out, letting the front door slam behind you; I felt ridiculously light.

It had not been easy persuading Pa I needed somewhere of my own to live in London. Once I'd found the gallery job, I went to see him.

'Yes?' he said, not looking up from his papers when I entered his study.

'I want a flat in London.' I had not meant to sound impudent. I'd practised a gentle introduction and a persuasive argument, but somehow face to face with Pa, I'd resorted to a combative tone. I wanted to be taken seriously. I didn't want to slip back into being the errant child.

'I'm sure you do. Wouldn't we all?' Pa glanced up at me from where he sat behind his desk, pen poised over his paper. He clearly had things to do.

'Now that I'm back from Milan, now that I have a job, it would make sense instead of paying rent. Please.' God, I hated grovelling.

Pa gave me a cold eye, stretching out the pause. 'If I had enough cash to buy you a flat, I'd get the roof fixed or the windows done.'

'I need to be in London for my work.' I stood in front of his desk.

'I don't understand. Why did you move back from Italy, Tina?' Pa sounded bored. 'There you were, safely tucked away, doing your own thing. Why come back and rock the boat?'

It wasn't that I couldn't stay in Italy. I could have. I enjoyed my job at the art gallery. It was good fun, though not as challenging as when I started. Then there had been so much to learn, and all in Italian. I had made plenty of friends in Milan, but suddenly I hankered for home. I wanted the familiar. That weekend in France with you, Max had been the catalyst. You suggested I come back, and I realised I really did want to come home. After all that time away, I would need somewhere private, somewhere safe, and my own.

'I want to be taken seriously. I need to be independent.' I said to my father.

In the end, he relented and gave me enough for a flat in a rather seedy part of Earls Court, but it was all mine. My space alone. Above and below me were rented flats. Filled with the noise of stumbling feet and irritating snatches of half-recognised tunes. The stairs were steep to the front entrance, where the paint peeled in great strips from the plastered portico. The hallway was unkempt and full of bicycles. But once I had climbed the stairs to the flat and closed the door, I was in a world of my own creating. It had been my home for the last five years, my refuge and escape.

Forever

It was not a good summer.

'The radiator is cold in Gareth's bedroom,' said Meredith when she came down to the drawing room before supper, 'it's freezing upstairs.' She wove between the chairs to stand in front of the fire, Pa's concession for the unseasonable cold weather. Meredith's crossed arms and hunched shoulders made her look as though she was trying to suck all the warmth from the fire to herself.

'No need to have the heating on; it's June,' said Duncan. 'We must truly have acclimatised to life in the U.S. if we can no longer tolerate a standard English summer.'

'The boy needs to toughen up. I turn off the heating at the Spring equinox, always have done. House needs to breathe,' said Pa. 'Need to preserve the furniture for future generations.'

Although his smile looked relaxed, Beth, standing beside her brother, saw his jaw move slightly; she could almost hear Duncan's teeth grinding.

'Thank God I managed to provide a son and heir. At least I achieved that!' said Duncan.

'Surely, it wasn't that hard?' murmured Beth to her brother.

'Of course not,' he whispered back running a hand up over his forehead and through his hair. 'Though Meredith can be very unaccommodating.'

Beth had never seen what Duncan saw in Meredith, but then she hadn't felt she was supposed to. Meredith was perfectly nice in a puritanical sort of way. Horses for courses, she had always thought. Beth had always liked Meredith, perhaps because she didn't feel threatened. Her arrival in Duncan's life hadn't altered Beth's relationship with him. And Meredith, despite her religious associations, had a sharp, observational mind that interested Beth.

'Dry air causes the wood to dry out and crack,' said Ma looking at Meredith, 'and a cool temperature is so much better for your skin too.'

'Don't take that personally, Meredith. I'm sure Ma didn't mean *your* skin,' said Duncan.

'No, of course, I didn't. I meant …' Ma looked shocked that anyone would misconstrue her words, but Beth saw her mother's eyes sparkle. Didn't Ma like Meredith? Ma was welcoming, but she seldom did anything with Meredith, and they didn't share many interests. Did Ma merely accept Meredith as the future of the family, Duncan's wife, and Gareth's mother?

'You all look lovely: so young and fresh.' Ma sounded less than sure. Beth saw Meredith looking at her reflection in the large mirror above the mantlepiece. She was pushing the skin on her jawbone back towards her ears in a move Beth found familiar. Meredith dropped her hand quickly when she caught Beth's eye in the mirror. Beth gave her a grin.

'Would you like a drink, Meredith?' Beth asked, raising her own gin and tonic as a suggestion. Meredith's reflection smiled back and nodded. As Beth mixed the drink, she said, 'When I go up later to check on Laura, I'll put an extra blanket on Gareth's bed.'

'No need,' said Duncan, 'the boy needs to toughen up.'

Beth hoped it was just the jetlag speaking. If her brother was going to be this tetchy for their entire stay, it was going to be exhausting.

At dinner, Duncan asked if his parents had any summer plans.

'Your mother and I will be heading off to the South of France with friends at the end of the month,' said Pa. 'It'll be good to see the sun. Will you be going somewhere?'

'I only get ten days' vacation each year, so no,' said Duncan.

'But of course, you have the sun all year. It must feel like you're on holiday every day,' said Pa.

'But you're here for less than a week!' said Ma.

'Well, although I'd love to spend all my vacation here, it's good to have time in hand. Perhaps to explore the States, and sometimes

I take days off to go along to Gareth's school open days,' said Duncan.

Beth saw Meredith roll her eyes.

'When we leave here, we're going to Wales for a few days to see Meredith's parents before I head back. Meredith will stay on to see more of her family. Back in Austin, I'll catch up with work and things before Meredith and Gareth arrive home.'

'You could get a job here, then you could see family all the time,' said Pa, 'you'd like that wouldn't you, Meredith?'

'I don't think that will happen anytime soon,' said Duncan. 'I'm enjoying my work and love living in the States.'

Duncan was behaving like a man who picks a fight with his girlfriend so she will break up with him. Except Beth knew it was a hiding to nothing, her parents would never let Duncan off the hook of being the only son. Families are forever, after all.

'How are you getting on in Austin?' Beth asked Meredith.

'To be honest, I still struggle. Duncan is always meeting people through his work and is a natural networker. Although I meet other mothers at Gareth's school and am volunteering at St Luke's, I've found it hard to make long-term friends. Americans are lovely but can be superficial.'

'You'll always have a job waiting for you at Farthingale and Parteger, you know that don't you?' said Pa to Duncan.

'You'd be better finding someone who really wants to do that job, Pa. I mean, how about Beth?' said Duncan.

'How about you?' said Meredith to Beth. 'How is F & P treating you?

'I'm enjoying it. I feel I'm really getting to know the different parts of the company and how they fit together. Being in personnel has been interesting. It's a small department at F & P, but I'm getting to meet so many people in the company. I've a good handle on the diverse aspects of the work now and an understanding of labour laws.'

'Gosh,' said Meredith. 'It sounds as though you are ready to fly.'

'So ready,' Beth said smiling at Meredith.

'What are you two whispering about?' said Duncan turning towards Beth. 'Where's Max?'

'He'll be down at the weekend.'

'And when's Tina coming? We'd like to meet this new boyfriend; sounds serious.'

'Freddie? I'm not sure if he's the one, a bit nouveau,' said Ma. 'Have you heard from Tina, Beth?'

'Honestly, she's hopeless. I'm constantly ringing her and leaving messages; she never gets back to me. I've no idea what she's up to … Max used to sometimes see her and occasionally took her out for dinner, but now he says she's always out with Freddie and hard to get hold of.'

'How awkward,' said Meredith sipping her gin as she looked out the window.

'It'd be a shame if she didn't come down. It's not as though we are over often,' said Duncan,

Tina

I took the tube to Sloane Square. As I exited the station, a bus pulled up, and I jumped on. I had discarded the past, and you, Max, I was going to see Freddie. The Kings Road was slow with traffic. I didn't want to be stuck on the 19 outside Boots. I wanted to be with Freddie. I was tempted to get off the bus and walk. I thought it might be faster. Freddie was going to show me his house for the first time, and later, we were going out to dinner at The Pheasantry.

'Lousy for public transport,' Freddie said when I arrived. He met me at the gate, and we walked up the short path. 'I don't believe in buses! Luckily, there's residents parking here. I found a spot down the road.'

The house was quaint, bijou.

'Belonged to one of my aunts,' Freddie said as he opened the front door, fiddling the key in the lock. The paint was faded and flaky. It looked as though it had once been a hunter's green. 'Left it to me in her will, the sweet old biddy.'

The hall was dark, although it had the original tiled floor. The walls were covered in magnolia woodchip wallpaper. I resisted the urge to run my fingers over the lumps and bumps.

'You should see in here,' Freddie said.

The sitting room was floral, filled with saggy armchairs and crammed with a great many ornaments. Freddie threw his briefcase and paper into one of the chairs.

'What about some bubbly?' he said. Freddie disappeared down the back stairs. I wandered around the room; everything was slightly shabby. It felt as though Freddie's aunt had just wandered out of the room to fetch her reading glasses. Freddie returned with a bottle of champagne and two floral-etched flutes. There wasn't space to put anything down without moving some little figurine or other out of the way. We had to create our own space in the crowded room.

'What shall we drink too?' Freddie asked when he had uncorked the Bollinger and filled our glasses.

I searched the carpet for something more engaging than the ubiquitous "cheers", but nothing that would imply too much commitment.

'To new beginnings,' I said, looking up at him.

'Yes, to the start of something new. To change, change is good,' said Freddie. Our glasses chinked. It was a symbolic moment for me, I had longed for change, and now it had come. Goodbye, Max! That was what I was really drinking too!

We stood and sipped our drinks. The room looked down into the tiny back courtyard, where a few plants struggled in their broken pots.

'Not much of a gardener,' said Freddie, noticing me looking out the window. 'Fancy a tour of the rest?'

The kitchen was pale yellow, the bathroom avocado green.

'Needs a woman's touch,' said Freddie, smiling at me.

'Needs more than a touch,' I laughed. 'But this room is usable.' I pulled him into a bedroom.

Freddie sat back against the bed's padded, piped, and ruched floral headrest. I lay on my stomach beside him. The old quilt was shiny and smelled of years of dust. I was still in my stockings, propped up on my elbows, sipping my champagne. Freddie got up, slapping my bare buttock as he did so.

'You're right, a complete overhaul. Can't do a thing, though, waiting for probate. Aunt's will is tied up in some complicated trusts. She's the first to pop her clogs; need to wait for her sisters to join her before I can change a thing.' Freddie rolled his eyes heavenward, then searched for his trousers on the floor. 'Right, we'd better get going ...'

'Well, the house, like its current owner, certainly has potential. And when it is done up, to my satisfaction, it'll be worth a bomb.' I rolled over, swung myself upright and began to pull my dress on.

I waited for Freddie in the sitting room with my coat on while he locked up. I was thinking how the second bedroom of this little house could be perfect for Laura to come and stay. I picked up a figurine, a delicate shepherdess dancing with her sheep, herding them with her crook.

'You can have that if you like,' said Freddie returning to the room.

'Oh no, I couldn't, and what about probate?'

'They won't miss that,' he said. 'Wrapping the porcelain in a piece of his newspaper. He tucked it into my bag and gave me a kiss.

'Reminds me of my mother,' I said. 'Thank you.'

Notice

The kitchen was noisy. Beth had been clattering around since she'd got back from dropping Laura off at school. The washing was on, and the dishwasher was loaded. Beth threw the last of the breakfast things into the tray, added the tab, banged the door closed, and set the machine going. She could whip round the house with a duster, but she'd done that yesterday. Beth went through to the living room with a cloth and the vacuum cleaner, looking for something to do. She flicked the duster at Churchill. He was an easy mark, leaving a trail of grey hair wherever he rested. Now, he took his time, stretched, arching his back. He gave her a dirty look before stalking off to find a cosy spot in a different room. Beth clapped the cushions together and hoovered up the strands of stray cat hair left behind on the sofa, before wondering what else she could do. Beth looked around the room, everything was in its place, it all looked perfect. She wandered back into the kitchen, she could wash the kitchen floor again, she supposed, or clean out all the bedroom wardrobes and take any old clothes to the charity shop, but that seemed too much, too exhausting. Perhaps, instead, she would just sit down at the kitchen table and cry.

She had been furious since Pa had suggested she hand in her notice at Farthingale & Parteger. Beth hadn't even had the dishonour of being sacked or made redundant. Instead, she'd been forced to leave, as if it were her own choice. It was so unfair! All she had done was her job, extremely efficiently.

Duncan was right; the company was old-fashioned. She shuddered at the memory of excruciating meetings. Once, when Beth had finished her presentation and had lost her proposal to a sarky comment from a senior manager, one of the older partners had patted her on the knee in consolation.

At Farthingale & Parteger, Beth hadn't been the only woman. Most of the administrative staff and the finance department were female, but no one in senior management. The women didn't mix with the male employees but would clump together in the canteen at lunch and head off for drinks together on a Friday evening. Everyone was kind to Beth, but they all knew she was a Parteger, even if her surname was Templeton, and no one was ever completely relaxed when she was around. Beth would never be one of the girls, but neither was she treated as the heir apparent.

Beth knew she could be the new P of F & P. Her father was thinking of retiring; everyone knew that. She had worked at the firm for over five years. Why wouldn't she be asked to take Pa's place on the board when he retired?

Beth booked a slot to speak to Pa with his secretary. Beth wanted to do this properly.

'Pa,' she said. 'Ma mentioned you were thinking of retiring. How do you feel about that?'

'Well, the firm is in a good state, and I am happy with the predicted outlook,' said Pa leaning back in his chair, twiddling his pen, and gazing into the middle distance. 'So, I have, from time to time, been considering what I want to do next.'

'I think, if you do step down, there should still be a Parteger on the board. Family representation in the family firm.' This was an excellent place to start, something they could agree on.

'Well, that would be my preference too, but I've already been through this. I've written to Duncan again, but he refuses to engage.'

'That wasn't exactly what I meant,' said Beth trying to keep the exasperation out of her voice. 'I was hoping that you might consider putting me forward –'

'I don't think –'

'To carry on the family interests, I could look after things for you.' Beth tried appealing to his ego. Her father got up and crossed the room to open the window before returning to sit at his desk again.

'Would you like to be on the board? Is it something you could really see yourself doing?' said her father in a tone that he might have used when she was six if she had said she wanted to be an astronaut. 'You don't have a particularly good attendance record. I know you have had the odd sports day to go to, but slacking off is the sort of thing that gets noticed.'

'Unlike golf,' Beth couldn't help muttering.

'What's that? Business gets done on a golf course, often the casual comradery at the club leads to commercial opportunities. Also, you haven't had a senior management role and being on any board requires experience as well as commitment.'

'None the less, I would like to be given the opportunity.' Beth sat up straighter and tried to keep her tone level; not raise her voice. 'As Laura heads off to boarding school in September, I shall be able to give more time to the company. I have worked in several different departments now and have on occasion –'

'And to be on the board ... well, it takes someone who can command respect from other board members.'

'But I feel this should be my role within the company,' said Beth, trying to strike a confident note, show conviction. 'It is the only job I want to do.'

'No need to raise you voice, Beth.'

'Sorry.' She had thought she was being assertive. 'I just want you to understand what it means to me.'

There was a long pause while Pa stared hard at the blotter on his desk as if trying to decipher the future from the random ink smudges and stains that had soaked into the absorbent surface. Then, at last, he looked up.

'Well, if there is no other job that you find you could possibly do in the company, then I suggest that your time here is over,' he said with a finality that astounded her.

And that had been that. Beth had left her father's office in a daze, ending up in the ladies loo on the back staircase, locked in a cubicle, stifling her sobs whenever anyone came in, gasping for breath when a loo was flushed, or the hand dryers raged.

Beth couldn't quite understand what had happened. The last time she had met her mother for lunch in town, Ma had said she was looking forward to Pa pulling back from the day-to-day running of the business. Beth had bought into Ma's opinion as though it were fact, and coupled with her own wishful thinking, Beth had moved precipitously and demolished her chances. Perhaps she should have asked for a stint in senior management first, but it was too late now. She had thought she was in control, had her life sorted, but all her plans had been wrenched apart and now she was at home, without a goal, or a purpose. Beth felt half the person she had been only a month before.

'You do realise, there's no need for you to work,' Max had said at breakfast. 'With my salary –'

Beth, in fury, put up her hand to silence Max. 'That isn't the point,' she said as calmly as she could. In the silence, she could hear her teeth grind. Beth had to accept that she was very thankful they were comfortable, but that was neither here nor there.

After cleaning the kitchen again, Beth called Penny and asked her over for coffee. Penny said she was busy preparing a mood board for a client but could pop over after lunch before picking the kids up from school.

While she was on the phone, Beth heard a thud. She knew what that meant; an over-excited bird had flown into the window. Looking out, Beth couldn't see anything untoward, perhaps it had been a glancing blow, and the bird had flown off. When she had finished talking to Penny, Beth went outside to check. Amongst the lavender under the kitchen window, she found the tiny body of a blue tit. It didn't look damaged at all, perfect in every way, the vivid colours of the feathers looked fresh and clean, but the bird was totally unresponsive. Beth fetched a trowel and dug the little body into the earth where it lay. The fox would probably dig it up and make off with it, but she did the honours anyway. When Beth straightened from her task, she saw the bird feeder was empty. She refilled it with fat pellets. Then she did some gardening to fill what was left of the morning, marching around in the crisp breeze, hacking at anything that looked vaguely past it or leggy.

'What's the emergency?' asked Penny as Beth made them coffee.

'Oh, nothing,' said Beth, piling cookies from the cooling rack onto a plate. 'Just finding it difficult to be at home on my own.'

'No thanks, trying not to snack quite so much these days.' Penny waved away the plate. 'It was rotten, what happened, but it was weeks ago now.'

'I really thought I might be able to do some good.' It hadn't just been about the glory, about proving she could do it. She didn't want to be one of those women who get a degree and then sit at home doing nothing. Beth wanted to work and work at F & P in particular.

'You could still use your qualification, find a bookkeeping —'

'Accountant, I'm a qualified accountant!'

'Yes, sorry, don't shout, you know what I mean,' said Penny helping herself to a cookie. 'You could get another job.'

'But I want to work at our company. My family has been involved for generations.'

'Any job you got elsewhere would prove your ability, and later you could take those skills back to F & P.' Penny took another cookie. 'You shouldn't leave the plate in front of me.'

'You are quite right,' said Beth, moving the plate. 'I suppose I could.' Penny really didn't get the point. Beth didn't need to be told what to do; she needed to rage. 'Talking to you always helps,' Beth added. Speaking her thoughts aloud, made it easier for Beth to know herself. Now she could see; it was all about the anger.

'Or that charity your father suggested? These are seriously good.' Penny licked the crumbs from her fingertips.

'I'd rather find something myself.'

'Well then, maybe you should double down on that charity you already help. Look, I'm sorry to rush,' said Penny. 'But I need to get going. I'm constantly juggling these days.'

'Would you like to take some cookies for the kids?' asked Beth, bagging up a dozen.

After Penny had left with the cookies, Beth made a mental list. Max's work was frightfully important. Everyone loved him at his hospital. Duncan had earned his promotion and was planning on moving to San Francisco. His life was full of change and all very exciting. Tina, well, Tina was Tina. She was an expert at doing nothing. Otherwise, how could she stand working in that dull art gallery all day, every day? Penny was very, very busy and always in a rush. As Beth washed up the coffee mugs, she glanced out the window. The birdfeeder was once again hectic with blue tits. She was glad she had filled it. She sighed and nibbled on a cookie. Everyone, it seemed, was busy except for her.

The Perfect Present

Usually so decisive, Beth was struggling. She had decided the siblings should give a joint present and had taken on the task of trying to find something they could all agree would be a suitable gift to give their father for his birthday. It was his seventy-fifth. If they could only agree, they could get him something outstanding.

When she had broached the subject to Duncan, he had sounded unconcerned, his disembodied voice hesitating and echoing on the long-distance line from Texas. His only suggestion was a bottle of whisky. When Beth pushed him to be more imaginative, he came up with several different esoteric and hugely expensive brands of whisky. It seemed such an unoriginal idea. Surely, they could come up with something more meaningful.

'Well, if you have a better idea Beth, you run with it,' Duncan said. 'You're the one doing all the leg work, you choose.'

Beth had an idea, but when she talked it over with Tina, she poo-pooed the suggestion.

'I don't know why you think he'd like that,' she said. 'You know it's not his thing. Just because it's your idea of a fun night out.'

Then Tina had suggested getting Pa's portrait painted by an Italian friend of hers.

'If we could find a good photograph, she could paint from that.' Tina said.

Beth arranged to meet up with Tina at Fortnum & Mason's for coffee to make a final decision. The train was late, and Beth couldn't find a taxi. As she walked along the pavement, Beth felt sticky and dowdy. She always forgot it was warmer in London and she wished she had worn her smarter blazer instead of her heavy coat. The traffic roared past, and Beth rued the day that you could hear a cab coming by its diesel engine. She found herself twisting around at the sound of every deep motor, but it seemed everyone drove a diesel these days. In the end, she hopped on the bus.

When she arrived, late and flustered, she spotted her sister across the room. Tina looked serene. Her chair was surrounded by shopping. The cord handles draped over the prominent brand names stamped across the subtle shades of the crisp, card bags. Tina sat upright and was on her phone. She was staring into the tiny pink gadget in front of her as if it was a crystal ball.

'Sorry, the train ...' Beth slung her coat over a spare chair.

'No worries, give me a minute. I'm just replying to Freddie. He's asking about Henley.'

The white tablecloth pulled askew as Beth squeezed onto a padded chair. When settled, she smoothed the ruckled linen back into place and put her handbag on the adjacent seat. Tina was still tap, tap tapping away, her painted nails catching the mobile's keys. Beth picked up the menu, not that she needed to; she'd have a pot of Earl Grey, black and weak.

Tina put down her phone as the waitress approached.

'Earl Grey?' said Beth.

'And maybe we could share one of those millefeuille that they do so well here?' said Tina and smiled her small secret smile. Beth beamed back, happy to have a moment of connection. They both sparkled at the idea of custard and pastry.

As they drank their tea and squished custard out of the pastry with the side of blunt forks, Beth showed Tina the photographs she had brought. Beth had struggled to find a picture of Pa on his own. She had come across one of him sitting at his desk in his study and another in the garden. Neither were very detailed.

'These are useless,' said Tina, 'couldn't you find anything better?'

Tina had brought some images of her artist friend's paintings to show Beth the style. Beth could tell at once that the idea was hopeless.

'Not sure Pa would like something so … cutting edge,' said Beth. Honestly, Tina was so removed from reality.

'You don't think he'd like it, or you don't like it?' asked Tina.

Tina was infuriating. They'd been having a good time and now the spell was broken. Tina made Beth feel unsophisticated, always had, even as a teenager. Tina had this way of glancing sideways at Beth, giving her a sly look, taking her in and then turning away; it was exasperating. Now she had limitless funds; thanks to Freddie, Tina was insufferable. It was as if Beth couldn't have valid ideas or preferences of her own. Beth felt an overwhelming desire to sponsor a donkey or a child in Africa for their father, something altruistic and non-confrontational.

Tina

We had been given the pink room. Huge roses bloomed on the chintz curtains, and the fringing on the swags and tails trailed on the carpet. The covered headboard of the bed matched the curtains, and roses flowered again on the scatter cushions. Now that I was in a proper relationship, I was upgraded from my attic lair. For a time, I wondered if my mother wanted me to be kept a child forever, sleeping upstairs in the old nursery while my sister and brother were downstairs being grown-ups.

Now, without you holding me back, Max, I had caught up with myself and could be the person I was supposed to be. Freddie had given me that. But however much Ma would like it, and however much Freddie liked my family and their big house, I knew he wouldn't want to stay the night at Nether Place. I needed to give Ma our excuses.

As I walked across the landing to the top of the stairs, I smiled to myself; what did the family really make of Freddie? An entrepreneur? A self-made man? An upstart? You, Max, I knew thought him worse than that, but I tried to persuade myself that I didn't really care what you thought. I'm sure Beth considered me beyond the pale now that Freddie was there to indulge me. I did hope so. I no longer dressed in hand-me-downs. My old retro look, unearthed in the clothing sections of charity shops, was in the past. Now I was invested in looking chic, my heels too high, and my clothes handwash only. My matching handbags were not big enough for anything more than my credit card, phone, and cigarettes. Nothing sensible, nothing suitable; it gave me real pleasure as I dressed in the morning to choose clothes that would satisfy me precisely because they were impractical.

I shook my head as I went downstairs to find Ma. My freshly styled hair bounced, and the touch of the curled ends stroked my jawline and gave me joy. The more polished I was, the more it amused me to think how infuriated you and Beth must be. I still could not understand how Beth could be so happy with you and make such an excellent home for Laura. It used to make me feel deficient that I could never be that person. But now, I don't have time to think about the past and what might have been. Now, I feel I know who I am, and you avoid me, Max, where once you would have drifted close and teased. Now I teased you.

Freddie and I had only been together a few months when he asked if I would like to go away with him. You had never taken me anywhere, Max, unless you count that pub in Yorkshire - hardly the same.

'Somewhere exotic,' Freddie said. 'We can have some quality time together.'

He took me to The Seychelles. We were staying in a lovely cabana that overlooked the beach. Underneath the palm trees, Freddie proposed. We were married on the white, sandy beach. I wore a pale, shimmery kaftan we bought in the hotel shop. I was barefoot. I pushed my toes into the cool, gritty sand to feel grounded. Could this really be happening, beneath such a beautiful, turquoise blue sky.

He had prepared everything in advance. How did Freddie know I'd say yes? I don't know. I don't think I've met anyone who said 'no' to Freddie. It was beautiful and romantic. Freddie had organised everything to perfection. Now, I belonged.

'Why hang around,' Freddie said. 'I want to know everything about you. I want to be with you always.'

And I wanted to be part of Freddie's life. I had done enough waiting on the side lines.

When we got home. I was so excited to tell everyone, but it was Pa's birthday. Our flight was delayed, everyone was soaked by the time we arrived, and somehow the moment passed.

A Happy Birthday

Beth needed to check over the proofs for the charity tombola invitations and then double-check the mailing list before contacting the printer. This afternoon it was her turn to collect Laura and her friend from school and drop them off at their ballet class. When the phone rang, Beth was thinking about what they needed to take with them the next day; they were going down to Nether Place for Pa's lunch.

'I've ordered two beef fillets for tomorrow from that smart butcher in Smithfield,' said Ma, 'I thought I'd get it locally, but it seems I've left it too late. Could you pick it up and bring it with you when you come tomorrow? Now you're not working, I thought you'd have plenty of time.'

Beth sighed. Of course, she could. Ma was right. Beth had all the time in the world. It would mean a trip up to London, but if she had to, she could manage. Before she altered her plans, she rang Max to see if he could collect the meat for her; Smithfield wasn't so far from the hospital. His secretary answered the phone.

'Sorry to disturb you,' said Beth. Miss Pritchard sounded out of breath; she must have run for the phone.

'We are frightfully busy here,' said Miss Pritchard. 'This is a hospital; we don't run personal errands. We don't do favours.'

'Of course not, I'm sorry.' Miss Pritchard had an uncanny knack of making Beth feel irrelevant and excluded from Max's important work. The sting nettled more since Beth had been demoted to housewife. It had been blissful to have an acceptable if uninteresting answer to the recurring inquiry of, "what do you do?". Working in accounts was one up from not working at all. Being a mother was not sufficient; there was supposed to be more. The most important job in the world, as women kept being told, on the condition that they didn't expect any applause. Sometimes Beth felt she would be given more respect if, when asked, she replied that she was a kept woman; at least it would sound interesting.

In the end, Beth shelved the tombola mailing list and asked Laura's friend's mother to take the girls to ballet. That gave Beth enough time to get the train into London. She found the butchers and picked up the beef that was packed ready for her collection. She also bought some amazing looking steak for their supper. Then she zipped back to collect Laura from the friend's house and returned home and get food on the table. Max was not staying over in London nearly so much lately. More family time was good, but she'd had to up her dinner menu options. Beth wasn't happy serving Max the sort of simple supper dishes she and Laura usually ate midweek.

Beth was driving. She paused before starting the engine. Max looked at her.

'Beef times two, gift, husband, daughter, all present and correct.' Max said.

Beth smiled and turned the key in the ignition.

'I can't believe your father is seventy-five already; time flies,' said Max. 'When did Duncan and Meredith arrive?'

'They flew in mid-week,' Beth said, 'they should be over their jetlag by now, ready for the big birthday lunch. I hope Meredith is happier this year. She hasn't hidden her frustration and loneliness before.'

'Quite a challenge. Not like you, darling, always calm and in control.'

Beth glowered at Max before glancing in the rear-view mirror. Laura had been given Max's Walkman and headphones so she could listen to something on the drive, but Laura was reading a book Tina had given her. Beth couldn't understand how anyone could read in the car, but Laura seemed engrossed.

Ma greeted them on the doorstep. In the kitchen, Mrs Simms, having heard them arrive, was already getting the rolling pin out of the drawer. The pastry was out of the fridge, the mushroom mixture cooling in the sink. Max and Laura, who had followed Beth through to the back of the house, were told to take some punnets and were sent to pick raspberries in the walled garden.

'I'll come back and help you with those when I've said hello to everyone,' said Beth to Meredith, who was peeling a vast pile of potatoes at the sink.

Beth left the kitchen to find the rest of the family and followed the Persian runner back to the front of the house, wandering past Ma's splendid flower arrangement in the hall. She found Pa with Duncan and Gareth in the dining room by the sideboard.

'Happy Birthday, Pa,' said Beth. Her father deferred to her kiss.

'Hi there,' said Duncan coming over to hug her. 'How are you? Gareth and I are helping Pa decant the wine,' said Duncan. 'Pa is giving Gareth a lesson in bottle-opening and pouring techniques. I was just going to check that there's enough champagne in the fridge.'

'I'll come with you,' said Beth, 'Mrs Simms has given Meredith a formidable pile of potatoes to peel. I must help. Any sign of Tina?'

'No,' said Duncan. 'Ma said she'd phoned earlier to say their plane was late. They should get here in time for lunch ... but if not, to start without them.'

'How are you coping now you are no longer working?' asked Duncan as they headed back to the kitchen. 'How are you getting on with Pa?'

'As though nothing had ever happened,' she smiled. 'As though daughters working for the family company had been an aberration best forgot.'

'Ah well,' said Duncan. 'Onwards and upwards.'

Knowing Tina and Freddie were on their way, Pa insisted on waiting for them to start lunch. When they arrived, and everyone was together, Duncan suggested they take a photograph to commemorate the occasion. Mrs Simms was called away from her preparations to wield Pa's heavy black camera. They all smiled. Everyone was very jolly by the time they went through to lunch, but it would be a big meal with plenty of food to soak up the alcohol. Beth went to help Mrs Simms carry lunch through.

'If your mother had only let me know lunch would be late, I could have delayed the start of cooking, and everything wouldn't look so tired,' Mrs Simms said.

'Don't be silly, Mrs Simms. It all looks splendid, as always,' Beth insisted.

Despite Mrs Simms's foreboding, lunch was delicious, and the beef was cooked to perfection. Gareth had taken his grandfather's instructions to heart and was very helpful, leaping up to make sure everyone's glass was brimming. It made it hard to count how much you were drinking if your glass was constantly topped up before you had drained the last drop. As the designated driver, Beth decided she must leave her glass full. It seemed such a waste, but there was no other way to stop Gareth. Looking around the table, Beth thought her father looked happy, content to be surrounded by all his family. Duncan and Meredith were no more querulous than usual. Max was the irritable one today. He did not seem as engaged by her mother's talk of potentilla versus philadelphus. Beth had always thought Max saintly with his long chats with Ma about plants. He could generally spin out his meagre knowledge for at least one course. His interest in gardening was genuine, but his experience was superficial, but today he seemed distracted and did not seem to be listening to her mother. In contrast, though jet-lagged, Tina and Freddie looked very happy. Tina glowed. It was a long time since Beth had seen her sister so radiant.

'Laura,' said Beth sharply after they had finished their main course, flicking her eyes towards the kitchen. Laura broke off explaining to Gareth about the witches and wizards in her book, and she and Gareth helped clear the table. While the presents for Pa were brought forward, Duncan went to get more Champagne from the kitchen for the birthday toast. He filled the flutes on the sideboard and passed them around the table, so everyone would have a drink when they came to toast Pa's health. The children helped Mrs Simms carry through the fabulous birthday cake, replete with candles and surrounded by raspberries.

After the candles had been blown out, Pa began to open his presents while Ma cut the cake. Duncan had given his father a bottle of whisky. Beth had bought opera tickets for both her parents, and Tina gave one of the paintings her friend had painted. Then it was time for birthday toasts; Pa rose, holding his champagne flute.

'Thank you, thank you for your kind gifts,' said Pa, 'Now, I just wanted to say a few words about retirement,' a chuckle rippled around the table. 'F & P has touched all our lives ....'

Beth supposed was only fair; it was his birthday. Pa embarked on a long and rambling speech about his long, illustrious career.

'Hear, hear,' they all drank his health and clapped in unison as Pa announced his decision to stay at the company in a non-executive role.

Then Duncan stood up to give a toast, a reply to his father. Duncan praised his father but then dared to mention Beth and her contribution to F & P and how unfortunate it was as she had been asked to stand down. Beth was mortified. It was good of Duncan to champion her efforts but talking about what had happened after the event wouldn't help. Duncan ended with a toast.

'To Beth, the man I could never be.'

While Beth was wondering whether to drink to this surprising tribute, she saw Freddie half rise in his chair, holding his glass.

'There is someth –'

But Meredith interrupted Freddie, leaping up from her chair, which toppled backwards and crashed to the floor.

'I have a toast to make too,' she said, 'as we are all being candid. To Duncan,' she raised her glass, 'my husband, the man who never was.' She paused looking round the table to see the effect of her words. 'I'm leaving, Duncan. Come on, Gareth.'

Gareth held his fork, balancing a mouthful of cake in mid-air. He was staring at his mother in amazement. 'But I haven't finished my cake.'

'– now,' said Meredith, and Gareth dropped the fork and, in a daze, followed his mother out of the room.

Silence filled the room. Duncan collapsed into his chair. The reverberations of the slammed door petered out in the heavy air.

Then they heard the car engine, a crunch, and the clatter of scattered gravel as Meredith took off down the drive.

Beth tried to weigh up what had just happened, but all she could think of was that she was sure Meredith had drunk too much to legally drive. Meredith had given no hint that she was going to do anything so outrageous and had said nothing to Beth while they were peeling the potatoes. Perhaps Meredith didn't know what she would say and do until the moment arrived. Poor Duncan. Maybe he would be able to patch things up, maybe it was just a row. Duncan looked devastated and perplexed, affronted, but perhaps also just a tad relieved. She caught his eye, and he smiled weakly and raised his half-empty flute.

'Que sera,' he said and drained the glass.

'What the hell is going on?' asked Pa, who was still standing. He searched around the table as if to find meaning, his gaze settled on Freddie, 'Did … did you have something you wanted to say, Freddie?'

'… No, no, not really.'

'Shall we have coffee in the drawing room?' said Ma, rolling up her napkin and sliding it into her silver napkin ring.

Part 4

'Hello, Darling. How are you? Lovely to see you.'

'Hello, May-May.' Laura took the photo album from the shelf. She wanted to ask May-May about a photograph of her mother and uncle, Duncan, when they were young. Sharon brought in tea, and Laura settled in the chair next to her grandmother and flicked through the pages of distant family events to find the picture she wanted. Laura glanced covertly at May-May. Her grandmother stretched her fingers into the warmth of a patch of sunlight.

'I do love how sunshine slides in low and warms the heart,' May-May said. She turned to look at Laura and smiled. 'Is this your confirmation?' She pointed to a photograph in the open album that Laura was about to pass over.

'Yes, it was held at school, in the chapel. Do you remember?'

'Yes, yes, I do. The headmistress gave a very dry speech,' May-May laughed. 'You must have been about twelve, thirteen.'

'I was in lower 4th, so, yes, I was thirteen.'

The chapel was painted white inside and out, like the rest of the school buildings. Every morning there was a short service for assembly and a full service on Sundays; attendance was compulsory. A red carpet ran down the central aisle and up the steps that led to the communion rail. Pupils would file in by form to their allotted row. The dark wooden pews had been polished over the years by students running their hands over the finials and sliding along to find their seat. The chapel was a place of hushed chit-chat and boredom. Apart from a very few, the whole year was confirmed.

'Afterwards, we all went out to lunch at a pub.'

'The Lamb and Ferret,' said May-May. 'How strange that I remember the most obscure details but forget important things.'

'Mum and Dad were there, and you and Grandpa.' Laura pointed to the shadowy figures looming in the background of the old photo.

Laura remembered she had felt quite peeved that day. Although it was her confirmation, it had been a day that seemed to revolve more around the grown-ups.

'I've booked,' her mother had said to the sullen girl at the bar when they arrived at the pub, 'Templeton for seven.'

Laura had been given gifts, a gold crucifix from her parents and a bible from her grandparents. Tina, her godmother, had given her an Italian handbag, which Laura had thought most sophisticated.

'I should take that home,' said her mother, scooping up the bag. 'It will get ruined at school.'

Laura had not seen the bag again; her mother had said it was unsuitable for someone her age. Laura must remember to ask her mother what had happened to the handbag. She must be old enough to have it by now.

'And here is Tina. Who is this with her?' asked May-May.

"That's Freddie, remember?'

'Oh, yes, him. I can't think where she found him.'

'This is one of my favourite photographs of Tina,' said Laura turning the page. 'You have the same one, but larger somewhere, don't you? In a silver frame.'

May-May drew the album closer. 'Oh, yes. I have the portrait version. It's here by the little shepherdess on the side table.' May-May peered at the photograph and pointed at the dog in Tina's arms. 'The little brute.'

'I love Tina's coat.' Laura took a closer look at the photograph. Tina looked like a model, her handbag hanging from her elbow, a ball of fluff under her arm, and a cigarette in her other hand.

'May-May, is that your coat Tina's wearing? The fur you were wearing for my christening?'

'Yes, I do believe it is.' Her grandmother took a sip of her tea. Laura watched the little fish of lemon swim on the surface of the clear golden liquid. May-May replaced her cup and saucer on the table, the fish riding a wave.

'After your christening, Beth said to me, "You can't wear fur anymore, Ma. It's not done." I told her what rubbish. After all, the coat had been in Dennis' family for years. Those little critters would have been long dead whether they were a lovely coat or not. But Beth was quite insistent. You know how she can be.'

'Mum can be stubborn.'

'So, Beth made me promise to give the coat away. She said, "I don't want some animal rights person throwing red paint all over you, Ma. Just get rid of it. Give it away. You can't sell them anymore. Even Oxfam won't take them." I told her not to worry. I would find it a good home.'

'So, you gave it to Tina?'

'Yes, after your Christening, Tina was heading back to Milan. It was November, getting colder, and I knew she would look fabulous in the coat and cherish it. So, I gave it to her. Back then, they were much less picky about these things on the Continent than they were here.'

'Ha! What did Mum say about that?'

'I don't think I told her.' May-May gave Laura an arch look and smiled. 'I thought at the time there was no need. Nothing to do with her, really.'

'And the first time Mum found out was years later when Tina wore the coat to my confirmation.'

After the service, the atmosphere had been prickly at the pub. Laura had not been interested in the details at the time; she had been sulking about the banished handbag. But she remembered the tone of the talk becoming sharper as lunch progressed. By the time the coffee arrived, things had simmered down. May-May burbling soothing stuff while Laura's grandfather paid the bill. They had all left rather quickly. Her parents were taciturn in the car. Laura had been quite happy to be dropped back at school.

'Mum can't have been pleased.' Laura said, refilling May-May's cup with tea.

'I don't suppose so. Now I think about it, there was a bit of a to do, but it wasn't as though Beth *wanted* the coat.'

May-May's gaze lost focus. She stared into her tea. Then, after a while, she said. 'But I held on to my astrakhan. Fabulous coat, so useful for funerals.'

Laura remembered the heavy black coat. If she closed her eyes, she could recall the musky, camphor scent given off when it appeared from her grandmother's wardrobe. Years ago, she must have been about twelve, she remembered playing fancy dress, wrapped in the astrakhan, sitting on the Persian carpet in her grandmother's bedroom.

'Have you seen her?' May-May had said. She was at her dressing table, a dark silhouette in front of the window, peering into the mirror, adjusting her hair.

'Meredith? No,' her mother had said as she placed a small vase of flowers on the dressing table amongst the silver backed brushes. 'Tina said she'd had a postcard from Duncan. I'm sure you heard his news too.'

'Yes, he's moved to San Francisco.'

'And has a new partner, Robin.'

'Yes, partner, that's an odd, formal word to use, isn't it? I don't know why Duncan doesn't just say girlfriend.' said May-May. 'No word about whether he'll be back for a visit?'

'No.'

The stiffness of the fur had surrounded Laura, the A-line skirt spreading out like a dark pool, she flapped her arms in the heavy, bell-shaped sleeves, and a musty scent of moth balls, dust and old perfume was set free as if by a spell.

The coat reminded Laura of a Christmas years before, when she was really young, about nine. Laura had been given the Narnia books by her aunt Tina. One Sunday afternoon, while the grown-ups were sitting in front of the fire in the drawing room, Laura had run through the house and searched all the wardrobes she could find at Nether Place. She had slipped down dark hallways, been caught in patches of sunshine from tall windows, and hopped through sporadic clouds of sparkling dust. Laura dared herself to go into far-off, seldom-visited spare bedrooms. She inched open creaking doors and crept into forgotten rooms, hoping to find secrets, a cupboard full of fur coats and a magic world beyond.

Laura had even ventured through the plain brown door and up the narrow steps to the old servant's rooms. She didn't think she had ever been up there before, certainly not on her own. It wasn't that it was forbidden. It was just that there was no call for her to go there. Near the start of the stairs, a step had screeched. Laura had waited, holding her breath, clutching the thin wood bannisters. Listening for any response from behind her. Anxious that her mother might come and ask her what she was up to. Her eyes straining upwards in case, perhaps, like Digory and Polly in the Magician's Nephew, she had woken some spooky ghost or demon in the attic that would drag her off to some different world. After a moment of silence, Laura continued upwards. Off the short corridor at the top of the stairs, she found a few deserted children's rooms with sloping ceilings and dormer windows that pushed out into the sky. Not much was left in the rooms that must have belonged to Duncan and her mother. The bedroom, which had been her aunt Tina's, was much more interesting. Laura spun on the central purple floral rug before she began to examine the room. There were still a few bright, fragile clothes in the closet and so many books in the bookcase. Laura bounced on the bed, and as she settled, noticed a pink, sparkly book on the bedside table. She picked it up and ran her fingers over the bumpy jewels stuck on the cover. The book fell open in her hands; it was a diary.

Although the loopy, open writing was easy to read, the comments were about people Laura didn't know and the glued in cut-outs from magazines were old-fashioned. In the top right-hand corner of each double page was a number with a smiley or frowny face next to it. 8lb 2, frowny face, 7lb 10, smiley face. What did lb mean, she wondered? Laura flipped through the edge of the pages with her thumb and watched the smiley faces dance. Then she heard her Mum's voice calling dimly from far below. Earlier Laura had helped Mrs Simms ice gingerbread men, it must be teatime. Laura closed the book, put it back on the little table by the bed, the quest for magic worlds forgotten, and raced downstairs.

2000 – 2005

Divorce

Beth shuffled through her cards. She wanted one with a religious feel. She knew Meredith would appreciate that, though maybe as she was divorcing Duncan, she wasn't as devout anymore. For years Beth had gradually been choosing Christmas cards that were more secular. It seemed to go with the times. But Meredith she felt would still feel a card with religious overtones was appropriate. Rootling near the bottom of her stash, Beth found a few not too dog-eared cards with a nativity scene and a generous sprinkling of glitter. Beth looked at the card, opened it pen poised, and paused. What on earth was she going to write? Maybe she should wait till she received a card from Meredith? Then Beth could respond in kind, but that might seem like she was only replying because that was the polite thing to do. In the end, she wrote a cheerful note about Laura starting boarding at Beth and Tina's alma mater, saying she hoped Gareth had settled well at his new school in Wales too. Beth didn't want Meredith to feel deserted by the family just because she'd left Duncan. After all, though no one was saying much, the little Beth knew indicated that Duncan was mostly to blame.

After that awful lunch, poor Duncan had returned to the States alone. Beth had tried to talk to him before he left, to find out what was going on, but he avoided everyone. It was as though Meredith had been put in a box, never to be opened again. When he got to

Texas, he terminated the house rental in Austin, sending everything Meredith and Gareth wanted back to the U.K. Then Duncan moved to San Francisco. Throughout, Beth called Duncan regularly. She was worried that he would get depressed while he was in the house on his own, having to sort through and pack up his life with Meredith. Then she was worried that he would be in a new city without any friends. Duncan had been upbeat but reserved. It was only bit by bit that Beth understood that Duncan wasn't alone at all. One life was over, but another had begun. Duncan had hooked up with Robin so swiftly that Beth had to assume they already knew each other quite well.

The next day Beth received a Christmas card from Meredith with a letter about all she had been up to since the dreadful birthday lunch. The sort of letter that, despite being fulsome, gave very little detail, but it did give a phone number. Beth decided to call.

'Well, it should be fairly straightforward,' said Meredith. 'I'm suing for divorce, but it will be perfectly amicable. Duncan appears to have moved on completely, not that I'm surprised. Just rather miffed that I am so quickly ancient history. I suppose our lives really separated years ago, and now I think about it, I can see that we were just going through the motions.'

'How is Gareth? Is he taking this change in his stride?' asked Beth.

'Oh, Gareth is fine. Children are so adaptable, aren't they? I've sent him to an independent day school here. I'm not in favour of private education myself, but I thought the teachers might have more time and be more sympathetic, what with Gareth switching to the British education system and he has important exams looming. Of course, Duncan will have to pay, which gives me the teeny, tiniest bit of pleasure.'

'How is school working out for Gareth?'

'Well, he's had run-ins with a couple of his teachers, par for the course with Gareth, I'm afraid. They are so uptight here compared to what Gareth is used to in Austin. But we moved at a good time.

He joined at the beginning of the run-up to GCSEs.'

'And how are you, Meredith?'

'I'm just fine, Beth, thanks. Never better. Glad to be home. I've joined a local choir. Early days, but there's a nice baritone I fancy. The only thing I miss about my previous life is the Texas weather.'

When Beth had finished speaking to Meredith, she thought she should not be partisan and should phone Duncan too and see how he was getting on too, but when she rang him, only the automated voice of the answerphone replied.

'Robin and Duncan are not in. Please leave your message after the tone.'

Freddie's House

What a quaint, charming home this could be. Beth stood in the courtyard outside the kitchen and looked up at the darkening sky. The garden was a bit of a well, but Beth was mentally filling pots with shade-loving plants and encouraging climbers to grow up a new trellis on the back wall. Of course, having had a tour of the house, she had decided that the kitchen and the bathroom would have to come out. The electrics would probably need to be updated too. The light in the front sitting room had blinked when Freddie flicked on the switch.

'Uh-oh!' said Freddie, chuckling as though dodgy house electrics were a minor inconvenience. 'Need to get that looked at.' He had arrived after them, back from work, coming in the door as Max and Beth stood with Tina in the narrow hall. It was a crush. It seemed as if Tina didn't know what to do, how to move them on. She was wearing the sort of slinky, bias dress that Beth would think twice about wearing as a nighty. Beth had been wondering if they should invite themselves further in when Freddie arrived and took over, ushering them into the sitting room and taking their coats.

'When did you move in?' asked Max as Freddie handed him a whisky.

'Over a year ago now. Don't know where the time goes. Should have done more, but it's been crazy at work. As you know, the house was my aunt's, and we're still waiting for probate to be finalised, it's taking forever. And, well, I wanted to wait till we were married, so Tina could have her say too. It's probably a good idea to see how we use the house before we decide on anything radical.'

'You could take these doors out,' said Beth as Tina opened the folding doors to the adjacent study. 'Join the front and back rooms properly with a steel beam. It would really let the light in.'

'It's definitely on the to-do list,' said Tina, who seemed more assured, now Freddie was back. 'There's so much we'd like to change, to make the house our own.'

'Trouble is, knowing where to start,' chortled Freddie.

'I often wonder, if everyone in the street took out the dividing wall, would a terrace like this collapse like dominos?' asked Max. 'It is the first makeover step that everybody seems to do these days in small Edwardian houses.'

'Comforting thought, Max,' said Beth. In her mind's eye, the room was already opened up. Gone was the faded, floral wallpaper and the short curtains that dusted the tops of the terrible 70s radiators. In Beth's imagination, the whole area was now painted the palest yellow, perhaps rag rolled, with full-length darker yellow curtains with rusty fringing that matched the painted cupboard Beth's mind tucked into the alcoves on either side of the fireplaces. 'You could ask Penny to help with the interiors,' she said. 'She's got a really good eye.'

'I don't think I have a bad sense of style myself,' said Tina.

'I didn't mean you wouldn't do a great job!' said Beth. 'Just a suggestion.'

'A recommendation of a builder might be more useful,' said Max as they climbed the stairs to view the bedrooms. 'Though I can't help you there, I'm afraid.'

'This is our suite,' said Freddie.

'And here is the spare room. I thought when it is done up Laura could come and stay,' said Tina.

'Of course,' said Beth, thinking over my dead body. 'What a charming room it could be.'

'Come downstairs,' said Tina to Beth. 'I've got something to show you.' Beth followed Tina as she teetered down the narrow stairs to the basement kitchen, where an area had been fenced off, and the floor was covered in soiled newspaper.

'Isn't he adorable?' said Tina leaning into the pen and scooping up the tiny ball of fluff that had wiggled across the floor towards them, causing the soiled sheets of newspaper to skitter and slide on the linoleum floor. 'I've called him Bitsy because he's such an itsy, bitsy little person. So adorable, don't you think?' She cuddled the dog up towards her. He wriggled in her arms, reaching out his tongue to lick her face. 'So cute, kissing mummy.'

'Adorable! A handbag dog,' said Beth, trying not to shudder as the puppy's tongue slobbered over Tina's lips. 'Can I take a look at the garden?'

'Not much to see,' said Freddie, who, with Max, had followed them downstairs. Freddie opened the back door letting in some fresh air. Beth passed him and stepped outside and breathed deeply. Beth thought the house had such potential and she should be glad that Tina was happy with Freddie. She wasn't jealous of Tina's prospects and plans. Beth had her own stable, secure life. At the same time this was exciting, except for the dog. At last, Tina's life had momentum. Beth heard the faint chime of the doorbell. After a moment or two, Max joined her in the courtyard.

'It's suppertime,' he said.

As they stepped over the threshold back into the house, Max nearly tripped over Tina's little dog.

'Sorry little fellow.' Max bent over to pet the puppy, but it turned and growled a tiny baby growl. Max straightening quickly, laughed. 'Good for you, take on the world.'

'Bitsy, behave!' said Tina, kneeling for a moment at Max's feet as she scooped up the dog, kissing it on the head. Beth saw Max look at Tina's bent head and the swift glance between them as she rose, then Tina's sly eyes slipped to the dog, and she turned to put Bitsy back in his pen. Max appeared uncomfortable, even guilty, not an emotion Beth associated with confident Max: he must have thought he'd hurt Tina's dog. Beth smiled to reassure him.

'Little blighter needs to learn some manners,' said Freddie, bringing shopping bags of cartons downstairs.

'As the kitchen isn't up to much, I ordered a takeaway,' said Tina. 'You don't mind, do you?'

'Indian,' said Freddie. 'My favourite.'

'Delicious,' agreed Beth. They sat around the Formica kitchen table. Tina opened the cartons of spicey, brown stews, while Freddie fetched plates and cutlery.

'So, Max any plans for cutting back your workload?' asked Freddie as he filled their wine glasses. 'You doctor chappies usually clear off out of the NHS as soon as you can.'

'Fifty-six isn't near retirement,' said Beth, the way Freddie had of asking a normal question seemed so loaded, it put her on edge, besides Max was in his prime. 'Can you pass the naan?'

'And I already split my hours between the NHS and private work,' said Max with a calm Beth didn't feel. 'Have done for years.'

The little dog began to sniff and scratch at the paper on the floor of his pen.

'Max has always been good at compartmentalising his life,' said Tina. 'Have you tried the chicken?' she added passing the dish to Max.

Max's chair wobbled on the uneven floor as he took the plate; Beth smiled at him, really Tina was too much. 'Yes,' she said. 'Max has always managed to keep his work at work; his home life is sacred.'

Tina got up to attend to Bitsy, who was now whining. Beth took a breath of the cool evening air that seeped into the kitchen as Tina took the dog out to the patio.

'But you're right,' said Max. 'I will gradually move over into more and more private practice.'

'Freddie has an exciting new project. He has decided to start his own fund,' said Tina returning Bitsy to the pen and joining them at the table.

'What does that mean?' asked Max. 'Are you starting up on your own, starting your own business?'

'Ah ... Tina is being generous,' said Freddie. 'Probably the time to do it. I should be braver, but no. I've been given autonomy over a new fund, that is, my own fund within my current company. It's what they like to do. Have independent traders working for themselves under their name.'

'But still, quite a responsibility,' said Beth.

'Well, the buck will stop with me, so I will have to make things work. But I have experience in the field, stock picking and so on, it should be fun. Just need to build interest with investors so I have some real money to manage.' Freddie chuckled. 'I already have some loyal followers.'

'Was that a dog?' asked Max on the train home.

'Almost,' said Beth.

'Didn't like us much.'

'I didn't like it much either,' said Beth, watching the lights passing outside the window as the train slipped through the outskirts of London.

'Made quite a stink for such a little thing. Baby substitute, I suppose.'

'Really?' said Beth, watching Max's expression in the window. The train rattled over some points, and his reflection bobbed up and down like a boat on a swell. 'You don't think they'll have children? Tina's still young.' Tina was obviously happy with Freddie. Surely, they would want to celebrate their relationship with a child. Beth understood the satisfaction of creating a family. If Tina and Freddie had a baby, Beth would feel her own relationship with Laura was secure. For, now that Tina was married, she was in a position to offer Laura a home.

'Freddie won't want children. He likes being the centre of attention. And with his new business venture, this new fund, what's it called, Gravity Financial Services or something. He'll be working hard, looking to build up the capital and all that.'

'I was talking to Tina about the house. It's a shame Freddie isn't more interested in doing it up quickly.' The nick-nacks and flowers that Tina had placed around the rooms did not change the impression that the house still belonged to the aunt. Despite the many candles that glimmered in damp corners, the whiff of old lady remained.

'Freddie doesn't seem very practically minded,' said Max. 'I don't think he's that bothered about the house for all his talk.'

'I wonder how Tina will cope, living in that mess, with Freddie out all day and working late.'

'Do you suppose she'll get a wallpaper stripper and set to work herself?' said Max with a grin.

'And ruin her nails? I don't think so! I see her sitting, happily sunk into one of those awful, saggy sofas, reading interiors magazines and dreaming of all the work they'll do one day. She'll be sipping Earl Grey with that fluff ball curled up in her lap, cutting out all the pretty pictures, making mood boards and keeping everything in a folder. Like she used to keep photos of pinups in her teenage diary. Tina will tidy all her plans away, so they won't upset Freddie when he gets home in the evening, but she'll be getting ready for when the work begins. Tina likes being prepared.'

'Is that what you do?' asked Max. 'Scheme behind my back and, when the time comes, present your ideas as a fait acompli.'

'Of course not, darling. I don't have a devious bone in my body,' smiled Beth.

'I don't believe you do,' said Max patting her on her knee. 'I'm sure they'll be very happy. They are made for each other.'

'And Bitsy too. Don't forget Bitsy!'

Gliding out of the blackness of the countryside the train approached the lights of the station and home.

'Have you got the car keys?' asked Max. 'I'd like to get home pronto. Indian food never really agrees with me.'

Tina

'Well, that was a surprise!' said Freddie as we headed back to Chelsea in a cab through the cold winter streets.

'A good surprise?' I asked.

'Well chosen,' said Freddie leaning over to kiss me. 'Thank you.'

'What was it about a musical comprised entirely of Abba numbers that made you nervous?' I asked.

'You were right, you were right. It was great fun.'

At the last minute, I had managed to get tickets for Mamma Mia for Freddie's birthday. We were up in the gods, where the seats themselves seemed to lean in towards the stage. Standing up there, I felt I might pitch forward and fall onto the actors. Seemingly without apprehension, Freddie swung around as we looked for our seats. He was amazingly agile and light on his feet for a large man. I could barely hear Freddie when he ran up and down the stairs at the house. I would tease him that he could be a cat burglar if he ever needed another job.

I had grown up with Beth playing all the Abba songs. I wonder, does she still play them, Max? When she was a teenager, Beth saved her pocket money and bought all the albums as they were released. When Beth was home from school, she would commandeer the record player in the drawing room at Nether Place.

You know the cabinet, it sat adjacent to the drinks table. It fascinated me when I was young. It almost looked ordinary, but it was a deceit. The polished wood-effect veneer was so shiny, much glossier than the real wood furniture. There were no handles, the double doors opened with a gentle push and a pop to reveal on the left, the record player, and on the right, the cream radio. Underneath was storage for L.P.s with vertical dividers, and a long low speaker ran underneath. You can imagine I was not allowed anywhere near this cutting-edge and delicate media centre, but when Ma was in the drawing room listening to her piano concertos or playing the baby grand then I would take off my shoes and Ma would laugh as, in my socks, I would entertain her, slipping and sliding, dancing across the parquet floor.

When Beth was home from school in the holidays, everything would change. Pa did not appreciate the rollicking beats and lyrics that cascaded through the house. He would rise from his favourite chair beside the fire, fold his newspaper, slap it on the arm of his chair, and stomp off to his study, muttering about his elder daughter's lack of taste.

I used to hide behind the sofa and eavesdrop on Beth and her friends as they laughed, gossiped, and listened to the L.P.s. Beth seemed so sophisticated and, as a child, all I had wanted to be was Beth, and to be the fortunate owner of all the Abba records. How my goals have changed, although I still like Abba, I no longer want to be like Beth. I do not intend to be deceived by my husband.

As the cab lurched around Knightsbridge, past the bright windows of Harvey Knicks announcing January discounts, and down Sloane Street towards Peter Jones, Freddie was happily whistling Waterloo under his breath.

'You know,' he said. 'Now that we are together in the house, you could sell your Earls Court flat. It must have rocketed in value since you bought it.'

'It has. Even Earls Court has come up in the world. But I can't,' I said. 'Pa insisted it was put in a trust. It's not mine to sell. The flat goes to Laura eventually. That is if anything happens to me.'

'Ah,' said Freddie. 'No matter.'

'Why? Is there a problem?' Freddie had never asked me about my money before. All his talk had been about his Gravity Investment Fund and what he could offer me.

'Oh, no, nothing at all. I thought you might be impatient to improve things at the house, buy some new furniture. But we can wait for my end-of-year bonus. It had just occurred to me that it would be a good project for you if you wanted to get on with things.'

'I have the rental income from the flat. Most of that goes on the day-to-day stuff and my bits and pieces.' The income I got from the flat was very useful. Freddie was a big thinker, but the reality of living bored him.

'No, no, it won't be long, won't be long at all, before I get some finances together. Everything is going very well, raising lots of funds. It'll be no time, and we can start work on the house and get it all shipshape.'

'You know, Freddie, it's not important to me that you have a massive income. I'm happy just to be with you.'

'Ah, that's very commendable, but you must admit, it's fun to do all the glam events and travel when and where we want to. If you can bear it, in the short run, I'd rather leave the work on the house and enjoy our life together.'

He leant towards me, holding onto the taxi strap so he didn't slip, and kissed me, his other hand warm on my thigh.

You would be surprised, Max. You, along with everybody else, saw Freddie as a bon viveur, but I knew he wasn't, not really. Although Freddie liked to look the part, when we were alone together, he enjoyed the few things we had and the little things we did together. He told me about his unhappy childhood and how it had scarred his confidence. I noticed how in front of family and work colleagues he felt the need to show off. What he wanted was the envy of his friends. It was as if he needed to see a reflection in their faces that confirmed who he was.

The cab pulled up outside the house, and Freddie leapt out to pay the driver. I cautiously edged myself out of the purring taxi onto the icy pavement. I steadied myself, holding onto Freddie's arm.

'Take care now,' said the cabby as he pulled away. It was late, and the road was quiet. As the taxi turned onto the main road at the end of the street, Freddie turned towards me and like in a movie, kissed me slowly under the streetlight.

Flying Lessons

'I've had the most wonderful letter from Duncan,' Ma said. 'Let me see, where did I put it? Here we are. Look, what do you make of that?'

Ma passed Beth a photograph of Duncan. In the picture, the sky was incredibly blue, Duncan was standing beside a light aircraft, holding a certificate. He looked a little wild, his hair ruffled as if by the breeze. He looked inordinately happy.

'He's got his pilot's licence! Isn't that fabulous? Did you know he'd been learning?'

'I knew Robin had given Duncan a flying lesson for Christmas last year. A sort of one-off experience. But I didn't realise he'd gone back to learn properly,' said Beth. 'Wow! That really is something.'

'So lovely to hear from him and see him looking so happy.'

'Isn't it,' said Beth. She had come down to Nether Place to visit her parents. Somehow, these days the house felt a bit neglected. She supposed, as her parent's lives slowed down, there was less hustle and bustle. 'I think Duncan forgets how much we miss him.'

Without Meredith to prompt him, Duncan had not been so diligent about visiting the family. After a business trip to Europe, he might tack on a couple of days here and there. Duncan would scoot into London, perhaps to sign papers for Meredith at her lawyer's office, perhaps to see Tina or Beth for lunch, dash down to visit his parents overnight and then vanish back to California. Robin's family was local to San Francisco. When Beth talked to Duncan it seemed that Robin and Duncan were a complete unit content in themselves. They did not appear to need anyone else.

Similarly, Tina and Freddie were ensconced in their new marriage. Beth asked her mother if she'd seen much of Tina lately. Had Tina been a virtuous daughter and been to visit, perhaps more often than Beth.

'Those two love birds! They don't have a moment to spare. They are so wrapped up in each other,' said Ma with a laugh.

'Do you think they'll have children?' Beth couldn't help thinking that if Tina had a child with Freddie, then she would have no need to lay claim to Laura. An idea that had taken hold and kept Beth awake at night. She worried that now she was married, Tina would want Laura to live with her and Freddie. Or Tina might get it into her head to tell Laura her true parentage, perhaps when Laura was twenty-one, or maybe at eighteen, or even sixteen. That was only a couple of years off.

'Oh, I haven't really thought about it. They seem so young,' said Ma.

'Tina is over 30 now, and I believe Freddie is at least five years older.'

'I think you have too much time on your hands if you are worrying about Tina and Freddie's sex life,' said Ma.

It wasn't Ma's fault, but Beth did have a great deal of spare time. She had not looked for another job after she left Farthingale and Parteger. She felt too raw. Beth was incensed with the unreasonableness of it all. At first, she had found it hard to be in the same room as her father, but she got over that; she had to. At family gatherings, it had not been difficult; she could easily hide, be busy helping her mother in the kitchen or in the garden.

Anyway, her father was much more interested in what Max was up to or Freddie's opinion on this or that. As time passed, she realised her confidence had taken a knock. Beth had always thought she wanted to work to stretch herself intellectually, to keep engaged with the world, and to have a modicum of financial independence, but suddenly those things didn't seem as important. She felt apathetic about working for anyone else. Beth only wanted to work for the family and, her ambition deflated when she wasn't allowed to. And of course, because Max had done so well, she didn't have to work, so now she didn't.

When Laura started boarding school, Beth found herself at a loose end, so on occasion, she would come down to Nether Place for a couple of days, particularly if Max was suddenly working late and staying over at the flat in London. When Beth visited, her father often seemed preoccupied, disappearing into his study or, since his partial retirement, going up to London to stay at his club. Beth thought her mother must be lonely, but if Beth had arrived spontaneously, as often as not, her mother, not expecting her, would have made arrangements to do something else.

'How lovely to see you, darling. But what a shame, you should give me more notice. I have lunch at the bridge club today.'

Or ...

'I hope you don't mind too much, darling, but Olive Johnson has asked me to make up a four.'

Beth would find herself scrabbling for lunch in the kitchen while chatting with Mrs Simms. Then Beth would mooch in the drawing room, or if the weather was good, she would wander out into the garden and might come across Burr, in the spring, dipping pea seeds in paraffin in the greenhouse for planting, or, if it was autumn, he might be in the long border of the walled garden, lifting the dahlias.

Shortly after Beth had arrived that afternoon, her mother left to give old Miss Hampton a lift to the doctors, so Beth telephoned Duncan. He was heading out the door to work. She could hear the commotion in the background signifying the beginning of his day.

'It is fabulous, Beth,' said Duncan. She heard him gulp. 'Sorry, running out the door, just finishing my coffee. Bye!' He yelled to someone in faraway San Francisco. Robin, she presumed. There was a thud of a door. 'It is amazing. The sky is so blue, and there is so much of it. When I'm flying, I feel totally, truly free. I love it.'

Crumble

They had been summoned to Nether Place for a family dinner. Beth finished her crumble and eyed what was left in the dish. Mrs Simms had excelled as usual. There was a bit left, maybe enough for two. Ma pulled the dish towards her as if she was about to offer seconds but then hesitated and was distracted. Instead, she turned to Max, who was on her right and asked him about lawnmowers. Freddie was sitting next to Pa, the white collar on his blue city shirt open, his neck rashed where the tight neckline had worn a groove earlier in the day. Now, released from work, Freddie was relaxed, playing with his glass, and leaning back, laughing at something Pa had said. Then, in a seemingly confidential move, Freddie leaned in towards Pa as though to let him in on a big secret.

At the beginning of the evening, Beth had heard Pa ask his standard son-in-law question, the one that came after the rhetorical, 'How are you?', and a slap on the back. The question came as everyone was seated, and proper conversation could begin.

'How's work?' Pa had asked Max, the senior son-in-law, as they sat with their pre-dinner whisky.

Max had his story ready and told her father an amusing tale about a surgeon friend who was constantly outraged by misuse in the system. Max had chosen well; Beth knew her father would enjoy fraught tales of skulduggery at the hospital. Later at dinner,

Pa turned to Freddie, who had endeavoured to make investment sound as entertaining as the fight for life and death that Max faced every day.

Now pleasantries concluded, Pa could lower his guard and enjoy his dinner and wine, knowing that he had done his duty, and been an attentive father-in-law. The table was covered in the debris of a campaign well fought, and the family looked rosy and happy in the soft glow of the candles. Pa beamed. Max asked her mother, radiant in the soft light, about the garden. Tina had that inscrutable, cat-like look on her face that made Beth think her younger sister was listening to some private monologue in her head. Beth wanted to slap her, wake her up. She had hoped Tina would be more approachable after she married. And sometimes Tina would be more open and there would be a glimpse of a possible, fragile bridge between them, it was almost a tangible thing, a suspension bridge of concurring ideas and shared memories. Then at other times, like tonight, Tina was as mysterious as ever. It was as if she was coated in shellac not a crease or a wrinkle, even her hair sat perfectly. She was polished and sophisticated with all the wealth that Freddie showered on her. Tina's diamond flashed as she played with her napkin ring, rolling it back and forth absentmindedly beside her table mat. Her ring was a corker and Beth couldn't imagine how they had missed it at Pa's birthday. Of course, there had been a lot going on that day.

'Doing well, doing well. Gravity Financial Services looks like it is going to be a winner. Accounts up over 20% since April.' Freddie roared, pressing his sausage-like fingers to his lips to stifle a belch. 'Everyone's happy. Very happy.'

Freddie leant across the table and grabbed the dish of leftover crumble. Beth watched as he took the spoon and offered some to her father before finishing the rest, scraping it into his own bowl before returning the serving dish to the table.

'Course, we are only a small concern, less than a dozen employees. Pass the cream, please, Beth,' he said with a genial smile.

'Come on, Beth,' said Ma, 'don't just sit there with your mouth open. Pass the cream.'

Max, who was nearest the jug, handed the cream to Freddie before continuing to ask her mother about an orchid he had been given.

'No, no, no, no, couldn't possibly.'

Beth watched Freddie swab his face with a handkerchief he'd slowly pulled from his pocket like a conjurer.

'Family defo a no-no. Only under extraordinary circs. Investments go down as well as up, you know. Couldn't take the chance,' continued Freddie, rolling back in his seat so he could stuff his handkerchief back into his trouser pocket. 'Though we are doing particularly well. I mean, there's ...'

For a moment, Beth fancied she saw a wolf-like flash, but then Freddie resumed his usual expression of candid bonhomie.

'Thought we'd celebrate quarters end. We're off to New York next week on Concorde. Thought I'd give my beautiful wife a treat.' Freddie gazed across the table at Tina with admiration, then glanced at Beth and winked.

Beth turned away in horror. 'So, what are you going to get up to in New York, Tina?'

'Unfortunately, Freddie has some meetings. As the weather forecast isn't great, I'd hoped we might just hole up in the hotel room and ignore the Big Apple, but I will just have to brace the weather and go shopping to amuse myself.'

'What's good for the goose is good for the gander,' Freddie chortled.

'Well, you'd be a silly goose for not getting out and exploring the city. What an opportunity,' said Ma.

After dinner, in the drawing room, Ma was telling Beth how long she needed to boil marmalade. Beth glanced at the clock. Tina stifled a yawn, her red nails catching the light from the fire. Beth slithered forward to the edge of her chair, leaned over, and slipped her demi-tasse onto the black and gold tray her mother favoured for after-dinner coffee.

'Max, we should make a move.' said Beth.

'What do you think, Tina? You've hardly said a word all evening,' Ma asked.

'I think Beth's right,' said Tina. That'd be a first, thought Beth. 'We should get going. It's getting late. We can't leave Bitsy alone for too long.'

'So, the nurse said she'd let me know by lunchtime!' Max finished up his anecdote.

'How amusing,' said Freddie as though he had heard the joke a hundred times.

'Bravo!' Pa slapped Max on the back with approval as though he had never heard the story before. Tina would probably accuse Pa of being false or hypocritical, but Pa was an indulgent host. He had been indoctrinated in the language of social particulars and wouldn't let one of the boys feel a fool.

'All right, darling.' Max added, waving his glass in her direction as she rose from her chair.

'Come on then,' she said, returning from the hall a moment later.

'My driver speaks, and lo, I obey!' Max swallowed the tail end of his whisky, plonked his glass down on the tray and took the coat that Beth was holding out to him.

Tina and Freddie also made to follow them out. Freddie still talking to her father, shaking his hand as they said their 'goodbyes'.

'Well, come in, come into the office, by all means ... We can have lunch.' Beth heard Freddie say to her father as she and Max walked through to the hall.

'I do hope your father doesn't do anything foolish.' Max said to her as they drove down the drive and out through the gates onto the main road. 'Crumble was delicious, wasn't it?'

Tina

The flight was fabulous. First, there was the Concord Lounge, which was very sleek and splendid. The plane was already at the gate, an aerodynamic, white dart.

'Pretty smart, eh?' said Freddie, sipping the complimentary champagne as we looked at the sleek plane through the floor-to-ceiling windows. Free champagne, Max, you'd have loved it.

I looked around, the other passengers were mainly polished businessmen, but there were a couple of families, glamorous parents, and well-dressed children. I wondered who would pay for their kids to fly on Concord?

The plane was tiny, with only two narrow seats on each side of the aisle. There was hardly room for Freddie to stand or to sit. He had to squeeze in next to me. We each were given a pack of Concord memorabilia, a pen, a notepad etc., in a folder, all very stylish. And then we took off with a woosh. The flight was noisy but so smooth and so high. Looking out, I could see the curve of the earth. At first, I thought it was distortion from the window, but no, the captain announced, we were so far above the earth we could see its arc. It was the most extraordinary thing.

'Out of this world,' said Freddie.

The flight took hardly any time, only a couple of hours.

'No time to get jet lag,' said Freddie, and he was right.

While we were in New York, we stayed at The Mark. I did some sightseeing and spent some time exploring 5th Avenue, while Freddie was hobnobbing with companies he thought might be interested in his fund. Most of our evenings, we met up with friends of Freddie, but for our final night in New York, Freddie took me to dinner at The Rainbow Room, high up in the Rockefeller Building, up on the 65th floor. I was wearing one of the new dresses I'd bought at Henri Bendel's. We were sat by the window. I don't know how Freddie got the best seat in the house, but somehow, he always did. The view was dazzling, so many lights, so many iconic skyscrapers.

'Looking lovely, my darling,' said Freddie kissing my fingertips. We turned to look out of the window together. 'It's a helluva town,'

Successful trip?' I asked.

'Very.' Freddie grinned back. He took a slug of the Californian chardonnay. 'It's going to be a decent year. I mean, we'll see if everything that has been pledged is realised, but I have a good feeling about things. We can only go up from here. This year is going to be fantastic.'

'Amazing.' I pushed my salad around a bit. 'If the fund is doing so well, should we put some of our own money in?'

'Double down on the business? We could ... generally, it wouldn't be considered sensible to have all one's eggs in the same basket, but the markets are doing tremendously well currently.'

'Well, I do have a tiny amount of savings. I don't think I've mentioned it before, but I'd like to put them into your fund.'

'Endorse the old boy, eh?' Freddie wiped his mouth with his napkin as the waiter removed his empty plate. 'Well, I would be flattered by your belief in me and honoured to oversee your investment if you were to place it in my care.'

The savings account had all the bits and pieces which you, Max, had given me over the years. I don't know why you thought I needed paying off. You could have convinced me by telling me my silence would prevent my family from being hurt. Needless to say, I had not talked about you, you and me, that is, to Freddie. Once it was over, I realised it was all too sordid to speak of. I was too embarrassed. Anyway, Freddie didn't seem too interested in what I'd been up to before I met him. Our lives were all about the here and now. I never asked him about his past, either. Freddie only told me he had grown up not really knowing his parents, who remained in South Africa while he was sent to a beastly boarding school in England.

I thought of the old savings account as money for Laura. I had saved all those payments - your bribes, Max. They sat, slowly growing, untouched. Now, I thought, if I could put that money somewhere where it could get a decent income and reinvest the dividends, I could build something extra-special to give to Laura one day.

Dishes

'Glasses first, please,' Beth called through the open door. She could hear Max stacking crockery.

'Good to see your parents,' he said, returning with some dishes. 'Wish it didn't stress you out quite so much.'

'I wasn't stressed,' said Beth. 'Why would I be stressed?'

She took the plates from him and began putting them in the dishwasher, discretely rearranging those that Max had already loaded. Honestly, any idiot could see that wasn't the optimal place to put side plates. Did Max really think she enjoyed playing this sort of game?

'Where is Laura? Shouldn't she be here, helping,' he asked, smiling broadly. He had been watching her rearrange the plates. 'Has she run off to her room at the sight of all this washing up?'

'You know she has to study for her exams.'

It was the Easter holidays, and Beth had asked her parents to come to them as Laura was home. The darling golden-haired sprite who Beth adored had begun metamorphosising into an adult, and it was not an easy transition. Laura had dyed her hair black, still a natural colour, so permitted by the school, and taken to being taciturn and undemonstrative. Beth ached for the hugs and laughter that used to fill the house when Laura was home. Instead, the charged silence that radiated from Laura's bedroom made Beth tiptoe in her own house.

'Hm. Shall I make a start on the hand washing?' Max had brought through some serving dishes.

'Thank you, darling, but do you mind? I'd rather. Could you collect all the glasses? I'll do them first.'

Max would fill the sink with soapy water and clean the frying pan first, then wonder why everything else was covered in a fine layer of grease. And Beth would have to rewash everything when he wasn't looking. Reading medicine, he must have covered some basic science. She supposed it was a long time ago now.

'Dennis seemed to have aged somewhat,' Max said as he left the room.

'Pa?'

'But your mother doesn't age a bit. She was on fine form, as usual,' he said, returning with sherry glasses from the sitting room. 'Though you'd never know if she wasn't. She'd rather die than let on if she had a broken leg or if you had put out the wrong forks.'

Beth blanched. Had she? Of course, she hadn't. She scowled at Max.

'Don't worry, it was all perfect, darling. It went very well. The right forks, in the right place, at the right time,' he added, giving her a kiss before returning, smiling, to the chaos of the dining room.

Beth put on her rubber gloves while hot water filled the washing-up bowl in the sink, bubbles rising. Max returned with more debris.

'Not there, darling, that's where I'm going to drain the glasses.'

'Bit worried about what your father said about Freddie's venture. I thought the family had agreed not to invest.'

'I thought so too. As Tina's investment is doing so well, he must be tempted.' Beth stood the tall glasses upside down on the drainer. 'She did look fabulous last week, didn't she? Gorgeous tan.'

'Must say I can't see what she sees in him,' said Max. 'I shudder just thinking about him touching her.'

'Freddie? I guess, after all those years of gadding around, she wants some security.' Beth knew what Max meant, there was something distasteful about Freddie, something vaguely greasy.

'Ha! you mean --'

'Don't pre-suppose what I mean!' Beth did not sound as shocked as she'd wanted to. Tina *had* flitted around for years as if trying to complete some Sisyphean task: to find the right man. Beth was glad Tina was settled now with Freddie; whatever Beth's own impressions might be. He had come along with his large personality and solid bulk. He had given her the security she must crave, the lifestyle she coveted, and that ring! They had the house in Chelsea that had so much potential. They did the season, the flower show, Henley, and Wimbledon, where Tina wore such fabulous outfits. Beth had seen the photos.

Of course, it had been different for Beth. She had been lucky. She had met Max early on and she'd never felt the need to look around, to cast her glance further. One was enough, and Max had proved, well, almost perfect.

Tina

Beth had been angling for an invite for tea at the house, but Freddie and I hadn't had a chance yet to do the work on it we wanted. It was mine, and Freddie was mine. I didn't want to see my idyll reflected in Beth's cynical eyes and know she would hurry back to tell you all about it. Beth was up in town to pick up some school uniform for Laura from John Lewis, so I suggested Beth join me when I took Bitsy for his walk and then we could get a cup of tea at the Serpentine Café. We met outside the Queensway tube station and walked into the park towards the Round Pond.

'Can you walk in those heels?' asked Beth as we set off.

'These? These are normal,' I said. 'Just wedges.' I let Bitsy off his lead. 'How's Laura?'

'Fine. She's really enjoying her new school and seems to have taken to boarding like a duck to water. Quite a relief.' It was unseasonably warm. Beth loosened her scarf; it had turned into a beautiful afternoon. 'Of course, I miss not having her at home. Children are such a joy …. even a teenager.'

'Ah…' Did Beth really know the meaning of the word *miss*? I had missed Laura every day of her life; when I had a moment that is. And of course, I wouldn't know if children were a joy to have at home, though if we ever got the house fixed up, I would be able to offer Laura a place to stay.

'You ... you're not tempted to, er, have a baby ... with Freddie?'

'No, I'm not sure I have the patience. And Freddie's not interested, it's not on the cards.'

'Oh! Don't you mind?' I mean. 'Wouldn't you – every woman wants … don't they?'

'No, only you. It's every woman's right to choose. Freddie let me know before we married.' I was glad to clear the air. I knew Beth had been dying to ask me for ages. I had seen her struggle to find the right moment. Her words were clumsy, as if they had been stuck on the tip of her tongue for too long. 'My previous experience of pregnancy wasn't exactly … rosy,' I added.

'Ah, no, I suppose not,' said Beth. 'Good that Freddie was upfront …'

'Freddie has been totally honest with me.'

'Lovely to have a puppy then.' Beth gestured towards Bitsy. 'Won't he run off?'

'No! He's very friendly. He's little, so he doesn't go far. He always comes back.'

'Who will look after him when you are in Milan?'

'Freddie will take care of him. I'm only going for a long weekend to see the girls.'

'Your usual trip. It's good you've managed to keep up those friendships over the years. You were so young when you went out. All your friends will have ended up doing different things.'

'Yes, there is a lawyer and an architect in the group, and another started out as a buyer for one of the large stores but has crossed over to work at one of the big design ateliers.'

'And how's Freddie and his fund?'

'All good, thanks. Freddie's very busy at the moment. He's got something big coming up.'

'But he'll be able to look after the dog?' asked Beth.

'So he says and he's not let me down yet.' Beth could be so tiresome.

We had circumnavigated the pond and walked in amongst the striped deckchairs near the bandstand. Bitsy was scrabbling around beneath the chair of someone trying to have a sandwich. I called him over, and we moved to walk under the trees, away from the groups of people enjoying the sun. Beth didn't ask me what I had achieved or how my career had panned out. I didn't ask her how hers had gone, either. We knew everything we wanted to know about each other. Neither of us needed to go over tedious, contentious ground. We neared the Albert Memorial and turned towards the café by the Serpentine.

'How's the house?' Beth asked.

'Fine,' I said. 'How's yours?'

We walked on. After a while, Bitsy came and walked beside us. I picked him up, it was hot, and he was exhausted.

'Gosh, we have been lucky with the weather,' said Beth, as though there wasn't anything else left to say.

Bust

Max and Beth had been summoned to Nether Place on their own. Instead of joining them, Laura had gone to spend the day with a friend. Just as well, thought Beth; despite the cheerful sunshine, lunch had turned out to be a sombre affair. Pa was not there to greet them as usual, only appearing when Mrs Simms sounded the gong.

Ma was overly bright. She asked Max to get drinks as Dennis was indisposed.

'He'll be joining us shortly. Just got some papers from F & P to see to,' Ma explained.

Ma could talk fascinatingly about nothing to anyone forever and be glamorous and entertaining throughout.

'I was going to give you pheasant for lunch, and then I remembered I didn't have any quince jelly, and your father doesn't like one without the other,' Ma said.

It was impossible for Beth to break through her defences and find out what was going on. When Pa did appear, he was more reserved than usual but accepted the whisky Max poured for him to take into lunch. Throughout the meal Pa, normally not one to waste time or words, would start a sentence but never quite get to the point.

'The thing is ...' Pa started before tucking into his plate of sea bass. 'I mean, if only I'd ...'

'Pa, are you feeling all right?' Beth asked as the conversation petered out. Her father looked depleted somehow. There seemed to be less of him. He was sunk lower in his chair and shuffled his cutlery in his large hands as if he had forgotten what it was for.

'Would you like some salt, Beth?' said Ma. 'You know your father has had so much to think about,'

Beth passed the salt dish, a blob of clay with a thumbed indent, that Laura had made in Primary school.

'Thinking about what?' said Max. 'This is an excellent Chardonnay, by the way.'

'Good, good, glad you like it. Well, I should have ...' Pa continued. 'I could have ...'

'Could have?' asked Beth. 'Could have what?'

After lunch, Ma disappeared to the kitchen to get coffee. In the drawing room, Max and Beth settled next to each other on the sofa across from Pa, who sat supported by his large wingback chair. Pa concentrated on the wine glass he had brought through from lunch, which he spun in a desultory manner.

'The thing is,' Pa said. 'I've been asked to stand down from F & P.' The glass in his hand spun faster. 'I've made a few hasty decisions and been asked to go.'

'What?' said Beth. 'But your father started the company with Mr Farthingale's father.'

'That doesn't count for much now, it seems,' said Pa. 'But as consolation, if I go quietly, I can name someone in the family to replace me on the board.'

'Oh,' said Beth. Was this the moment, the moment her father would acknowledge her?

'That's why I wanted to ask you, Max, if you would be prepared to take my place.'

'Oh,' said Beth. She couldn't believe it, but Pa looked so shattered she couldn't bring herself to object. It was true, if she had found some other work that had added to her C.V., as everyone had suggested, instead of descending into a monumental strop that rivalled one of Laura's, Beth would be in a stronger position and might feel she could complain. But she had always known that without Pa's endorsement she would never be asked on the board at F & P and Pa had made perfectly clear that Beth was never going to get that whatever she did.

'Well,' said Max. 'It really ought to be Beth, don't you think?'

Pa looked out the window.

'If there are any issues at F & P, Beth would be the one to make sense of it,' said Max. 'She's a qualified accountant and has worked at the company. I'm a consultant, a surgeon. I don't know anything about business.'

'It's true, there have been some accounting irregularities,' said Pa, his gaze returning to the unlit fire.

'Oh, Pa, what has been going on?' asked Beth. If Pa had raised money against the value of F & P shares, he and the family owned, that was one thing, but if he had used company funds, that would be a disaster.

'But I feel this is a job for a man,' said Pa. 'Someone with grit, who can stand up to the board. I thought of Duncan, of course, but I know he won't come, not even for an emergency. He's not interested in what's been built here.'

'What's happened, Pa?' asked Beth. Her heart was sinking. As she listened to what her father was saying, she thought about all the missing words. What had her father done? What had the board said? Did her father really believe she couldn't handle this, or did he still think the fault lay with the board who would be more inclined to take a man seriously? She looked at her father; he looked so old and vulnerable. She couldn't ask, now was not the moment.

'You know I put some capital in with Freddie's fund? My investment in Gravity Financial Services was doing very well. I had some strong dividend returns.'

'Until you didn't,' said Beth.

'Yes, that's the sum of it. Freddie suggested I invest more. He said the bigger investors were making bigger returns.'

'You didn't borrow from F & P, did you, Pa?'

'Well, Freddie said, we were bound to make a big return. Just a matter of time.'

'How much did you lose?' asked Beth.

'Too much.' The room went quiet. 'Everything,' said Pa looking up from his shoes. 'Anyway, I haven't been able to get hold of Freddie. I spoke to him last week, and he said not to worry, he would redeem my investment, said it might take a couple of days. He'll probably be back in the office on Monday.'

'And Tina is away, isn't she?' said Beth. 'It's her annual trip to stay with her girlfriends in Milan. She doesn't get back till later in the week.'

'Yes, couldn't be worse timing.'

'Oh, Pa,' said Beth. 'You could say it couldn't be better timing.' Her father looked as grey as she felt.

Max sat very still beside her, and then he reached out and held her hand.

'Have you told Ma?' Beth asked.

'No, no need to worry your mother. I'll give Freddie a ring on Monday. I'm sure he'll be able to explain everything. Probably just a glitch in the system.'

Beth thought they'd be lucky if they ever saw Freddie again, he was probably gone for good.

Hospital Run

'He'll be fine, you'll see,' said Ma. 'Strong as an ox.'

Beth was driving Ma to the hospital. Pa had been taken in.

She had been due to visit her parents that day. So, when she got the call, she only needed to whizz around the house, locking the doors before collecting up all the bits and pieces laid out for her to take with her. The traffic was atrocious. You never knew how it would be, but today of all days, at this time. Irritated by the argumentative commentary on the radio, Beth listened to one of Laura's old audiobooks; it was the only CD she could find in the car with one eye on the road. When she had first heard this story, Beth had thought she could listen to the mellifluous voice for hours. Now, she wasn't so sure. Although the familiarity of the soothing tones washed over her like a rolling tide, trying to pull her into the story, Beth's anxiety about Pa kept breaking through. A sharp flint on the beach impervious to the action of the waves. If she breathed deeply, she felt a restriction in her chest and a sob would bubble up. Beth sighed to swallow the ache and willed the traffic to move forward. Finally, she reached the Crawley exit. In the end, the journey only took about five minutes longer than usual.

At Nether Place, Ma was waiting for her on the front doorstep. Beth got out of the car and opened the passenger door for her mother. Beth hoped that if she could ensure all the little things went smoothly, then perhaps the big thing would also work out.

'He was fine at breakfast,' Ma said as Beth nudged the car out into the traffic at the end of the drive. 'Mentioned he was feeling a bit tired. He said he'd spend the morning reading the paper and not take his usual constitutional. Go out after lunch when he felt up to it.'

'When did you realise something was wrong?' asked Beth.

'When I took him his coffee.'

Elevenses were always taken at ten-thirty at Nether Place. Beth had never asked why.

'I went into the study, he looked a little grey,' said Ma. 'As I put down his coffee on his desk, I asked him how he was. He said he felt a tightness. I didn't like the sound of that, so I phoned the surgery. They sent an ambulance round straight away.'

'What did the paramedics say?'

'Very helpful, asked whether your father was a DNR.'

'Do not resuscitate?'

'Yes, that's right, the young man explained as they took your father out to the ambulance.' said Ma. 'It was quite alarming. Your father told them he was perfectly fine and could walk, but they sat him in a wheelchair and fitted an oxygen mask on him. It distorted his face. He didn't look right.' Ma pulled a handkerchief out of the bag on her lap, dabbed at the corner of her eyes, before folding and putting it back, snapping the bag shut. 'I told them, of course they must resuscitate. It's just a blip. He was fine at breakfast.'

Whatever Ma said, Pa had not looked great lately. He had seemed to be carrying a layer of grey under his skin. The bankruptcy had destroyed him, and the family were crippled financially. Beth couldn't stop wondering if Pa had allowed her that seat on the board, could she have made a difference. She should have fought harder for the role. She could never decide if it had been a test and if she had persevered her father would have seen her determination and supported her, but perhaps he would never have been persuaded that she could do the job. In the end it was her choice to stay at home. Beth took a deep breath and concentrated on the road.

They drove through the market town, and Beth picked up the blue 'H' signs that took them to the hospital. At reception, they were told Mr Parteger had been taken by ambulance to the General.

They got back in the car.

'Really, I can't think why there's all this fuss,' said Ma. 'But, I suppose, at the General, he will get better care.'

By now, it was school run time, and the roads were busy. Beth tried not to drive too fast because she didn't want to seem anxious and worry Ma, but also not to drive too slowly because she was anxious and wanted to get there.

At last, they broke through the town and got on the by-pass, only to hit rush hour traffic. By the time they arrived, it was visiting time at the General, and Beth circled the hospital car park twice before she decided to leave the car in an unmarked space at the end of a line of legally parked cars. Beth felt exhausted and they hadn't even found her father yet.

At reception they were asked to wait. A doctor would see them directly. Beth suggested they go to the café and get some tea and a sandwich.

'But we'll miss the doctor,' said Ma. 'We should wait here for him like the receptionist said.'

After half an hour, sitting in the draft from the main door, Beth went to find the café to get some takeaway teas. She used double cups, but even so, her fingers were getting quite uncomfortable by the time she reached her mother back in reception and the sandwiches she was carrying pressed under her arm looked squashed and unappetising.

'No sign of the doctor?' Beth asked, passing her mother one of the cups. 'I'll go and see if the receptionist can tell us what's holding things up.'

'Good idea,' said Ma taking a sip of her tea. 'I can't imagine what might be keeping him.'

'Any moment,' Beth said when she returned from the reception desk.

Another twenty minutes passed before Beth saw a white-coated doctor approaching them down the corridor, her coat flapping, her heels clicking. She looked sombre but moved with purpose, stalking towards them down the hall. She could be for anybody; she could be on her way anywhere. Beth watched as the doctor went to reception and the girl behind the desk pointed in Beth and Ma's direction. The doctor turned and slowly crossed the hall towards them, bringing with her a scented cloud of disinfectant.

'Mrs Parteger? I'm Doctor Bradley, I've been treating your husband.' The doctor was apologetic. 'We tried everything, but ... Mr Parteger had a second heart attack in the ambulance on the way here. By the time he reached us ... there was nothing we could do.' The doctor finished speaking. Beth took Ma's hand.

'But that can't be,' her mother said. 'He was perfectly fine at breakfast.'

Wake

The last time they had all been at Nether Place together, the day had been dry and clear. There were high, wispy clouds that looked as though they would rather be somewhere else, in someone else's sky, with someone happier. It was too good a day to have such sad business to attend to. Beth watched the hearse leaving, wheels scrunching, bearing Pa over the gravel for one last time as his coffin was carried to the church. They followed in the hired limos with dark-tinted windows. Beth, Duncan, and Tina with Ma in the first car. Max with Gareth, and Laura in the other.

During the service, Duncan gave the eulogy. He spoke about how Pa had dedicated his life to his family and Farthingale and

Parteger. Pa had caught the tail end of the war and afterwards stayed on in the Royal Engineers. He had been stationed in Cyprus. Pa was in his late twenties when his father died. He returned home and joined the family firm. It was about this time that he met Ma, Esme, May-May to the grandchildren. Dennis had been taken by a friend to a concert in London. There was a spare ticket; someone had dropped out. Unmusical Dennis shouldn't have been there. Shouldn't have been the one to meet the exotic, beautiful piano soloist, but he had. They had had a long and happy marriage, an enviable union. Pa had been a lifelong, upstanding, and engaged member of the local community. Duncan told some charming anecdotes. He didn't mention money, the family fortunes, or Dennis' subsequent heart attack.

Stepping out of the cold church into the colder March air, Beth's sharp heels stabbed through the icy gravel of the path. She was wearing the shoes that Tina had given her for her fortieth. Beth hadn't worn them before. She wasn't sure that this was the right moment, but they would give her the confidence to face the day, to meet any F & P shareholders who might turn up. Beth wanted to feel empowered. If only her toes didn't feel like ice, crushed into the sharp points of the shoes. As it was, she had only seen young Mr Farthingale in the distance, in the church; she hadn't seen him later.

The family followed the vicar as the pallbearers carried Pa, out of the church. Ma supported by Duncan went ahead of Beth and Max. Tina accompanied the children. The rest of the mourners trailed behind as they crossed the uneven grass to reach the Parteger plot. They lined up by the grave, awkward in their distress. Ma looked frail; Duncan had her hand tucked into the crook of his elbow. Tina, her head swathed in an elegant veil, stood beside them. Even on this day, Beth felt infuriated by her sister. Tina looking so chic was an affront. She should appear contrite after all the family had been through because of Freddie. Beth held tight to Max's arm. The congregation gathered around them, heads bowed, faces hidden beneath dark hats, scarves pulled by the fitful breeze, tissues in hand. Beth had thought there would be no crying. In the past weeks, she had shed more tears for Pa than she thought possible, but here she was, weeping again. Max, beside her, put an arm around her.

After the burial, they thanked the vicar, shaking hands in turn. By the time they were on the move, Beth's toes had become stiff blocks that burned as she walked back to the car. Duncan held Ma's hand. He held on to her as if she might be caught by the gusting wind and be blown away.

When they returned to the house for the wake, Beth saw Laura and Gareth slink away into the garden. She followed Duncan and Ma up the steps to the front door. Everything outside, in the garden and the wide world beyond, was the same, just as it had always been, startlingly indifferent to Pa's passing. Nether Place, however, seemed bereft. There was a crumbling chip in the stone threshold, and as the door opened and the panes of glass flashed in the fitful sun, in the corner of one, a distortion of the refracted light drew Beth's eye to a small crack that she hadn't noticed before. Nether Place seemed to be falling apart without Pa there.

Duncan settled Ma in the old wing chair next to the fire, Pa's chair. From that comfortable spot, Ma received the friends and tenants who had come to pay their last respects. Duncan hovered nearby protectively. Beth and Mrs Simms circulated with canapés amongst the mourners who gathered in clumps around the drawing room. Max handed out drinks. Tina stationed herself by the French window, cigarette in hand, letting the smoke drift out through the open door. Tina held herself aloof. She was sleek in black; her veil had been discarded but she still looked elegant. Tina seemed to be holding herself apart as if to observe the room, but today, the day to mark their father's life, Tina was being kept separate by the family. Since Freddie had vanished, Beth had barely spoken to Tina. Beth found she could not countenance her sister without thinking of the pain Freddie had caused. Beth thought her views about what had happened would soften, but the truth was keeping Tina at a distance was an easy habit to maintain. Now, as she looked at her sister silhouetted in the window frame, Beth felt a pang of guilt.

When, at last, the last guest had left, Max sank into the threadbare Georgian sofa by the fire near Ma.

'Okay?' he asked Ma.

'Like something a little stronger than tea, Ma? A sherry?' asked Duncan. He was standing next to the drinks' cabinet. 'Max?'

Ma shook her head, but Max said, 'Yes.'

Duncan tinkered with the bottles and glasses, then approached, and handed Max a whisky before joining him on the sofa with his own drink.

'Beth, can't you stop?' Tina said.

Beth was collecting plates and glasses that had been abandoned around the room. Tina tossed her finished cigarette butt out onto the terrace, slunk over to the drinks cabinet, and made herself a gin.

'Are you going to the kitchen to weep over the washing up?' Tina asked Beth as she returned to her place by the window and began rummaging in her bag.

'Won't take a minute. I won't be able to relax until this is out of sight,' said Beth, determined not to respond. She piled the dirty cups onto a tray on the sofa table.

'You shouldn't worry.' Duncan said. 'Mrs Simms said she would be back in the morning to clear everything up.'

Beth watched Tina balance her glass on the table by the window. Beth hated minding, but she hoped the glass filled with ice was dry and wouldn't leave a ring. Tina lit another cigarette, picked up her gin, took a sip, and stared out into the garden. As Beth circled nearby, looking for any remaining glasses, she could hear the children's voices through the open window; they must be nearby. Beth wondered if Tina was watching them.

'I just want everything to stop. To stand still for a moment.' Tina drew in her extended arm, pale and blue-veined, and inhaled.

'Keeping busy takes my mind off things,' said Beth. Tina suddenly looked weary, defeated in her isolation, and sullied by cigarette ash.

'Martha and Mary,' said Ma. She turned to Duncan. 'Actually, darling, I think I would like that drink.'

'What'll it be?' said Duncan pushing himself up from the complaining sofa.

'A G & T, thank you, darling,' Ma said.

'I'll have one too,' said Beth. 'I'll take this through and be back and join you.'

When Beth returned from the kitchen, she brought a plate of leftover canapes. Duncan was back on the sofa by Max, and Ma had her drink. Beth noticed how her mother sat; her ankles crossed, her fine hands held the glass, which caught the light from the fire and sparkled as if it were a jewel, but her eyes were dull. We are all falling in on ourselves she thought. Pa has gone, and we have lost our rudder. Beth gave her mother first choice of the nibbles before placing the plate on the coffee table.

'Why didn't you bring Robin? It's about time we all met,' Ma asked Duncan.

'We thought about it, but I wasn't sure this was the right occasion.' said Duncan, looking into the remnants of his whisky. 'As it is, I will have to fly back tomorrow.'

They sat in silence, the ice tinkling in their glasses as they sipped their drinks. After a moment Ma spoke. 'You know, I think I might go upstairs and have a rest before supper.' She placed her half-finished drink on the table beside her. 'Today has been very wearing.'

'Of course, Ma,' said Duncan.

Duncan escorted Ma from the room. At the threshold, she looked back.

'You know, I can't believe he's gone,' Her hand touching her pearls. 'He promised he'd always be there, that he'd always look after me.' Then she slowly turned, and Duncan helped her up the stairs.

Beth joined Max by the fire, curling up beside him, letting his presence comfort her. The killer shoes were already there, tucked under the sofa where she had kicked them as soon as they had returned to the house. Max took her hand in his, their fingers interlaced.

'I don't know why Duncan didn't bring Robin over. It might have cheered Ma up. Meeting her would have been a distraction,' said Beth.

Tina turned back into the room and stared at Beth.

'Oh, for goodness sake, Beth, you're such an idiot,' said Tina. 'Do you have to have everything spelt out to you? It's obvious - Robin's a he! Didn't you know? You must have known.'

Beth felt a wave of knowledge wash over her.

'Oh,' said Beth. They sat in silence. Max squeezed her fingers. How foolish she felt.

'Did you know?' she asked him.

'Suspected it,' he said with a nod.

'You never said.'

'Well … what was there to say.'

Beth turned back to the fire and watched the flames flickering, dancing this way and that changing from one shape to another. The more she thought about it, the more obvious it was. How had she not known? She should have asked. She sighed, she never seemed to notice the important things. How thoughtless of her. Why hadn't Duncan told her? Then she thought, perhaps he's tried. But Max was right, what did it matter. Duncan was her brother and she'd love him whatever. Beth wondered if her parents had guessed, despite Duncan's efforts to obfuscate. Now, it was too late to ask Pa, not that she was sure how she would have started that conversation.

With the door open, she could hear the grandfather clock in the hall. Time ticked away. Tina's cigarette smoke circled back into the room.

After a few minutes, she heard Duncan's footsteps returning, becoming louder, as he crossed the hall parquet. Beth wondered if she should say something but knew she couldn't, not now. Apart from being an inappropriate moment, to say anything would give away that she hadn't understood something so elemental about her beloved brother. That she hadn't been aware was a distressing shortcoming, but Beth was also piqued that she wasn't the confidant she thought she might have been.

'Well, what's to be done with the place?' Max asked as Duncan picked up his drink and settled in the chair recently vacated by Ma. Beth and Max had already discussed the possibilities for Nether Place. It had become apparent that Pa had managed to gloss over or ignore the upkeep of the house for several years. Perhaps that was why he had become so entranced by Freddie's get-rich-quick scheme, to get some cash to do up the house. However sentimental the siblings were about the family home, it was an old, neglected house that needed a lot of money spent on it. They all knew the answer.

'I've arranged for a valuer to come Monday, but he'll be hard pushed to find anything worth a farthing. Pa had already gone through everything with a fine-tooth comb,' said Beth sitting up straighter. Pa, trying to hide the worst of his financial problems, had sold off bits of this and pieces of that, anything he could get a price for. It was a wonder they hadn't noticed, but anything of significance had been hidden from view in cupboards and drawers. Now there was nothing of merit left. Poor Duncan, Beth thought, a difficult inheritance, hard decisions. No one wanted brown furniture or the sorts of family odds and ends that remained in the house. The only thing of value was in their memories.

'I shouldn't think there's a complete, untarnished set of anything left,' said Duncan looking over the room. Beth looked up at the rectangular patch of unfaded green wallpaper above the piano. Last year, a family portrait of her great grandparents by some minor Victorian artist had hung there.

'You'll need to sell, I daresay, as quickly as possible,' said Max.

'Surely, we can't sell,' said Tina.

'Surely, we must sell,' countered Duncan.

Beth uncurled her legs. She flexed her feet. They looked vulnerable through the gauze of her stockings, delicate morsels caught in a fine net. She wriggled her toes, the thought of losing Nether Place, losing all the memories – this little piggy has none.

'Either way, it's not your choice to make,' Beth said, standing and returning to her collection of dishes to be taken to the kitchen. 'You already had your inheritance years ago. You don't get to have a say.' Tina had her flat, Beth would get her residual part of the trust. They were immune from the financial burden that was Duncan's lot. But there wouldn't be anything extra.

Beth gathered the remaining coffee cups together for Mrs Simms. They had been tucked away in every corner, hidden behind photographs and ornaments. The lengths people had gone to hide their discarded crockery was extraordinary. She glanced at Tina, who kept her position by the French window. Her lighter clicked as she flicked it off after lighting up yet again. Tina inhaled and, on the out-breath, lifted her chin as if to challenge the room, as if her life depended on it. For a moment, she looked inconceivably haughty, standing on the threshold, her blonde hair glowed warm, her face lifted into the pale sun that sifted through the open doors. Tina's eyes narrowed slightly against the smoke as she exhaled.

'Anything interesting to be sorted? Odd requests?' asked Duncan.

'Nothing untoward,' said Beth turning back towards her brother. 'The bequests for Mrs Simms and Burr are a bit on the stingy side, but if we get a good price for the house and if there is anything left when we've settled with the taxman, we could up that a little.' Beth swept up a final stray cup onto the tray, 'that is if you agree, Duncan?'

'They've looked after the house forever. We couldn't have coped without them.'

'And they've been indispensable, supporting Ma,' said Beth.

'We must make sure Ma has somewhere to live. I'm sure you've all noticed how much she has aged, quite beyond what one might have expected,' said Duncan.

'She has been devastated by Pa's death,' agreed Beth.

'I must say you do seem to be relishing the role of executor, Beth. I'm glad at least Pa had the sense to put you in sole charge of this one thing. I'd never cope from the other side of the world.'

'The solicitors have been very helpful. On the subject of where Ma should live, I thought we might be able to do up Burr's old cottage, once he's left, for Ma, finances allowing.' Beth paused and looked at her watch. 'We'll need to get going soon. Max has work tomorrow, and I'll need to get Laura back to school.'

The chatter of the children had grown louder and now filtered into the room from the garden with the late afternoon sunshine.

'What about you, Tina? What are you going to do next?' Duncan asked.

'I will go back to the flat and wait.'

'You've still had no word from … Freddie, then?' Duncan asked.

Tina stubbed out her cigarette on the outer stone frame of the window and threw the butt away amongst the lavender. She turned slowly back into the room.

'No,' she said, flicking her hair. 'Nothing.'

'For the best, probably. It was a turn-up for the books finding out that house of his was only rented. It must have been difficult for you to discover the locks had changed when you got back from Milan. Must have been pretty rough. At least you are not on the streets, with your flat on in Earls Court. And you have your ring.'

'Zirconia,' said Tina tossing her fingers, so the ring caught the afternoon light.

'Ah …' Duncan finished his whisky in a gulp and placed his tumbler carefully onto a matching, pre-stained cup ring on the wooden table beside him. None of them wanted to talk about it.

Beth and Duncan couldn't face the impossibility of Tina's financial situation. She had brought it on herself, after all. She was young enough and able enough to get a job; they were not liable for her finances. It was she who had put them and their mother in a risky situation. Ma was their responsibility.

'I'd better call Gareth in. I need to return him to Meredith before nightfall, and she turns into a witch.' He laughed as he struggled out of the sofa. 'Not really.' Duncan added with a grimace.

'We'd best be heading back to the real world too,' said Max standing.

Beth felt a surge of pride in Max, still so fit and healthy. She slipped her hand into the crook of his arm, and they exchanged a smile before joining Duncan, who was now with Tina at the French window.

The garden looked idyllic. Burr had appeared briefly at the reception and given Ma an awkward bow before retreating to the walled garden. He had worked hard to perfect the lawns for Major Parteger's last day. They looked out now, calling for the children. Beth had always loved this view, the interaction of shadow and sun on the grass. Looming fingers of darkness created by the shadow of the huge cedar were slowly inching over the lawn as the sun progressed, as though catching on individual blades of grass.

Gareth must have seen his father as he came quickly back to the house, his long legs striding up towards them as if eager to be gone now the day was done. Beth had not registered how tall Gareth had become; he was almost the same height as Duncan. She wondered what the cousins had got up to in the garden. The families had spent so many summers together in Ma's beautiful wonderland. The days were filled with picnics, dens were built in the woods, and they had mucked about in a dingy on the lake and romped across sunlit lawns. Seeing them now, for a moment at a distance, she realised they weren't children anymore. Laura seemed to change every day, and Gareth was thinking about university. Beth knew he had taken his SATS and was applying to study in the States. She wondered what Meredith thought about that.

This would have been a farewell tour for Laura and Gareth, to say goodbye to their favourite haunts. They knew the house would be sold, and this was their last chance. Beth watched Laura trickle back up to the house. She dawdled behind her older cousin as if reluctant to leave the smooth, green lawns of childhood behind.

Debts

Beth heard a car's engine and, standing by the frame of the window, peeled back the curtain. Tina stood wavering on the gravel, her sharp heels intermittently dropping between the pebbles. She grabbed her bag from the back seat and drew a note from it to give the driver. Tina gave the car door a shove; it banged shut. Then she picked up the little dog that was moseying about on the front lawn. The taxi reversed out the front gate.

'Darling, will you get the door? I'll put the kettle on,' Beth said. 'It's Tina. We have a long afternoon ahead of us.' She turned to him. 'Listen, if she gets ... you know ... I always seem to manage to say the wrong thing.'

Since their father's funeral, Beth found Tina increasingly unbearable. She was unfriendly and a grating reminder of the dreadful Freddie. There was something unattractive about Tina being so needy and yet so ungrateful at the same time. And she couldn't be eating enough; Tina had passed from slender to gauzy but was now scrawny. Beth couldn't say anything without her remark being taken by Tina as criticism or an insult. Now, Beth only saw Tina when they were both with their mother. While they sought probate, Ma had moved to a rented, rather uninspiring, but adequate newbuild in the village. The last time Beth had visited, and Tina had been there, Beth had realised that Tina was trying to get her mother to pay for something or other. Beth had had to step in. Ma had nothing as it was. Beth felt so annoyed that Tina wasn't helping herself but scrounging off the rest of the family. It wasn't on.

'I'm so worried about her,' Ma said. 'I wish she'd eat properly. I'm trying to cook her lunch once or twice a week, but she just messes with her food. I even asked Doctor Hunter to lunch once when I knew she was coming so he could, well, advise, but she didn't show up. And she's depressed, that's obvious, but what can we do. I can't very well ask the doctor to lunch every day just on the off-chance Tina will be there.'

Nothing we do makes a difference, thought Beth. Everything we have tried has been rebuffed. Tina ought to get a job and, stop moping around, pull herself together; no one else could do it for her.

'Don't worry, I can sort her,' Max said as the doorbell rang. 'If she becomes demanding, I can handle her. I've managed before, you know.'

'You are a saint.'

Max answered the door.

With the kettle on, Beth came back through and greeted Tina, who gently dropped Bitsy to the floor and parked her bag on the sofa table.

'Hello,' she said, pecking the air on either side of Beth's cheeks.

Beth smiled. Tina looked gaunt, her eyes large and glassy, but she was beautiful as always, pale, and ethereal, like a porcelain ornament, and she smelled gorgeous. Scent never lingered alluringly around Beth as it did with her sister. Beth glanced at the shaggy, white mophead of a dog and thought how much she despised the horrid, yappy thing.

'Don't worry. He's already *been* outside. He should be alright for a bit.' Tina strolled around the room. Beth glanced out the front bay and wondered where in the front garden the dog had done its worst.

'You've rearranged things,' Tina said, turning to Beth. 'This was in the drawing room at Nether Place, wasn't it?' She ran her fingers along the smooth wood surface of the sofa table.

'Yes,' said Max.

'You said you weren't interested in anything from the house,' said Beth. Why did she sound so defensive? All three of them had had their say at the time. Duncan wanted nothing, living so far away and not relishing the cost of transporting anything across the Atlantic. Tina had said she despised the idea of chopping up their parents' lives and sharing everything out. As her siblings obviously didn't think she deserved anything, Tina wouldn't take anything. She was exasperating.

Beth went to rescue the boiling kettle whose whistle carried down the hall crying for attention like a bawling baby. She wondered what Tina hoped to achieve by coming to the house unannounced. Her arrival felt portentous, as if a miasma lurked in her perfume that would be left behind and wreak havoc. Surely, whatever it was, it wasn't their business anymore. Beth brought the tea tray into the living room and settled down to pass round cups.

'Well, isn't this nice?' she said. Even to her own ears, she sounded just like her mother.

Tina wouldn't sit; she paced the room. Beth could almost hear the cage-bars rattle. The dog followed at Tina's heels, back and forth between the garden window and the door to the hall. Every time she turned at the window, Tina looked as if she would fly away, if only she could. Occasionally, as she passed the sofa table, she would pause and look in her handbag as though to find solace there. She was probably looking for her cigarettes, but Tina knew Beth's rules.

Beth poured a cup of tea for Max and set the cup on the table by his side. It gave her a sense of stability to place it there. She hovered for a moment.

Tina paced. Max sat. Beth lingered. She knew Max was trying to look nonchalant. He was relaxed in his chair, sitting back, his legs stretched out in front of the fire. His elbows on the armrests, his hands clasped. But one finger had escaped his grip and was tapping on his other hand. Beth placed her hand on his shoulder. They were a team.

Beth went back to the tea tray. Why was Tina here? When would Tina start talking about whatever it was, she wanted to say. Beth poured her sister a cup of tea.

'How are things?' Beth asked into the awkwardness that clogged the room. She stopped Tina mid-stride to hand her the cup of tea. 'How is it to be back working at the gallery again?'

Tina paused, took the cup, and looked like she might say something – but said nothing.

'No millefeuille, I'm afraid,' said Beth.

Tina didn't smile, Beth sighed. She watched Tina take a sip of tea, pursing her carmine lips, before abandoning the cup on the sofa table.

'I'm thinking of moving back to Milan,' Tina said making her way to the window, the little dog in her wake. Beth retreated to her chair near Max. She glanced at him, hoping for a conspiratorial nod, a sympathetic smile, but he didn't look at her. Max was nearing sixty, but his face had hardly changed, just as strong, maybe a little looser round the edges as if his features were working free. His eyes were paler now, softer, no longer that startling blue that had entranced her when they first met. He was watching Tina as she crossed and recrossed the room.

Tina stopped in her stride, facing away from them, looking towards the window, and said, 'When we married, Freddie suggested that going forward, we put the finances of any new venture we engaged in together in our joint names.'

'Ah,' said Beth, her mind scrabbling to imagine how large those debts might be.

'What does that mean in practice?' asked Max. 'Does that mean you are liable for Freddie's debts?'

'Well, our joint debts. Obviously, I lost my savings when Freddie absconded with the fund that I had invested in. Apart from that, the rent on the house hadn't been paid for 18 months. Our life together was a mirage. It turned out, everything was on the never, never. Also, Freddie emptied our joint accounts and --'

'Do you know where he is?' asked Max. 'Have you had any news at all?'

'No, probably South Africa. I think he must be there. I know Freddie has some business contacts in Johannesburg. And, of course, the parents he would never speak of.'

Tina looked in her bag, and this time, took out a cigarette and lit up, drawing a long desperate breath before continuing her pacing. Beth watched Max. Max watched Tina. The entire speech Tina had not looked at either of them at all, as she walked, her eyes seemed to trace the picture rail round and round the room.

'I signed anything Freddie asked me to,' announced Tina.

'Such as?' asked Max.

'Oh, well, apart from the house, the cars and the yacht.'

'The yacht!' said Beth.

'Perhaps …,' said Max.

'Oh,' Beth said, blinking at him. 'I seem to have forgotten the sugar.'

None of them took sugar in their tea, but neither Max nor Tina contradicted her. Beth left the room. In the kitchen, she picked up the dishcloth and dried the already dry washing-up that was resting on the draining board from lunch. Beth passed the plates round and round through the cloth in her hands. She looked out the window at the squabbling bluetits busy on the birdfeeder. She always wondered if they were a family group on a mission or individuals all brought together by need, competing for the fat. A yacht? When had Tina and Freddie bought a yacht?

Beth heard the front door slam and a car engine growl. She returned to the sitting room. Max was now hunched, looking at the fire. She collected Tina's undrunk tea with her half-smoked butt, the filter-stained lipstick red, lying abandoned on the saucer and placed it on the tray.

'That didn't go so well then?' she asked.

'Not so well. I told her we couldn't help. It's too much. It isn't going to happen. We have Laura's school fees to pay, and then there'll be university. Tina's on her own. We can't be responsible for her debts; we can't be responsible for Freddie's debts; we can't afford to be. She brought this on herself. I did warn her.' He coughed, pulled out his handkerchief and wiped his nose. 'You don't have to worry, darling; we don't owe her anything.'

'We don't? Good, I guess,' said Beth. Somehow Beth didn't think that was quite true. After all, they had had the joy of Laura, but Max was right, they couldn't pay all her debts and Freddie's as well. Who knew where that would end? They'd be ruined too. 'Was she upset?'

'No more than you'd expect.' For a while, they sat together, staring into the fire.

'I did write her a check to finance her move to Milan.'

'Oh?'

'Not very much, just a couple of thousand. To pay for her flight and so on ...'

'Well, I'm sure that was the right thing to do.' Beth tipped her teacup towards her. She had all but finished; a few tea leaves remained in a soupcon of liquid. What were you supposed to do, turn over the cup, turn it three times on the saucer, pick it up and read your fortune. She was turning the cup for the third time when Beth heard the tip, tip, tap of tiny claws on the hard floor. Tina's little dog entered the room, came towards them, snuffled, and settled on the rug between them. Beth looked at the dog with dismay. Bitsy looked up at Beth and wagged his tail. What was going on, Tina must have made a mistake, could she not afford dog food now. Beth got up and went into the hall. After a moment, she came back.

'I think Tina must have taken your old MG. The keys aren't in the key tray by the door, and there is no sign of the car on the drive.

Tina

Well, Max, who'd have thought you were such a soft touch. But thank you, I suppose. When I got back to London I paid in your cheque and paid off the outstanding bills on the flat. In the morning I set out early.

I drove up to Harrogate before heading out onto the moor. It was a glorious day. The low, early sun sparked tantalising glints through the trees like hope beckoning. I stopped to fill up with petrol on the way and checked that the spare can was full too. I knew your flash sports car would eat up fuel on the long drive.

We had once spent a whole weekend here together. You drove through the night, against the glare of headlights zooming south, to a part of the world where there would be no one that knew us, no one at all.

I almost missed the road. The single track I turned onto was not marked. When you and I came here, you had driven with assurance. Now, it occurred to me that you must have been here before. I wound down the windows and let the cool wind blow away the thoughts of others.

The road was remote and wound up and over the hills. As I drove, I recognised the spot that overlooked the river, where we had stopped for our picnic. It had been a beautiful day that day too. With sunshine filtering through bright green spring leaves that leant over us as we stretched out on the travel rug you spread on the bank.

I drove fast and thought about the past. When we had first met so long ago, I had been enthralled. How my life had changed, things hadn't turned out like I had supposed they would. You had stolen my life and Lara. You had kept from me what was mine through lies and deceit. Were you protecting your reputation or shielding Beth. Would you ever tell her the truth? Beth and I have both been your victims. I drove faster than the road could tolerate. The wheels of the roadster slid over the edge of the tarmac on the bends, spitting out angry waves of gravel.

Freddie rescued me from your conniving. Of all my suitors, he was strong enough, a taker who could take me away from you. But I didn't realise he would take so much. I have lost my family, my home as well as my dreams. I thought I had a future with Freddie. All my hopes have turned to fears. There is nothing left. The tarmac came to an end. You won't help, can't help, who cares which? Beth refuses to engage and turns away from anything conflicting or difficult, as always. I feel I am only half a human being. I have no maternal instinct and despise myself for putting myself before my child. Life is so complicated. I pulled up onto short, sheep-munched grass. At least you and Beth have looked after Lara, and the flat is now secure for her.

I was in a place of such remoteness that I could finally leave my thoughts behind and feel alone. I got out of the car and walked along a track that twisted over the moor, my calves brushing against the tired yellow grass that bowed across my path. I walked as though it were a joy to be alive, walked until my heels were killing me. I heard the lonely cry of a buzzard high above, searched and found it, a dark scratch against the pale blue sky. I took off my shoes and, dangling them from my hand, returned barefoot to the car. I tossed my heels onto the front seat and took out the can. The liquid slid over me as I poured it through my hair, the smell of it foul and heady. The can, empty, I dropped it to the ground. I searched in my bag for my cigarettes and my slim, silver lighter. I breathed in the cloying sweetness into which I already seemed to be dissolving. My fingers stumbled over the flint, but the flame held firm at last as I lit my cigarette. Then I leaned against the bonnet of the car and looked out over the wilderness while the flames leapt up my arm, fitting like a glove.

Part 5

How dark the drive had become; the trees had filled out and had been allowed to spread, and bushes crowded the tarmac. The roundel had gone in front of the house, and gravel now extended into the front lawn making a generous car park. For the care home management team, gardening was not a priority. Most of the old herbaceous borders had gone, but the lawns looked good. Laura could hear the drone of a mower as she paid the taxi driver and headed towards the front door.

May-May was sitting in the wing chair looking through a brochure.

'Hi May-May, how are you? What have you got there,' asked Laura as she took off her coat.

'I don't know, really,' May-May looked up and smiled. 'I went for a walk and picked this up on my way back through the hall.' She held out the glossy pamphlet to Laura.

'Oh, it's for here. It must be the new brochure for Nether Place. You know, as a nursing home.'

'No wonder it all looked, well ... how silly of me. I was trying to think where I'd seen ... it all looked so very familiar and yet, somehow ....'

'Don't worry, May-May. It is confusing. You get halfway down a corridor, and there's a fire door, and access has been cut off. You are not the only one who finds it bewildering. Mum said she was trying to get to Dr Simpson's office the other day and ended up in the old laundry.'

'Most days, I just meander back and forth to the dining room.' May-May leant towards Laura as though to share a secret. 'I share a table with Lady Wetherstone, you know. But today, when I passed through the hall, I heard a man's voice coming from your grandfather's study, so I wandered in.'

'That must have been unsettling,' said Laura. 'The room is so different now. It doesn't even smell the same. I can't believe the developers threw out all grandpa's old books and bookcases and then covered the walls with wallpaper of library shelves. I noticed a sign on the door calling it The Library now.'

Once, Laura had asked her mother if anyone had ever read any of the books in the study. Mum had said the older books were her great-grandfather's and, as far as she knew, hadn't been touched for years by anything other than the feather duster of Mrs Simms on her weekly go-round.

'It was a bit surreal,' said May-May. 'I realised it wasn't Dennis talking long before I got there. Dennis never raised his voice. However, Major Whittaker has become quite deaf, and for a second, I was transported back ... I thought I must replace the flowers on the hall table and check that Mrs Simms is aware that Dennis has a visitor who might stay for lunch. I suppose that's why I was so disorientated when I picked up the brochure.'

Laura flicked through the flyer of sunshine-filled photographs. Everything was the same, but also so, so different. No wonder May-May was confused.

'Gosh, it says here that there are all sorts of activities you can do and clubs you can join. I didn't realise there was so much going on. Have you tried any of these?'

'There's a gardening club, I try not to despise their efforts,' said May-May. 'But really, they haven't a clue. Burr would be furious with what they've done in the walled garden.'

After Laura had gone, May-May picked up the jaunty booklet again and studied the photographs. It seemed only a moment since Nether Place had been her actual home. She had loved being chatelaine of a house with such strong family traditions. When she was young, she had so wanted to be part of something bigger than herself, to belong to something greater.

Nothing lasts forever, she sighed, however ancient and solid the foundations appear. When Dennis died, she was so ashamed of how cross she became. Of course, she had been terribly upset that he died but also furious with him for leaving. She had thought that they would be together forever, and then, he wasn't there. She was told grief got easier with time, but she still missed him dreadfully. Thinking of a joke or a memory, she would turn to share, but there was only emptiness; Dennis had gone. Sometimes in the night, she would lie in drowsy sleeplessness and feel that if only she looked hard enough, she would be able to find him. She would fall into a restless sleep, and then in the morning, he wouldn't be there all over again. It was ghastly. Even now, when years had passed, that wretched feeling of loss could take her by surprise.

At the time, there had been an issue with the family finances, which made everything so much harder. She had wondered if wills were explicitly designed to be contentious and had decided to clarify her own, not that there was much left to leave. She hadn't done anything of the sort, of course, but she really must.

May-May hated seeing the children bicker over the remnants of the estate. At the first hint of a disagreement, Duncan had disappeared off back to the States. Then, Beth and Max had ganged up against poor Tina, who had lost everything herself. At that time, May-May had been living temporarily in a horrid little rented house that Beth had found. Tina had come to visit. She would spend most of the time with tears pouring down her face; on good days, she merely moped. When she left, Tina would always say what a joy it had been to see her mother and how helpful it was to have that emotional support. May-May had been at a loss to know what to say. It had been heartbreaking. How hopeless she had felt that she couldn't do or say anything that could help. Poor darling, darling Tina, her baby. Now Tina was gone, too, and there was nothing May-May could say anymore that would make anything better ever again.

However, changing his will so that Beth was the sole executor had been a clever move on Dennis' part. Beth was so organised, and Duncan no longer wanted to be involved. When the house was sold, Beth had secured one of the cottages on a temporary lease.

It had been bliss, rather. The developers had updated Burr's Cottage, and everything was new. The house was modest, and she could reach everything and look after herself. It was like playing house after running Nether Place. And if anything went wrong, May-May just picked up the phone to reception, and a man would arrive and fix the washing machine, or whatever it was that had gone wrong. Darling Mrs Simms had come in once a week to give the place a clean. She had even done the odd bit of cooking too, filled the deep freeze. It was marvellous. Then, unfortunately, Mrs Simms had moved away to Eastbourne to be near her ailing sister.

After that, May-May had been just fine for a while. Beth was forever popping over, but it hadn't been quite the same as having Mrs Simms around. Then May-May had stupidly tripped over the edge of a rug while carrying a cup of tea and had done something to her hip. By the time she had been allowed out of the hospital, after all the endless checks and forms, May-May discovered that she no longer lived in her lovely cottage but resided at Room 2, Ground Floor, Nether Place Nursing Home.

2005 – 2012

The MG

Meredith had written immediately after Tina's death. The usual sombre condolences to Ma but to Beth, Meredith had written a much more informal letter. Duncan must have told her. Beth would have contacted her before the funeral, but Meredith already knew. She had written to say how sorry she was, but she wouldn't be there. She had no intention of being anywhere near Duncan. After all these years, Beth was surprised Meredith's animosity towards Duncan would trump being there for the family. Perhaps she didn't think of herself as a Parteger anymore, and Beth supposed, Meredith had not been that close to Tina. But still, how deep rejection must sit in the psyche, burying itself inside the pocket meant to be used for self-esteem.

When they heard about what had happened to Tina, Beth and Max had been together. She remembered the crushing horror and suffocating disbelief that had crowded in on her as the police had asked them questions. Interrogated them before they had been told the facts. It had been terrible. Thinking about it now brought back feelings that she wanted to forget. Her indignation at the thought of either her or Max being culpable threatened to outweigh her grief, and stray strands of panic would thread through her brain and catch her by surprise. But it wasn't the horror of what had happened and how they had been told; it was the loneliness she couldn't bear. When Tina was there, Beth didn't have to see her or agree with her or laugh with her. By being her sister and being there, just by existing, Tina had been a part of who Beth felt she was. Beth had been someone who had a sister, and now, she wasn't. As she held her pen, ready to reply to Meredith, Beth was overcome by awful images and wondered what she should write. Beth sighed. It had been the car's number plate that had brought the police to Beth and Max's front door.

That afternoon, Beth had heard the front door click shut.

'Hello, I'm back,' said Max.

Then the doorbell had rung. Max was ushering the police into the living room as Beth came down the hall towards the front of the house, Bitsy in tow, to see what was going on. The officers shook her warmly by the hand and almost smiled. For a fraction of a second, Beth thought the female officer looked disappointed. She presumed they must be there about the MG. She was right.

'But, no, no, don't leave,' said the male police officer. 'You may be able to shed some light, Mrs Templeton.'

They sat by the fire, looking at each other. The police did not want tea. They did not smile anymore. The policewoman sat next to Beth on the sofa, near enough to touch her. Beth kept her hands on her lap.

The police wanted to know why Max hadn't immediately reported such a special car missing.

Max told them his sister-in-law had borrowed the car. He didn't know where she was taking it or when she would return it; she hadn't said.

'Was that something she was in the habit of doing?' the police asked.

'No.'

The police asked Beth if she knew whether her sister had any connection to Yorkshire, near Horsley, or reason to drive there. She didn't, Beth said.

Then the police said a body had been found by the car. It had not been identified yet, but it was young, female; forensics were ongoing.

The policewoman beside Beth leant in closer, her hand crept across the floral print of the sofa towards Beth.

Beth felt her eyes lurch from side to side, hunting for a rational meaning; her breath caught in agonised suspension. Beth knew the answer before she could process the emotional response. Her mind could assess, could tell her who's the body must be. Tina would not have given the car to anyone else. If there was a body with the car, she knew whose it was and still, her thoughts careered, searching for an alternative before she gave way to certainty.

Was the death significant, the police wondered?

Beth now understood what it meant to turn pale; she felt the blood drain out of her face. She was still finding it hard to breathe. That was when Max asked the police to leave. He told the officers that they were both very happy to answer any questions the police might have but that right now, they needed time to come to terms with the awful news. As they rose to leave, Beth realised that the police had thought it was her body in the ash and that perhaps Max was guilty. But guilty of what, it was an accident surely. She thought of Tina alone, in the car. Had the car gone off the road? Poor Tina. Beth hoped it had been instant. But the police should know Max had nothing to do with this.

'I was here,' Beth said. 'I was here the afternoon Tina took the car. She was unhappy. We tried to help her, but she took the car, and left.'

The officers looked at Beth, then thanked her and went away.

When Max returned from seeing the police out. They stood by each other, not touching, numb. Beth's mind didn't seem able to compute what she'd been told. She realised the body must be Tina's, who's else could it be? She knew Max would be thinking the same, horror and disbelief. And the assumption that they were in some way implicated, that there had been foul play. It was horrendous. Max looked stricken, still holding onto the mail he must have picked up from the doormat when he got in from work. She had not noticed before. He held onto the bundle of letters as though they tethered him to reality.

Beth went to the phone and called Tina's number as she had done when they realised the car was gone. It rang, and rang, as it had that previously. There was no option to leave a message.

They didn't speak beyond banal trivialities. They did not talk over what must surely have happened, what might have happened, but it had to be Tina, didn't it? But if they didn't talk about it, perhaps it hadn't really happened at all. They half-heartedly ate supper and went to bed beyond comfort. In the morning, surely, it would all be proved a dream.

When she woke, Beth was groggy and confused. Max had given her a pill, and she had dropped into a dreamless, unrefreshing sleep. Drowsy, before she could gather herself, the truth of the day overtook her and howling, she turned back into the comfort of the duvet in the hope that the familiar would ease her pain and she might fall back into oblivion. She didn't succeed.

It seemed inconceivable, but if it wasn't an accident and Tina was that unhappy, perhaps she had taken her own life. Maybe it was carbon monoxide poisoning; that was a thing, wasn't it? A sleepy, peaceful way to go. Beth thought carbon monoxide might induce ghastly headaches. Also, the old MG probably would not be airtight enough to create a seal, and anyway, Tina was going to Milan to start over. Tina had a plan; she wasn't suicidal. Beth wished she hadn't thought of that word. Suicide.

Beth managed to rouse herself and get downstairs, Max was already up and had put the coffee on. The paper was open. Max had highlighted a short paragraph that mentioned that a dog walker had found a charred body by a burnt-out car on the moors. The words didn't make sense. It must have been an accident, a horrible, horrible accident, a crash. Burning to death was a punishment for medieval heretics. A slow, tortuous death. Poor, poor Tina. Beth couldn't imagine it. The awfulness was indescribable. Thank God, the article gave no personal details. Thank God Laura was away at boarding school. Beth poured herself some coffee and went to find Max, who was lighting the fire in the living room.

'What are we to do? What do you think happened? She seemed happy enough when she left here, wasn't she? She was going to Italy,' she said. 'It can't have been …'

'What? Suicide? I've been thinking about that too,' said Max, standing up from the hearth. He kicked the logs that burned fiercely, devouring scraps of paper in the flames.

'You said she had plans.'

'She gave me no inkling that she might … that this might be something she would do. She definitely gave me the impression she had a plan.'

'We must contact the school. They must tell Laura. And I must go and see Ma. Try and prepare her for what has happened.' Although the pain inside Beth was coming at her in waves, making her feel nauseous, each surge successively greater, leaving Beth feeling in danger of being swamped, it was important Ma had someone with her when she heard the news. Besides, Beth needed to be practical; it would help.

'What are you doing? It's a bit early to be lighting the fire, isn't it?'

'Oh,' said Max. He looked ravaged from the night. Moving oddly, awkwardly. 'I thought we'd probably be in all day and might need a bit of warmth. I had these letters to burn, so much trash in the post, flyers …' He gave the logs another kick to settle the wood onto the flames already consuming the torn papers. Beth looked at the pink and blue letters and leaflets in the grate. 'Are you going to be alright?' he asked. 'Do you want me to come too?'

'If we both go, it will seem too ominous. I just want to warn Ma that something might have happened. That we don't know anything for sure.' Beth fetched her coat from the peg in the hall. She returned to the living room. 'I will probably bring Ma back with me, so she's with us ....'

'Will it be worse ...'

'No, better, much better to be together.'

'If you're sure ...'

'And we ought to sort out how we tell Laura.'

'Laura ...'

Max seemed to be unable to finish complete sentences anymore. He reached out to the mantlepiece as if to steady himself, although he wasn't falling.

'A traffic accident, don't you think? We can say it was a horrible, horrible accident. As far as we know, it's the truth. Well, practically the truth and much more manageable.'

'If you ... you ... you ...'

Beth thought Max was being unusually uncoherent and he was a strange colour, although he had every reason to be pale. It was going to be a challenging day, and she wanted to get to Ma as soon as possible, but as she left, Beth found herself turning back into the room.

'I can't ... I ... I ...' stumbled Max.

'You know, I'm going to give Mrs Simms a ring and see if she can be with Ma,' said Beth. 'I think I'd rather be here with you.' As she watched one side of Max's face began to drop.

Beth read over Meredith's letter again. She wanted to remind herself what was written and how she was going to reply.

Yes, it had been a shock to hear about Tina, and yes, it was a horrible way to go. And dreadful when the police told them the actual cause of death. It had been a relief there hadn't been much in the press. Yes, her mother had been distraught, had taken a knock back, but Burr's cottage was available and well equipped. Mrs Simms was with Ma now, living in. And there was always the support of the nursing home just across the garden and a room available when the time came. Yes, it had been a terrible blow when Max had a stroke so soon after, and yes, she supposed it was guilt over Tina's death that had contributed; after all, she had used Max's car. Yes, it had been extremely lucky that Beth had decided to stay at home that day.

Gravy

Beth stirred the gravy, waiting for it to boil. Round and round. Nothing was happening. She turned from the watched pot, swept up the potato and carrot peelings and tossed them in the compost bin. A ripe sweet, pungent smell lingered after she had closed the lid. She should empty the bins when she'd added the leftovers from lunch.

She looked out the window at the damp, dark day. Leaves had gathered around the barbeque like eager teenagers outside a pub. She saw the blue tits clamouring at the bird feeder, struggling to get at the last blobs of fat.

I must fill the bird feeders after lunch too, after I empty the bins, while I'm wearing my wellies, Beth added to her mental list. I'll sweep up the leaves tomorrow if the rain holds off.

Beth turned back to the gravy; now, it was claggy and sticky.

'Fuck!' She muttered, 'Fuck, fuck!' She whisked the gravy harder than needed.

She added more water from the kettle and whisked till the sauce was smooth again. Round and round.

'I can't, I just can't do this …' She howled at the extractor fan. She blinked a tear and stared hard at the now re-thickening gravy, biting her lower lip. The house seemed to creak before settling down after her outburst. The silence from the living room seemed to intensify. Then she heard the creak of Max heaving himself up out of his chair and the slow tap, tap of his cane accompanied by that hesitant shuffle as he dragged himself down the hall, followed by the tip, tip, tap of Bitsy's claws. Then, finally, Max edged his head around the frame of the kitchen door. Showing her the good half of his face. Oh, Max, she had never thought of him as vain, but then, life had always been so easy for him; he had looked good from every angle. It was only now, when he had lost his physical rigour that he played games. Tried to fool her into thinking he was as he always had been. That he was still worth loving.

'Everyfing all right, darling? Did you drop something? I heard you call ….'

'No, fine, yes, everything's fine. Almost lunchtime. Sorry it's taken so long. Couldn't get the gravy to do its thing.' She turned off the stove and turned to beam at him. 'But it's there now.'

'Good, good, well, th-that's all splendid fen.' Max shuffled from foot to foot. He clutched at the door frame securing his balance as the dog danced between his feet.

There was a triple beep from the oven.

'And there, that's the meat done. Lunchtime!' She said brightly as she undid her apron.

'Anyfing I can do?'

'Oh, darling, could you just check if I put serving spoons on the table? I'll bring lunch through now.'

Once the home assessment team had been round, Max had come home from hospital. Since then, Beth had been his sole carer. Lovely Grace had come round from the health centre to make sure Max had settled in and popped back after a week or so to check up on him again. After that, Beth was on her own. Occasionally she'd get a phone call from the surgery to check Max was alright, that he had his prescription. No one phoned to ask Beth how she was, if she was managing, but, of course, she was. That was what she did best. It was odd to be in charge of the household, paying the bills, making decisions, and doing all the things Max had always done. She was organised, but she'd never had sole responsibility. They had been a team. Now Beth was adept at surreptitiously helping Max, preparing the way, chopping up his food, trimming his nails, reading him the paper, and in the bathroom. She was careful to allow him to feel as though he was coping. She was unendingly cheerful. It was a full-time job.

Initially, Max had been back in their bedroom. After a few nights, Beth moved to the spare room to get some sleep. She hadn't realised how much space Max would need and how much huffing and puffing would carry on all night. Poor darling, he really was in a state. Beth and Max had to get used to bed baths, bedpans, and all sorts of indignities. She had wished she could look away; poor Max was mortified. But with work, his condition improved. After a couple of months of intense physiotherapy, he had gained some mobility and Max moved downstairs.

The next half term, when Laura was home, she helped Beth move the single bed from the smaller spare bedroom into Max's study on the ground floor. They had to make space, move the desk and chair, and the old, green sofa was now in the garage. Beth pushed Max's desk and chair into the corner and piled on top all the boxes of papers stashed in and around the room. The feng-shui of the study had been ruined by moving the furniture and adding the bed, but it would work. Max would have the freedom of the ground floor.

It was a nightmare to get Max downstairs. Churchill watched them navigate the stairs from the upstairs landing, wrapping his tail around his toes. When he had seen enough, he unravelled and stalked off. Bitsy yapped and scrabbled at the bottom step.

'Solly,' Max moaned as they helped him out of bed and off the stained incontinence patch.

'Solly,' as he overbalanced and squashed Laura against the wall.

'Solly,' as his feet tangled, dragged, and he almost brought them all down.

He was heavy, his body without purpose. They all stumbled on the final stair, Bitsy running around their feet. At least, they had been bringing him downstairs. It would have been impossible to get him up. Poor Max, once so capable and upstanding, proud of his physicality, brought to this.

'Solly,' he sighed as they helped him into his new bed.

Laura had been a saint. She shouldn't have to see her father like that.

Once installed downstairs, Max's health did improve. He could stand by himself with the help of the new riser-recliner chair in the living room. And he could walk with his stick, though his bad leg constantly dragged. It was a relief; Beth could now get him to the car on her own and take him to his physio and other clinics. If he didn't have to tackle the stairs, Max had a modicum of independence.

'It was lucky you called the ambulance so quickly. A speedy response is critical in stroke cases. As it is, the permanent damage shouldn't be too bad,' the doctor had said.

'If he attends all his clinics and does all the exercises, he should get almost 90% functionality back,' said the physio, and Max did. Max was almost Max again. Almost 90% of Max was back, with Beth, in their house, all day, every day.

Arrangements

Beth was driving, Laura was with her. It was raining. They had brought Bitsy too; he was in the well at Laura's feet. Every so often, Beth could hear Bitsy snuffling, complaining at having to share his spot with Laura's boots.

Beth had brought a cardboard box of flower arrangements. Bright daisies dyed intense rainbow colours, predominantly vibrant blue and violent pink interspersed with desultory sprigs of fern. Laura had the box balanced on her knee. The previous day Beth had helped at her final charity do. It had been the last hurrah. She wanted to spend more time with Max.

'Will May-May really want all of these?' Laura asked.

'You know she loves flowers. These were table arrangements at my charity lunch yesterday. I popped a tenner in the collection box and took the lot.'

'But still, eight?'

'Your grandmother has always said she could never have enough flowers.'

Though, Beth had to admit, the arrangements did look a little dog-eared, and Ma was still discerning enough to know the difference between real flowers and these, but they were just a bit of cheerfulness.

'I don't know anything about gardening, but these arrangements look as though a mad axeman has decapitated the flowers outside a petrol station and clumsily stuck the fallen blooms into green sponges,' said Laura.

'Oh, that's harsh,' said Beth. 'They're rather jolly, really. There are a couple left, not quite as nice as these. I put them in the boot. I thought you might like them for the flat.'

'Thank you,' said Laura.

The summer after Laura left school, Beth told Laura that she had been given Tina's flat. When Tina died, as Laura was a minor, Beth had rented it out, deciding to wait until Laura was eighteen before telling her about her inheritance. The rental income paid for Laura's university. Now, Laura had moved into London and was decorating the flat in Earls Court, making the place her own.

When Beth had first worked through the accounts, she had realised that Tina had used the money Max had given her for her supposed move to Italy to pay off the outstanding debts on the flat; the amounts tallied. Beth found it hard to reconcile the generous, thoughtful benefactor Tina was to Laura with Beth's notion of Tina being a flaky spendthrift. Tina had seemed so young and irresponsible. How difficult it had been to talk to her. How enigmatic Tina had been. Beth had always assumed that Tina had something to hide. Beth had never been invited to Tina's flat. Beth had asked Max to visit her sister sometimes when he was up in London to check she was alright, but he had never given Beth much detail.

When given the flat keys, Beth had expected to find evidence of a terribly unhappy, messy life with confirmation of unfulfilled relationships, chaos and clutter. Certainly, Freddie's house had been a mishmash of neglect and ultimate disaster. But Tina's flat was only a little dusty from being empty for the few months during probate. There were few personal belongings; the flat was clean and tidy. It was obvious Tina had a plan. She hadn't left a note, the police had checked for that, but everything was in order. The flat was a haven with calm, cool colours in complimentary tones. Beth sat on the low sofa, brushing her hand along the soft velvet pile. She felt very peaceful sitting there. She was impressed by what Tina had achieved in this tiny flat. Beth couldn't imagine how Tina had ever lived with the hectic Freddie. Perhaps she could manage because she had a private refuge. Beth could see the advantage of that. Here, Tina could be herself. Beth laughed, wondering who Tina might be afraid she was being compared to and who was judging. Then Beth felt a flash of shame. She had felt superior for years while feeling insecure under the glare of Tina's gaze. Now, she had to admit that Tina's life had a substance of its own, and her motives were sincere.

The car coasted along comfortably in the slow lane of the motorway. Busy people with places to go stream past them in a hiss of spray. The car wipers swished and clicked.

'How is the flat? Have you finished painting?' asked Beth.

'There's just the kitchen to do.'

'Well, it's tiny, so that shouldn't take long. I rather thought you might have asked that nice chap from work to help you. Would take half the time.'

'He's not a friend, Mum. Just a colleague.'

Signs loomed announcing exit after exit. At last, it was theirs.

Beth took the turning, and the car scythed through the puddles at the edge of the road as they eased round the corner.

'And how is your job going?' asked Beth.

'Well, I'm just a trainee, so I don't get to do anything very exciting yet. But I like the company. It's fun to be involved in something creative.'

'I'm never quite sure what the company does.'

'Well – ' began Laura.

'I mean, they don't actually make anything useful, do they?' said Beth.

Laura sighed and didn't elaborate. Beth was reminded of her interactions with Tina and bit her tongue, she must hold back, not presuppose.

'Sorry, darling,' Beth said. 'I jumped in there rather.'

The car crawled through the centre of the market town. Bitsy began to whine. Laura rearranged the flower arrangements, so the box felt more balanced on her knee.

'How about you, Mum? How have you been? How's Dad?'

'Well enough. I'm ... we're managing. I can make it work with the agency help coming in twice a week.'

Max could be demanding, wanting to spend time with Beth as she did all the ordinary daily things. He would stand at her elbow smiling genially, watching whatever she was doing, whether she was looking for a stamp for a letter or washing up the dishes. The weekly shop had become a nightmare. The time it took to get in and out of the car, let alone get around the shop, was tortuous; even laying the table for lunch could be fraught. Being accompanied everywhere by Max required the patience of Job. His condition had slowed their life to a glacial pace, yet Beth was run ragged. Looking after Max gave her self-validation, but it was frustrating. She loved Max and found time spent with him worthwhile, but at times she had to fight her rage at the mindlessness of her life. And, although she had no time to herself, she realised she was lonely. Her friends had stopped calling. Whenever someone telephoned, she would always condition any get-together with if Max doesn't need me, but he invariably did.

'It's a shame you are giving up your charities,' said Laura.

'Well, your father's health and happiness are the most important thing to me right now.'

Beth could hear Bitsy snuffling around; he was becoming agitated.

'I do hope we get out of this traffic,' said Beth. 'What are all these people up to? What can they all be doing? We don't want Bitsy having an accident in the car.'

Laura shifted her feet away from the grumbling dog.

'God, Mum, he's gross.'

'I've never warmed to him either,' said Beth. 'I don't know where Tina found such a snarly creature. Pretty I suppose, if you like that sort of thing. And loyal, follows me everywhere.' Like Max she thought.

'Sounds exhausting. I don't know why you kept him, Mum. Didn't see you as a dog person,' said Laura. 'Is Churchill still outraged?'

'He is still extremely offended. Churchill has retreated and rules the roost upstairs in cat heaven. Bitsy is a downstairs dog.' Beth sighed. 'He is hideous, but he serves a purpose. Reminds me of your aunt, not that I'd ever forget.'

Bitsy was her penance. After all these years, Beth would still, in the early hours, wonder if there was anything she could have done or said that would have stopped Tina from doing what she did. Even when Beth convinced herself that one single thing wouldn't have changed anything, she still felt she was partly to blame. A lifetime of microaggressions fuelled by Beth's jealousy of her younger, prettier sister.

It didn't take long to clear the traffic in the end and the car swept out of the town and on and up to the house. A large modern sign in neon colours on the old rusty brick wall read "Nether Place Nursing Home", and underneath in smaller writing, "your comfortable home from home".

'Never fails to surprise me,' said Beth.

'What? The sign ... or everything?'

'All the changes, I keep forgetting and expect Nether Place to be back like it was like it should be.'

'Me too,' said Laura.

They parked in the car park in front of the house. Beth reached behind Laura to grab an umbrella and Bitsy's lead from the back seat.

'Duck,' said Beth as she swept the brolly over Laura's head, before handing her the lead. 'Pop this on him, will you.'

Then Beth opened her door and, shaking out the umbrella, ran around the car to collect Bitsy. It was still raining, a cold drizzle with a sloppy wind that caught one unawares. While Bitsy rummaged in the bushes, Beth stood in the damp and watched Laura run with the box of flowers across the forecourt and up the steps to the front door of Nether Place. Laura lurched to avoid the puddles, leaping as gracefully as a gazelle. It had been different when Laura was a toddler. Then she would run towards and skip into puddles delighting in the splash. On their wet weather walks, they would inspect every pothole and muddy patch. Ma had given Laura her first pair of wellies. Beth still had them in the loft. The material was deteriorating; it had become stiff and cracked. Now Beth marvelled at the size of the tiny baby pink and white boots. Had Laura ever had such small feet. Beth had come across the wellies recently when looking out some slippers for Max. When she had bought them a couple of years before, Max had refused to wear them, they were too frumpy, but now they were ideal house shoes.

Once Bitsy was done, Beth grabbed her bags from the back seat of the car and dashed after Laura into the nursing home. A blast of rain chased Beth into the house but was cut off by the gentle 'whump' as the front door closed behind her. Laura was waiting for her, dripping slightly on the door mat.

'Hello, Mrs Templeton ... Laura,' said the nurse behind the reception. 'She's having a good day. Shall I bring through some tea?'

'That would be lovely, Sharon. We could do with a cup, thank you.' Beth turned to Laura, still holding the box of flowers. 'Right, now, remember, be cheerful.'

'I'm always cheerful,' muttered Laura.

Beth sighed, and bit her tongue for once, now was not the time. Laura was being amazingly helpful visiting her grandmother particularly as Beth was so busy with Max. Now together, they would be cheerful. They crossed the hall to Ma's room.

'Beth and Laura! Darlings, how lovely to see you. And you've brought the dog ... marvellous.'

'Hello, Ma!'

'Hello, May-May.'

'I've brought some flowers from my charity lunch to brighten up your room,' Beth enunciated clearly, then more quietly to Laura. 'Darling, take them out. Put them round.'

'Where?' asked Laura.

'Why anywhere, everywhere,' said Beth. 'How have you been, Ma? I have been busy with Max. He insisted on coming to the shops with me on Monday. To carry my bags. He's so thoughtful. We had a lovely time meandering around.'

Beth chatted about her week to Ma, putting a bright spin on things.

'Max is so much better now he's downstairs. I'm trying to persuade him to help me clear out his papers.' She laughed. 'He doesn't seem to have thrown anything away, ever!'

Laura lifted the arrangements out of the box one by one and squeezed the flowers between family photographs and ornaments. Bitsy followed her, sniffing at the furniture. Beth took one of the better set of flowers to place on Ma's bedside table. To sit beside the photograph of Pa. Beth slid the flowers between Ma's water and her books.

'Very ... bright,' said Ma.

'I thought you'd like them,' said Beth. She loved the spectacle of the furniture now covered with the arrangements of artificially brilliant button-eyed flowers. She thought her mother would be amused too.

Laura stood up, having wedged the final arrangements onto the side table between the delicate china shepherdess and that rather gorgeous picture of Tina at Laura's confirmation; she was wearing Ma's fur.

'Darling, you'll never guess, but I remembered,' said Beth as she settled in a chair and organised herself.

'Remembered what?' asked Laura.

'Your handbag.' Beth handed over a shopping bag.

'My handbag? The handbag!' Laura opened the carrier and took out a buff cloth bag. She pulled at the cord at the neck of the branded sack and took the bag out. It was very smart and very chic. Laura turned it this way, and that. The smooth leather caught the light.

'Very pretty,' said Ma.

'You were right,' Laura said.

'That seems unlikely,' said Beth smiling.

'You made the right call. It would have been ruined at school.' Laura grinned, and Beth beamed back.

'Cool, cool,' said Laura, opening the bag; the clasp gave a satisfying click. 'Wow.'

Inside, Beth could see the black bag was lined in a rich purple silk.

'What a gorgeous bag,' said Ma.

'It's the bag Tina gave Laura at her confirmation. Do you remember Ma? The one I'm afraid I confiscated. Tina always gave such lovely, but exorbitantly expensive presents.'

'There's a card,' said Laura.

'Oh,' said Beth, trying to sound surprised not worried. 'Really?'

Laura opened the stiff envelope; the card was printed with

abstract red and purple flowers. Beth tried to keep breathing. She wondered what Tina wanted to say to Laura all those years ago.

Laura read the message out loud,

> Best wishes on this special day.
> What a blessed reason for us all to be together.
> There is nothing to compare
> with the joy and comfort that being part of a family gives.
> All my love, your aunt, Tina

Beth sighed. She felt as though Tina had given her a gift too. Beth had always been fearful of Tina's power. That, one day Tina would take Laura aside and reveal her true parentage. Nights before they were due to meet up as a family, Beth would lie awake thinking that this would be the day Tina would say something and then would lie awake the next night wondering why she hadn't. It couldn't just be as Max suggested, because he'd asked her not to. Beth realised that perhaps Tina thought it was best for Laura not to know, not to question her stable upbringing. Laura had had a happy, secure childhood; everyone could see that.

'Darling Tina, so thoughtful,' said Ma. 'I do miss her. I keep thinking she will walk through the door.'

'Yes, I think of her often, too,' said Beth. 'Tina was more thoughtful than I ever gave her credit for.' She turned to reach out to her mother, but Beth noticed Ma's eyes were closed. At that moment, the door opened.

'Ah, Sharon, lovely, tea.' Beth kept talking. She wasn't sure if her mother really was asleep, but it was essential to be present, even if her mother was not. Bitsy started scratching the carpet, reaching for something under the wardrobe. Beth raised her voice.

'Ma, are you awake? Tea?'

Guilt

The little dog skittered around Beth's feet as she sat at the kitchen table drinking her coffee and munching on a digestive.

'Oh, Bitsy,' she said, looking down into the desperate eyes. Bitsy did a little dance, paws sliding sideways on the kitchen tiles. 'You cannot have a snack whenever we come into the kitchen. Even if I do.' She took a bite of her biscuit. Bitsy reached up on his hind legs balancing with a paw on Beth's shin. 'Otherwise, you will end up a roly-poly, like me, and Tina would be furious.'

Beth sighed, Bitsy, the last link, a living memory. Penny had said she should give the dog away and move on, but Tina had left Bitsy with Beth. Looking after Bitsy consoled her. It had almost been a comfort when Beth discovered how organised Tina had been. Her death hadn't happened because Beth didn't talk to Tina properly at that final dreadful tea. Still, she could have done more, should have done more. Beth's last memory of Tina was her fine hand, like bone china, in a fleeting movement, placing her teacup with that stain of carmine lipstick, on the sofa table as she walked past, her hand floating on without the cup. It was as if Tina was gliding into whatever the future might hold, leaving the dregs behind. The dregs included Bitsy, and Beth was there, as usual, to tidy up. Every time Beth passed the sofa table, she would caress the wood where Tina's fingers had lingered. A homage to her sister. In truth, Beth didn't want to move on; she wanted there to be no escape from her guilt – or from Bitsy. Beth dropped the corner of her biscuit onto the floor and took a sip of her coffee.

Besides, with Max's condition, movement in the house had slowed until it seemed time was stopping altogether. Beth found it harder and harder to push through the torpor. She was getting older too, over fifty now, just, and she hated having to slow down. She felt it would become a habit, and she was ageing disproportionately. Apart from the two mornings when the help came and Beth went to visit Ma or do some shopping, there were two moments of each day when Beth was free. The first was when she took Bitsy for a walk at the crack of dawn before she helped Max get up. They would zip around the block; it was long enough for a lazy dog and a lazy woman. Beth would greet anyone she saw; it was contact with the wider world. The other time was now her little ritual. Beth felt the cup, warm in her hands, the room cool. It was a relief to breathe, to not have every stifled breath drawn through desert, dry air. The house was far too hot, but Max was less mobile and felt the cold, so he liked to turn the thermostat up. So, whatever the weather, as soon as she had fed Max his lunch and made him comfortable, Beth would retreat to the kitchen closing the door to the rest of the house. She would be on her own, just for a moment, for just as long as it took to have a cup of coffee. While the water boiled, she would open the back door and fling the windows wide. Beth would get rid of the stifling invalid air and, with it, her frustration. Then, after her break, she would close everything up, and she could return to being the person she wanted to be with Max and join him in the living room where she had left him with the paper.

Beth took another sip of coffee. There was a faint cry from the front of the house. She heard a low thump and listened for a moment, her mug in her hands. Then she put down her cup and rushed down the hall to Max, Bitsy at her heels. Max was in his study; he had fallen. She had left him in his chair in the living room. He must have got up and crossed the hall to look for something. The study floor was covered in a mass of folders and papers that had fallen from his desk.

Beth had to phone for assistance. She couldn't lift Max without help, but she didn't have to wait long for the paramedics, who whisked Max away.

The doctor confirmed that Max had had another stroke, this one more serious than the first. Even so, Beth begged for Max to be allowed to come home.

'We've been together for so long; we still enjoy each other's company.'

'It will be much harder to look after him now. You'll need help. And I'm afraid, this time around, Mr Templeton won't be much company.' The doctor studied Max's notes and, without looking up, said, 'I hope you're not doing this because you need a sense of purpose, Mrs Templeton. There are other things you could be doing.'

'For richer, for poorer,' Beth said. 'We have had such a good life together. Max has looked after me and provided, given me a child. We created a family together. Now I feel it is my turn to care for him.'

The doctor agreed to Beth's request, but before Max was released from care, she needed more medical equipment in the house, a hospital bed and so on. Beth hated the apparatus of sickness, but if it meant Max could live with her, she would manage.

The following Tuesday, Beth was up early. She wandered around the house, followed by Bitsy. The council had arranged to deliver the hospital bed and a wheelchair for Max.

'The delivery will be sometime after eight in the morning. Between eight a.m. and six p.m.,' said the woman on the phone. 'Will you be in?'

'Not a problem,' said Beth, 'I'll be here. That will be fine.'

Midmorning, Beth took a ginger nut from the jar to go with her coffee. As yet, there was no sign of the council team. She took her cup through to the front of the house, so she wouldn't miss someone at the door. Beth sat in the living room in her chair by the empty grate and nibbled her biscuit. She twisted the magazines on the coffee table into a neat rectangle and straightened up the square coaster her mug was on to match. Then rising, Beth smoothed the cushion on Max's riser-recliner. It was an ugly chair. If only it could make up its mind what it was, perhaps she could like it better.

Beth wandered across the hall into the study, followed by Bitsy. A clean rectangle of carpet yawned where Max's new bed would go. The rest of the floor was heavily stained where it had borne the demands of Max's illness, spots and stains splashed here and there. After Max collapsed and was taken to the hospital, she had piled the fallen papers he had dislodged back onto the desk, balancing everything together. Beth looked around the room. There remained an air of confusion, of hasty decisions and actions, but remnants of former happier times persisted. The ashtray on the mantelpiece was flanked by photographs of Laura and Airfix models. Each Christmas, Laura had given Max a kit, and they would spend the holiday putting them together. Framed medical certificates covered the wall, and a few bits of golf memorabilia cluttered the surface of the bookcase, which was stuffed with medical tomes and journals. This was Max's domain; Beth had never been allowed to touch anything. She had to resist the itch to straighten and smooth.

'Don't touch anyfing,' he said. 'I like it like vis. Everyfing is vere it should be. Vere I know vere it is.'

Gently, Beth put out her hand, touched the rim of the desk, running the tips of her fingers along the rolled edge. Perhaps now she could slowly make a start while she waited for the hospital team. Surely Max wouldn't mind. He would hardly be in a state to read papers or correspondence. Beth picked up a stack of files and boxes from the desk and returned with them to the living room. She sat the papers down on the coffee table, nudging her mug aside, and began to go through them. A pile to keep, a pile to burn, and a pile of things she didn't know what to do with. She'd make a start, to keep her occupied until the collection service arrived. Gradually, she added to the three piles, and when done she went to get more papers. The piles grew higher and slid together, at least the throw away pile was the largest.

The bell rang; they had come. Beth leapt up to get the door, shutting the yapping Bitsy in the living room. It was lunchtime. She would, after all, be able to visit Max later on that afternoon and tell him the good news; that he would be home soon.

When she returned from seeing Max, Laura rang.

'Oh yes. He's so much better, darling, quite comfortable, waited on hand and foot. All those pretty, young nurses to look after him. He's in seventh heaven,' said Beth. 'Yes, he was awake. No, he can't really make himself understood. Hopefully, that will improve. But he will be home soon; that's the important thing.'

Max was home. Laura came at the weekend to see her father to help Beth get him settled back into a routine. Beth organised private nurses to come two more mornings a week, but Beth still wanted to do most of the caring. There was much more caring to be done. Max was now bedbound, unable to move much beyond the odd inflexion of his right arm and a slight contortion of the right side of his face that could be a smile or a grimace, but either way gave a jaunty charm to the otherwise leaden mask that had replaced his previous self.

When Beth fed Max his puree at supper, it reminded her of feeding Laura as a toddler, and she had to restrain herself from making aeroplane noises.

'I think this is pork, darling,' she said as her hand hovered with the spoon above his mouth. 'Delicious, hmmm?' And she sent the food zooming towards the gash that was his mouth. She then whipped the edge of his lips with the side of the spoon.

'All gone, darling!' she said. 'No more, we can't have you getting any heavier.' After Max's first stroke, he had gained weight. One of his few pleasures was food, as he was tall, a few pounds didn't matter, but if he put on much more weight, he would be impossible to move if he needed turning or to be taken anywhere.

Later, Beth fed Bitsy. Then she started preparing the chicken she had taken out of the deep freeze for her own supper, but the effort defeated her; it went back into the fridge. She'd cook it in the morning and whizz it up for Max with some vegetables. Instead,

Beth gathered some crackers and cheese and carried them through to Max's study so she could keep him company while she ate. Beth manoeuvred her way through the papers on the floor to sit at the desk.

Every day, Beth would sit with Max and tell him about who she'd met that morning on her walk or how Ma had been if she'd been to visit. That morning she'd taken Ma some of the lovely lilac bush that Max could see if he looked out his window, the one that came from a cutting from Nether Place. Max didn't turn to look out the window. As she talked Beth picked up a folder and a bunch of papers to go through from Max's desk. Max lay there, unable to move, unable to join in the conversation, but Beth kept going, as if things were as they had always been. She had cleared the chair and part of the desk, she burned or binned the rubbish, but the piles on the floor of 'keep' and 'maybe' kept growing. She was making more mess trying to be tidy. Beth took the pile of 'out' papers to the living room and knelt by the grate to light a fire; she burnt what she could. Why had Max kept an invoice for cleaning the chimney from twenty years ago? She scrunched up the bill and tossed it on the bright flames beginning to lick around the dark logs. Collecting more obsolete bills, Beth chucked them on the fire, fanning the flames with the bellows. Once she was sure the letters had caught, she put the guard in front of the fire and, her face glowing, she left Bitsy snoozing in the warmth to return to Max.

He was propped up, lying in the same position, whether awake or resting. Beth had managed to get a small television balanced on the bookcase against the wall at the end of his bed. It was on constantly, on a sports channel, in case Max could understand. Beth hoped he would find the movement of the screen images stimulating and the commentary better than her endless babble, though she kept the sound down low when she was in the room. Beth wasn't sure Max cared. He usually had his eyes closed and leant back on too many pillows. He needed to be sitting up to prevent pneumonia. Max was moved twice a day and washed at night when the care-worker came; Beth helped, they did it together. Beth would try to keep Max moving a little each day, so he was comfortable. She tried to keep him upright while preventing him from sliding down the bed. It made her wretched to think how Max would hate all this intervention. The mundanity of this minor care would infuriate his medical sensibilities. It was survival, not science. His whole life, he had been so independent and enjoyed being in control. She wept to think how outraged he would be at the intrusion. Beth tried to focus on the good memories, the striding out, the winning at tennis, the enjoyment of golf. She thought of how she had known when he was in the house, in another room, working on papers, writing, or reading. Now, after this second stroke, with his mask-like face and irritable grunts, Beth felt she had lost him. Sometimes, only sometimes, mainly when Laura was home, Beth thought she saw a flicker of interest or recognition. Then she thought he was there but was so disgusted with life that he had decided not to pay attention.

Beth turned back to the mess on the desk. She spotted a brightly coloured old cigar box hidden halfway through the next pile of folders. Beth tugged at it. The elastic band that circled the red and yellow box perished as she pulled it. She picked up the pieces of elastic and threw them in the bin. As she straightened Beth looked up and saw Max had his eyes open.

'Hello, darling, look what I've found.' She held up the box so Max could see. 'Do you remember? You were given this such a long time ago. When you operated on that poor child. What was her name? Jenny, Jenny something-or-other.' It had been a tricky but successful operation she remembered Max had been pleased at the time.

Max made a grunt. Did he remember?

'All right, darling?' Beth put the box down, went to him, and smoothed his sheets; he was quite silent and still now but alert. She held his water up so he could reach the straw with his dry lips.

'Better?'

Beth returned to the desk, she cupped the old box in her hands and traced her fingers over the raised gold medallions that framed the lovers' embrace. A golden-haired girl leant out over the stone balustrade towards her lover, who was climbing up towards her on the flimsiest of gold ladders: Romeo y Julieta, the star-crossed lovers.

After the cigars were finished, the box had sat on Max's desk. Beth had never wondered what Max kept in it: pens, pencils? She glanced across at Max; he was watching her. Beth smiled at him and lifted the lid. Inside there were letters, old letters from years ago. An assortment of envelopes, in different coloured ink, in a variety of hands addressed to Max at the hospital.

'Oh, Max, you rogue. Are these old love letters?' Beth asked.

Lilacs

May-May was asleep. Her face looked faded. Her hair was flat; it had lost its perm. Laura left her bag in May-May's room and fetched a coffee from the machine in reception. When Laura returned, she settled down in the chair that faced the bed. Laura took out her book. After a while, the dregs of her coffee cold in the cup, Laura closed her book and rose to leave. Her movement must have woken May-May, who stirred.

'Hello,' said Laura.

'Hello, darling! Lovely to see you. I'm so glad you've come.' May-May's eyes wandered as if she lingered in a half-forgotten dream. 'But goodness, it's been a while. I didn't think I'd get to see you again. How have you been?'

'May-May, it's me, Laura. I was here a couple of weekends ago. How are you?'

'Laura, how lovely. Are you sure?' May-May pushed herself up to get a better look. 'You look so grown up. For a moment, you know, I thought you were Tina.'

'Yes, May-May, it's me ... sorry.'

'Well, it's lovely to see you, darling. No need to be sorry. It was just for a moment there, with the light behind you ... I get so confused these days.' Her grandmother made to reach for her water glass on the bedside table. Laura stepped in to help. 'Thank you, darling. I get terribly thirsty; the air is so dry in here. Tell me, how are you? What have you been up to?'

'I was emailing ... chatting to Gareth during the week. He says he's going to try and come over this summer.'

'He's done well, hasn't he,' said May-May. 'For years, he seemed so loud and uncoordinated, so easily distracted. I couldn't see him managing to concentrate on anything. Yet now he's what? Something clever in computing?'

'Yes, he is. He loved his programming degree and now has that fancy job in Silicon Valley.'

'I'm so glad he's enjoying life.' May-May leant forward. 'Can you help me, darling?'

Laura pulled out the pillows and puffed them up, rearranging them so May-May could sit more upright. May-May was so thin and brittle but seemed much more awake now she'd had something to drink.

'And you, darling, are you happy too?'

'Oh ... yes. I'm a bit worried about Mum and Dad. But Mum will sort things out; she always does.'

'It must be so difficult at home now your father is ... not himself.'

'It's really sad. I'm going over as often as I can. Dad is really incapacitated. After that second stroke, he can't do anything for himself. But when I look in his eyes, I know he understands everything that's going on.'

'Beth mentioned that too.' May-May pulled a handkerchief out of her nightdress sleeve and dabbed her eye. 'Always running, can't get them to stop ... your mother also said she was talking to

Duncan about his upcoming trip.'

'Yes, it's so exciting they are going to visit this year. They want to see family, of course, but they also want to tour around.'

'So, it's to be a proper holiday, not just a flying visit tacked onto a business trip. I am so longing to meet Robin. It seems so odd that they have been together for so long now, and we've never met.

'Gareth said he's planning to tie in his trip with Duncan and Robin too. They're coming over in June, aren't they?'

'June? Are you sure? What month are we now?' May-May reached for her juice and Laura handed her the glass. 'Thank you, darling.'

'April, nearly May.' Laura looked around the room, wondering if May-May needed a rest. 'I see Mum brought you some proper flowers this time, some of her lovely lilacs.'

'Yes. They smell divine.' May-May reached out her hand as though to caress a bloom, but the flowers were across the room. 'Those flowers are from an off-shoot I gave her from the tree at Nether Place.'

'Is the tree still here?' said Laura. Her grandmother looked bewildered. 'Remember, we are at Nether Place, in a ground floor bedroom.'

'Oh yes. I've moved back in, haven't I? Back into the drawing room.'

'Well, a bit of it anyway.'

'But I get the French window.'

They laughed together and looked out across the lawn. It was a sunny afternoon, and the shadows of the tall cedar stretched across the grass.

'Are you feeling a bit tired? Shall I go and give you time to rest?'

'Oh, my darling, do stay. It's so lovely to have company, and I have all the time in the world.'

Laura looked at May-May's pale grey face. Her eyes were ringed by dark shadows of purple and yellow, and her lips were almost colourless. Her undressed hair was thin, and Laura could see May-May's fragile scalp through the stray strands, causing her to look even more vulnerable.

The door opened, and a nurse Laura didn't recognise came into the room waving a thermometer.

'I'm afraid I'll have to ask you to leave, Miss. It's time for Mrs Parteger to have her check, and then it'll be time for her dinner.'

Laura kissed May-May goodbye. Her grandmother's pale face was cool where Laura's lips touched the skin.

'See you soon, May-May.'

Pandora's Box

Inside the Cuban box were a collection of letters, separate bundles bound with elastic bands that had grown loose over the years. The first bunch were written in royal blue ink. The script looped its way across the top envelope, the paper, old and yellowed. They were addressed to Max at his old consulting rooms and postmarked London. Beth had a thing about reading other people's letters, it wasn't on, but this letter was old, dated years before she knew Max. And how amusing, why had he kept them, she wondered. She opened the first envelope the old paper crackling slightly in her hands.

> Darling,
> I can't wait to see you. I don't think Matron suspects a thing, but I will be extra careful, as you suggest.
> I am involved in an intrigue - how exciting!
> xxxx Josie

'Oh, Max, you naughty boy!' Beth laughed and waved the note at Max. Did he smile back? Perhaps the hint of a grimace.

Darling
Today when you passed me on your rounds, you were careful to ignore me, but I felt a spark between us - did you feel it too?
xxxx Josie

My Darling
You won't be late, will you? I'll be on the corner of York Road after my shift. I can't wait! My heart is a flutter!
In haste
xxxx Josie
P.S. I must be back before nine-thirty as Matron will be checking us in tonight.

Beth sighed, silly love letters from a student nurse. Josie wasn't in such haste she couldn't add all those extra kisses. Max, you rogue. Beth picked up the next bundle, a slightly later date, darker ink, more upright, tighter writing.

Darling,
When you held me and looked at me, I felt as though you could see right into the deepest part of me. Your eyes, the deepest, bluest of blue, can read the depth of my passion like a book. Your hands moved over me like you were covering me in cream. I can't wait for us to be alone together again.
Til then, yours with deepest love, Perdie

Beth decided not to read any more of Perdie's letters; there was only so much ardour she could take. The dates of the following bundle overlapped the dates of the previous bunch.

Darling,
Don't worry. Perdie will never understand you, like I do.
I know how clingy she can be and how you will need to
let her down gently. Somehow, I will manage to share
you until it will just be us and we can be alone together.
All my love, Lois.

A few letters later, Lois seemed to be less understanding.

Dear Max
You must accept that I can no longer be a part of Perdie's
obsession with you. She cannot give you up. You must
finish with her decisively for our love to blossom. If not,
it will be over between us!
Love, Lois

Beth was glad to see that Lois was taking control of the situation. Perdie had to go. The next bundle began a couple of years later. Max had had an internship abroad before returning to the U.K. to complete his training, which might explain the gap.

Maxwell, my Darling,
I am looking forward to our time away together. Driving
to Yorkshire in your MG to the magnificent Horsley
House, how splendid! We shall have such fun! I have
told Mark that I am going on a girls' weekend.
with love Amelie

Only one letter from the sophisticated and seemingly otherwise attached Amelie. Why did Beth know the name, Horsley? It would come back to her later. Beth skipped ahead. There was a group of short, efficient notes from a Louise. Beth had met Louise, a pretty nurse. It had been when Beth and Max were first engaged. Beth had visited Max at the hospital, they were going to the theatre; Beth had gone to pick Max up to make sure he wouldn't be late.

Max after work Red Lion don't be late. x Louise

Max, I'll wait in the back stairwell, see you later. x Louise

These notes were not dated, but as all the bundles were neatly kept and otherwise chronological, Beth could assume when they had been written. Beth had known Max had played the field before they married. She had known the nurses were easy. Max had told her. He had not been shy about his conquests.

Not for the first time, Beth wondered if Max had married her only because she'd said 'no'. These love letters seemed to affirm that. Her fingers slid through the bundles. The dates of the postmarks on the envelopes ticked forward, crossed the date of their marriage. Beth paused; she had always assumed that she had nothing to fear from previous girlfriends. After all, she had won the game and married Max. What had seemed a lark, looking through past correspondences, now felt sleazy and made her feel diminished. These letters implied a different side to him that she had never seen and didn't recognise. A side that he had pursued despite their marriage. A more adventurous facet of his personality that enjoyed risk. A part of himself he didn't share with her.

There were a few more bundles, more letters, different handwriting, newer whiter paper, same ardent messages. Beth sighed; somehow, she wasn't surprised, and yet, she had never suspected. All those late meetings and dinners in London, she felt so stupid. Beth had been so understanding of Max's work commitments and so compliant. She seldom stayed at the flat, but when she did go, there had never been anything to suggest anyone else had ever been there. Beth had never questioned, so he'd never lied; he didn't have to. She couldn't believe she'd made it so easy for him. She had been so naive she felt partly to blame. Hadn't her mother always said a good marriage was worth working for? Should she have done more? Had she had been complacent?

Why had Max kept the letters for so long? Trophies? Perhaps it gave him some erotic pleasure just knowing they were in the house. The thought that Beth might discover them at any moment. She'd never known. She'd never guessed. She'd never looked. Beth stared at Max. He stared mutely back. Beth looked at the bundles on her lap. She fanned them out. Was that Miss Pritchard's handwriting; just one note. Honestly, Max, she looked at him again, aghast, even Miss Pritchard, that uptight, hard-faced bitch. Beth picked up the note and opened it.

> What constitutes a good work-life balance? I think you have managed to find the sweet spot, Max. Certainly, you and I have an excellent working relationship. Our team hums along with the best ratings in the department. Could this be because of our partnership? I feel so close to you that I seem to be able to sense when you are in the building. And your idea that we share an office has brought not only efficiency but also an enjoyable frisson to the working day.
> Evelyn x
> P.S. You really must stop your wife from phoning the office – she always calls at the most inconvenient times!

Evelyn, Evelyn Pritchard, Beth had never known her first name, now she would never forget. Max's glassy eyes slid sideways. Beth was furious; she felt she should leap up and strike out at him. Her jaw ached, Beth looked away took a breath and tried to relax. Max had taken her for the fool she was. What an idiot she had been. All the time she had thought she been building something strong, something she could be proud of, something for both of them, something for all of them, Max had been undermining her.

She had been holding her breath. Beth sighed, letting the air seep out between her pursed lips. After all these years, she should not let the loathsome Evelyn Pritchard get to her. Beth would not read any more of these tiresome letters; she would take them all through to the living room and burn them. The fire would still be hot. She gathered up the bundles, needlessly taking care to put them in the right order. Then she took the box and the letters across the hall to the living room and knelt by the hearth. First, she threw the pretty box onto the fire, pushing it firmly down into the coals and ash with the poker, holding it down until it was immersed in flames. She sat back on her heels and watched it burn, the gold decoration on the lid emitting a blaze of blue and green. Then she tossed the bundles of letters onto the fire one by one, trying not to think about what these women had meant to Max.

Beth threw the final bundle onto the fire and was leaning in with the poker in her hand to ram the letters further into the flames when the band around the wad snapped and the charred topmost letter slipped off the pile onto the hearth. Beth dropped the poker and picked up the letter to toss back into the grate. As she did so, the envelope turned over in her hand and Beth, with a gasp, recognised the handwriting. She froze for a moment before picking up the poker to try and salvage any other letters from the flames. She knew there had been more envelopes in this final group, at least ten, perhaps a dozen, but her frantic scrabbling in the ashes only caused the flames to flare up higher. There was now nothing left but ash.

Beth sat still in front of the hearth and held the scorched letter. Perhaps, is she didn't move, time might seep backwards, and the evening begin again. Then Beth began to rock back and forth in sorrow as, with dust smeared fingers, she turned the envelope over, and over again, until her hands were a uniform ash grey. The handwriting was unmistakably Tina's, in her favourite turquoise ink. The post mark was smudged, 19 something, so at least ten years old. Beth couldn't bring herself to open it, not yet. The carriage clock on the mantlepiece struck; she glanced up, it was eleven. Despite the heat from the fire, she was cold. Beth felt as though the face of a glacier had collapsed on top of her. Opening the cigar box had been a catastrophe. As if a wall of ice had fallen, ice so clear she hadn't even noticed that carrying a flame, she had walked into the base of a crevasse. Without reading the letter, she knew what it must say, what it meant. All the letters Max had kept were the same. Suddenly, it was as if she had always known. In disgust, she almost threw this last letter on the flames too.

Beth didn't want to know the truth, but her thoughts ran to dates and moments when paths had crossed – opportunities. How had she not known? Beth couldn't tell if she already knew the truth. It felt as though she must. The clues were there when she looked, all those nights Max stayed over in London, and that time in France. If she did not know, she should have. Did it come to the same thing? What a fool she was.

Beth returned to the study, still holding the letter. She stood in the doorway. She looked at Max lying prone in his hospital bed. Beth watched him for a while; he didn't move. Finally, she switched off the light but stood a little longer in the wedge of light from the hall. Max didn't move; he didn't sigh, he didn't make any sound at all. Beth left the room, closing the door behind her. She would not, could not, countenance him any longer.

Once Beth was in bed, her mind refused to calm. The anger stirred and disturbed, kneading her brain, shame overlay fury, sadness interleaved with loss and misplaced pride. She should have felt this raw a long time ago. The fact that she had been so callow made her angrier still. How could Tina have done this to her? Beth tossed in her bed, turning as if trying to unturn the thoughts her mind was busily twisting. Her head searched for a cool, clean spot on her pillow untainted by bad impressions and wicked implications.

For years, hours had stretched out endlessly as Beth had looked after Max. The house quiet as if waiting, Beth tiptoeing, Beth holding her breath so as not to disturb. Bending to please Max, to care for him the best she knew how. Now, time had raced forward faster than she could have imagined. For Beth, so used to measuring every movement against the will of Max, what he wanted, what he needed, the new whirlwind of her thoughts felt inappropriate. Beth was exhausted, wide awake, and furious.

As the hours passed, marked by the tinkling clock, Beth felt heavy, a stone sinking down into deep dark water. The burden of her thoughts and the weightlessness of the house, no longer a home, but a shell, seemed to rise around her as she plummeted. Her life, the marriage that she had been so proud of, had been a sham. The void that now filled her was a tangible thing. By the early light that began to seep into the room, Beth could make out the surviving letter on her bedside table.

Pearls

Laura had come with her mother to Nether Place. For once, Bitsy had been left behind. Mum had been in a really, really bad mood lately. She was visiting May-May much more often. Perhaps Dad's ill health was getting to her, and she needed to get out of the house. Laura sighed; it was great to be given a lift; the train could be a nightmare.

When they arrived, Laura went straight in to see her grandmother while her mother was called away by the nurse at the reception desk to have a chat with Doctor Simpson.

'Can you open the door, darling,' May-May said. 'I like to hear the birds.' She was in better form, sitting in the old wing chair by the window.

Laura unfastened the latch and slipped through the French window into the sunshine to hook the door open, so it didn't catch in the breeze. The lavender was beginning to come into flower. As she brushed past the bushes, the scent encircled her. When she came back inside, May-May was pulling at her pearls.

'Darling, can you help me?' Laura leant over and carefully unhooked the diamond clasp and safety chain. She handed the warm pearls to May-May, who held them in her cupped hand. The beads glistened against the pale fingers, emulating the ivory skin of May-May's bloodless hands.

'Darling, here.' May-May took Laura's hand and placed it over her own, then turned their hands over together, so the pearls dropped into Laura's palm. 'Will you take them? I would like you to have them.'

'No, May-May, no. They're yours. I've never seen you without them. They belong to you.'

'Darling, things go missing sometimes, and I'd like to know that you had these. They were your great Aunt Eliza's, and now I feel they should belong to you.'

'Put them on,' said May-May.

Laura fastened the warm pearls around her neck, pulling down the neck of her sweater to show her grandmother.

'Lovely,' said May-May.

'Thank you, May-May.' Laura tucked the pearls away and sat beside May-May in the nursing chair. Before she could start a conversation, her mother burst into the room.

'Hello, Ma.' Beth placed her bag on the bed and then dragged a chair over to join Laura and May-May by the window.

'Goodness, who opened the window! Are you warm enough, Ma?' asked Mum, leaping up and tucking the rug tighter around May-May. 'Laura, could you go and see if you can find Sharon and ask if she has a minute and can bring us some tea?'

When Laura returned to the room, her mother seemed to have lost her mind.

'Well, I'm going to have to report this to the management.' Mum was ransacking the bedside table. May-May had her eyes closed. She was still in her chair, wrapped in a rug in the sunshine.

'Is everything alright, Mum?' said Laura. 'Sharon said she'd bring tea through in a minute.'

'Your grandmother's pearls are missing. She can't remember what she's done with them, and I can't find them anywhere.'

'I'm sure I had them this morning,' said May-May, turning back into the room and opening her eyes. Her hands moved to her neck and stroked her bare collarbone.

'I can't believe it. You always wear them, Ma. We can't have lost them; they have been in the family for years.'

'Mum, Mum, calm down. May-May gave her pearls to me. Don't you remember May-May? When Mum was talking to the doctor, you gave me your pearls.'

'Did I, darling? That was clever of me. I'd completely forgotten. I'm so glad you have them. They belonged to your great Aunt Eliza you know.'

'Ma gave her pearls ...' said Mum, looking up, suddenly still. 'She gave them to you?'

'Yes, Mum. It's fine, look.' Laura pulled down the front of her jumper so her mother could see the necklace.

'Oh! That's marvellous!' said Mum. 'But you could have told me sooner. I've been frantic.'

At that moment, the door opened, and Sharon backed into the room carrying a tray of tea things and looked around to see where she could put the tray.

'Everything alright here, Mrs Templeton? You look a bit flushed.'

'Yes, thank you,' said Mum. 'I just had a bit of a fright, but all's well.'

On the way back in the car, Mum said, 'You know, your grandmother has never given me anything, ever.'

Custard Cream

The room was hot. Beth stood close to the window, the cold beyond the glass calming her. She watched the couple at number 43 dash across their front pathway, through the squall, to their car and drive away. After a while, a delivery man arrived in a van and carefully protecting them from the weather, carried some flowers, artfully tied in brown paper, up to number 45. He returned to his van and drove off. It was so still and quiet in the room. Outside, the world swayed in the wind. Fresh green birch leaves torn from the trees spun across the dark grey tarmac of the road.

Earlier, when she had come in from walking Bitsy, the private carer, now employed full-time, had pulled Beth aside.

'He's very low, Mrs Templeton.' Beth made to go to the kitchen. The nurse moved slightly in front of her to make sure she understood. 'It won't be long.'

'Thank you, I'll call my daughter,' said Beth sweeping the nurse aside as she strode down the hall, swathed in her enduring anger, tears pricking her eyes.

The morning after she had discovered the Cuban box, Beth had woken late. She had slept through her alarm and any noise Bitsy might have been making in the kitchen. Beth had roused and staggered downstairs when she heard the carer arrive. Beth fed the dog, made herself a coffee, and retreated upstairs, pleading a cold.

Beth climbed back into bed, placing her coffee cup on the bedside table next to the letter. Churchill appeared and jumped up beside her circling till he found a warm spot and tucked in close beside her. She absentmindedly stroked the cat while she picked up the singed envelope. Beth considered the consequences of reading the note and the danger within. In all the love letters Max had kept, Beth had picked up the idea that the women had been chasing Max. Had Tina thrown herself at him too? Had Tina loathed or loved

Beth so much that she wanted her husband? To take him from Beth, to have and hold what was hers, an insincere form of flattery. Beth had hesitated the night before but had known she would have to read the letter soon. Beth smelt the charred paper, she may as well get it over with, she already felt like Eve after Adam bit the apple. Beth had to look, or she might convince herself that she had imagined the box, the letters, everything. After all, she had chosen to believe what was convenient over what was self-evident in the past. Beth thought back to every time she knew Max had been alone with Tina. Now she examined every interaction; there seemed to be clues peppering every memory.

'Wouldn't want your sister catching cold in her games kit. That skirt really is a bit short,' she remembered Max once saying. 'She'll get unwanted attention if she's wandering around like that, showing off those long legs.'

It had all seemed so innocent. Max would drive the car round, Tina would jump in the MG and off they would zoom to some school sports event or to drop Tina off with friends, and Beth would have a peaceful moment to catch up with Ma in the garden.

Beth sat up straighter and carefully opened the letter. The envelope was intact, it had been cut with a knife by Max, not torn. The letter was a single sheet. Beth unfolded the stiff paper holding it flat so she could read Tina's unmistakable rounded, loopy script that tore across the page as if the words had been hurled at the paper.

> Max
>
> Once I would have done anything you asked. Once I believed you were everything I needed. You made me believe that I was all you wanted and that I had something no one else could give you. Not even Beth. I did things I shouldn't have done, didn't want to do, but I did them for you. I thought that's how grown-ups behaved. I look at my body now and I see where you

have been, and I loathe my own skin for having been touched by you. I thought you were the world, the universe. And in return you took everything, my virginity, my self-confidence, but most precious of all you took my baby, my Lara. I gave up everything for you and you took it all, without a backward glance. You twisted what I thought I wanted and turned my love for my sister into a competition. It turned out that the prize was Lara and Beth won. And then you grew careless and now it is over, and you are furious, and all you care about is that your game is spoiled.

Yours never again, Tina

Beth read and read again. She fell back into her pillows, her fingers loosened, allowing the letter to fall to the ground. Beth gasped and gasped again. Was this how it felt to reel from the shock of a betrayal. Churchill rose like an apparition roused from the depths, arching his back to show his dislike of being disturbed. He fled the bed as Beth leant over the edge to grapple for the letter. Beth felt betrayed.

Beth remembered when she had first held Laura. She was like a pearl; she glowed with the new life coursing beneath the surface of her skin. She was so perfect, so vulnerable, so soft. It had been a moment of such magic, such possibility. For those first few days, Beth had not been able to leave Laura alone. How could Max have taken this precious child from Tina? How had Beth been so blind to Tina's pain? Beth had mourned over her own miscarriages, but when Max had brought the baby home that autumn, Beth had barely thought about Tina. Now Beth was ashamed. She had been complicit in Max's cruelty. Beth had been so excited to meet Laura. She had waited for a baby for so long. Tina had always seemed to hold herself apart and be disinterested. Beth had thought Tina was glad to be rid of the baby, to not be tied down, or held back. Beth had not thought beyond her desires to consider that the only way

Tina could cope with her loss was to withdraw. Beth rued the missed opportunity to reach out to Tina. Tears streamed down Beth's face. She didn't know if she was crying for Tina or herself.

Beth had been in Max's room for over half an hour now. She hadn't said a word. Neither had Max. Slugs of rain now pelted the window, sliding down the glass, leaving a watery trail. She held Tina's letter and tapped it against the sill. Beth wondered what was in those other letters, the ones she hadn't managed to save from the fire. She wanted to know, needed to know every sordid detail: it infuriated her that she couldn't know. Beth glanced at Max. She thought about the fire that Max had made the day after the police had told them about the car being found. Letters had been among the papers burned. At the time, she had thought they had been circulars, but now she wondered if Tina had written a letter to Max, and he had concealed it in the flames. A final note from Tina might have confirmed that her death was indeed suicide. A letter like that would have been incendiary. It could have released Max from the implication of guilt for Tina's death when the police were considering murder, but at the same time, associate him with her motives that would reveal the affair. What a quandary Max must have been in. No time to assess the damage the note might incur. Of course, Beth had defended him to the police, prevented anything unpleasant from being uncovered.

His eyes were closed, but she could tell he was awake. She had looked after him for so long, she thought of the years and years and sighed. His breath rasped in a way that implied he was ignoring her. Beth thought that Max might have been curious. He had seen her read the first letters and then seen her holding an envelope at the door. Beth had given over his care entirely. She hadn't been able to look at him, let alone look after him; she'd been so furious. Now she was here, Max might have wanted to know what she had been up to. At the very least, Max would like to hear about Laura. He used to perk up when she came to see him bringing news. Beth turned back to the window.

Max grunted.

My, how are the mighty fallen.

The rain was heavier now.

Max grunted again. Beth stepped back from the window and watched the mist from her breath fade from the pane. Then she turned and looked at him. Max looked back. She noticed it took effort for him to drag the dry air from the hot room over his cracked and blistered lips. His mottled grey hand, which lay on the beige blanket of his bed, almost lifted. Twitched, then moved a fraction more decisively. The sound that was once his voice scratched the silence of the room. Was he trying to say something to her, something that could explain or make amends or was he just thirsty. Beth tried to feel empathy; this was her husband, she had loved him once, but she would need time, more time than Max had, to come to terms with what he had done.

Beth moved away from the window. Max's rheumy, lizard eyes slid after her as she crossed the room. Beth held up the letter so Max could see, would understand. What she had thought was the truth, her life with Max, had been a lie. Why had she trusted Max. She had been manipulated, as well as deceived. Now she understood why Max had persuaded her not to tell Laura that she was adopted when she was eighteen as Beth had intended.

'What would be the point,' Max had said. 'Genetically, you and Tina couldn't be closer, and I'd rather Laura wasn't told that I am not her father.'

Beth approached Max, still holding the letter up so he could see. She leant over and with fury, she brandished the envelope in front of his nose. She had to be sure he understood that she knew everything. Max's eyes slithered to the envelope.

'See, see! I know all about you, you and your … treachery.' Beth shook the letter hard in his face. Then she pulled back and looked down on him with scorn. She slipped the note into her pocket.

Next to Max's glass of water with a straw, on the bedside table, was a plate with two custard creams. Beth looked at the biscuits. She picked one up and took a bite. She considered Max while she finished her mouthful. Beth was annoyed. She couldn't tell if he understood. He lay there, large, and solid and seemingly intractable. He gave no indication of repentance. She needed resolution; it was what she craved.

'Nothing to say, Max?' She waited.

His lips opened slightly; his breath rasped.

'No matter,' said Beth, leaning over him, she pushed the rest of her biscuit between his teeth and left the room.

Older and Wiser

Beth tidied up the mugs and sat close to the bed, taking Ma's hand in her own. Beth wanted to feel her mother, wanted Ma to know she was there. She needed to be everything to Ma. Like Tina had been.

Tina and Max, Beth had thought Max was her saviour. He had interceded between Beth and the frightening unknown. They had been a team; a good team and they had faced the world together. At least she had thought they did. Max had helped pull her out of the circle of jealousy and spitefulness in which she danced with Tina. Of course, Beth didn't behave any better and nor did Tina, but at least Beth had a refuge. Max was good at reassuring her, listening to her grievances. He could put everything into perspective. Would intercede, calm down the rhetoric, transform their sniping into conversations. Beth could be civil if Max was there. He was good with Tina too, suggesting books to read or films she should see with her friends. When they were down at Nether Place for the weekend, she remembered Max being only too happy to give Tina lifts to the cinema or offer to drop her off at hockey matches. Beth had thought Max brought them together and had ironed out the sisters' differences, now she wondered if Max had worked to keep them apart.

Everyone loved Tina.

'Ma, are you awake?' asked Beth. 'I wanted ... wanted to know why ... it always seemed to me that ... was Tina your favourite?'

Silence filled the room. Beth stroked her mother's hand. Then Ma took a long slow breath and opened her eyes.

'Tina wasn't my favourite,' Ma said.

'But Tina was special. You treated her differently. What was it about her ... that I didn't have?'

'Oh, my darling,' said Ma squeezing Beth's hand as she opened her eyes. 'I treated you differently because you were different.'

'Well, I was older.'

'Yes, older but also wiser. You have always been sensible, so self-contained. I never had to worry about what you might get up to. You are like your father, strong, loyal, and decisive.' Ma took a long, ragged breath. 'That, I think, is part of the reason Max was so happy with you. He wanted someone who would support him. He gave the appearance of being in control, but he needed you with him to be that person.'

'I recently found out that Max had affairs.'

'Oh darling, I'm so sorry, that is very hurtful. Are you sure?' Ma stared at her through rheumy eyes, as though trying to pull Beth into focus, to see her clearly.

Beth nodded.

'I suppose he wanted to prove to himself that he could be and have everything. But you must remember he couldn't be Max without you beside him.'

'I should have known he was unfaithful. I'm such an idiot for not suspecting. When I think back there were signs. I was just too trusting.'

'Don't be ashamed, my darling,' said Ma. 'It was humiliation that defeated your father in the end. Shame is corrosive. You have to accept what happened, you can't go back and change anything. And what is love without trust.'

'Max seems to have slept with anyone, even … I mean … I never guessed what was going on.'

'Did you never question? I used to wonder if your father ever did … but I decided not.'

'Of course not.' The unsettling image of Olive Johnson on her prancing filly popped into Beth's mind from the day of the hunt so long ago.

'Of course not.' Ma almost laughed. 'You know, he was really torn over your involvement in Farthingale and Pateger.

Beth felt herself bridle at the memory. She took a deep breath; she didn't feel anything else could be said that would add to that episode.

'Yes,' Ma went on. 'It wasn't that he didn't think you were capable. He thought you were very accomplished and had balanced the work and family obligations with aplomb.'

'But …,' said Beth.

'But he thought the other directors were not ready for a woman on the board.'

'He could have let me find that out for myself.'

'He anguished over that very point, but in the end, he wanted to protect you. They were his colleagues and friends, but he felt that the environment wasn't suitable … he didn't want you to get hurt.'

It did hurt. She had been hurting ever since. Her father didn't think she was on an equal par with Duncan and so she had chosen to back down and look after her family. Now she had to reconsider what that meant.

'And Tina?' Beth asked.

'Tina was like me; she needed looking after. I had Dennis. Tina was a frail, clever girl, but she lacked perseverance. Tina would bounce from this to that. Her fussy eating used to worry me, and she had frightfully unsuitable friends. I felt I needed to keep an eye on her. To keep her safe.'

'Safe from what?' asked Beth.

'Herself! Of course, it was impossible. Tina was always out and about and so pretty; she was always attracting the wrong sort of attention. I couldn't watch over her all the time.'

'No,' Beth sighed. 'I guess not. Just as I couldn't keep tabs on Max.'

'You were sure of yourself but scared of the world. You needed Max too, to bring you adventure. Tina was afraid of who she was but curious about the world. She needed to be kept safe. I often wonder what more I could have done.' Ma paused and closed her eyes, breathing slowly, then she sobbed, her agitated fingers plucking at the bedspread. 'I miss my baby girl so much.'

'I know,' said Beth patting Ma's hand softly. 'I know, but it was a difficult time for you, with Pa gone. Losing a child must be something you never get over.'

Ma fell silent. Beth thought she must be asleep.

'What shall I do about Laura? What shall I tell her?' Beth asked, not expecting an answer.

'I think ...' Ma roused. 'It would be good for Laura to have a positive memory of her father, don't you?' Ma looked at Beth. 'Family is so important. You don't want to lose Laura. The best kept secret is one you learn to forget.'

Ma closed her eyes again and patted Beth's hand.

'Don't worry, my darling, and don't blame yourself. In any relationship, you are only half of the equation. Life is a riddle to sort out as best we can.'

Old Fox

Beth was so weary her body lay heavy on the bed as though it had given up. She thought it would be easy to be alone, without Max. She had slept for so long with half an ear waiting for the inevitable cry that she wondered now if she had forgotten how to cast off. The house was quiet. Then Beth heard the clock downstairs strike the hour. She rolled over and turned her pillow, looking for a smooth, cool surface.

At the funeral, Beth thought that people would question her anger and think her cold. The rage still stormed inside her, but as she stood beside Laura, who had been so strong, Beth had realised that one intense emotion, from the outside, must look very much like another. Their friends came to give their condolences and Beth could see that they assumed it was grief that consumed her. And, she was grieving just not for the Max they had come to say goodbye to. Beth was mourning the Max she thought she knew and the marriage she thought she had. When it was over, and everyone had left and after Laura had gone back to London, Beth had sat in the silent house that no longer felt like home and wondered what she should do. Nothing precipitous, they, whoever they were, always advised, but Beth had felt as though she was standing on the cliff edge for a while.

Lying in bed not expecting to sleep, Beth looked across the room to where her dressing table mirror reflected the pale gloom from the streetlight that seeped around the curtain. In front of the mirror, a photograph of their wedding day rested amongst the lotions and potions she haphazardly applied every morning and evening. Beth did not have to see the picture clearly to know the smiles. Max, with ridiculously fluffy hair facing her, looking down at her upturned, enraptured face. A lifetime ago when Beth believed in love. Beth wasn't sure why the picture was still there, a testament to her naivety perhaps. Beside it, there was a photograph of Laura.

Beth could not understand how she had never noticed the resemblance between Max and Laura. Since Beth had read Tina's letter, Beth could think of nothing else. At the time, when Laura was growing up, it would have been preposterous to entertain such a thought. Now, whenever she saw Laura, Beth found herself staring, ticking off the similarities. It wasn't just Laura's eyes that were blue. The blue that had drawn Beth to Max in the first place. But Laura's mannerisms, the way she smiled, how could Beth have been so blind? She felt a fool, all over again. The insidiousness of the whole affair crept under her skin and ate at her soul; no wonder she couldn't sleep.

Beth felt a sudden, stifling heat and threw back the covers. Her body reminding her what age she was. After a moment, she sat up and swung her weary legs to the bedroom floor. She had finished her water. A walk to the kitchen would help her cool down. Beth picked up her glass and, with a sigh for lost sleep, lurched stiffly to the door. God, she felt old.

In the dark kitchen, Bitsy thumped his tail but didn't get up. Beth stared at the reflection of the woman in the black glass of the window as she waited for the water from the kitchen tap to run cold. There were bags under her eyes, and the gloomy light gave her skin an unbecoming grey tone. The outside light flicked on, dazzling her. A fox had triggered the outdoor sensor. Caught in the orange light, it turned and gave her a cold stare with bright reflective eyes before heading into the darkness at the back of the garden. As she left the kitchen, Bitsy wagged his tail again, snuffling in his bed. Beth looked at the little dog, getting on now too, and a cloak of sorrow swept over her. How she missed Tina. How she missed Max, the Max she thought she knew. Beth trudged up the stairs.

On the landing at the top of the stairs was a black and white picture of the ghostly view of the cedar overlooking the lake at Nether Place. Max had taken the photograph from the terrace outside the French windows the morning before the contents of the old house were auctioned. They had arrived early at the house and wandered from room to room, winding between lots ready to be sold. It had been miserable seeing all the old familiar things packed up and ready to go. As they left Pa's study, Max had picked up Dennis' old camera. No one used one anymore; phones were so much easier, but it was a throwback moment. While Beth ended up in the kitchen following the smell of coffee and found Mrs Simms, Max took the camera out onto the terrace and was taking photos with the last of the roll of film. Beth brought him a coffee, and they had watched together as the mist rose off the lake and the sun broke through. After a cold start, it was going to be a beautiful day. But Beth knew the pale still waters that began to reflect that sunny last day were dark and murky up close. If you stared into the depths, the water was green, deep, and busy with mysterious life.

Beth woke feeling anxious, as though she had forgotten something. She could feel the weight of Churchill curled at her feet. She must have left the bedroom door ajar when she crept back into bed. She opened her eyes. The room was still in shadow, but dawn now lit up the wall around the curtain. Beth feeling hot again, searching for coolness in the sheets, stretched out and gave Churchill a shove: he landed on the floor with a snarky hiss.

How she wished she had just once heard Tina out; listened to what she had to say. Beth should have listened, but she had always walked away. She had been frightened of confrontation. Maybe it would have cleared the air if they had talked. There would have been no room for deceit to take hold if they had been honest with one another. Beth lay on her back; a tear slipped down the side of her face and trickled into her ear. Had there ever been a moment when something she could have said or done might have changed what had happened?

Shepherdess

Beth sat with her mother; Ma was sleeping. Her face was calm but had lost substance; she was fading. Beth thought about when Ma had been young and glamorous and the life she had lived; the life they had all lived. Beth didn't remember her own childhood being happy or unhappy. Either way, she wasn't sure life was supposed to be one long blissful encounter. Beth had been content and reached adulthood. What more could she ask?

When they first met, Beth had asked Max down to Nether Place to meet her parents. In the mess and muddle of the family, Duncan with his new girlfriend, Meredith, Tina with her school friends and all the dogs, Beth saw how easy it was for Max to fit in.

Max had been with Beth through thick and thin. He made her feel part of a team; with Laura, they were a family. Her best memories were of Laura' growing up, watching her playing with friends, learning about the world. Ma popping over to share a cup of tea in front of the fire, small children romping around them. Time at Nether Place and holidays together. It was all about family, and Max was there in the background, handing out drinks, putting plasters on grazed knees, and holding Beth's hands during difficult moments. Beth with Max had been complete. Once Beth fulfilled her own and her parent's expectations, her life seemed more straightforward.

Except now Beth knew she had been an innocent in a world which had turned out to be anything but. Now she had to accept her life had been an illusion. Was it a straight choice between celebrating the happy marriage she remembered or accepting that her life had been a charade. It didn't seem that simple, Beth couldn't decide what was real. Would she have preferred to live with the truth? What then? If she had known about Max's affairs sooner, what choices would she have made? What life would she have lived? Should she have been more self-reliant, lived her own life instead of immersing herself in the lives of others. Beth thought about Tina's letter, tucked into the inner pocket of her handbag. Beth wished she had never read it. If only she had not opened the box, and all the letters had been consumed by fire.

They were so appealing, the bright, innocent days of the past. Back then, Ma had been full of energy. Now, Beth examined her mother's pale fingers, fluttering, yearning for life. Beth began to stroke her mother's hand softly but firmly.

'I'm here, Ma,' Beth said.

The door opened, and Laura burst into the room. Startled, as she turned, Beth caught her rings in the candlewick counterpane of Ma's bed.

'Sorry I'm late, Mum. The train was delayed. How's May-May?'

'Hello, sweetheart. No discernible change. She is just slowly and gently leaving us.' Beth smiled at her mother and squeezed her hand. 'Now you're here, I'll whizz out. I left Bitsy in the car, he'll need a run around, and I'll pick up a sandwich. Do you want something? We can catch up when I get back.'

'No, I'm fine, thanks. Do I need to do anything?' Beth saw panic in Laura's eyes.

'Just sit with her. She'll know you're here. I won't be long.' Beth kissed Laura and left.

Laura looked around the room and put her bag down by the little nursing chair she liked near the French window. She didn't want to sit in the wing chair that had been moved near the bed; that was May-May's chair; it wouldn't feel right. Laura paced the room looking at the old photographs and ornaments her grandmother had cherished. Laura paused by the round side table and picked up the pretty china shepherdess. There was not only a chip in one of the frills of her dress, her crook had snapped off, also, one of the sheep had lost its horns. It was far too delicate and pretty for Laura's taste, and a shame it had been chipped, but the sweet face of the statuette was a perfect reflection of her grandmother.

'You gave me that, do you remember?' May-May whispered from the bed. Laura nearly dropped the figurine.

'Hello, May-May,' Laura said, carefully placing the ornament back by the silver-framed photograph of her Aunt Tina before turning towards her grandmother. 'I thought you were asleep.'

'It's lovely to see you, darling. I've been thinking of you so much. I did so want to see you.'

'It's lovely to see you too.' Laura approached the bed and took May-May's hand.

'What have you been up to? Always so busy, my darling. My pretty, pretty girl.' Her grandmother's voice was low and raspy. 'No dog today?'

'No, May-May, no dog. It's me, Laura, not Tina,' she said, but May-May didn't hear her; she had fallen back asleep.

Laura was standing by the bed. May-May held her hand softly, time passed. Laura didn't feel she could move. May-May's breath flowed gently in and out.

Sharon and a doctor came into the room. It was Doctor Bannister. May-May had introduced him to Laura to on a previous visit, presenting her as her unmarried granddaughter.

'He's frightfully nice and single too,' May-May had said. Doctor Bannister hadn't seemed the least put out. Laura supposed he was more used to such introductions than she was.

'How is she?' he asked, smiling at Laura. 'Comfortable?'

'Yes,' said Laura, letting go of her grandmother's hand and standing back so the doctor could go near the bed. 'I'm sorry, my mother's not here. I'm sure she would have liked to talk to you. She shouldn't be long.'

'If Mrs Templeton gets back before my shift finishes, she can ask for me at the desk, and I'll be happy to have a chat,' said Doctor Bannister, taking May-May's pulse.

Laura noticed how frail May-May's wrist looked in Dr Bannister's capable solid looking hands.

'All good,' said the doctor, gently placing May-May's hand back in the bedspread.

Sharon replaced the orange juice on the side table with a fresh jug, and the doctor and nurse left. Laura paced the room again. She stopped by the photograph of Tina. Laura picked it up and took it across to the oval mirror on the wardrobe door. She held the picture up and compared it to her reflection.

'I'm back,' said her mother. 'I managed to catch that nice Doctor Bannister as I came in. He really is terribly nice. So much younger than Doctor Simpson, but I'm sure he's just as competent. He said Ma was as comfortable as possible.'

Her mother hung her coat on the back of a chair and came and stood beside Laura in front of the mirror. Her mother smiled at Laura's reflection. 'What are you up to?'

'May-May woke up briefly. She thought I was Aunt Tina. She's made that mistake before.'

'Your grandmother has been a bit confused for some time now.'

'I was just looking at this photo of Tina and comparing it to my reflection.' Laura held the photograph once more in front of the mirror. The three of them in a row, Laura, Mum, and Tina's forever youthful picture between them.

'This photograph must have been taken when Tina was in her late twenties. There's a strong family resemblance. If you were worried, I can confirm; you are a Parteger through and through,' said Mum, smiling. 'But look, you have your father's beautiful eyes.'

'May-May said something about, "it had all been for the best, hadn't it? Anyone could see how happy the baby was in a proper family." What was that about?'

'Well ...,' said Mum. 'You know ... I'm not sure. Your grandmother's mind is floating backwards and forwards. She could be poised at any moment in time. Perhaps even before we knew her. Knowing what's going on ... finding out the truth can be intriguing, but it can also be unsettling.' Her mother gave her a hug.

'Gareth and Duncan aren't going to get here in time, are they?'

'It doesn't look like it,' said Mum.

Laura put the photograph back, and they sat down, her mother in the wingback chair and Laura in the little nursing chair. Sharon brought them mugs of strong, milky tea. Laura looked into her mug and wondered if builders asked for 'builders' or whether they just said tea.

Alix

In her hand, Laura held May-May's little prayer book. She had picked it up from the bedside table where it lived beside May-May's photograph of Dennis. Laura had loved her grandfather, but he had seemed autocratic and distant and smelt of cigars even though he didn't smoke. Sometimes she thought he was waiting for her to grow up before he would take any notice, but by the time she was older, she was away at school, and her grandfather had become infirm. Laura turned the prayer book over in her hands. The burgundy leather cover was worn soft with use, and the gold embossed Cyrillic lettering faded. In a keen moment, Laura had joined the Russian club at school, but she would struggle to read this faded archaic text. May-May had never flaunted her Russian heritage nor encouraged her family to learn her native tongue. Instead, she had wholeheartedly embraced being British and venerated her adoptive country.

May-May slept, she was sleeping more and more. Mum had asked Laura to be there, so May-May wouldn't be alone. Absentmindedly, Laura flicked through the prayer book's gold-edged pages, the delicate paper almost transparent. A stiff inch square, black and white photograph fell from the soft leaves onto Laura's lap. It was of a little girl, a toddler. Laura picked it up. For a moment, Laura thought it was Tina as a child, but that couldn't right. Laura turned the photograph over. On the back, something was written in pale, faded ink. Laura searched her memory to translate the letters, 'A'. 'L'. 'I'. 'X', 1953. Alix? Laura's heart paused as she tried to think. Wasn't Alix the name of May-May's Russian doll? Why would her grandmother have an old photograph of a child in her prayer book? Laura knew what the answer must be and was trying hard to rearrange what she knew about her grandmother. Laura turned over the photograph and studied the child's face. She wondered what had happened to the little girl, where she was now.

Laura heard the door open and slipped the picture back into the prayer book. She wasn't sure why she hid the photograph, but this felt like a secret May-May had shared with her.

'Hello,' said Mum. 'How's she doing?'

'Just sleeping.'

'Thank you for keeping watch, darling. It means so much to me.' Mum busied herself, taking off her coat, dumping her bags.

'No bother,' Laura said.

'Oh, you've got Ma's old Russian prayer book. You should keep that if you like. I doubt your grandmother will have an opportunity to read it now.'

'Thanks,' said Laura dropping the little book into her jacket pocket.

'Why don't you go get some fresh air, take a walk around the garden. I'll watch over her now.'

Laura got up, ready to hand over the bedside chair. She swept a stray strand of hair behind her ear as she leant over May-May and gave her dry cheek a kiss before sauntering out through the French windows onto the terrace and into the sun.

Ripples

Laura sat on the stone steps that led out from the tall French windows. They were smooth from years of use. At the edges, weather-rough lichen stretched its yellow and green fingers from cracks and crevasses. Blue lavender nodded gently from garden beds on either side, its scent drifted towards her.

The silence of soft footsteps on carpet seeped out from May-May's room where Laura's mother was moving gently, waiting. Laura leant forward and played with the gravel at her feet sorting, selecting, favouring the round orange pebbles that felt smooth in her hands. She lined them up along the edge of the top step, one for each time she had visited her grandmother, the smallest first. The largest pebble for today she held in her hand, tossing it, feeling it's weight. She looked up and out across the lake to the far hills, purple and blue in the distance.

Laura wandered across the lawn towards the lake, passing under the giant cedar. She walked out onto the jetty, leant out over the handrail, and stared deep into the water. After a while tiny minnows separated themselves from the weeds, and she could see small shoals of fish nipping mindlessly around their underwater business. Laura pulled her focus back to the surface and stared at her dark, watery reflection. The pebble was heavy in her hand. She dropped it through her fingers. Ripples broke across the water, fracturing her image into wavering shards. As she watched, the wobbly features of her reflection were restored, and the lake became calm.

Float Away

Ma seemed agitated, her mind chasing some indeterminate dream. Beth could see her mother's eyes tracking back and forth under closed eyelids. Beth released her mother's hand, thinking perhaps she had been holding it too tightly. Her mother woke and turned towards Beth lifting her head as if she carried the world.

'Is that you?'

'Ma, I'm here. It's me, Beth.'

'Oh, Beth. Can you help me, darling? Where's your father? Do you know?' Ma asked, as though from a great distance. She struggled for breath, 'someone said he wasn't well. I've been so worried about him. Do you know where Dennis is?'

Beth leant in and took her mother's pale fingers in her own hand again and kissed them.

'It's alright, Ma, don't worry.' Beth stroked her mother's brow with her other hand. 'Don't worry. He's fine. You'll see him soon.' Her mother looked so pale and light as if she might float away.

'Are you sure?' her mother whispered. 'that's good ... that's alright then.' Her mother closed her eyes and leaned back in her bed. Her breathing eased. Beth sat quietly beside her. After a while, Ma's breath slowed and slowed until it quietly stopped; suddenly, softly, Ma left, and Beth realised that she was alone. Beth still held Ma's hand. Her body lay as it had a moment before, but everything was different. This was no longer Ma. Beth placed the parchment hand she held in hers carefully on the blanket. She looked at the pale, worn-out, gaping face. She ought to fetch the nurse, but Beth didn't want to leave, in case Ma hadn't really gone, in case she changed her mind and came back.

Beth waited, but the room was silent. Her mother had gone.

So had Tina and so had Max.

What had Ma said about secrets? Beth took Tina's letter from her bag and ran her fingers over the address, Tina's writing, Max's name. Beth tore it up, over and over, into as many tiny pieces as she could. Then she stood up and dropped the shreds into the bin. She looked at her hands, old hands, not pale claws like her mothers had been twisted by arthritis, but old wrinkly hands, nonetheless. Beth looked at the gold ring, tight on her fat wedding finger. She wrenched it off, twisting it over her swollen knuckle. Beth held the ring, turning it, watching it catch the light from the window, and then dropped it in the bin to, where it slid among the torn strips of paper and disappeared.

Beth hadn't noticed her tears; she found a tissue and wiped them away. Then she returned to the bed and kissed her mother's forehead, gently brushing back her hair. Beth rang the bell for the nurse before going to look for Laura, scattering the row of pebbles on the steps as she stepped out into the sun.

Printed in Great Britain
by Amazon